SHH

JOCELYN DEXTER

Angela Elizabeth Herickx
28th September 1932 – 17th June 2014

1

At first glance the fifteen-year-old boy looks as if he is standing propped up against the iron railings with his head resting on his chest. His arms appear to be holding him up, cradling the rails, with his forearms hanging down. He perches like a marionette whose strings have been cut, leaving him formless.

It isn't until you look a little closer that you see that the boy is balancing on tiptoes; an impossible position to maintain for any length of time. But look closer; his arms are impaled by the spikes. They pierce through his scrawny biceps. It could be a crucifixion. His head lolls to one side. Lift it and there is no discernible face. It is pulp. Swelling hides his eyes. His nose no longer has a bridge but is splattered across his face, his nostrils only identifiable by two bloody holes, disconcerting in their position – now haphazardly rearranged on his face and no longer symmetrical. If you were feeling artistically inclined, you might describe his face as a Picasso; an ill-fitting montage of features, misplaced and oddly set.

His ripped and broken lips hang open. If you look carefully you would just be able to see that something is hidden within the hole that had once been his mouth. A hearing aid rests against his three remaining bottom front teeth, the plastic tube from the aid protrudes slightly, as a worm looks appearing from under the soil, seeking rain. His right ear is completely demolished, bootprints leave clear imprints upon the side of his face. His left ear hangs by a sinewy knot of gristle and lies next to one of the displaced nostrils. He resembles less a boy and more an unimaginably mismatched jigsaw. Assembled with a maniacal fury. It leaves a demented chaos of a child.

Were you to lift his shirt and jumper you would see a blaze of colours; red, purple, black. More bootprints in shocking welts that stand angry and livid against his skinny frame. A rib sticks out from his pale skin, shocking in its rude display of internal anatomy. If you carried on your examination you would find bruises covering his entire lower body: his knees are clearly no longer where they should be.

Had you been working your way from the top of his body to the bottom, your last sight, and thus your lasting memory, would be his left ankle. It has been so crushed that his foot faces the wrong way. If you were being whimsical you might think the boy looks as if he has been caught in some deranged half pirouette.

Kicked and stamped to death. You wouldn't have to be medically qualified to reach that conclusion. The damage is there for all to see.

If you dare to look.

But if you are sensible you would not look at all, but hurry past and leave his discovery to some other poor soul.

If you were sensible, you would close your eyes and you would never look back.

You would run.

Run for the hills.

If you were sensible.

2

———

1 YEAR LATER – MAY

Annie Black was thirty-seven and profoundly deaf.

She hurried home from work, head down, sweating in the early evening heat.

Worried about her friend, Sarah, and her son, Toby. He was fifteen, deaf and missing. Annie wasn't one for platitudes, for soothing noises. Nor was she a liar. How could she say to her dearest friend, 'Don't worry, it'll be alright?' She knew it might not be. The longer Toby's absence, the worse the outlook. Annie knew it. Sarah knew it. So why pretend? Although naturally, both she and her friend *did* pretend. Coddled themselves in fakery. Indulged in hope. But now Annie forced herself not to be overly precious about it. It needed to be said and so she said it. As she walked, she whispered it out into the night air. *Toby might be dead.*

Toby had last been seen on Thursday night on his way to the Deaf Club. Now, forty eight hours later, and still nothing. Forty eight hours – the magic number of hours when the case went from 'missing boy' to 'let's still pretend everything's fine'. Let's lie.

Tonight, she planned on getting home, changing, and making her way to the Deaf Club. A Saturday night – it should be full. She would ask questions that had already been asked by the police, but she expected better answers purely because she had access.

Nine o'clock and the night was heavy and oppressive. Annie could feel thunder in the air, waiting to explode, the smell of the coming rain sweet. A strong breeze whipped through the air. She lowered her head, intent on her destination and not being able to hear, could only imagine the noise the wind made as it swirled around her, throwing paper, plastic bags and an old polystyrene coffee cup aloft, spinning them in an upward spiral. An empty cigarette packet scudded across the pavement, two crisp packets tumbleweeded alongside it. Pulling her sleeves down over her sticky flesh, she swatted away a hovering ball of midges, her skin slick with sweat from the intense early summer heat.

She stopped and looked up the length of her quiet but familiar residential road: the light was gloomy and the lamp posts only made the dark darker. As she walked, her skin prickled and her mouth went dry. A quiet dread sat heavily in her stomach. Where the bloody hell *was* Toby? His disappearance felt like a countdown.

Annie reached her building – a Victorian mansion block on the corner – and ran through the large gap in the wall for both cars and residents. She slid on the dusty pea shingle drive where residents' vehicles were parked neatly in rows.

As she manoeuvred herself between two cars, the sharp smell of body odour washed over her. The very physical presence of another person entered her world. She knew immediately that she was in trouble. In a part of her brain that still functioned rationally, she realised that someone must have been hiding behind one of the cars; crouched down – waiting. Waiting for her, or for anyone?

It didn't matter. Because it was too late to react, too late to run, too late to stop something from being pulled down over her head. It took a moment for her to recognise it as a plastic bag, as it tightened around her neck and the drawstring was pulled.

She couldn't hear and she couldn't see. Panting, eyes wide open, mouth stretched wide, she was plunged into the dark, black hole of her worst nightmare. Blindness. And with her sight taken away, abject terror kicked in.

The man pushed and pulled her to the ground. On the way down the side of her face hit a car, her knee crashed onto the shingle, and his weight pressed down on her. She felt the lump of her now-useless mobile hard against her hip, out of reach inside her jacket pocket.

Automatically she let out a cry, not sure whether she actually made an audible noise until she felt the vibration of her vocal cords. Grunting like a beast being led to the slaughterhouse. Stupid with fear. Dumb with shock.

Panicking, she inhaled. Inhaled too much and too quickly. Felt the plastic whoosh into her mouth with a vacuum force, filling it instantly. The bag stuck to her nostrils, to her face, to her ears and to her chin. She could feel it on her tongue, slick and smooth. The plastic shaped itself into a mould of her features, her mouth open, screaming in a silent O, the contours of her nose and eyes feeling pronounced, as if she had hermetically sealed herself in. A perfect replica of her face, now cast in plastic.

One of the man's fingers pressed onto her parted lips on the other side of the bag – shh. She recoiled at the intimate touch. Felt his fingers try and pry apart her mouth, pushing and poking – wanting access through the plastic. Instead of biting it, she withdrew her neck; reeling it in like a tortoise.

Her hands grabbed at her throat where the string bit into her neck, trying to stop the suffocation.

Giving in, she made herself stop gulping at air that wasn't there. Settled for taking tiny little inhalations. Just enough to live. Her lungs screamed, shouted, cried out in agony, in pain, in fear – on fire: burning.

Knowing that she was close to passing out, Annie suddenly felt the man loosen the bag by slipping his hand between the drawstring and her neck. Desperate for oxygen, she sucked in greedily, ignoring the obscene feel of his gloved fingers as they brushed up against her face like furred slugs. Trying not to sob in gratitude, Annie lay on her side and regained a more rhythmic in, out, in, out breathing pattern. Feeling the pain-free movement of her lungs.

She felt his fingers playing with the cord, but she forced herself not to react. Played dead. He slipped his fingers inside the bag and stroked her cheek. And then he patted it. Twice.

Still rigid, unable to relax yet, she breathed in the glorious air that seemed to fill her space like an unexpected wave. Luxuriated in life given back. Celebrated the fact that she wasn't dead.

After a while, lying there, her head still dressed in plastic, Annie felt him gone. The wind rippled over her body. She waited a minute, just to make sure, and then her hands found the knot that the man had left. Fumbling like a child, her fingers finally managed to undo the tangled cord and she ripped the bag from her face and stood up. Circling slowly, she made sure the man had gone.

She waited for the heat from her flushed cheeks to leave her. Coming to a standstill, she remained there, still holding the bag. Shaking. Shaking, but breathing.

And very alone.

The whole thing could only have taken three minutes. Maximum.

Exhausted and terrified she ran the remaining ten paces to her flat door, just as the sky split open and the first fat raindrops fell, instantly soaking her. Fumbling with her keys, she fell inside her front door.

Her deafness had never defined her.

Until now.

3

———

Question: *What's the best way to frighten a Deaf person? I know that sounds like the beginning of a joke, but it isn't. It isn't funny at all.*

Answer: Turn the lights off.

To deny a Deaf person light is laughably effective. It frightens them. They just cease to function. It's most satisfactory. And it's so simple. Simple is always best. Always capitalise on what you are presented with. Take away what helps someone, and then destroy what is left. Make the most of what you have and what they do not.

Deafness makes sight an essential commodity. Crucial. And as sure as night follows day, darkness will break them. Turn off the lights; take away their safety net. Free fall.

And here's the added bonus. Denying the Deaf light takes away their ability to communicate. With one flick of a switch, you render them completely useless.

Deaf, blind and cut off. They become beast-like in their panic, they forget to think. They can only wait for rescue.

I know very well the power of sensory deprivation. I was the recipient of it. Punished as a child for unknown crimes, shut in a cupboard under the stairs for periods of time that seemed endless.

My father would drag me by the ear down the hall to the cupboard. My grandmother would sit there, fat and regal, clapping her hands with glee. Silently watching. Such sport. Daddy would tie my hands and ankles with masking tape and wedge my special hearing aids deep into my ears. He would then tape my mouth. He would smile, pat me on the head, put his index finger to his mouth – 'shh'. Then he would lock the door.

That first time my father inadvertently left a chink of light visible between the bottom of the door and the carpet. It was my grandmother who discovered this one rogue light source. It was consequently blocked up. Mummy helped.

I was four.

What do I remember? An all-embracing darkness and the taste of salt from my tears, which would trickle down the back of my throat.

And the smell, always the same. Dampness and musty old coats that had been shoved into the back of the cupboard and left. My urine would add its own unique aroma. I would feel the hot trickle between my legs. I remember that feeling of warmth turning cold, damp – making my shorts stick to my legs. The smells would mingle with the taste of salt, and I would sit and wait for someone to let me out.

Of course, one must not forget my grandmother's role in the amusing daily adventure that was my childhood. She certainly played her part – an integral one. With gusto.

They called me 'Cupboard'. I was always under the impression that my grandmother instigated both the name and the game. She ruled the household, pulled the strings and all obeyed. No one challenged her. Certainly not me.

But I didn't forget.

I concede that it was most assuredly my mother, father and grandmother who gave me the starting point for my current venture, but I have added a much-needed sophistication to the whole proceedings. I am now turning My Game into a little tribute to the teachings of my three blood-related guardians. And am passing it on to others.

My own personal torture worked well on me. With a little added artistry, it will work well on others.

Especially with Annie. I think she got the idea tonight. The Game, after all, revolves around her. She is central to my project and thus I bagged her with some considerable delight this evening. Made her Deaf World just that little darker, her world just that little smaller. Think of it as a sample of what I will do to her. Currently I have given her something to only think about. That is sufficient for the time being. Later she will feel under siege. And later still... well, let's not be premature.

Overall, I think my family would all be proud of me now; of that I'm fairly certain.

I don't include my brother, Ewan, in this game that apparently so delighted my parents and my grandmother. He had no idea of what they did. I never told him. The older generation kept their fun to themselves. But who really knows? Maybe he was in on it with them. I shall never know, and does it really matter? It wouldn't change anything. They're all dead now.

But I learnt something very important.

I learnt how to be invisible.

If I crept quietly around the house, and made myself physically smaller, forever keeping a low profile, what point would there be, banishing me to the cupboard? I might as well have been there already. My very existence was negligible.

My parents stopped locking me under the stairs when I was ten. They had achieved their goal. I knew how to not be there. I was an expert in not being noticed.

Something for which I thank them now.

4

———

Everything inside Annie silently screamed but she forced herself to face the two policemen who sat opposite her. Immediately she got into a sipping rhythm with her wine. No, not sipping – gulping. Swallowing alcohol fast and furiously. Desperate.

Her life had been wounded by Toby's disappearance and was now further fractured by a stranger's attack. No, more than fractured – demolished.

'I'm DI Crabb, and this is DS Peters. May I call you Annie?'

She nodded, focusing on his mouth movements. He was in his early fifties and his face so oddly constructed that it looked like a child's doodle. His eyes were sad, brown and long-lashed. He swept his palm over his bald head and wiped away drops of rain that sat like beads of perspiration on his freckled skin. He said, 'You texted your flatmate, Scarlet, saying that you'd been attacked. She rang us and explained what had happened. She also said that you were deaf. Do you need an interpreter?'

He spoke overly-slowly, pronouncing every separate syllable as he smiled encouragingly at her. Annie smiled back, feeling trapped by the politeness of it all. 'She's on her way back. And really, no to the interpreter. I'm fine. I lip-read. And there's not really a lot I can tell you anyway. But I'll try.'

She felt herself speaking in staccato bursts and watched Crabb cock his head imperceptibly as he attuned his ears to her voice. People had told her that she sounded as if she were underwater; slightly adenoidal. But being unable to hear her own voice, her words could only ever be an imagined sound. Crabb smiled again, trying to put her at ease. She noticed with surprise and as if from a separate and very distant universe, that he had dimples that transformed his plain face and his expression into something youthful and sweet.

Crabb said, 'Tell me what happened. And breathe.'

Words careered and bounced around inside Annie's head. *A man put a bag over my head and tried to suffocate me. He hurt me. My knee's grazed. I think I've got a black eye. My neck's sore. He tried to kill me. I don't know why he did it. I couldn't breathe. It might be someone I know. It might be a stranger. I might be a random victim, or I might be a target. He scared the shit out of me. That's what happened.*

She sucked down air and said, 'I've just been attacked by a man.'

'Describe it to me.'

'He put a bag over my head. Tried to suffocate me.' Her normally good speaking voice felt distorted with panic. Few people had problems in understanding her, but she could feel that her pitch was all wrong, fear making it off-key, too loud, the words becoming more indistinguishable as her volume increased.

Annie felt unable to engage with the newcomers: her head remained cut off, as if it were still covered with a plastic bag. Normally, in her everyday life, things were black and white. Now everything felt kaleidoscopically chaotic with colour.

Catching sudden movement in the periphery of her vision,

Annie startled and leapt up: wild fear slammed into her stomach, making her guts turn and spin. She dug deep and swallowed the vomit that had come up and soured the back of her throat. When she realised it was only Eric, his face appearing on the other side of the conservatory cat flap, his nose pressed to the glass, she swallowed and shakily sat down again. He flew into the room. As he went to pass her, running across the Persian rug, frightened by the wind and rain outside, she caught him, sat back down on the sofa and pulled him onto her lap. A temporary but instant comfort.

He coiled himself like a striped pretzel on her lap and settled down, head on paws. He smelt wet. She bent and buried her face in his fur, slipping her fingers under his red collar with its silver disc inscribed with his name. She cupped his chin with her hand. The vibration of his purring soothed her. Or maybe it was the alcohol. She knocked back two thirds of her glass of wine. Topped it up again.

Keeping Eric on her lap and speaking quickly, signing with one hand out of habit, wanting the telling over, she gave a blunt, straightforward account of the attack, and of course, the near suffocation itself. No emotion. No feeling. Just a string of facts. Which were few; embarrassingly short on detail.

Unlike hearing people, Annie didn't just look. She looked and she *saw*. Really saw. Big difference. Her specialist subject – all that is visual. Problem was – she'd seen nothing tonight. Absolutely fuck-all.

'I didn't see him, I can't really add anything other than he jumped me outside; I think he'd been hiding behind one of the parked cars. He put a bag over my head.' She shrugged in defeat: 'Sorry, that's all I know.'

'Nasty,' Crabb said.

DS Peters' conker-coloured curls swayed as he shook his head in sympathy, his eyes downcast, inspecting his shoes.

Now that the words had been spoken out loud, the fact of her attack now out there, the enormity of what had happened felt like a slap in the face.

'He smelt of sweat,' she said.

Crabb crossed his legs and Annie flinched with the unexpected movement. Her mind flatlined. She put her empty glass on the rug.

'When the bag was over my face, he touched me.'

Out of the corner of her eye, she caught the young sergeant's conker-coloured eyebrows as they shot up his face like a bomb had gone off.

'No, no, I don't mean like that. I mean he patted my face and sort of stroked it.'

'Meaning?' said Crabb.

Annie felt, with relief, the first stirrings of anger. Faint but there. 'At the time, I just hoped it meant goodbye. But now I don't think so. It felt more like he was saying, "goodbye *for now*", or "until the next time", "thanks for the laughs, must do it again". Something like that. I really don't know. Thinking about it now, it felt a bit like he was letting me know that he was the one in control and there was fuck-all I could do about it. He was showing off.'

She hadn't been able to defend herself. The fact that he had made her feel weak was almost as bad as the attack itself. She said, 'The whole attack seemed controlled, measured. He'd thought it out. Confident he wouldn't get caught. He was fast and efficient. It all felt very calculated. Not rushed or panicked.'

She heard herself speaking matter-of-factly, instead of describing a man attempting to suffocate her. Crabb held his head to the side, his jowls almost resting on his shoulders. Leaning forward, he balanced his elbows on his knees: 'You think he'd done it before?'

'Yes, I suppose so. It wasn't exactly routine, but it also didn't feel as if it was a new experience for him. He was quite calm about it. Considering what he was doing. Bastard.'

Anger. *Finally*. Better late than never.

'It felt like... like inflicting pain on another human being was nothing particularly out of the ordinary for him. It was nothing that made him behave in a panicked way, the very physical violence of it was nothing new. I'd expect that, wouldn't you? For him to react to suffocating someone, with an emotion, like excitement, or rage, or hate. But I felt none of those from him; it felt almost mundane. It was all very calm. For *him* it was calm.'

Realising that she was rambling, feeling hysteria threaten, getting more angry, she made herself stop talking and watched Crabb nod. He said, 'Do you know anyone who might want to hurt you? Anyone you're personally, professionally or romantically involved with?'

'No, no and no. I might have pissed someone off along the way. Who hasn't? But nothing that would deserve a bag over my head.' She laughed but couldn't muster up any humour to go along with it.

'No problems with anyone?'

'No problems with anyone *that* much.'

'I'm just thinking that stranger attacks are relatively rare. Can you think of anyone who may bear you a grudge, dislikes you for some reason, anything like that?'

Annie shook her head. She paused, not enjoying having to talk about her personal life. It was precisely that – personal. Equally she knew that she couldn't really avoid giving away a little information – there was no reason not to, other than her own self-imposed privacy laws. 'I'm a window dresser and work with Scarlet. She's a make-up artist. And my attacker wasn't a smoker. Scarlet is. My attacker just stank of sweat. So, I know it wasn't her.'

She smiled at the absurdity of Scarlet being her attacker, and

Crabb smiled back at her. 'You see, you remember more than you think. He wasn't a smoker. It's something.'

On a roll now, Annie wanted it all out in the open. 'And I don't have a partner.'

'No recently dumped boyfriends, or unhappy exes?'

'No.' She inhaled slowly. 'And it wouldn't be a him. It would be a her.'

Crabb waited a beat, his eyebrows furrowed in confusion. She watched as understanding of what she was saying sank in and then he said, 'Any unhappy female exes?'

'No. And no, Scarlet's not my girlfriend. Just flatmate, friend and professional colleague. And anyway, my attacker wasn't a woman.'

Crabb changed tack, surprising her. 'Do you know a boy called Adam Jacobs?'

She didn't have to think about it and quickly shook her head, saying, 'No. Who is he?'

'A fifteen-year-old deaf boy, murdered last year. We never found his killer.'

Clasping his hands together, he asked, 'And how about a deaf boy named Toby Coleridge?'

Annie sucked in air, feeling as if she were inhaling the entire room. 'Of course I know him. I've known him since he was nine years old. He's the son of one my best friends. He's missing.'

'I know he's missing. I'm working the case.'

Annie leant forward, as her heart trampolined inside her chest: 'What do you know? Is he alive?'

He didn't answer her directly. 'Adam was killed one year ago, and his case is still open. My case. Toby's still missing. Again, my case. We don't have anything concrete to follow-up on. At this point I don't know where he is. But I do think Adam's murder and Toby's disappearance are linked.'

Annie felt herself deflate. Just the mention of Toby's name

had made her hopeful. Unrealistically so. She sat back into the sofa and said, 'Are you saying there's someone going around attacking deaf boys?'

'That's what I've been asking myself, yes. But clearly you don't fit the victim profile. He didn't kill you, you're not fifteen and you're a woman. I've got a murder, a disappearance and an attack. I'm making a leap including you in the pattern, but I don't think a big one. At the moment, you're a possible.' He smiled as if to soften the blow that she may be included in such a bleak group of people.

She said, 'Adam and Toby *must* be linked. Same age, both boys, both deaf. Me? Well, only you know the statistics of stranger attacks on women. Deaf women. You tell me.'

'I don't know. Although you weren't murdered, it's the level of violence used against you that worries me. And the fact that you're deaf, like both the boys. It's the timing that's disturbing. A deaf boy, *who you know well*, goes missing and your attack happens two days later.'

She looked at him, studying his face. 'If it's the same man who's done something to Toby, who killed Adam, why the year's gap?'

'Again, I don't know.'

'*Do* you think Toby has been killed?'

'No, I don't think that.' He clearly did think that and he dimpled at her again, trying to take the truth away. But she could read the lie in his eyes. His avoidance of direct eye contact, his skittering gaze, his shifting feet, the crossing of his arms.

'Tell me how you know Toby,' he said.

'I used to teach percussion at the Deaf School. I gave Toby drumming lessons when he was nine. Anyway, I met Toby's mother. Liked her. Helped her with her signing. For Toby's sake.' She smiled. 'She's still not very good, but we became friends.'

She leant forward and held on to Eric. Aware that her

posture was challenging, she said, 'Come on, tell me the truth. You *do* think that Toby is dead. If Adam's dead, Toby's dead. You don't have to lie to me. It's an obvious conclusion to make. Toby goes missing; you can't find him. You're just waiting for his body to turn up. He's exactly the same type of victim as the first boy. Same age, same disability. Then I'm attacked. We're all deaf.'

'But only Adam is dead. And we don't know anything solid about Toby's whereabouts. I'm just kicking around a theory. I don't know anything for sure. Apart from the deaf connection, I'm most worried that you know Toby. Too many bloody coincidences.'

'But I didn't know Adam. How did he die?'

Crabb hesitated for a second then said, 'He was kicked to death.'

Annie found her brain stutter to a halt, unable to picture the image; it was too grotesque, too brutal: how could a man *kick* a boy to death?

A hot Eric slithered off her lap and collapsed in a puddle on the floor in front of her. Annie felt like joining him – running on empty now, with her emotions temporarily overloaded, all she wished for was an end to the questions and to meet her desperate desire to be horizontal. She was having to concentrate on Crabb's lip-pattern. Strangers were always harder to lip-read until she got used to the way they moved their mouths, the turn and tilt of their heads. All their own little facial idiosyncrasies.

Her eyes felt gritty from staring at his mouth; like little grains of sand were embedded in her pupils. She told herself to get a bloody grip, wanting to finish this tonight. Give as much help as possible. To help herself, to help Crabb, to help the boy called Adam, and most of all, to help Toby.

A thought suddenly and unexpectedly occurred and she wondered why it hadn't come up earlier. Thinking back on the man jumping out at her, she remembered that the weather was stiflingly hot, so when he'd put his bag over her head, why had he been wearing gloves? She realised that it could mean only one thing: 'He was wearing gloves. The man who attacked me. He came prepared. It was premeditated.'

Crabb blinked slowly, said, 'It sounds premeditated, I agree.'

He didn't offer any words of kindness, but she felt his need to know, to *really* know what was going on, driving him. He said, 'Problem is, at this stage, I can only speculate about the killer of Adam. Your attacker. Presuming they're one and the same. We have no real leads. Toby's disappearance is a high-profile case with a lot of press coverage. We've followed up on every single tip or sighting that we've had. And there's been many, as you can imagine, but nothing relevant. So far.'

He rotated his neck as if it were stiff. Looked at her. Peters lifted his head and smiled sympathetically at her. Under the gaze of four eyes, she felt on show, like something fragile, pinned under glass. Crabb said, 'Anyway, are those the clothes you were wearing when you were attacked?'

He pointed at her, his finger going up and down, encompassing her clothes from head to toe. Then took in her wet hair and understood its relevance. 'You've had a shower.'

'Sorry. Had to. Felt dirty.' She tipped her head to show direction. Said, 'My clothes are there, on the chair. Do you want them?'

He nodded.

'And I'll need you down at the station tonight. I'm sorry, I know you're tired and upset, but your attacker might have left trace evidence or fibre on you, or on your clothes. You didn't scratch him by any chance, did you?'

'I wish. Anyway, I've scrubbed myself clean.'

He closed his eyelids for a fraction too long, unable again to hide his disappointment. He glanced down to avoid her gaze, as if this was all very personal to him. A personal failure. Lifting his face, he said, 'You're the first real lead we have, as de-human-ising as that sounds. This might help Toby.'

'You don't have to persuade me. I'll come.'

The two men stood. Crabb put his hand on her arm and said, 'You sure you're alright?'

Annie blinked once for yes. Wondered how she'd last the final indignities still to come at the police station. She held her hand in the air, stopping them. 'I forgot something. I'm not sure if it's important or not. The man put his fingers to my lips, tried to put his finger *into* my mouth. Stuck his finger in between my lips through the plastic bag.' She shuddered at the memory.

Crabb looked strangely at her. 'Really?'

Annie nodded. Crabb looked intrigued. Tried to camouflage the expression by wiping his hand across his face. Then he said, 'It seems to me the question we need to ask is, if all these inci-dents *are* linked, then why *didn't* he kill you? He could have, easily. But he didn't. He chose not to. Why let you go? Why *aren't* you dead?'

Goosepimples speckled Annie's arms.

5

It was early Sunday morning.

The pond on Hampstead Heath was relatively small and the water murky; stagnant and foul-smelling. The area was surrounded by trees; secluded. A police photographer teetered on dry land, leaning forward precariously, taking photographs of the floating body from every angle. A grey blanket skulked at the bottom of the pond, only visible as it undulated against the stony bank, one corner stuck around a broken branch that was keeping it in place.

Crabb watched the naked body of Toby as it bobbed in the water. The boy was instantly identifiable from the photograph his mother, Sarah, had given him.

The police photographer bent at an awkward angle to take another shot, and inadvertently plunged one foot into the pond. The water rippled over Toby's body, nudging him against the cement bank. His head bumped against the side making an oddly intimate noise – a quiet thud, followed immediately afterwards by the sound of metal scraping against stone. It was as if all other noise disappeared, the voices of officers faded into the background, the song of birds momentarily stilled. Only the sickly noise of the implement protruding from the boy's ear was left, grinding out a disturbing sound; in time with the rhythmic pulse of the water.

'For Christ's sake, get the boy out now. Enough pictures. Get him out now,' Crabb shouted, feeling his cheeks flush in the early morning light. Seven o'clock and already his day was miserable. Couldn't be any more miserable. Miserable and humid, the rain had been and gone and the sun had not yet burnt through the cloud. But it persevered. The air was already uncomfortably sticky. He lit up a cigarette and inhaled deeply.

The sight of dead children upset Crabb every time he had the misfortune to see one. It just wasn't right.

The scene of crime officers dragged the boy from the water, shooing away a flock of ducks that had started to peck at Toby's bare feet. A dirty white football floated away; fallen leaves sticking to it like plasters on an injury. A small plastic yellow boat bobbled on the surface of the pond, looking incongruously jolly as it sailed past the corpse.

They laid the dead body on a clean plastic sheet, under a hastily erected tarpaulin. All the SOCOs and the police officers stood back, made physically awkward by the sight of a mutilated young corpse. They had all worked together for years as part of major task forces; and the majority of officers here had worked together on Adam's murder. Now the policemen and women stood like strangers at a party; awkward, almost embarrassed.

They made way for the pathologist, and backing away, they fanned out and disappeared like ephemeral beings, ready to begin their fingertip search in the area around the pond and in the water itself. They would work with the SOCOs to see what was worth bagging and tagging, what may or may not be connected to the crime.

Crabb stood over the body. Raw emotion rarely took up visible residence in the faces of a major investigation team. Too many disgusting deaths seen by too many disgusted policemen. But with a child – it was always different. Dead children felt like a contradiction in terms.

The boy had a plump and dimpled stomach and a strawberry birthmark on his left hip. His soft roundness made him look much younger than his fifteen years. Wet ringlets of hair haloed his head, the drips running from his body and pooling around him.

His mouth was sealed shut with masking tape. It was wrapped around and around his head, sealing his mouth shut.

They watched in silence as Dr Harry Moore bent over the body. Crabb desperately tried to concentrate on the beauty of Moore's hands, trying to ignore the ugliness of the corpse. Beautiful hands, alive and agile, contrasted harshly with the still form of the dead boy. Moore's fingers, bony but fragile, danced over the body. His long fingers flitted softly and quickly over the boy, poking and prodding, almost caressing him.

Crabb had forgotten how much more dead a child looked compared to an adult.

Unsettled, he turned away, not wanting to see the rectal temperature being taken. It seemed such an intrusion on a body already defiled. He turned back into the huddle as Moore sat back on his haunches.

'It's pretty obvious what killed him,' Moore said bluntly.

Crabb looked at the metal skewer embedded in the boy's left ear, its end protruding – lethal, harsh. Cold, bright steel.

'Based on visuals only, it looks like your common or garden variety of skewer used primarily for barbeques. Kebabs, that type of thing. Unless the tip, which is not visible, is something other than appearances suggest, I'd have thought that anyone could buy one in any number of kitchen or DIY outlets,' said Moore. 'But that's your problem, not mine.'

'Would he have died instantly?' asked Crabb.

'Well, there are a few hesitation marks visible at the entry of the ear canal, whether because of incompetence or nerves, impossible to tell. However, the main thrust of the skewer, which your murderer got right in the end, would, I suspect, have killed him outright. Difficult to say until I cut his head open.'

Crabb inwardly winced at the pathologist's words. Next to him, DCI Docherty stood stock-still – his usual immobility striking. As if he wished he wasn't here. Although superior in rank, he was more than happy to let Crabb take the lead. The DCI was more of a desk-man, a politics man, delegating from the safety of his office; a weak and ineffectual officer – a yes-man: uninspiring. A stupid pig of a man – but with a tired, given-up streak. A lethal combination. Crabb assumed Docherty was only here now because of the high-profile nature of the case.

'Was he killed here?' Crabb asked the pathologist.

'No.'

Crabb waited for further explanation.

'Come on, Moore, how do you know the boy wasn't killed here?' said Docherty. 'This isn't twenty bloody questions.' He barely moved as he spoke, his fat body trussed up in his tightly buttoned suit, his Father Christmas beard giving the false impression of geniality.

'See the signs of lividity? The bruising on his buttocks and the back of his thighs? I suspect he was killed whilst sitting in a slatted chair; see the striped bruising?' Dr Moore rolled the boy onto his side, and outlined them with his gloved hands. 'And he was left there for some hours, after being killed.'

There was silence as the assembled men pictured the scene: Crabb sure that each of them had very differing internal visuals going on, all of them adding in their own unnecessary imagined extras.

'There's evidence that he was bound at the wrists and ankles by some form of twine or cable ties. Something like that. See there, the bruising,' Dr Moore said, pointing at the pale skin at the wrists and ankles, now tinged with soft colours.

'More bruising on his left wrist than his right. Odd,' said Moore.

'Any sign of sexual assault?' Docherty asked, his tone neutral – going through the motions.

'Again, impossible to say categorically either way, but on superficial examination, no, it doesn't look like it.'

'He definitely didn't drown, then?' Docherty clarified.

'He definitely did not drown, no.'

'Time of death?' said Crabb.

'Not committing myself at this stage – makes a difference that he's been in the water. Not for long, but long enough to bugger up his core temperature. I'll let you know all the details after I've done the post-mortem. Stomach contents should help with time of death.'

Crabb listened, vaguely repulsed by the dry and academic tone with which Dr Moore chose to talk about Toby Coleridge. A good pathologist, no doubt about that, but he lacked any sense of humour, even black humour, and had little, if any, social graces. Crabb could not recall ever having seen him smile. He was a cold sod, but maybe one needed to be, bearing in mind his job.

'I wonder why his mouth's been taped,' said Dr Moore, striking an almost conversational tone.

Crabb watched with morbid curiosity as the pathologist neatly cut through the grey tape with a scalpel. His gloved fingers probed inside the boy's mouth, parting his lips gently.

'There's something in his mouth,' the pathologist said.

6

———————

Crabb said, 'What is it?'

'Looks like pencil shavings. Green pencil shavings.'

'What does that mean?' said Crabb, not really expecting an answer.

'I'm just telling you what I found. What it means, I have no idea,' said Moore.

Crabb walked away from the group, aware that his DCI followed. Docherty said, 'Skewer in the ear. Pencil shavings in the mouth. A ten-a-penny nutter.'

'Nutter or not, it's a very organised and passionless murder,' Crabb said.

He thought about the body and the method of killing – it seemed clinical, too well-thought-out to be a random killing. Too much time and effort had been expended in the execution. It looked like a careful murder, followed by a careful body-dump: the second in a series in his opinion. Crabb shook his head feeling baffled and sad.

But intrigued.

Docherty caressed his white beard and said, 'Or it could be a deaf thing. A hate crime. You know, hatred of the deaf. Skewer in the ear.'

Crabb ignored his superior stating the bleedin' obvious, and said, 'It *could* be a hate crime, but I think it's much more than that. Clearly it's linked to deafness. A skewer in the ear – that's symbolism that can't be ignored.'

Crabb hated murder. But he couldn't deny that it was exciting. There was no other word for it. The anticipation of all those people he was yet to meet in this investigation: lying, crying, pretending, surviving, *feeling*. He almost relished the challenge before him. He knew it sounded cruel, but that was why he was good at his job. He enjoyed it.

His thoughts turned to Sarah Coleridge, the boy's mother. He shook his head with sadness for her. Her already half-known suspicion had just become a hard truth: her son was dead.

And of course, there was Annie's grief as well. He tutted in frustration. He liked Annie. Liked her a lot. A strong woman, not used to being a victim. Of anything or anyone.

He'd been more than a little taken with her eyes; a duck-egg green. She'd engaged warmly with him when she'd relaxed, by somehow softening them. And then, when the mood had taken her, when the shock took over, her eyes had not engaged at all. They'd become almost reptilian. He'd watched in fascination as they'd gone flat and sightless – shutting him out. Strangely, the scar that ran from her right eye to the corner of her mouth didn't detract from her beauty, but rather enhanced it instead.

He suspected that when he got to know her better, and he would, that he'd like her more and more. He could tell that she was a non-conformer. Different. He liked that.

Late last night, he'd dug up what he could find on her. The background check had all been very mundane. Nothing to suggest that her home life had been anything other than normal.

Ditto her adult life. Using the few names of friends she'd given him, he'd found precisely nothing that even raised an eyebrow on any of them either. Not a trace of Annie Black in the system. An utter absence of criminality. Just an existence. Like most people. Except he knew she *was* different. In a good way.

For good measure, he'd also checked Scarlet with the same total non-red flag response.

Bringing himself back to the present, he said, 'This murder is cold and calculated. Unlike Adam Jacob's murder which showed only unadulterated anger – pure bloody fury: overkill. And there was something placed in Adam's mouth – his hearing aid. Now we have something in Toby's mouth; pencil shavings. And a seemingly well-thought-out, organised murder. No anger or particular emotion obvious.

'Now factor in the attack on Annie Black last night: her attacker touched her mouth. He made a point of touching her lips. Attempted to insert his fingers. He couldn't leave anything inside her mouth because he left her alive, but he made a point of bringing attention to her mouth – the next best thing to leaving something inside it. I think it's another reference to deafness. Deafness, speaking, not speaking. Something like that. The killer has a signature, a focus on the mouth, and at this point, I don't know what that means. Two dead deaf children, the same age and gender; two completely different murders. But one killer. One attacker.'

Crabb lit up a cigarette and said, 'I think our killer has evolved since Adam's murder. Accelerated suddenly. Improved his technique.' He pulled at his sweaty shirt, the sun finally coming out and its strength making him prickle with heat under his armpits. Getting no answer from Docherty, he said, 'I'll go and inform the mother.'

The harsh and abrasive finality of death. It was *always* a surprise when the news was broken. Even when it was expected.

Death came with a sodding great exclamation point. Not a comma, a blip, a pause, but a total and abrupt ceasing-to-be. A bloody great full stop.

Before leaving, Crabb said, 'Just to bring you up to date, sir, you'll remember that I've interviewed Toby's family: the mother, father and brother–'

'I *am* up to date, Crabb.'

Crabb continued, 'And they all alibi each other, supported by a record of phone calls from the mother to her sister, and a neighbour who popped round to see the father, Jonathan, on Thursday night. Paul, their hearing son, was at home all night.

'But *I* want to tell Sarah, not her husband about Toby. I suspect that she'll be the one to identify their son. He's a coward. And a complete shit.'

DCI Docherty smiled smugly, Crabb having extricated him from any emotional mess. Relieved that he now didn't have to deal with a mother of a dead child, he said, 'And after you've informed the victim's mother, I'll give another press conference. And we won't be mentioning what's in the boy's mouth. On that note, do you have *any* idea what the objects left in the mouth mean? A hearing aid, and pencil shavings. What do they mean?'

'I don't know. And I'm not telling you your job, but don't give too much away about the murders will you, sir? I think it better if you don't link up Adam. Or mention Annie. Keep them out of it. We don't want a full-scale panic on our hands in the Deaf Community.'

Docherty raised his eyebrows briefly and then feigned a smile and mock-punched Crabb on the shoulder. Pretending a camaraderie that wasn't there. Had never been there. But there was a viciousness behind the punch. 'Don't tell me how to handle the press, Crabb. Just don't.'

Crabb ignored him, noticing that despite the early hour, the media was already hovering at the edge of the trees. It was a big story: missing deaf child – now dead deaf child. An investigation like this needed publicity when the time was right. Docherty would do the press conference. His bloody Santa persona oozing concern, he'd droop his eyes in mock empathy, and appeal to the masses. It was a shame that if you looked closely, his eyes would give him away every time. They were like dark, black little beads hidden in his pudgy face – utterly soulless.

But PR wise, the DCI could play the game and preen with the best of them. Pity he lacked the balls to get his hands dirty with anything real.

Now, like maggots, the press were crawling ever nearer, pushing, jostling. Hungry for a story. A dead deaf boy. They wouldn't be disappointed. Stories of dead children always sold papers. Being deaf just made it juicier.

The voices of reporters shouting out inane questions could be heard across the pond if Crabb turned his head and actively listened. But he ignored them.

Turning to leave, Docherty grabbed Crabb's arm roughly and whispered into his ear: 'I expect you to work hard on this, mate. This is going to be big news. Keep me briefed. I want to know *every*thing. Don't forget who's in charge here.'

Crabb looked at him. Docherty would take all the credit for Crabb and his team's work.

'Do *not* piss on my parade, Crabb. I will not tolerate this case going tits-up. I want this wrapped up as soon as possible.'

Crabb left the scene, feeling a little older and a little soiled from the morning's events.

7

———

My upbringing would be described by anyone as odd. But thinking about it from an adult's perspective, it clearly shows that the general oddness within which I found myself, really wasn't my fault. Not at all.

Even when I was little, I had always preferred my own company. And that seemed to suit all of us. Ever since I had first learnt to read, I could be found, tucked into the alcove in the kitchen, lost in a book; impervious to anything that might be going on around me. If my head was not buried in a book, I would be drawing.

I felt more of a real child when I was on my own. When I was with my family, I felt like an after-thought: a mistake — an unhappy accident.

I was an appendage. A floating piece of extraneous matter, who had no real connection to the rest of the family. As soon as the family were all together in the same room, I seemed to become a non-person. That always struck me as odd. I never fitted in. It was as simple as that. I'd obviously got used to it, as the years went by. But it was so unfair. I know that sounds terribly whining, especially now as an adult I recognise that, but really, my life Was Not Fair.

After the cupboard years, I was allowed to roam the house freely, unnoticed and unbothered. I was used when needed, but other than that, I was left to my own devices. Lonely and ignored, I lived my childish life on my own. Taught myself about the big outdoors, about the world outside our house and the people who inhabited it; quickly realising that I was most assuredly not the norm. But I got used to it.

I remember feeling that it was especially wrong when I had to start learning all about my mother's gynaecological problems. It started when I was about eleven, maybe twelve. Post-cupboard. When my mother started going into graphic detail about her ovarian cysts. I didn't understand and I felt intuitively that I shouldn't have to understand. It was inappropriate. I was too young. She had to explain it several times to me before I got it. It was embarrassing. Too much information for such a little child. My mother; cruel and perverted and totally incapable of love.

But this odd life was all that I knew. It was my thirteenth birthday that changed everything. Without wanting to sound overly dramatic, it was literally life-changing. It changed the course of events that would shape our lives. The entire family was never the same again.

Life-changing events should be of grandiose proportions, set off by something great, be it good or bad, but something important at the very least. This was all so mundane. So trivial. A reaction to something so silly, really. That's what I remember most. What a stupid, idiotic and childish reason to change the course of one's life.

But as I discovered, life is like that.

8

———

alf past nine on Sunday morning and Annie felt like
crap. Raw. At risk.

'See you later, and good luck,' said Scarlet.

Annie pointed at her own face: 'Are you sure you haven't
made me look like a bloody mannequin? All this make-up.'

Scarlet tilted her head. Often her answers came in eyebrow
movements only – like some weird kind of semaphore. She only
spoke if her eyebrows failed her. Now her brows rose a quarter
of an inch and stayed there. The rest of her features remained
set for a moment before her forehead furrowed, and she said,
'You're just not used to it. You said you wanted to camouflage
your injuries. Job done.'

'Okay, I believe you. And thanks for coming to the police
station last night. You didn't have to.'

Scarlet shook off Annie's words; embarrassed – eyebrows
rigid, cowed into submission by a single thank you. She turned
her back – escaping. But smiling.

Thirty minutes later the taxi dropped Annie off outside the
Deaf School. Dora Potts, the matriarch and unspoken leader of

33

the Deaf Community had texted her this morning, demanding that Annie come and join in.

The Deaf were out in force. Toby had gone missing between his house and the Deaf Club, passing the school on his way. No one knew at which point he'd disappeared, only that he'd never arrived at his destination. A group of Deaf men and women walked the length of the street, pinning posters of Toby to trees, sellotaping his photograph to lamp posts, to bins, to trees and to walls. Knocking on doors.

As she stepped from the cab, Annie felt cellophane-wrapped: the after-effects from her attack felt tangible and visible to anyone who looked at her. Memories of suffocation immobilised her.

She bent at the waist, struggling not to gasp for air. Hyper-vigilant, she watched the feet of everyone within her visual circle, checking that they weren't advancing; noticing the laces of a shoe, some pink-varnished toes in a pair of blue flip-flops, a weed sprouting from a crack in the pavement. Straightening and turning, she bumped into Edward, a man in his thirties with bad skin, who smiled and signed, *'Hunt, join, you?'*

Nodding, not knowing him well, she didn't smile in return. Found his barely concealed enthusiasm disturbing. She went in search of Dora. Instead she saw Ben Downing walking towards her. Toby's tormentor.

Annie made herself remember that Ben was just a child. Reminded herself that he was only sixteen. He saw her and sauntered over, his walk a cocky teenage swagger. He was tall, stocky and had a heavy, plain face with a basin haircut.

Ben looked stupid but his eyes gave him away. They glittered with an intelligence. He vaguely frightened her, although she couldn't quite put her finger on that trickle of unease she always felt around him. Maybe it was because he disguised his feelings too well. She found him disconcerting and difficult to read. He'd grown since she'd last seen him. Now much taller than she, he must be nearly six foot, and his large cumbersome body adopted a more confident stance than she'd remembered. Unbidden, she imagined him squeezing tight on a plastic bag, holding it over her face until she couldn't breathe. She inhaled deeply, telling herself not to be so stupid. *He's only a boy.*

He was only one year older than Toby but seemed almost adult by comparison. He glared back at her with equal dislike.

Ben signed, '*Boy gold? You here, search? Where, where?*'

'Come looking for golden boy? I wonder where he could possibly be?'

Ben used British Sign Language: unlike Annie, who used Sign Supported English. Most of the people here were BSL users. She personally preferred to follow English grammar, as her father had taught her. Forced her to sit on her hands as a child, making her speak. It sounded cruel to others, but she'd loved her lip-reading, speaking and vocabulary time with him. Couldn't be more grateful to her father. If not for him, she'd have no voice.

BSL syntax was quite different. A truncated but rich form of English, with nuances and often meaning coming from the facial expression. In the eyes of the Deaf Community, her sign language usage made her little-d deaf. She wasn't deemed deaf *enough* to warrant the label, big-D Deaf, not *proper* Deaf, although she was profoundly so. As far as she was concerned, deaf was deaf.

'When did you last see Toby, Ben? Did you see him on Thursday night?' she signed.

He shook his head lazily. 'No. Definitely not. Would have told the police, wouldn't I? That Crabb copper interviewed me.'

'Why do you hate Toby so much?'

Ben laughed, bent his knees and threw back his head as if her signs were the funniest thing he'd ever seen. 'Because he's a sissy, that's why. A big fat mummy's boy. But I didn't hurt him. I just teased him – that's all. Why would I hurt him? What would be the point? He's more fun when he's there for me to tease. If I really hurt him, I'd take away my own fun. And that would just be stupid don't you think?'

'Were you at the Deaf Club on Thursday evening?'

'No.'

'Did you see Toby that night?'

'No. Who are you anyway, the fucking police?'

Annie angled her head to the side, trying to read his facial expression. But he kept his face rigid, gave nothing away. He was strangely talented at revealing nothing. Annie could usually spot a liar at a hundred paces.

Ben looked back at her and signed, 'You know I don't like you, don't you? You with your great big clever voice. You make me sick. You look down on us – the proper Deaf. We're not disabled. Not like blind people. We don't need fixing. Doctors are always trying to repair us – like we're broken.'

He drew his lips back. 'You're not one of us.'

He took a puff of his cigarette and wiped away a line of sweat that had gathered on his upper lip with his index finger. As a grand finale, he added, 'I bet you think *you're* disabled.'

She wanted to scream at him, 'Of course I'm disabled, I'm fucking profoundly deaf.'

But she didn't bother. Couldn't be bothered. This was about Toby, not Deaf politics.

'Where's Dora?'

He simply pointed over Annie's right shoulder. She swivelled on her feet, and first saw only Martin, the caretaker of the Deaf School. He smiled briefly at Annie and then peeled away from Dora, leaving the older woman to approach alone.

Dora Potts moved imperiously, as if holding court: majestic in her demeanour, and arrogant in her bearing. She was a morbidly obese woman with her body and face stretched to capacity. As a result, she looked younger than her fifty-nine years. She held a Chihuahua in her arms as if it were a baby. It shivered and its bulbous eyes looked on the verge of weeping.

Dora's battleship bosom-and-bottom manoeuvred itself across the road with no discernible effort on her part. She gathered her folds of fat in hand as she moved ever nearer to Annie – a wobbling but strong presence gliding across the tarmac as smoothly as a razor through stubble.

'*Long time not see, you. Happy you here,*' Dora signed.

'Happy to see you're taking advantage of my voice,' Annie signed and smiled politely, not bothered that she was playing this game. If Dora wanted to be queen bee, that was up to her. It didn't affect Annie. It was the best time to take advantage of the voice Annie had, and she was happy enough to be used by Dora. The huge woman beamed at her, both of them aware that Dora was playing her trump card, and unashamedly using the very thing that Annie had that Dora disapproved of: her ability to speak. The woman's fat fingers flew through the air: 'We might need your voice, but it doesn't mean the Deaf don't *have* a voice. *I* am their voice. But using your speaking voice, well... it makes it less official than using interpreters. It will appeal to the hearing community from a Deaf perspective.'

Annie nodded her agreement, only wanting to talk about Toby. She didn't want to talk about her own attack which in the light of day, compared to Toby's situation, suddenly felt trivial. She was still here. Toby wasn't. She'd tell them all later when she had to. If she had to.

Dora carried on: 'Thought now was a good time to talk to people. It's Sunday morning. The police may have missed people when they asked around about Toby on Thursday evening. People might have been out at work, at the pub, whatever. We owe it to Toby to ask ourselves. He's one of us. We've got to find him. And you can do the asking for us. Although we do have interpreters here: both Sam and Harry.'

She smiled smugly. Annie bowed her head, smiled back.

For such a large woman, Dora's hands were extraordinarily delicate and she signed with a natural elegance that belied her size, her fingers flitting through the air as if playing an instrument. Annie found herself pleased to see her and things felt slightly less haphazard in Dora's presence. Safer. However big-D Deaf the woman was, Annie secretly liked her. Admired her. Trusted her. She could be a bitch, but she was kind. Despite herself.

'Did Ben go to the Deaf Club on Thursday?' Annie signed with her back to Ben, who, she was aware, still loitered in her shadow behind her.

Dora's eyes drifted upwards as she thought, also ignoring the boy behind Annie. Slowly she shook her head. Annie wondered where Ben had been. Wanted to quiz him further. She turned, ready to really question him, gloves off, when she realised that she couldn't see William. His absence was enough to stop her and she signed, 'Where's William? I'd have expected him to be here.'

'I don't know. He'll probably turn up later. I did text him.'

After a cursory glance around for William, not overly concerned, Dora signed, 'Have you met that detective, Crabb? He came to the Deaf Club on Thursday evening. Sarah called the police, frantic when she came to pick Toby up, not knowing that he hadn't even arrived. Crabb interviewed all of us. Lucky that Harry was there to interpret for us. But Toby's mother, desperate she was. Poor cow.'

Annie already knew all this but answered, adopting the sign that Dora used for Crabb – first two fingers of each hand held together, tapping the thumb: like pincers. She signed, 'I've met Crabb. He's alright. Nice. I liked him.'

Dora pursed her lips in a moue of distaste. 'He was okay-ish. Considering.'

'Considering what?'

'Considering he's the police and he doesn't have a clue about the Deaf Community.'

'Explain it to him then. He's hearing. It's a new world for him. Help him.'

'I did. Toby's my priority, but Crabb needs to know how it is. Needs to understand about us. The Deaf. Our World.'

Annie felt irritation but simply signed, 'That's okay. He's not threatening your world. Remember, it's all about Toby. That's all that's important. Fuck the Deaf World. It's not a war, Dora. Crabb's trying to help. Help him.'

Dora nodded, her neck creasing into folds, and her chins wobbling. It was as near an acknowledgement of Annie's truth as she could expect.

About to ask if Dora had found any information out about Toby, Annie caught sight of an old woman in her peripheral vision, standing at her door, holding on to the door frame of her house. Even from where she was, Annie could see the woman pointing at Ben, her outstretched finger accusing.

Annie turned to Ben who stood, staring at the woman, frowning. She looked at the house opposite her and counted back down along the street: the woman stood outside number twenty-two. Feeling a frisson of excitement, Annie started moving towards her. Dora followed, her dog still clutched to her bosom.

Annie stopped as she felt the vibration of her mobile in her pocket. She held her index finger up to Dora in a stop-wait gesture and read her text.

Come now. They've found Toby. Come to my house. Get a taxi.
Sarah.

9

———————

Annie watched Sarah's hands on the glass. Watched the sweat from her fingers leave a damp trail on the partition; the partition between them and Toby's lifeless form. The dead boy's body was laid out on a cold slab, a white sheet pulled up tight to his chin; his face in profile. Her friend's knuckles were white with the pressure she exerted on the glass, the beds of her fingernails stained an unnatural grey.

Sarah's posture was rigid, but her head trembled. But only if you were seeking out signs of her distress – and Annie was. She didn't know what else to do. Her friend's head was like a too large sunflower: on a too-frail stalk with a huge flower head struggling in a too-strong wind. Her normally perfectly groomed hair was covered by a crumpled headscarf. With the loss of Toby she had become somehow less. Less Sarah.

She suddenly dropped her right hand from the glass and clutched Annie's left. The heat and moisture of Sarah's palm quickly transferred itself onto Annie's outstretched hand. They gripped their fingers tightly together. Annie's world was always silent, but this was a different silence. A forever and desperately lonely quiet.

40

Sarah gently let her head fall slowly forward until her forehead rested on the glass. The movement almost dislodged her dark sunglasses but she didn't bother righting them. Her entire body remained tense, but it seemed to hum as if she were an old violin being plucked for the first time in years. Other than that, she remained completely still, one hand holding on to Annie's, the other splayed onto the dividing pane, separating life from death. Mother from son.

Sarah's usually beautiful and fine features now appeared harsh and gaunt. Seeing her friend like this made Annie's own grief redundant. Forbidden. Although Annie desperately wanted to cry, her throat aching with the effort of holding it in, she wouldn't allow herself to burst into tears. She didn't deserve that luxury. That right belonged to Sarah alone.

Annie blurred her vision by gently squeezing her eyes, keeping them only partially open. Giving her only a softened vision of Toby. She blurred her heart, keeping it untouchable and blurred the pain. Became a blurred spectator only. Incapable of taking in the grief of such a young boy.

And yet one tear escaped from her eye. She felt it slide down her cheek and she swiped angrily at it. Pretending it was not there; making it not there.

Sarah turned her head and Annie lip-read, 'His hair's all wrong. He'd have hated that. It should be slicked back, not all flattened down like that – with a parting. They've got that wrong. Toby liked his new hairstyle. He left one loose lock of hair so that it fell down his face – at the front. Silly, really. But he'd be so upset if he could see how he looks now.'

Sarah let go of Annie's hand and gently placed her own back on the glass. Almost caressed it. She patted it softly as if in farewell and turned to Crabb, who stood awkwardly at the back of the room, his eyes downcast, his body language screaming out his discomfort. Sarah said, 'Thank you, inspector. That is Toby. Now I'd like to leave.'

She turned and walked from the room, not turning back, waiting for neither Crabb nor Annie.

Crabb caught up with her and gently guided her with his arm at her elbow. Annie went to take her hand on the other side, but Sarah shook her off. Crabb led them into an office with soft furnishings, two armchairs, a sofa and a small coffee table. Everything felt muted; the walls painted a sickly green. The supposed calming colour of all institutions. It didn't calm Annie. She thought the space a transparently 'I'm sorry for your loss' room, but sank gratefully into a chair, placing herself opposite Sarah and the policeman. Hardened herself, forced herself, protected herself by becoming a clinical observer only – not a participant. Crabb said, 'Could I get you a cup of tea?'

Sarah didn't even bother to shake her head, but said, 'How did he die?'

Annie watched Crabb preparing to lie. His eye blink was slow, as if he were forming the words in rehearsal in his head, before perhaps dumbing them down, missing something out, creating something less horrific, something more acceptable to a mother of a dead son. Finally: 'He was stabbed.'

'Stabbed where?' Sarah seemed unreachable, her face immobile, eyes hidden behind the black shade of her glasses – no tears visible on her cheeks.

The two words hung heavily in the air as again Crabb seemed to struggle with the answer. 'In his ear. We'll know more when the post-mortem has been done. I don't think he would have suffered.'

Annie bit the inside of her cheek, wanting the distraction of physical pain. She was beyond tears now. Her heart had closed: sobbing wouldn't even come close to how she was feeling.

Crabb's last sentence had come with an almost imperceptible shake of his head, a gesture in complete contradiction to his verbal statement. An unwitting negation of his words. Annie briefly closed her eyes, not wanting to see any more. When she opened them she saw that Sarah had taken off her headscarf, revealing dishevelled and unwashed hair. She slowly and deliberately folded the cloth into a neat rectangle. She then unfurled and re-folded it, this time into a triangle – Annie could feel herself and Crabb both inextricably drawn to this rather odd form of origami playing itself out in front of them.

Sarah looked up at Crabb and said, 'It's all my fault. Toby shouldn't have died. It's my fault. I lied to you, inspector. I told you that I wasn't feeling well, that that was the reason that I hadn't driven Toby to the Deaf Club. But I was talking to my sister, Amy. On the phone. I wasn't ill. I was laughing with Amy. *Laughing*. Giggling like two stupid children. I didn't know what would happen. How could I? I just waved Toby off. I assumed he'd be alright. It's an easy walk, it was still light. He's fifteen. He's not a child. It's just that I'd promised him a lift that night. I don't know why, but I did. He usually walks, but I should have driven him. If I hadn't been so selfish, wanting to chat with my sister, he wouldn't be dead now. It's all my fault.'

Crabb said, 'It is *not* your fault. And talking to your sister on the phone is hardly selfish. As you say, Toby had done the walk before on his own, many times. Do *not* blame yourself.'

'My husband, Jonathan, could have given him a lift, but that would have been asking too much. Now *he*'s a selfish bastard if we're bringing up blame. He never did anything for Toby. For Paul, my other son, yes. But not for Toby.'

Annie watched as Crabb sat back, shocked at her outburst, clearly not expecting it. 'Why's that? Didn't your husband get on with Toby?'

Sarah's body tensed and her fingers flitted back up to her sunglasses. 'Jonathan never really bothered with him. Was embarrassed by Toby's deafness. He never even bothered learning to sign. And anyway, he was drunk that night. Incapable of driving. Incapable of being a father. Talking to some ghastly neighbour who'd dropped in for a free drink.'

She frowned and her face tightened as she readjusted her glasses.

Annie thought that Sarah might as well have sent up a distress flare. Her body language gave her away at the mere mention of her husband. Every time she mentioned Jonathan, her hands moved involuntarily to her glasses. Annie knew what they were hiding. What they often hid.

That was the annoying thing about the hearing. They relied *too much* on words, when there was so much more to communication. Annie was pleased that Crabb *did* in fact look. She saw his face relax as he understood. 'Does your husband hit you, Sarah?'

In answer, she took the glasses from her face and revealed a greenish, yellow bruise around a swollen eye.

'There's no point in pretending now. What's the point? He's been hitting me for years. But he never hit the children. Just me.'

Crabb's lips tightened in restrained fury, but he said nothing. Hoping perhaps for more from Sarah. Obligingly she added, 'I wouldn't describe my husband's relationship with Toby as particularly close.'

She stated this boldly, as a simple fact, but Annie could see a mixture of shame and then hatred cross her features. Sarah pulled her shoulders back.

'Anyway, it doesn't matter now. I shall be taking Paul with me up to my sister's place. I shall be staying there for the time being. Jonathan can rot in hell. I will not grieve with him. I shall grieve with my son and my sister. Let me know when I can have Toby's body back. I shall need to make the necessary arrangements.'

Annie leant forward and placed her hand on Sarah's knee.

Squeezed it and watched as tears suddenly started to fall from Sarah's eyes. Like a wet sheet, they continued to tumble out, a torrent of grief. Not identifiable as singular drops, but instead a solid curtain of tears, a waterfall unleashed. Not bothering to wipe her sadness away, she said, 'Toby was such a gentle boy. Popular. Kind. Perhaps a little immature for his age, but that's not a bad thing, is it? He was just a boy. A little boy. My little boy.'

This time, Sarah allowed Annie to take her in her arms and hug her. Annie wanted to hug her to death, to stop her pain, to bring Toby back, to make it all better again. None of that was possible. She kissed Sarah on her cheek and said, 'If you need anything, Sarah, anything at all, you know where I am.'

Annie knew that was trite, but she couldn't think of anything else to say. Impossible to find the right words. The right words didn't exist. Sarah stood up, still semi-locked in Annie's embrace and although her tears still flowed, her face and mouth didn't look as if she were making any sound. She was caught in her own anguished world, and Annie felt Sarah shaking from deep within her, as if her core were crumbling.

Sarah pulled away and put on her glasses again, said, 'What you can do, Annie, is come home with me now and distract my shit of a husband, while I pack. Other than that, you can help Crabb find the bastard that killed my son. Show Crabb the Deaf World, make them talk to him. It was Toby's world. Even I wasn't included in that part of his life. You are. Make the Deaf open up to the police.'

Crabb said, 'Why do you assume that Toby's murderer is from the Deaf World?'

Sarah stopped at the door, taken aback by his question. 'I don't know really. When I went to the Deaf Club to pick up Toby, they were concerned. Kind. Worried for me. For Toby. But they seemed to shut me out when I asked about Ben. He bullied my son, as I've already told you. But the Deaf closed ranks. I'm not saying it's Ben – I've met him; he's just a boy. But... I don't know. I just assumed whoever took him is Deaf.'

'I've already talked to Ben. As you say, he's a bully, but still only a boy,' said Crabb.

'A big boy,' said Annie.

Crabb ignored her, paused and changed the subject. Said, 'Did Toby like drawing?'

'Drawing? Not especially, no. He liked the drums.' She smiled at the memory and then frowned. 'Why are you asking about drawing?'

Crabb waved her question away. 'It's not important. Just following something up.'

Sarah didn't listen, desperate to leave. She turned the door handle. 'I need to go. Now. Please, would you give me a lift back? I've got to go.'

Her tears had come to a stop and Sarah had entered into just-getting-through-the-next-minute stage. She used her innate politeness as a crutch and opening her bag she handed Crabb a piece of paper. 'Here's the name and number of an interpreter who's agreed to work with you whenever you need him.'

Annie took the sheet of paper from Crabb, and read the name. She nodded and said, 'Sam. He's an excellent interpreter. He'll do a good job. Either him or Charlie.'

Sarah said, 'When Sam heard that Toby was missing, he offered his services, which was kind of him. I've known him for years, and Toby liked him. So I want him. I barely know Charlie.' She picked up her bag. 'Forgive me. I really do have to leave.'

Sarah reminded Annie of those dried and flattened flowers that she had pressed between the pages of a heavy book as a child. The colours always vanished and looked watered down and diluted as time passed. Sarah walked ahead of Annie and

Crabb, wanting the distance, needing to be gone from this dreadful place – almost running.

Hoping that she was whispering, had got the pitch right, Annie said, 'Do *you* think the killer is deaf?'

'I don't know. But I'd assume he knew Toby. Toby wouldn't get into a stranger's car, would he?'

'He was a naïve child. Sweet. But a bit scared of the hearing world when he was alone. So, yes, I agree. Toby must have known his killer, who must have been deaf. Toby couldn't lip-read.'

'Will you help me? With the Deaf Community? When I spoke to them on Thursday at the Deaf Club, they were a little... I don't know quite the right word.'

'Frosty.'

'Yeah, frosty. Will you help? Like my sort-of consultant, but just between you and me. Nothing overt.'

'Of course. And you have to understand about the Deaf. Deafness is like being in an exclusive gang that's somehow separate from the hearing world. Special. That's definitely not how *I* feel, but it's the way the Deaf Community works. Hearing and Deaf. Them and Us.'

'Which are you?'.

'I keep myself firmly and squarely in my own camp. Them, Us, and Me.' She stopped walking and said, 'And what's with the drawing thing?'

'What? Oh, nothing. Really, nothing.'

'You're lying.'

Crabb stopped and looked at her. Said, 'And how are *you*?'

'I'm fine. It's Sarah you have to worry about. It's her who's lost her son. I was just a friend.' Tears suddenly and unexpectedly flooded her eyes. She allowed them to fall freely. 'I loved him.'

He placed his hand on her shoulder and said, 'I meant, how are you after your attack?'

'Oh, that.' Annie almost smiled but couldn't get her chin to co-operate. 'I'd almost forgotten. Feels like a million years ago. It's nothing in comparison to Toby's death. Nothing at all.'

Crabb gripped her arm and looked her straight in the eye, said, 'Annie, I want to reiterate my opinion that you, Toby and Adam have a common enemy. Something that ties you all together.

'I want you scared because scared means you'll be careful. It's one way of reducing the odds of another attack. Remember to be scared. It's important. Really important.'

10

———

My mother has been dead to me since I was thirteen years old, and I to her. She died in the very physical sense last year. At the beginning of April. We had not seen each other since I had left home at eighteen. I think she blamed me for everything that happened.

She even blamed me for the death of our cat, Snowy. Blamed me with silent looks. Naturally, the death of the cat paled into insignificance in contrast to the passing of my brother into the ether, but we both knew where the responsibility lay for the cat's unfortunate demise. On the very day that Ewan died as well. What are the chances? My mother was unaware of Snowy's torture. Although I of course knew only too well how it had suffered. Pointy sticks with sharp ends stuck up and down and through every orifice.

And then Snowy was burnt and left at the bottom of the garden. Still enough of it to be recognisable as once-cat. A pile of snowy ashes. It was never referred to again. After all, it seemed tasteless what with Ewan's death. Hardly worth an obituary. It was just a stupid cat.

I believe the word 'trigger' could be used, in terms of my mother's death, and its effect on me. I like the word trigger: it's nicely descriptive and implies that I coped with the shock of my mother's demise by *behaving like an errant missile: a bullet ricocheting about the place, with no direction, and no intended target. Maybe the word 'coped' is being a little generous to myself. My way of coping was to annihilate a boy – Adam Jacobs, as I later found out. But my behaviour was really rather repellent, for which I am ashamed. It was a mistake. It was an horrific and unwarranted attack. I can't blame him. His only fault was to be there. His misfortune. My punchbag. His untimely death. My fury. And ultimately, my luck. I wasn't caught.*

I had been so wrapped up in the unexpected aftershock of Mother's death, that I had lost control. At least I can admit that. But I shall not be making the same mistake again. And so far, so good.

Well, I say 'so far, so good', but that's not strictly true. I have had to kill again. But it wasn't my fault. And I was not driven by fury this time. Merely necessity. I believe that goes in my favour.

I had given this whole matter a lot of thought before I started. Care and precision had been crucial to the initial stages of my plan. Indeed, all the stages. But it's actually more than a plan. It's more like a blueprint for a complete overhaul. A renovation, if you will.

My lack of self-discipline shown with Adam Jacobs will not be repeated. His was an uncontrolled annihilation. As if I were a novice in the ways of killing.

Or more honestly, I had forgotten. Either way, it doesn't really matter.

Because I will not make the same mistake again. By definition, I can only improve. An apprentice no longer, but a master. My work will be something to look forward to. The anticipation something to relish and excite.

Sit back and enjoy. I know I shall.

11

Sarah held her son Paul in place in the hall with another kiss and a raised finger, silently forbidding him from following her. She swept into the sitting room, her face tight. Her husband sat on the sofa, with the conservatory doors open, a warm breeze barely making itself discernible. Crabb followed quickly and was in time to hear her say, 'I've just seen the boy from the pond. It's our son. It's Toby. He's dead.'

Crabb was aware that Annie had caught the words from her position at his side by craning her neck, and he saw her wince at the harshness. He watched Jonathan's face. He did not react to his wife's stark announcement. His expression didn't noticeably change, other than he closed his eyes and held them shut for a few seconds. Then he took in the statement with a small nod and tipped a glass into his mouth, the amber liquid disappearing with a pursing of the lips, and an inhalation.

Sarah left the room, grabbing Paul by the shoulder as she passed. Crabb watched the seventeen-year-old follow, his eyes vacant, his movements automatic.

Crabb said, 'I'm sorry for your loss, Jonathan, but I'm afraid I have to ask you a few more questions.'

Jonathan tipped his chin up, his eyes glassy. He took in Annie and said, 'And why are you here?'

'I'm just here for Sarah,' she said, looking uncomfortable and as if she were being intrusive. 'She asked me to come back with her,' she added.

'Why don't you go and be with her then?'

'I will, but I think she needs a little time with Paul.'

Crabb watched as Toby's father retreated further into his glass. He suspected that this retreat was becoming a permanent residence, and not just a temporary pit stop.

Crabb and Annie sat in stiff wing-backed chairs, whilst Jonathan semi-sat on the edge of the sofa, leaning back as if all he wanted to do was sleep. His body was defeated: his short squat thighs splayed wide open, one of his elbows rested on the armrest, the other held his glass in his lap. His face and skin had an unhealthy slick sheen to it, beads of sweat peppered his cheeks and brows, his features gaunt and remote. Spikey prematurely white hair sprouted from above each ear, and thick tufts sat at sharp angles in the middle of his head as if he'd been running his hands through it. Crabb couldn't help likening him to a troll stuck on the end of a pencil.

Moving forward and sitting upright unexpectedly, Jonathan thrust his chin in Crabb's direction and raised his eyebrows in question. 'I hardly think this is the time to be questioning me, if that's your intention. My son is dead.'

'I'm not questioning you. Just a little chat.'

Annie interrupted, obviously feeling she had to explain her presence. 'I know we're not the best of friends, Jonathan, but I can't tell you how sorry I am about Toby.'

'I don't need your commiserations. He's gone. What do you care?'

'I loved him, Jonathan. He was a sweet little boy. If there's anything I can do.'

Crabb saw her concentration as she lip-read him and then heard the clichés as they fell from her mouth. He was sure that Annie was aware that she had offered over-used condolences. But, as he knew, there really were no words that summed up, concisely and kindly, the death of someone else's child.

He leant forward, putting his face nearer to Jonathan's, feeling the warmth on his cheeks as the sun shone brightly into the room.

'Believe me, I shall do my absolute utmost to find out what's happened to Toby,' he said.

Jonathan grunted.

Annie asked, 'When did you last see him?' She held her hand up, stopping Jonathan from interrupting, 'And yes, I'm sure the police have already asked you all this. But I'm asking now. *I* need to know. I need to understand.'

Jonathan laughed. 'He's our son, Annie. Our dead son now. Not yours. What gives you the right?'

'Nothing gives me the right. I'm just trying to help. I was lucky enough to know him, that's all.' She repeated, 'When did you last see your son?'

Crabb, interested now in their dislike of each other, allowed her to overstep the mark, over-involving herself in what amounted to an informal police interview. Jonathan grudgingly answered her.

'At dinner, Thursday night. He buggered off as per to the Deaf Club. My wife was too busy on the phone with that sister of hers. Can't stand her. Anyway, that was it. Haven't seen Toby since.' He poured another glass of whisky for himself and took a large swallow. Thought and added, 'And now I won't see him again at all.'

Crabb said, 'Anything at all different about Toby, recently? Did you notice if he was worried or seemed frightened of anything?'

Jonathan seemed to give it real thought, throwing back his head and gazing at the ceiling. 'Even though you've asked me these bloody questions ad infinitum, I suppose I did notice something odd,' he said. 'But not really about Toby. I haven't mentioned it to your lot before because I couldn't see the point.'

'What was it? What did you see?' Annie asked. Eager. Too eager.

'It was Wednesday afternoon, the day before Toby went missing. I occasionally pick up Toby from school, if I finish early in the City. And I recognised that boy. The one that bullies Toby.'

He looked enquiringly at Crabb, who said, 'Describe him.'

'Looks like a bit of a retard, basin haircut, big for his age – I think he's in Toby's class. Maybe a year older, how should I know?'

'Ben,' said Crabb, 'and he's not a retard. He's deaf. Nothing wrong with his brain as far as I'm aware.'

He registered Annie's lips tighten in anger at Jonathan's word choice.

'Whatever. That's the boy, though,' said Jonathan. 'He can be a cold fucker. Rude. Over-confident. Sarah tells me that he bullied Toby. Whatever. I saw him standing with an older chap. Mid-twenties? Handsome bugger, if you like that sort of thing. A lot of muscle and glossy hair. Dressed well. Looked sharp. Probably gay. They were both standing on the corner. This must have been about four o'clock-ish? And Ben looked absolutely shit-scared. Crapping himself, not to put too fine a point on it. They were both signing so I couldn't tell you what frightened the boy so much. I don't speak Deaf. But my son, he was watching them.'

Crabb wondered who it was who had frightened the bully. And what had Toby seen? He needed to see Ben again as soon as possible.

'And then the young man left and that tart was comforting him,' Jonathan said. 'Comforting the boy, I mean. Ben.'

The word 'tart' conjured up nothing familiar to Crabb, and he looked to Annie for help. Saw her ball her fists and look down at her feet.

'Could you give me a little more to go on? Tart could mean anyone,' Crabb said.

'Yeah, she's Annie's mate. *That* tart. Deaf. Blonde. Big tits, curves in all the right places.' He carved out an hourglass shape in the air – his hairy knuckles making the whole gesture even more salacious.

With the description, Crabb remembered DS Peters mentioning the woman. Making the same shapes with his hands in youthful naïveté. Saying that she'd been a little pissed when he'd spoken to her at the Deaf Club on Thursday night.

Annie said, 'You mean, Fiona. *She* was comforting Ben?'

Jonathan had grown tired of the conversation and was fast diluting himself with alcohol. His eyes were blurred, soft, wet, but he leant forward, pissed and pissed off now.

'Get back to my son. I couldn't give a flying fuck about Ben. Or the tart. What you want to know is, did *I* kill my son? The simple and honest answer is – no, I didn't. As I've already told you down at the station. Did I like the fact that my son was deaf? No, I didn't. But I loved him.' He lit a cigarette and sucked wetly on the tip.

'My son is dead. My wife will leave me. Is probably packing right this minute – I'm not a complete fool. And she'll take my normal, healthy son with her, who, by the way, I also love very much. Good riddance to both of them. My family is destroyed. I have nothing left. And I have absolutely nothing to add to that.'

He poured another large whisky into his tumbler, the ice cubes chinking quietly.

'Oh, apart from, if the police find out exactly when Toby was killed, you can rest assured that I have an alibi. At work or here since Thursday; haven't left the house since Saturday morning. As you very well know, Crabb.'

Jonathan Coleridge's eyes, so bright blue that they made him look almost blind, gazed at Crabb and Annie. He took another drink, and closed them, saying, 'Goodbye.'

Crabb looked at him. Alcohol, impotent fury, a murdered son, and a suddenly-to-be absent wife and child had left an angry but sad character in its wake – God only knew what would happen to him now. He didn't like men who hit women but found himself feeling almost sorry for the man.

But not quite.

They quietly left the room. Annie touched his arm, shaking her head as if in dismay, and said, 'I forgot to tell you. There was a neighbour, opposite the school, when I was with the Deaf search party this morning, who pointed at Ben. Ben Downing – Toby's bully. Like she recognised him. You'll have to interview him again.'

He nodded, but she'd already turned from him, intent on her mobile, texting. Waiting. Looking worried. Finished, she turned her face to his.

'Who are you texting?'

Annie's face looked momentarily slack with incomprehension: she'd missed what he'd said so he repeated it.

'I'm trying to get in touch with Fiona. We have to speak to her. She must have seen something.'

'Do you know her?'

'Yes, I went to school with her. She's my friend.'

Before he could reply, Sarah came down the stairs, Paul walking behind her as if on automatic pilot. She struggled with two suitcases and Crabb rushed to take them from her.

She carefully placed an envelope on the hall table and smiling grimly, she walked out through the front door.

The press were waiting. A line of them, pushing and shoving. Ignoring them, she walked, her posture rigid, around the side of the house. She pressed the remote to open the garage doors and looked bleakly up at the sun as it beat down on her and her surviving son. Crabb saw her composure waver; small but deadly cracks threatened.

'Thank you, Crabb. You've been very kind,' she said. 'Keep me updated.' Turning to Annie, she smiled and kissed her on the cheek, hugged her briefly but tightly and said, 'Email me. Text me. Either. Let me know everything that's going on, okay?'

Annie nodded and Crabb saw Sarah's eyes bright with tears. She wiped at them absentmindedly as they slid down her face and got into her car.

Sarah ignored the bombardment of camera flashes as she sat behind the wheel, Paul next to her, rigid and pale, as she reversed out of the garage. *Her curtain call*, Crabb thought. The tiny staccato clicks of the photographic shutters sounded like quiet and far off gunfire.

He felt like telling Sarah to duck.

12

Crabb was outside Mrs Whorton's house; the neighbour Annie said had pointed at Ben. He stepped up to the door and rang the bell.

A curtain twitched at the window as he waited. Finally, he heard the muffled thump of shoes approaching the door. A woman in her seventies opened the door a few inches, a chain pulling taut as she peered through the crack. All Crabb could see were rheumy eyes which seemed to float around in a roomy face, a large beak of a nose, and pursed lips in a lined and baggy skin sack. All this framed with wisps of white hair like dry straw.

'Mrs Whorton? I'm DI Crabb. I'm investigating the death of Toby Coleridge. May I come in?' He showed her his identification.

'I've already talked to the police,' she said.

'I know you have. Would you mind letting me in? Just a few more questions. Won't take a moment.'

'No.'

'You're not in any trouble. I just wanted to hear what and who you saw on Thursday night.'

'I don't know what all the fuss is about. Why should I have to repeat myself again and again. Don't you people liaise with each other?'

'I'm just going over everything. And a child is dead, Mrs Whorton. Just tell me what you saw, and I'll leave you in peace.'

She made a snorting sound, and said, enunciating clearly as if she thought Crabb were slightly stupid, 'For the umpteenth time, I saw Toby walking past my house, past his school there, opposite.' She pointed. 'And behind him was that boy, Ben. Half past seven-ish, it was. I remember the time because my favourite television programme had just finished and I was hot. Went to the window to open it. Saw that monster of a boy.'

'Why didn't you mention it when we did the original house to house canvass? According to my records, you said you saw nothing. You didn't see either boy.'

She seemed irritated. Turning abruptly and looking down, she shooed back a white Scottie dog with her slippered foot, pushing him gently back into the house as he nosed her legs, trying to get out.

'I'm an old woman, I get the dates mixed up, all my days run into each other. Can't distinguish a Monday from a Friday. But I've given it some thought, and now I know I'm right. It was last Thursday. I was wrong before. So, what are you going to do – arrest me?' She snickered, showing yellowing teeth.

A disgusting, vicious woman, and Crabb instantly disliked her – distrusted her. Wanted to wipe the smile from her face but words failed him. He forced his own smile and said, 'How do you know the boys? Their names, I mean?'

'I know Toby. I let him get his ball from my front garden some time ago. He introduced himself. Nice boy. But when the police showed me the pictures of him, after he went missing, I got confused. It was only when the deaf lot came around that I recognised him.'

He found that hard to believe and wondered what game she

was playing. What she was hiding? And why? 'How about Ben. How do you know him?'

Her face became unforgiving, and she pressed her lips together. 'Everyone knows Ben Downing. He has a voice. Well, *he* thinks he has a voice. Sounds more like a mental defective. Grunts, whoops, not proper words. He likes to hang from the school gates like some... some gorilla, shouting out what I can only assume are meant to be obscenities. Nasty boy. It shouldn't be allowed.'

She rubbed her face and said, '*And* he kicked my dog. Little bastard. It really shouldn't be allowed.'

'What shouldn't be allowed? *Deaf*ness?'

He couldn't quite believe her unpleasantness, her bigotry, although that hardly described her toxic words. She grimaced at him, vitriol escaping through her pores, though she appeared happy with what she'd said. He ignored her lips as they remained curled in revulsion.

'You didn't see anything else untoward, or odd on that evening?'

'No. Look, really, you have to go. I don't want to get involved.'

'Involved in what, Mrs Whorton? What are you frightened of?'

He tried to gauge what she was lying about.

'Nothing, nothing. Goodbye, Mr... Goodbye.'

He placed his foot in the doorway. 'What are you lying about? Whatever it is that you are hiding, I don't have to remind you that this isn't a game. It's murder.'

'How dare you,' she said. A tiny gobbet of spittle flew from her mouth and landed on the lapel of his shirt. He forced himself not to frantically rub it away. 'Of course I'm not lying. What could I possibly have to lie about?'

'Only you would know that, Mrs Whorton. But one more question. How did Toby tell you his name? He couldn't speak.'

She visibly relaxed. 'He drew his name in the soil of my garden when collecting his ball. With a stick. As I say, a nice boy. Deaf, but nice. As nice as those types can be, I assume. You know what I mean – simple, or whatever the PC word used to describe them is these days.' She snapped her fingers together. 'Subnormal. That's the word. Subnormal. Now, again, goodbye.'

She slammed the front door, leaving him bewildered and angry.

He'd send in DC Bragen to re-question the woman. He'd tell the usually persuasive Bragen to lay it on with a trowel. All Crabb felt like was laying it on with a hammer.

Vicious bitch.

13

—————

After she'd left Sarah's, Annie had walked for hours and hours. Then she'd gone to the pub. She couldn't account for her day, or where she'd been. It was all a blur. She found it didn't really matter.

Sitting on a bench, she tried to stop crying. She couldn't erase the thought of Toby's body lying in a cold, steel drawer. To end up in a *drawer*. Like a pair of fucking socks. She bit down on her lip to stop the image.

Everyone would have heard of Toby's death by now. Digging her nails into her palm until it hurt, she brought out her mobile and texted Dora.

Get people to Deaf Club tonight. We all need to talk. 7.00. Ax

Then she sent another one to Crabb.

Meet me at the Deaf Club 7.00. We need to talk to Dora. Get Sam to come. Annie

The sun scorched her bare arms but she enjoyed the stinging sensation. Dora took only ten minutes to reply.

No prob. Told everyone to come. Urgent. Sorry abt Toby. Very sorry.

It was an hour before Crabb replied.

Will do. See you then and take care. Don't mention Adam Jacobs yet. Explain later. Let me do the talking. Crabb

She sent another text to Fiona, her fourth of the day, but there was still no answer.

While she was at it, she texted William. After a while, she decided that he also wasn't going to reply. Maybe he'd picked up someone on Friday night and was spending the entire weekend having sex, convinced he was in love. Had happened before. But still, his silence vaguely disturbed her. She was always the first to know of any new sexual encounter. She found herself a little hurt that he hadn't texted her about Toby. It wasn't like him.

It was a quarter to seven when Annie arrived at the Deaf Club. She threw open the door. It ricocheted back at her as it banged into the wall, nearly hitting her in the face on rebound. As an entrance it was dramatic and visually violent. Falling into the room with nowhere else to go – desired destination reached, she stopped. The eyes of the assembled Deaf people rounded with shock and as one their bodies jerked in their seats. She'd spread her fear and grief without even trying – felt it spread like an infection.

Stumbling three or four paces further into the room she stopped again. Reminded herself that all that mattered was Toby. His death, the memory of his body, gave her momentum. Brought her back to the here and now.

She held her hand up, palm outwards towards Dora in a stop gesture. *Give me a moment. Wait.*

But Dora didn't wait. Signed over the top of her Chihuahua's head, 'I'm so sorry, Annie. We're all sorry, aren't we?' She looked around her little fiefdom and waited for the nods.

The pockmarked Edward from the search was there – still bubbling over with his gleeful and inappropriate interest. He signed quickly, his hands stumbling with anticipation, 'Was he stabbed? That's what the television reports are saying. Where? Where was Toby stabbed?'

Annie preferred not to answer directly; signed, 'Does it matter? He's dead. That's it. Stabbed to death.'

In her periphery, she saw heads bow, shoulders hunch, eyes flicker downwards. A couple of women dabbed at their eyes with handkerchiefs. Her friend, Polly, in her fifties, always dressed in clashing colours of reds, pinks and oranges – an eccentric woman with a huge love of all things amusing – wiped her nose with the cuff of her floating, baggy shirt, and smiled faintly at Annie in recognition of her grief. Annie smiled sadly back, grateful to see her.

Then Annie flapped her hands in the air, making a huge gesture, arms cartwheeling around her body, wanting them all to look at her. Having got their attention she signed, 'Who would do that to him? Someone must know something. He was a little boy. Who hated him that much? Think. I want you all to think. Who hated Toby enough to kill him? Why him? Why not someone else? Why not another little boy? Why Toby?'

Frightened faces looked at her, turned to Dora for guidance. The fat woman signed, 'Come and sit down. None of us know the answer to your questions. But we'll find out. Together. We're strong as a group. Our identity as one will be a strength. It's nobody in our community – it can't be.'

'How do you know that?' Annie signed. 'Of course it could be. It could be anyone.'

She scanned the room, hopeful that she'd see William, but he wasn't there.

Neither was Fiona.

Nor Ben.

Charlie Blue, the interpreter, was there. Nondescript, he sat like a grey cardboard cut-out, neither nice nor unpleasant. Just there. Like wallpaper. He raised his hand in greeting and signed, 'Hello, Annie. How are you?'

'I thought Sam was interpreting tonight?'

Charlie shook his head and signed, 'I'm not working. Just came to express my condolences to the community. I know Toby was a popular boy. And I am so sorry. A dreadful thing.'

Looking over her shoulder, he signed and pointed: 'Here's Sam now.'

She watched Crabb shuffle in, accompanied by DS Peters, more briskly youthful in his movement. They stood, slightly unsure, next to Sam.

Sam was a regal-looking man, dressed in a suit; late thirties, thick dark hair, a pale complexion and a large hooked nose. He had high cheekbones and surprisingly well-defined eyebrows. As if he plucked them. The interpreter was an inch away from being handsome – there was just a little something missing. He dipped his head in Annie's direction, gestured the two policemen into chairs and sat in between them.

The Deaf manoeuvred themselves into a large semi-circle, making the two policemen the focal point, whilst simultaneously making themselves visible to each other around the chipped Formica-topped tables.

Crabb smiled and sat, lifting his hand in greeting to the group. Everyone took the time to introduce themselves, fingerspelling their names. Instead of looking at each person as they signed, Crabb chose to look at Sam, as if in order to hear, he had to face the interpreter, who sat at his shoulder, speaking the words of the Deaf.

Annie, not in the mood for social niceties, signed: 'Fiona's not here. Neither's Ben.'

She felt frantic, wanting to hurry, feeling time pressing, wanting to find the bastard who'd killed Toby, and needing to fulfil her promise to Sarah. She now signed and spoke, wanting to stress the importance of her worry directly to Crabb: 'Where *is* Fiona? Has anyone seen her? She's not answering any of my texts and I've been to her flat. Nothing. Where is she? Have you found her, Crabb? Or found Ben?'

'No, I've found neither and it's important that I speak to both of them. As soon as possible.'

Again, Crabb looked at Sam as he answered. The use of an interpreter was obviously a new thing for him. He hadn't quite grasped it yet. *Come on*, Annie thought. *It's not bloody rocket science. You're allowed to look at Deaf people when they sign and the interpreter will interpret. Hence his presence. Christ, Crabb. Get it together.*

Sam interpreted well and was a regular fixture in the Deaf Club. He was very big-D in his signing, matching BSL sentence structure well and effortlessly.

Martin, caretaker of the Deaf School and always trying to impress Dora. In his thirties, he was barrel-shaped and Annie always thought him transparent in his woeful adoration of Dora. He now sat as near as possible to the fat woman and laughed. Spelt out F-I-O-N-A on his fingers and then made the universal sign for drinking. Let his tongue droop from his lips in a parody of inebriation. Making fists with both of his hands, he banged the inside of his wrists together. Laughed again.

Annie lip-read Sam as he interpreted the meaning, putting

the signs and facial expressions into English, 'Fiona's probably pissed. Having sex with someone.'

And again, Crabb only had eyes for Sam; continually failing to look at the Deaf as they signed. *He'd learn. He'd bloody have to.*

Martin looked childishly at Dora, foolishly anticipating her appreciation of his anti-Fiona joke, whilst forever hoping her kudos would automatically rub off onto him just by his very physical proximity to her. Dora gazed through him as if he hadn't signed, making no reply, as if he hadn't communicated at all. Her face impassive, cold.

The caretaker coloured and his face drooped with disappointment, having failed to amuse her. His braces pinched his flabby chest into two breasts. *Nasty bastard.*

Polly threw a pink wispy scarf around her shoulders, and signed, 'Don't be disgusting, Martin. Fiona might have had a cochlear implant which you're all so against, but so what? There's no need to be so cruel about her. She's a sweet girl. Don't forget we're here because of Toby. To find out what happened to him. Just shut up.'

Annie watched as Crabb concentrated, listening to everything being relayed verbally into his ear by Sam. Polly turned to Crabb, signing, 'You were saying?'

Crabb listened to Sam before saying, 'I have a description of a man and was hoping one of you might recognise him. I haven't a lot to go on, but hopefully something might sound familiar to you.'

He waited and Annie watched Dora lean forward excitedly in her chair as Sam signed Crabb's words. The fat woman jumped in eagerly with her reply:

'Go on, describe the man. Was he Deaf? I know all the Deaf in these parts. Or if not them personally, then I know of them.'

Annie watched as Crabb struggled at hearing Dora's words being spoken by a man. *He'll have to get used to the interpreting process quickly*, she thought. Everything was annoying her. Nothing was happening quickly enough. The two policemen sat in silence, outwardly calm and in control. Crabb paused before choosing his words carefully. Annie couldn't bear it. She bit her lip and clasped her hands together to keep herself silent.

Eventually Crabb said, 'Mid-twenties, muscular, well groomed, well dressed, handsome, good hair. He was seen signing with Ben last week. Wednesday, four o'clock-ish. Outside the Deaf School. Doesn't of course mean he's deaf, but he could be. They clearly knew each other. Ben looked frightened of him. I know it's not a lot to go on as a description, but do you know–'

Dora held her hand in the air, extended her index finger and held it immobile in space, her eyes closed as if she were trying to remember something from a long time ago.

Annie felt like screaming with the suspense. Dora knew. Knew something. But she was taking her time. Annie was beyond frustration and concentrated on breathing. Deeply and slowly.

Don't scream. Don't hit anyone. Don't swear. Just wait.

14

Slowly Dora's eyes opened, gleaming with a knowledge as yet uncommunicated. Finally: 'Obviously I can't be sure... How could I be with such a vague description? It could be *any* young man. But I think I have an idea of who it *could* be.'

'Come on, Dora,' Annie signed. 'Who do you think it is? It's important. If you know, then say so.'

Dora cocked her head to the side, scratched her chin, shook her head slowly from side to side, stroked the head of her dog.

Annie stamped her foot and signed, 'Toby's fucking dead. Stop playing games.'

Dora's eyes flared in annoyance at Annie, but she signed quickly, 'If you're pushing me, I'd hazard a guess, judging purely on the fact that you say Ben was frightened and the man so handsome, that it was Theo.'

Annie felt like hitting someone. 'Who's *Theo*?' she signed.

'Don't you know? He hasn't been around these parts for years, but if it is him, Theo is Ben's older hearing brother. God, but he was a handsome boy. But nasty. Really nasty. Looked like a cherub but was more like the devil. Something bad about him. Couldn't put my finger on it, but deep down bad.

'And he just disappeared one day. Think his mother sent him off to live with his father. Yes, I remember him well. Always a natty dresser, even as a child. A cocky so-and-so, but really mean. Obsessed with his hair. And he always frightened Ben. Poor little beggar.'

Some faces suddenly took on a look of a dawning recollection. Annie signed, knowing that Sam would speak for her: 'I didn't even know Ben *had* a brother.'

'Well, that'll be because you don't come here often. Now you know,' signed Dora, relaxed – having, in her eyes, regained her supremacy after Annie's obvious annoyance at her. She brought her hands up again. 'Theo was, now let me see, four, possibly five years older than Ben. They didn't go to the same school. Obviously. As I said, Theo was hearing. But he'd come to the Deaf Club now and again. Not often. And always on his own – never brought Ben with him. Theo could sign well, I'll give him that. At least he had the decency to learn sign language for Ben's sake.'

Crabb said, 'Do you know anything else about Theo? Has anyone else seen him?'

Nonplussed faces greeted his statement, and the multi-coloured Polly asked Dora, 'Have *I* met him? I do remember a very good-looking boy coming here years ago. As you say, an attractive youth, aggressively cocksure. But I didn't know he was Ben's brother. Tall? With a sort of swagger?'

Dora nodded and signed, 'He didn't want people to know who he was, so I never told. He told me not to. I... he frightened me.'

She coloured at her own weakness. Dora was well-liked, her leadership taken for granted: the mother of all the Deaf. No one liked to see her embarrassed now. She shrugged her heavy shoulders and repeated, 'He was a nasty boy. But at least Theo learnt to sign. Unlike Ben's mother. A pathetic woman. Always drunk. No wonder Theo had to move away.'

She fondled her dog's ears, paused, confident that she had regained some composure, and signed, 'Theo would be twenty, possibly twenty-one now.'

Crabb said, 'When did he disappear?'

'I couldn't say with any degree of accuracy, but I'd guess, when he was perhaps sixteen?'

An absence of signing greeted her news. No one had anything to add except a few uncertain nods.

Dora continued, 'I make it my business to know the history of the Deaf in these parts. Their family background, their roots. It's important to know the cultural heritage that we have. Of course, I'm the only one here who has Deaf parents, Deaf siblings, and Deaf grandparents. A true Deaf lineage. I'm genetically Deaf. Grass-roots Deaf. Old school Deaf. Deaf through and through. Not many like me around.'

DS Peters' eyebrows furrowed in confusion whilst Crabb's lifted in surprise as they heard Sam's words. 'I assumed most Deaf people had Deaf parents,' Crabb said. Annie knew most hearing people thought this, but was irritated by the time it took to explain it to Crabb. Giving precious time to Dora, who answered, oozing pride and puffing up her already huge bust like a pink cardiganed peacock:

'That's what everyone thinks. But they're wrong. Ninety per cent of Deaf have hearing parents. Not me. I'm special. I'm *Real* Deaf.'

Annie quietly fumed, wanting to run and find Fiona, find Ben. Find Theo. *Do* something, instead of listening to Dora trumpeting her own fanfare.

And where *was* William? His continued absence worried Annie. They were great friends, shared a secret, always kept in touch. Out of everyone, she'd expected him to contact her about Toby. But he still hadn't. Not one text. Why not? He was the kindest man she knew. Even if he was 'in love' again, he would have been devastated about Toby. She signed to Dora, 'Where *is* William?'

Dora frowned: 'I don't know. He's such a nice man. Now you come to mention it, it *is* strange, him not being here. He's so involved with the children from the Deaf School. You're right, he *should* be here. I did text him. A couple of times. I heard nothing back. He didn't turn up on the search with us. And he wasn't at the Deaf Club last Thursday. He's a regular – always comes on Thursdays. He *only* comes on Thursdays. But not this last Thursday gone. Strange; hadn't struck me before. You can almost set your clock by him.'

She laughed and signed, 'But I don't suppose he's gone missing as well. He's an adult. Can look after himself. Anyway, *you* should know where he is. He *is* your boyfriend after all.'

She smiled and Annie smiled back, carrying on the lie that she and William had created. Annie saw Crabb look quizzically at her. She quickly shook her head just a fraction – *shut up, don't say anything. I'll explain later.* She hoped Crabb understood. Thankfully, he nodded imperceptibly back at her.

Martin pulled at his braces and said, 'Funny, I'm friends with Ben – the one you're looking for. He should be in school tomorrow if you need to speak to him.'

Really? Annie thought. *Really? Ben and Martin friends? I don't fucking think so.* This was just Martin's pathetic and transparent way of involving himself in the conversation, revealing something he thought was important. Trying to match the importance of Dora's information, but failing miserably.

Crabb nodded at Martin, taking it all in. Looked as disbelieving as Annie felt. Then he breathed in deeply and she wondered what he was going to say. His words surprised her: 'Do any of you know a young deaf boy, fifteen, who was killed last April. In Bromley. His name was Adam Jacobs. Have any of you heard of him, or of his murder? Maybe you knew him?'

Everything suddenly felt horribly out of control. What was Crabb thinking? Annie felt the people in the room go taut, still – shocked into immobility.

'What do you mean? Is Toby the *second* boy to have been murdered?' Dora signed, breaking the game of statues; her face suddenly pale.

'The second *Deaf* boy to have been murdered. What's going on?' signed Edward.

Dora was indignant: 'Why didn't we hear about this? Why wasn't it in the newspapers, like Toby's murder?'

Crabb looked embarrassed, his dimples abandoned: 'I'm afraid my superior at the time thought it was a hate crime, a one-off. I didn't agree, but I didn't have the clout to go nationwide with it; no authority. It was in the local papers at the time, and some of the broadsheets covered it, but it was never front page.'

He glanced around at them all and said, 'And now that we do have a second deaf boy, murdered, I thought you all should know.'

The Deaf as one seemed to curl in on themselves, pulling up the drawbridge as the possibility of being prey made itself real. Annie shuddered as she took in their frightened faces and felt completely inadequate.

Chaos peeked its head over the garden wall.

15

———

'We'll give you a lift back, Annie. Here, get in,' Peters said. He held the car door open for her.

Crabb insisted that Annie sat in the front passenger seat, and he got in the back seat behind the driver. Tapping her on the shoulder, he wanted to ask her about the conversation in the Deaf Club.

Annie held her hand up, and then turned on the interior light. Said, 'I can't see otherwise.' Shifting in her seat so she could see Crabb's face, she carried on, 'That went a bit tits-up. Now the whole community's terrified and I haven't even told them about my attack. Don't think I will now. What were you thinking? You told me to not say anything about Adam, and then you go and blurt it out yourself.'

'I changed my mind. Working on the same principle as keeping you safe. I need people scared, want them to stick together. I'm not sure what we're dealing with here, but whatever it is, better to err on the side of caution. Fear gets people talking. I thought of keeping it quiet, but it's better out there. I want people aware. I saw tonight how tight the community is. They need to stick together.'

'Yeah, tight and now completely freaked out. Well done.'

Ignoring her not-so quiet anger, Crabb said, 'You told me you were gay. Why does Dora, and presumably the rest of them, think that William is your boyfriend?'

He saw her sigh and ball her fingers into fists before stretching them out, like early spring shoots, taut but supple. She flexed them and then relaxed. 'It's no great revelation and far from exciting. I just don't like people knowing my business. I'm a woman, and I'm deaf. Neither defines me but I can't hide either of those facts. They say deafness is an invisible disability, but only until you open your mouth. When I speak, people think I'm special needs or have learning difficulties. I don't choose to add my gayness to the list.'

'I find it hard to believe that people think that of you.'

'Believe it. Who cares? I don't. But what I do care about is preserving what I can about my own identity. Who I really am. Who I choose to sleep with shouldn't matter, but if I was open about it, I'd just get another label. The Deaf Community likes pigeonholing people and is hardly known for its tact. Gossip is the thing that keeps it going. It thrives on gossip. Loves a good juicy secret.

'William is also gay. *His* secret. We just came up with the simple idea of pretending to be each other's partner, to protect each other's privacy.

'I often work as his interpreter when we go out to gay pubs. He can't lip-read, so I do the honours. And then when he's met someone, he's on his own. I presume with a lot of finger point-ing. Sex isn't rocket science – doesn't need a huge amount of verbal communication. He's a laugh. I like him. But in terms of our own privacy, better to keep our mouths shut, or more appro-priately, our hands zipped.'

She made the motion, drawing her index finger and thumb around her straightened fingertips on her left hand, starting at the base of the thumb and ending at the opposite side of her wrist. And then stopped abruptly.

Crabb said, 'And?'

Annie was quiet for a moment, opened her mouth to say something but then changed her mind and said, 'And nothing. That's it. Everyone thinks we're boyfriend and girlfriend. *No one* knows the truth. Except Scarlet obviously. So don't go blabbing.'

She hadn't been going to say that, he was fairly certain. She was hiding something, something about William, but she'd shut down. Her duck-egg green eyes completely barred him entrance: *Get out, no trespassing.* Annoyed, he changed the subject, trying to get a better feel for her, saying, 'Your parents are hearing?'

He already knew this from his background check on her but wanted her version. She nodded. He just looked at her, raising his eyebrows – quietly demanding that she continue. Forcing her to give him a little bit of her.

'Yes. Both hearing. If you take the belief of our great and glorious leader, Dora, I'm positively ten-a-penny deaf.'

'You don't like her?'

'I do actually. She's always been very kind to me. She's not as harsh as she appears. Just a game she plays. She's all mouth. Dora wears her Deafness like a badge of honour, creating her own hierarchy, placing herself at the top. Her big-D Deaf isolates her to some extent. The thing that saves her from distancing herself from the Deaf Community, is the fact that people love her. Including me. But she uses her deafness like a shield, not a treasure as she claims. I feel sorry for her.' She shifted, trying to get comfortable in her twisted position. 'But if you take away the Deaf crap bollocks, she's a kind, soft woman. You just have to disembowel her to find it. Once you know it's there, she still tries her best to conceal it. Don't know why she bothers. She's a transparent carer. It's what she does naturally. She cares. Wants to be everyone's mother. I *do* like her. When my own father died five years ago, she took me up like a pet. She loved me. Parented me. And for that, I'll always be grateful.'

'You love to hate her?'

'Or hate to love her. Both work. Same as my real mother, so no great stretch. Anyway, what's this got to do with Toby?'

'Maybe something, possibly nothing. Probably nothing. I just want to get a feel of how you do or don't fit into this community.'

'Well, now you know.'

16

Uncomfortable in the back seat of the police car, Crabb heard his mobile ring somewhere in his trouser pocket. He swore as he fumbled it out into his hand. Glancing at the caller ID, he saw that it was DC Bragen. He re-positioned himself directly behind Annie and turned his head to the window. If the call was what he was hoping for, this was private and definitely not to be shared with Annie.

'What have you got, Bragen?' Crabb said.

'Right, here we go. I'll bring you up to date on everything I've got. Think we've got the murderer on CCTV.'

Crabb waited.

'Someone was caught on camera at the top of North End Road, where it meets the heath, pushing a blanketed boy in a wheelchair very late on Saturday night. Well, early Sunday morning. Three minutes past three in the morning to be exact. As you know, the wheelchair was found dumped nearby. It's been scrubbed down with bleach. The same applies to the blanket found at the bottom of the pond. Bleached. We've got him veering off the road onto the heath proper. The man disappeared for about thirty minutes, and returned to the same point, without the wheelchair. And then he doubled back further down, back onto Hampstead Heath, and we lost him. Had a slight limp. His left leg. And he obviously knows the heath well. Avoided being picked up by cameras again. He just vanished.'

Crabb made a non-committal noise. Bragen said, 'Whoever it was, was wearing a cagoule, which covered him from head to foot. Also a scarf around the lower part of his face.'

Simple but effective. Nobody would have questioned the waterproofs – it was pouring last night. The scarf might have been a little excessive with it being so warm, but at that time of night, who'd notice or even care? Same with the limp – and easily faked. 'What about height?'

'About five-eleven.'

Crabb sat silently and tried to picture the scene. 'No forensics then?' he asked.

'The lab are still looking, but it seems unlikely. There were no fingerprints on the skewer itself.'

'Presumably the area's been checked for footprints, where he dumped the wheelchair? It was raining for God's sake.'

'You're right, but the killer went to a lot of effort to smear all his own footprints. Must have walked backwards with a stick or something, brushing and obscuring where he'd walked. Until he reached grass. He just left a mud-bath behind them.'

Crabb was quiet; thinking. Bragen interrupted the silence. 'Except he missed a size eleven bootprint he'd left.'

Crabb's heart quickened. 'Same tread as Adam's killing?'

'No. I checked with the forensics. But same size.'

Quietly Crabb bit his lip. How many men had size eleven feet? Millions. Bloody useless information. *And* he would have changed his shoes since the murder of Adam. He said, 'Check all the CCTVs for large vans. He would have needed a vehicle to transport Toby in a wheelchair. Find all sightings of vans or hatchbacks seen in the area at the time and cross reference them to those owned by the regular Deaf Club goers.'

'What, *all* of them?'

'Yes, all of them. Anything more on the pencil shavings found in Toby's mouth?'

Bragen paused and Crabb heard papers being shuffled again. He restrained himself from shouting at the man to hurry up. He wanted to talk to Annie again.

'Okay,' said the DC. 'The pencil shavings were from your bog standard pencil I'm afraid; nothing specialised. They were the type of coloured pencil you could buy anywhere: generic.'

Crabb grunted. 'And the post-mortem results?'

'According to stomach contents, Toby was killed yesterday, Saturday. Estimation is late afternoon some time. Strangely, the killer gave the boy food right before he killed him. Toby had eaten jam sandwiches, crisps, a pork pie, jelly and cake. Children's food. Like an old-fashioned proper tea. He was killed almost immediately after eating. Nothing was digested.'

'What sort of killer feeds a boy and then murders him?' Crabb asked.

He didn't expect an answer and didn't get one. Instead he asked, 'Cause of death?'

'The insertion of the skewer into the brain. I'm assuming you're happy with the layman's version.'

'I am.'

'Dr Moore said that it would have been possible to kill the boy with a skewer through the ear without any medical training. Just a good aim and possibly a bit of luck and a bit of power behind the thrust. Also, his hair was singed.'

'What do you mean, singed?'

'Exactly that. Singed. Burnt. Just a little, at the front.'

There was silence on the line.

'Are you still there?' asked DC Bragen.

Crabb grunted and said, 'Burnt hair. What does *that* mean? I just cannot believe that Adam was this man's first kill. Feels like he's warming up; Toby's killing is far more controlled.'

'Agreed.'

'Feels like the beginning of something. It's all so, I don't know, carefully *arranged*.' He paused and said, 'Tomorrow I want you to go around to Mrs Whorton. The old cow who claims that she saw Ben following Toby on Thursday night. She's a bitch, and a lying one at that. Interview her again. She didn't respond to me and just dug her heels in further. Find out what she's lying about.'

'Will do, sir.'

'And before I forget, anything from forensics on Annie's attack – outside her flat: anything?'

'No. If there had been anything, it was washed away in the rain.'

'Door-to-door canvass turn up anything?'

'Zip. Nobody saw or heard diddley.'

Crabb hung up, rolled down his window and lit a cigarette.

17

———

I had given them 'The Boy in the Pond'.

The bleaching of the wheelchair. The bleaching of the blan-ket. All that smearing of my bootprints. All the melodrama of dressing in a cagoule and the unnecessary scarf. I knew where all the cameras were. All I'd had to do was keep my face down, but instead I used a scarf. And limped, *for God's sake.*

And I undressed the poor boy. For effect only. Obviously. To temporarily give the police something else to falsely ponder upon. The possible insinuation of a sexual motivation. The whole thing was laughable. A farce.

Too, too dramatic for words. But it achieved its goal. It got the tabloids twittering, the broadsheets singing their psychobabble. Who is this monster, they asked? This man with a limp? This man who had undressed a young boy, leaving him as naked as a baby? Could they not see the lies? The posturing for the sake of it? Playing to the gallery? A silly 'extra' to My Game. The scarfed bogeyman with the gammy leg and unhealthy sexual proclivities. Completely meaningless.

I could have deposited the still-clothed boy on the heath completely undetected. But instead, I had chosen to play a little.

Allowed myself to be seen. And why not? Give a man a little fun. Why not?

The real death, the not-so fond adieu to the boy, was far from meaningless, however.

For me, the body in the water, in that pond – that specific pond: so symbolic – the symbolism paramount. It was the whole fucking point.

I would hazard a guess that the significance of the football was totally missed. Not even noticed. Assumed to be unrelated detritus. It was absolutely *related.*

But they will understand. In time.

The actual killing of this second boy, a real hands-on experience, had been so much more satisfactory than the mindless beating of Adam Jacobs. It had a certain resonance. A skewer, a deaf boy, an ear – God, the delights of a sophisticated imagination. And physically? Easier than I had anticipated. Other than his bothersome shying away from the tip, the skewer, once on target, had slipped in nicely. Perhaps the word 'slipped' is an exaggeration. More of a shove was required. I could feel the need to push against bone and gristle. Not for the squeamish nor the faint-hearted. But as I had anticipated, most effective.

The other one *had watched in silence. The apparent 'adult' in this Game, although he hadn't behaved in a very mature fashion. His eyes had bulged and vomit had spewed from his mouth. In a torrent. All over himself.*

But I have to take into consideration that he might have been just a little frightened. I couldn't really blame him for that. I should try not to be so hard on these incompetents who were attempting to play by my rules.

And failing abysmally.

I was now, albeit temporarily, back home. I hadn't moved in proper. Not yet. Being in situ *as I was, both my contenders had visited cupboard land. They each had a taste of being cupboard people. Not together of course. No point in being locked in the dark if you can minimise your distress by holding hands. They had gone in separately. Enjoyed the dark all on their lonesome. It had done its job and had worked its magic. It had completely terrified both of them. Amusingly so. Their unadulterated fear brought back memories for me. Not happy ones, but memories all the same. Nostalgia is not to be sniffed at.*

From the moment of their dual capture by yours truly, I realised that the older substitute was going to be trouble. Dug his heels in straight away – refused to even attempt to play the Game. From the Thursday evening until his late Saturday departure, he was, right from the start, 'deaf man walking'.

A shame. A real shame.

But what was so bothersome to me, what really Fucked. Me. Off, was the boy's utter refusal to comprehend the obvious. I made it oh so simple – had signed: 'Happy with your coloured pencils? Do you like them?'

A terrified shake of the head; confused, bewildered – useless.

'Aren't you pleased? Can't you find it in your ungrateful heart to enjoy them?'

Again with the shaking of the head.

'Can't you pretend, as I did? A little common courtesy wouldn't go amiss. I pretended. I had to. Now it's your turn. Say "thank you" for your present. This time you're not getting what you wanted. You're getting what I got. Crappy bloody pencils. And I said thank you when I was given them. I pretended. How do you think that made me feel? How does it make you feel now?'

I'd left his one hand free so that he could communicate with me, but all he did, all he signed, was, 'Please don't hurt me. I don't know what you want. Please stop. I want to go home.'

'Oh, but you are home. Finally. Your real home.'

But I tired quickly of trying, cajoling, persuading him to accept my present. Tired of insisting that he play My Game. Bloody little moron.

Bet he's sorry now.

Damn sure he's wishing he'd thanked me for my gift of coloured pencils when he'd had the chance.

But clearly, now it is too late for him.

He should have tried harder.

All I had to show for my efforts was the acquisition of two mobile phones, switched off. Dead and useless.

Much like the boy and the man.

18

Annie was exhausted after the Deaf Club. It was half past nine and the night was black, with puffy white clouds scudding across the sky. Humid.

She attempted to bolt from the car as Peters swung onto the pea shingle drive, but Crabb grabbed her shoulder, stopping her escape. He got out himself and opened her door, pointing at a female figure sitting with her back against the wall around the corner from Annie's flat. Said, 'Who's that?'

Annie squinted into the darkness where the girl had chosen to sit and clamped her jaws together in anger. Her friend, Fiona, sat crouched down, teetering on the balls of her feet.

Ignoring Crabb, she strode quickly towards her. Fiona, with her cochlear implant, could hear only slightly better after her operation, but not clear words: just noisier noise. The procedure had failed. Sighing at life in bloody general, Annie signed: 'Where have you *been*? Didn't you get my texts? Bloody hell, Fiona. For God's *sake*, what's wrong with you? Toby's dead and you go missing. Where have you *been*? Why didn't you answer me?'

Furious, Annie wanted to shake Fiona, get some reaction,

some proper reaction, instead of being faced with this vacant Fiona, who hadn't got to her feet and sat, in bubble-gum pink clothes, looking like a jelly baby in Lycra shorts and matching T-shirt. It took a while for Annie to realise that Fiona's face *was* reacting by its non-reaction: slack with shock and incomprehension. Annie squatted, taking no notice of Crabb, and signed, 'You didn't know, did you? About Toby?'

Fiona's eyes were rounded like dinner plate circles, staring, staring. Annie turned to Crabb and said, 'It's Fiona. She didn't know that Toby's dead.'

She held Fiona's hand and kept her face angled up to Crabb. Said, 'What do you want to do?'

She saw him sigh, rub his palm over his face and then: 'I need to talk to her. Can you interpret?'

Annie shook her head. 'Absolutely not. No way. It's not professional. I'm her friend and this is a police investigation. It would be completely inappropriate, and I don't *want* to do it. You'll have to call Sam.'

He bent and talked into his mobile, while Annie tugged Fiona to her feet. Hugged her. Overly made-up like an inflatable doll, Fiona's mouth was a perfect red cupid's bow – garish with cherry red lipstick. Earrings as large as consommé bowls swung from her ears. Annie felt vulnerable just looking at her. Fiona wasn't the brightest button on the cardigan, but Annie liked her. Fiona was kind, and kindness trumped stupidity every time. Her highly polished and veneered face only served to make her look available. To anyone and everyone male. Annie stared into her face.

Fiona blinked slowly, and signed, 'What happened to Toby?'

'He was murdered. Found in a pond on Hampstead Heath. Sarah knows, she's identified him. She's left Jonathan and is staying with her sister. You'll have to talk to Crabb.' She pointed at the policeman. 'Okay? Do you want me to come?'

'Come where?'

'To the police station. You're a witness. You saw something on Wednesday, outside the school. Do you want me to come?' The very marrow of Annie's bones ached with fatigue. Her body was full to the brim with too many horrors. Felt like a dam ready to burst. She bit down on her lip, attempting to stem the emotional leakage.

How could she not go with Fiona? She needed looking after. I *need looking after*, Annie thought, *but there's no time. Too much going on too quickly.* What little control she had pretended she had, was fast disappearing.

Crabb stepped into her line of vision. 'She'll have to come down to the station now to give a statement.' Annie saw him study Fiona, and then look back at her. 'Are you coming with her?'

Annie nodded, and watched in a detached way as Eric sauntered past, tail high. He took a detour and sniffed at Annie's legs. Sat. Waited. Slowly, she gently persuaded Fiona into Crabb's space, made sure she was moving in the right direction, and went and opened her flat door. Shouted for Scarlet who appeared suddenly as if she'd been waiting for Annie's return. Scarlet checked Annie over with a quick top-to-toe glance; taking in her physical appearance and checking for any added injury, her brows a jagged line of concern.

'I'm fine,' Annie said. Defensive.

'No, you're not. You're worried. What's up?'

She'd tell Scarlet about William later. Again, not enough time. Not now. Instead she said, 'Didn't Fiona ring the bell?'

'Yeah, earlier. She came in and I wrote down for her that you were at the Deaf Club, and I was expecting you back soon. She wrote that she'd catch up with you later. Refused to stay. Think she was a bit pissed. Not slaughtered, but merry in a sad sort of way.'

Fiona wasn't pissed now. Shock, death, murder, grief; life's little soberers.

Annie watched as Scarlet watched Crabb leading Fiona by the hand into the waiting police car. Scarlet frowned.

'What's going on? What's she done?'

'Nothing. She's just a witness. Will you be here when I get back? Crabb needs to check things out with her. She didn't even know about Toby.'

'Bloody hell. Poor bitch.' She pulled her hair back. 'I'll be here. Where else?'

She smiled, side-stepping Eric who tried clawing his way up her denim leg. Wearily, Annie turned and went and sat next to Fiona in the back seat of the police car. Their fingers clung together tightly, sweaty and moist. Needy. Annie wasn't sure who needed who more.

Twenty minutes later at the police station, Crabb escorted Sam into the interview room.

Crabb sat opposite Fiona, with Sam at his side. The interview room was bland but full of smells. None of them good. Stale. The air humid. It smelt of people and bodily fluids.

Annie sat in the corner. Crabb pushed a cup of tea towards Fiona. Did sweet tea ever really make anything any better? Annie watched as Fiona pushed it to one side and waited for Crabb to speak.

He said, 'I'm sorry that you had to learn about Toby's death so suddenly. It must have been a shock.' Sam's fingers formed shapes and moved through space, putting words into their visual form.

Fiona only nodded.

'Where have you been? We've all been trying to get hold of you.' Annie could see that Crabb was thinking: *It's been in all the evening papers, on the television. I assume all the Deaf are talking about it. How could you miss it?*

Fiona cast her eyes down, embarrassed. Shoulder shrug, a rigid body, and then her hands caught her face as she hung her head down. Everyone waited. Her posture was defeated, but in contrast, the large gold hoops that dangled from her ears, her lips that were painted a vicious red, made her appear visually hard and brash. A cheerleader on the edge.

'I wanted to talk to you about Wednesday afternoon. You were seen outside the Deaf School, talking to Ben,' Crabb said. 'Can you remember what were you talking about? Someone said it looked as though you were comforting him.'

Fiona looked vulnerable as if she might bolt at the first opportunity. She seemed unsure of herself. She watched Sam interpret Crabb's words and then sat quietly. Thinking.

'You haven't done anything wrong,' Crabb said. 'I just need your help.'

Fiona signed, having to rely on Sam's interpretation: 'Yes, I saw Ben. It was about four o'clock. Something like that. I was coming back from work. I work for a Deaf and Hearing Theatre group – keep strange hours, but it's a very good organisation. Well respected.' She looked proud, almost showing off, keen for Crabb to know that she was more than a pretty face.

'Anyway, I was meeting a friend, a teacher at the school, and was waiting for him. That's when I saw a man come up to Ben. I was on the other side of the road. I'd seen Ben talking to Toby. And then this man just appeared. Ben nearly jumped out of his skin. I think he was surprised. I mean, *really* surprised. Like it was the last person in the whole world that he was expecting to see. I remember the man pointed at Toby. He was gorgeous looking.'

She didn't bother making sure that Sam had finished interpreting. Had confidence in him. Then, 'Toby took his chance to escape. I couldn't blame him for that. He was such a sweet boy.

Ben had obviously been bullying him. Toby looked upset. You know, his body language. He looked sort of extra small.'

'Did the man talk to Toby, or just point?'

'No. Just pointed at him, and then Ben started signing to him, the man I mean, but I couldn't see what he was saying. Toby could though. He'd been watching before he scuttled off into his father's car. I was at the wrong angle to see any of the conversation itself. But I *did* see Toby's expression as he watched Ben and the man's conversation. He looked confused. No, that's not right. He looked frightened.'

Fiona wouldn't have seen the relevance, but Crabb was clearly thinking the same as Annie. Toby had witnessed an important conversation, a meeting, a *something*, between Ben and the mystery man – possibly his brother. It gave Ben motive. To shut Toby up? To stop a secret getting out? Impossible to know.

Crabb tried not to alarm Fiona, clearly realising that he was dealing with fragile, potentially breakable goods, and brought his questions round to safer territory. 'Can you describe the man?'

She laughed and wiped a tear from her eye: a clash of disharmony. Twined a piece of her hair around her fingers. 'Difficult to miss him, really. He was handsome. And I mean *really* handsome. Early twenties? Good-looking, like I said – well, beautiful actually. He was fit, had big muscles and his hair was highlighted: thick, really thick hair. It fell beautifully, swept over to one side. Like a model. Dressed like one too; skinny T-shirt, designer jeans, good boots. Hot.'

She smiled and Crabb nodded and smiled back. Fiona had a certain charm about her that Annie could see was appealing. She watched Fiona as she fiddled with the piece of black plastic attached to her scalp behind her left ear. Fiona noticed Crabb looking, and she immediately covered her cochlear implant with her long blonde hair.

'Anyway, Toby had gone by the time I reached Ben. So had the handsome man. He just turned and walked off – sure of himself. Like he didn't care about anyone but himself. Ben turned round and saw me. It was just us two. On the corner, alone. His face was white, I swear. He looked like he'd seen a ghost. When he saw me, he jumped. And then he just looked at me. Like I'd caught him doing something wrong.'

Again, Crabb nodded. Annie watched as Fiona started to relax and tried to settle back into the hard metal back of the chair, shifting around, finding it impossible to get comfortable. She crossed her legs; her Lycra-ed shorts clinging and accentuating her thighs. Her flip-flop dangled precariously from one foot as she pushed away from the table and crossed one leg. Her toenails were painted baby-pink and looked like tiny seashells. Physically, she appeared very summery and floaty – her face anguished and bewildered: a woman caught in a million contradictions.

Fiona started signing again, unprompted. 'I felt sorry for Ben. I just asked him if he was alright. He didn't really reply. I asked him who the man was and why he was so frightened, but he got all silly then. Pretended to be all hard. Said he hadn't been scared – it was an old friend who had taken him by surprise, that's all.' She shrugged in apology, obviously believing that she hadn't anything useful to add.

'Why didn't you mention this before?' Crabb asked gently, his face dipped to soften the accusing words.

Fiona looked embarrassed. 'I didn't really think about it. I didn't think it was important. And the police never asked if I'd seen anyone handsome. Just asked about Toby. If I'd seen Toby on Thursday. It just didn't occur about the day before. Stupid of me. I'm sorry.'

Annie shook her head back at her – *it doesn't matter*, and Crabb smiled at Fiona, told her not to worry. He was treating her with an odd soothing quality: the only possible way to treat her without fear of breakage. To shout at her would be too much like taking pot-shots at a drowning kitten.

Annie wasn't surprised that Fiona hadn't mentioned anything about Ben. But she wasn't operating from malice. Innocence was her guilty vice. She drifted through life, missing God knew how many important things.

Fiona looked down at her feet, avoiding eye contact with Crabb. Then she lifted her head, trying to look composed. 'Actually, I'm not being entirely truthful. I was a teeny bit pissed when I spoke to the police first time round, on Thursday. That's why I forgot to mention it. And then I just sort of forgot altogether.'

'Well, you've told me now, so don't worry too much.'

She smiled weakly at him. Grateful. Always grateful for any kindly crumb thrown her way.

Fiona blushed at this and then nodded in agreement, her thick black false lashes flapping up and down as her forget-me-not blue eyes blinked furiously.

Crabb said, 'Did you know Ben has a brother, Theo?'

Her eyes rounded in surprise, 'No. No, I didn't.' She waited a beat, then signed, 'Are you saying the handsome man was Ben's brother? God. He's so beautiful, and Ben's so... Ben isn't. But I like Ben.'

Her eyes had taken on a distant glaze. She looked sad thinking of the comparison.

She's like an ephemeral being, Annie thought, *infantile and pure, with no hidden agenda.*

Crabb paused, seeming sad at Fiona's sentiment, expressed vocally by Sam. Crabb had got more used to the interpreting process now, and virtually ignored Sam, confident that he would enable the conversation to flow between he and Fiona.

Fiona signed, 'Everyone's horrible about Ben. But I like him,' she signed again. 'He reminds me a bit of myself. Nobody understands him. But he's not that bad. Just stupid, you know, a normal teenage boy with problems. And we've all got problems.'

'Why don't people understand you?' said Crabb.

Fiona flapped her hands dismissively in the air. Suddenly embarrassed. 'Nothing really. Nothing important. I'm just a bit of an outcast. Like Ben. Me because I had a cochlear. That's it. No other reason. Other Deaf people don't approve. Apparently I should be proud to be Deaf. It's stupid. But I don't care.'

But Fiona *did* care. Cared hugely. She might as well have screamed out loud, 'Take me back into the fold. Accept me. Forgive me'. But she had no actual voice. Couldn't hear any better after the implant. An audiological pariah: neither Deaf nor hearing. She'd slipped through the cracks, Annie knew.

'And can I just clarify why you were at the school in the first place? Meeting a teacher, you said?'

'Yeah, me and Dave, one of the deaf teachers, he teaches geography, we have a thing. You know, a relationship. Sort of. Casual. That's why I know Toby and Ben. Toby better because I've seen him with Annie and Sarah as well. But I know a lot of the kids.' She laughed self-consciously. 'Always hanging about the school. I was happy there as a pupil. Before I had my cochlear. I like being there now.'

Crabb said, 'Were you with Dave this weekend?'

Fiona coloured but signed with her head high and eyes locking with Crabb's. 'No, I was with someone else. Someone I met at a pub. Hearing. Not a lot of conversation went on. Just drinking and you know...' She shrugged in a simple up and down movement, her face slightly flushed.

'Okay, that's fine.' Crabb was reassuring. He was winding up the interview. 'If you think of anything else at all, do get in touch with me, won't you?'

Watching Sam's interpretation, Fiona nodded shyly and floated up to her feet. Crabb walked her towards the door, Sam following; making sure that he remained opposite Fiona and next to Crabb.

Fiona nodded at Crabb, and signed as a farewell, 'You don't think it's Ben, do you? It can't be him. He wouldn't *really* hurt Toby. He's not *violent*. Just fucked up. No different from the rest of us. Damaged by life.' Poor, damaged Fiona. Annie watched as her friend finally signed, 'I do really feel sorry for Ben. I don't think he's had an easy life. There's something a bit sort of broken about him.'

Fiona waved at all of them, as she and Sam left. *Ben's broken like you*, Annie thought sadly, watching the door close.

Annie felt like weeping.

19

Annie couldn't think where she was when she woke on Monday morning. The sun wasn't where it should be, and a great weight pressed down on her chest. Sweating and with her eyes still shut, she felt around, and pushed at the instantly familiar lump, heavy and hot. Eric jumped off her chest and she opened her eyes.

She was lying on the sofa, caught in a slice of sunshine that sneaked through the curtained French windows. Moisture dotted her upper lip. She found her mobile on the floor, and quickly checked for messages. Nothing. Texted William. Waited. Nothing.

Sitting bolt upright, her feet tangled in a single cotton sheet which had covered her. It fell and balled as she moved her legs.

Scarlet walked in, flattened bed-hair, sharp, angular face with bony body, asking, 'What's up?'

Annie watched her lips move. Said, 'Can you do me a favour? Ring William's work. See if he came in this morning.'

Scarlet didn't question her, only held out her hand for Annie's phone. Annie put in the number and Scarlet spoke into the mobile. Annie watched her shoulders rise and fall as she talked, her head angled away from Annie. Facing her again, Scarlet said, 'No, he hasn't turned up today. Last time he was in was Thursday.'

The same day Toby went missing.

Annie said, 'He never misses work. Never. Come on, we're going round there.'

'Why?'

'Because I think he's disappeared. I should've gone round there last night, but I... Christ, I can't even remember falling asleep. Can we go in your car? Mine's still knackered.'

'No problem. Shouldn't you tell Crabb?'

'Not yet. William might just be in bed with a new lover. Don't want to embarrass him. Or he could be in bed with flu. Incommunicado for whatever reason.' She sounded desperate, even to herself. Knew nothing she'd just said was true. Highly unlikely, verging on she didn't believe it for a moment.

William never missed work, never took sickies.

Always answered her texts.

'I've got to find him, Scarlet.'

Scarlet eyebrowed her consent.

Ten minutes later Annie sat in the passenger seat of Scarlet's car. Her flatmate knew the way, so Annie didn't have to bother with directions. Took time out. Pretended all was as it should be. Colours danced through her closed eyelids, warm air blew in through the open window and she tried not to think of anything at all as the car moved along the road, turned around corners, rounded a roundabout and finally and too quickly came to a stop.

They had arrived. Reluctantly, Annie opened her eyes and was surprised that everything looked so normal.

Looked normal.

It was a quiet and currently empty cul-de-sac; no one on the streets. She had a bad feeling, and wished she'd asked Crabb to come with her.

Fighting the urge to turn and run, Annie instead strode up to the door and rang the bell.

Nothing.

'Can you hear anything?'

Scarlet put her ear to the pane of glass in the front door, closed her eyes. Shook her head.

Pushing her aside, Annie bent down, opened the letterbox, and peered through. Seeing nothing, she put her hand through and felt around. Searched with her fingers, scrabbled them against the wooden inside of the door. Panicked suddenly that the string was gone. But no, there it was. She pulled at it, lassoing it through her fingers until the key, tied at the end, fell into her palm. Looking into Scarlet's face, Annie caught a glimpse of fear skitter across her normally neatly arranged features. Annie's own expression mirrored her flatmate's. Bug eyed with anticipation. She turned the key.

The front door opened up into a dark corridor. Scarlet followed her, her hand on Annie's waist. She squeezed it, making Annie turn. Said, 'I don't like this. Feels wrong. Call Crabb.'

'Too late. Come on.'

The doors running off the main hallway on either side of them were all closed. The air felt musty: everything was still and felt like it had been undisturbed for some time. The corridor was thick with heat. The house felt neglected, lifeless. Stagnant.

As far as Annie knew, William had last been seen at work on Thursday.

Thursday.

Friday.

Saturday.

Sunday.

Now it was Monday.

A lot could happen in that time.

Grinding her teeth she gripped Scarlet's hand. Leading her on into something bad. Her stomach lurched as she walked. Deep down, Annie knew.

She opened the first door she came to: a small lavatory. It was, as usual, spotlessly clean and the corners of the toilet roll had been neatly folded so that the first piece hung down, shaped like an arrowhead. Closing the door, they proceeded to the next. Scarlet said, 'No chance he's gone on holiday?'

Annie didn't bother answering.

Gave up on trying to convince herself that all was well. It all felt bad. Very bad.

Finally they reached the sitting room. Scarlet almost banged into her as Annie stopped outside the closed door. All ground floor rooms except this one, searched. Placing her hand on the doorknob, feeling the dimples on the dented and battered brass knob, Annie breathed in, deep and long. Scarlet touched her wrist and said, 'What's that smell?'

Annie had hoped, stupidly, that her nose had been picking up an imagined odour. She had no reply. She knew what it was. They both knew.

The room was relatively large. Annie knew that William loved the bright light that filled it through the large sash windows. This morning, the room was bathed in sunshine but the action of opening the door caused a slight draught. She stood, watching the dust motes move in the sunlight. The draught had also disturbed the smell and made it an active floating thing – coating everything, including herself, in an indescribable, never-before-smelt stench. She covered her mouth with her hand.

She knew instinctively that it was the smell of decay.

Although she had been to William's house more times than

she could remember, she now saw the room as if for the first time. William was thirty-seven, same age as her, and here she and Scarlet stood, in a chintzy, old-lady type room. It didn't reflect his character, as if he were hiding behind lace doilies and the smell of camphor. Camouflaging his real self.

Again, everything was excessively clean and tidy, verging on obsessive. She knew what William had been doing: living a lie – presenting a staid, two-up, two-down façade. He couldn't be further from this pent-up, buttoned-up house, and she wondered why he'd bothered with the phony show of it all.

Blue curtains were held back with a gold brocade tie; a vase of dead daffodils sat next to a battered but comfortable armchair. Here the smell was worse.

She could see the back of a man's head. Without having to go any nearer, she recognised William's hair, the beginnings of a bald patch which he'd always been so self-conscious about. She felt sick and her legs felt wobbly. Disjointed limbs controlled by a lunatic puppet master.

William was sitting in the chair, his legs sprawled out in front of him. She watched as Scarlet stood forward and took command. Took prime position in the viewing process. Her thin, bony figure froze. Complete stillness consumed her. Annie found it hard to tear her eyes from the back of William's head. Too frightened to move any nearer.

Scarlet walked around to the front of the chair. She held her hand up to her, trying to keep Annie from advancing.

'You don't have to see this, Annie.'

Annie forced herself to ignore Scarlet's warning and walked around until she faced the dead man. Knowing that once she saw the dead body, she would never be able to unsee it.

It was William. She already knew that it was. But faced with his dead body she struggled to breathe. There didn't seem to be enough air. She gasped, turning her face away from the corpse.

She stayed like that for a couple of minutes, and then made herself do the impossible. She moved her head back and really looked.

The left side of William's face was nestled up against a cushion. His right side was not nestling against anything; would never nestle again. A skewer stuck out from his ear. The metal looked bright and cruel. His face was pressed into his other shoulder, thankfully making his expression impossible to see. His upper and lower arms had been positioned on the arms of the chair. They lay as if he were relaxing, watching the television, thinking quietly, about to pick up a book, wondering what to have for dinner.

His palms lay face up in his lap: two deep cuts ran vertically up each wrist. A razor was visible, cupped as it was in the semi-curled fingers of his right hand. The blade looked as if it had been delicately dipped in blood; a fine line of dull red could be seen: no longer wet and glistening but dried and more rust coloured than crimson.

There was so little blood that Annie found it difficult to process what she was looking at. His body was positioned to display a perverted nonchalance. His ankles were crossed: an outlandishly cosy position in startling contrast with his savaged wrists and head.

Apart from his brutalised head, the vomit on William's top spoilt the warped domesticity of the scene.

She was breathing fast, gasping, bent double, her hands on her knees.

'Fuck. William. Fuck, fuck, fuck.'

She sat down abruptly on the floor, faced away from the corpse, and silently screamed. Screamed in her head, until her ears hurt with the imagined noise. Didn't know how much more horror she could endure. How many more deaths she could deal with.

Gradually, through sheer force of will, she took hold of her emotions as if they were a bag of squealing live kittens. She threw them into a faraway mental abyss, drowning them. Cold, in control. Breathed in. And out. In and out. One, two, three. A final deep inhalation. Managed to stop her internal wailing. Swivelled around on her bottom and made herself watch Scarlet as she circled William. Concentrated on her face, wanting to see her reactions. Watched as Scarlet held her breath and reluctantly bent in closer to the body. Took in every movement that Scarlet made. She analysed her body language. It was the only way she knew how to cope.

How to avoid, to not feel, to keep on mentally running.

It was clear from Scarlet's reaction that the smell of decomposition was stronger close-up and she had to stop herself from gagging. Her flatmate held a hand to her face, covering both nose and mouth. Her hand didn't look like it was doing the job.

'Why are his wrists slashed?' Annie asked, not understanding why she had the capacity to ask such a brutal question, using the same tone as she would were she asking the price of lemons.

Scarlet moved her hand from her face and looked at Annie. 'It's not suicide, Annie. There's not enough blood. He didn't cut his wrists. It doesn't make sense.'

'I didn't think it was suicide. Not with the skewer in his ear.' She stopped and then said: 'It's how Toby was killed. Stabbed in the ear.'

Scarlet shook her head. Bewildered by the violence.

William's death felt jaggedly real, *sur*real, hyper-real. *Too* real. Now Annie had a duet of corpses in her head. Jostling for position. She wanted neither. Had no room for any more.

She just needed to keep it together for now. She swallowed and managed to say, 'Ring Crabb.'

Scarlet did and Annie sat there, on the floor, feeling numb.

Dead.

To everything.

All she allowed herself to feel was the line of sweat that trickled down her scar. She concentrated on it, imagined it following its course down the puckered skin on her cheek. Sweat was better than tears.

Sweat didn't hurt.

20

Crabb bent in nearer to the body. Tried to look at William's mouth. His face was wedged up against his shoulder. Keeping his mouth shut. Crabb put on gloves, wrinkled his nose at the smell of vomit, and gently turned the man's face, pulling down on his lower lip. Managing to part the mouth slightly, he leant in a little closer to get a better look. Once the mouth was open, he didn't touch or disturb the body further. Kept his hands clasped in front of him, as if in prayer.

He looked and looked, and then startled back. Almost screamed at the shock of what he'd seen. Or thought he'd seen.

'What? What is it?' DS Peters said.

Ignoring his sergeant, he had another look. Just to make sure. Knowing that his face was contorted in disgust and fear. He said, 'It looks like a dog's ear.'

'Jesus,' said Peters. 'A dog's ear. Christ. And poor Annie. That's two people she's close to, killed on the same weekend. No, *murdered* on the same weekend. What are the chances of that? Infinitesimal. You know Docherty will say we should treat her as a suspect.'

Crabb spoke through his teeth: 'If he does, he's an idiot.

Which we know already. It was a *man* seen with Toby in the wheelchair. A man. I've seen the tapes. It was a man. Remember Adam. A woman would not have had the strength to so comprehensively annihilate that boy with that much ferocity, that much power. Of *course* Annie's not a bloody suspect. She's a fucking victim.'

Peters' face reddened. '*I* know that. I was just saying about the DCI, that's all.'

Crabb held his palm out, facing downward – placatory. Said, 'The killer is a male, who's getting better at killing and who, for reasons as yet unknown, has Annie in his sights. I wouldn't be surprised if Docherty thinks she attacked herself.' Angry now, it was with relief that he stood back as Dr Moore entered.

Twenty minutes later, the house was teeming with SOCOs and Crabb once again listened to Dr Moore speaking in his matter-of-fact way. His words sounded like a dirge as he explained his findings. The pathologist had extricated the furry thing that had been sitting in William's mouth. He held it up to better examine it, with a pair of tweezers.

'Is it what I think it is?' said Crabb.

'I don't know what you think it is,' said Dr Moore.

Crabb said nothing.

'It's part of a dog's ear,' Dr Moore said. There was nothing in his demeanour to indicate that it was anything other than what he might have expected to find in the mouth of a corpse.

'At a guess, I'd say a Labrador,' Dr Moore added.

'And time of death?'

'Of the dog?'

Angry, Crabb waited it out.

'Well, decomp is under way, in this heat it's been accelerated, so I'd say he was probably killed at approximately the same time as the boy. The man, not the canine. On Saturday. Or not long after. I'll get my full lab report to the police after the post-mortem. But, of course, until I double check, I might be wrong.'

He waited a beat. 'Although I'd be surprised. I'd also say that he's only been dumped here in the early hours of this morning. Lividity proves he's been recently moved.'

Dr Moore was more forthcoming than was usual at a crime scene. He generally preferred to give his results and specifically the time of death after his post-mortem. He was thorough if nothing else. He was being uncharacteristically generous this morning.

It was obvious that *this* was not the primary crime scene. The house had clearly not been disturbed by anyone for some time. William's body was the freshest thing here. That's what they were missing. A primary crime scene. They needed to find the place where the killer had kept Toby and William. Where he had killed them. The killer needed somewhere private where he wouldn't attract attention.

He looked down as Dr Moore spoke again, 'The slashed wrists are for effect only. As I'm sure you can see. He was dead long before the wrists were cut.'

The pathologist turned his head and coughed, covering his mouth with his gloved hand. He put on a new pair and carried on speaking to Crabb's feet – not bothering to make eye contact again. 'One interesting thing, though. Remember on the boy's body. The bruising on his wrists? More on his left wrist than on his right?'

Crabb nodded.

'Other way round this time. More bruising on this man's right wrist, as opposed to the other. A quite marked difference.'

'So, the wrists weren't tied together. Tied *to* something. Is that what you're saying?'

'In my opinion, yes. But not both hands for the same amount of time. Hence the different bruise markings.'

'Any defensive markings on the body?'

'No. And none on the boy in the pond as per my report.'

'His name's Toby,' Crabb said.

Crabb stored the information away, thanked the doctor and started to wander about the place. Every room in the house was immaculate. He went back to look at the body. Something was niggling away in his mind, but it was just out of reach. He kneaded his brow with his fingers, tapped at his temples, trying to bring the niggle to the forefront of his brain.

It didn't work.

He did another tour of the house, opening cupboards and drawers. He looked under the bed and behind the curtains. Not entirely sure what he was looking for. Something missing that should be there, or something was there that shouldn't be. He went back again to look at the body. Were it not for the fact that William was dead with a skewer in his ear, the posing of the body made it an almost comfortable domestic scene. Sitting there with his mug of half-drunk tea on the side table, a tin of tobacco and a packet of Rizlas next to his unfinished drink. A lighter was aligned neatly next to the rolling papers.

Crabb frowned. Touched the mug. Obviously cold. But there was still tea in it. Half a mug. Would such a neat man leave an unfinished drink and not clear it away? Surely not.

The alternative was more disturbing. Had the *killer* made him a mug of tea? If so, why? William was already dead. He shook his head. Confused.

He grunted, frustrated. Desperate to retrieve the niggle from the depths of his brain. Desperate to talk again to Annie. Peters had made a good point: two murders of two close friends on the same weekend. It made Annie key to everything. Not a suspect, but he'd have to go through the bloody motions. Fucking pointless and a waste of time. But maybe Annie could shed some light on this murder. Maybe she knew something that she wasn't aware of knowing.

He only hoped that Scarlet could alibi Annie for the relevant nights. He remembered that Dora Potts had said that William had missed his usual Thursday night at the Deaf Club. If it turned out that William had disappeared on the same night as Toby, he'd have to ask Annie where she'd been on Thursday. After her attack, taking into account her whole demeanour, he hadn't thought it worth asking her for her whereabouts on the previous Thursday. He'd viewed her as only a reluctant and unfortunate victim.

He glanced up to find that Docherty had rolled into the room, putting in an appearance for appearance sake. The fat man nodded at Crabb. Combed his beard with his fingers. Said, 'Fill me in.'

Crabb did, and then said, 'I want Annie watched. A couple of men. She is *not* the murderer. But she is clearly *a* link to this investigation. I'm not sure how yet, but it's fairly bloody obvious now that she has a connection to all this. After all, my sergeant said so himself: how many people have two people they love murdered in the space of a couple of days?'

'Find out if she has an alibi. She's involved in some way.'

'Yes, she *is* involved. My opinion, as I've just said, is that she's *a* link. But not necessarily *the* link. But I'll tell you this for nothing, if anything, and I mean *anything*, happens to Annie, it'll be our fault. We need her under constant watch.'

'Prove to me she's not a suspect, and I'll see what I can do. Have to take into consideration the budget. We're running with a full complement of officers already. We're at bloody full capacity as it is. There isn't a bloody bottomless pit of gold coins at our disposal you know.'

'Do you want to wait until she *is* a victim?'

Docherty showed his teeth and thrust his chin forward,

saying, 'Watch your step, Crabb. Don't get uppity with *me*. Prove to my satisfaction that she is not directly involved in this. Other than being a "victim". Go and interview her now. In fact, make it official. Take her down the station to get her statement. Make sure you get it in writing, where she was from Thursday evening onwards. I'm trusting you on this. At this point, it doesn't exactly look good for her. How sure are you of her innocence? And don't give me any of your "gut" feeling crap either.'

'I'm as sure as I can be. Experience of people – and no, that's not gut instinct. The circumstances. Everything tells me she's absolutely not a killer. I think it's a little insensitive to take her down the nick. She's just seen the corpse of her boyfriend. And before that, Toby. A dead boy. Who she loved. She loved them both.'

Docherty shook his head. Irritated. 'I couldn't give a rat's arse who she loved.'

'*Really?*'

Docherty had the grace to falter, maybe realising he'd aired his real character too clearly.

'Don't twist my words. We need to cover our backs. Do every-thing by the book. Follow protocol. Take her down the station. Now.'

'Fine. I'll make it official. Callous but official. Don't you get it? She's being made to suffer on a very personal level. The killer is *involving* her. Whether she likes it or not.'

Docherty's face returned to bland and stupid. Cut off. Standing downwind of any whiff of police frailty. Crabb turned away. He hadn't thought it important that William's and Annie's relationship was not actually boyfriend and girlfriend. Not worth mentioning. Certainly not to Docherty. At this stage, he thought it irrelevant and there was no point in embarrassing Annie. According to Annie, no one knew that they were just friends. For the moment, he had no reason not to believe her. He addressed Docherty now. 'The obvious question is, who has Annie pissed off recently?'

'Find out. She has no connection to Adam Jacobs, does she?'

'No. There is *no* link between Annie and Adam. I investigated Adam's death thoroughly at the time. It was a murder committed without thought or planning. I thought the same then. I haven't changed my mind since.'

Crabb straightened himself and glared at Docherty. 'But now the killer's back on track. I think he wants to hurt Annie. He's baiting her. Targeting her. Call it what you will. I don't understand it. Not yet. The victims are all deaf; that is essential for the killer. Annie is also deaf. We *must* look after her.'

'It is our duty to look after *all* of the Deaf Community, Crabb.'

Smug bastard. He has no idea, Crabb thought. *No idea at all.*

Peters said, 'Surely the Deaf Club is the main connection between the two victims. Toby and William were both regulars there.'

Turning to the DCI, Crabb felt he had to spell it out for him: 'Actually, William only went once a week. In a nutshell, the killer needs his victims to be deaf. It's clearly a prerequisite. There is only one Deaf Club in the area, so where else would the killer go to find deaf people? I think it's just a place that offers up easy pickings. A pool of potential victims conveniently there for the taking. But I *am* convinced that both Toby and William went willingly with their killer. Meaning they knew him. There were no defensive marks on either body. So, one could presume from that fact, that the killer is a local man, or at the very least, he goes to the Deaf Club. Don't forget that DC Bragen said it was clear from the CCTV that the man was familiar with Hampstead Heath.'

Docherty nodded slowly and said, 'But Annie isn't a regular at the Deaf Club, is she?' He paused. 'Or is she?'

Fuck me. Shoot me now.

'No, Annie is not a regular at the Deaf Club. Fact. But more importantly, what is the link between Toby and William? I know William has some connection to the Deaf School, but we need to establish in what capacity.' Crabb shrugged. 'Annie might know. Anything else, sir? I need to speak to her now. Get her down the station.'

Docherty waved him away and Crabb turned to Peters, 'Get Bragen to make a list of all the names and addresses of everyone involved in this case.'

'Everyone?' He sounded incredulous.

'Yes, everyone. All the deaf, all the hearing, everyone that we've met. I need Bragen to find out if any of them have any second properties, garages, basements, holiday homes on the coast, storage units, allotments, warehouses, safehouses, shit-houses. Fucking tree houses. I don't care. Cover everything. Anything at all that we don't know about. The killer needs somewhere private where he can work undisturbed. Tell Bragen to find me that place.'

'We haven't even searched people's current houses. It'll take him ages.'

'Tell him to delegate what he can't handle. We can't go searching people's residences now. There's a small thing called a search warrant. We can't go barging into people's properties without probable cause. Tell him now. Straight away. We need a suspect.'

21

ow to my other house guest: William. I don't call him that because this is my life, my fantasy, my reality. To me, at this stage, he is not William. William just fills the shoes of my character: a good stand-in. Do not make the mistake of thinking me delusional, or in the midst of a psychotic break. I am well aware that William is William. Just not for my purposes.

The problem: the reality is not, thus far, living up to my fantasy.

All the boy had done was cry. Incessantly. Maybe it was my appearance that frightened him so. The man had no such excuse. He had age and experience on his side. He had simply displayed an obdurate stupidity that surprised me. I knew he wasn't essentially stupid — hence his inclusion. Well, that, and his obvious connection to Annie. That was crucial.

'What do you think I want most this year?' I asked the man.

'How the hell should I know?' he signed with his one free hand.

'But I've told you, again and again and again. Weren't you listening?'

'I have no idea what it is you want from me. From us. Why not let Toby go? Keep me instead.'

Oh, the heroics.

Again, despite my kindnesses, he merely looked baffled. Patiently, I signed, 'Didn't you get my not-so subtle hints? That all I wanted was a puppy. It wasn't a very fucking complicated request, after all. Surely you understood? Or maybe you purposely chose to ignore my request? Didn't I make it clear enough for you? Or were you just being a complete bastard? I never asked for anything except for that one time. And you denied me.'

He'd shaken his head in what appeared to be confusion. As if I were speaking in tongues.

I was filled with an all-too-familiar sadness. That nothing had changed. Nothing ever would change. Nothing at all.

22

'You've got to be kidding me, Crabb,' Annie said. 'I do *not* want an interpreter. You know I don't need one.'

'Yeah, well, my superior is insisting on it. Wants it all by the book. A formal interview. Sam's on his way.'

She folded her arms, angry. Still in shock. Didn't speak. Her face was devoid of any emotion other than irritation. And even that expression was fleeting. Didn't take hold. She was unable to even come up with indignation about having to wait for an interpreter. He guessed that it was insulting for her. Looking at her face, he couldn't find anything there at all. Just a blankness. Her skin the colour of alabaster. Her lips stretched tight and razor-thin. Her teeth clamped tightly together. He spotted the telltale sign of the muscle in her jaw clenching as she bit down, molars on molars. Finally, 'Are you interviewing Scarlet as well?'

'Yes. Peters is. Can I get you a cup of something?'

'Yeah, alcohol.' She was only semi-joking. Tilting her head up, she closed her eyes. Not playing.

There was a knock on the door. 'Come.'

Bragen popped his head around the door of the interview room. Crabb sighed: he'd been expecting Sam. 'What is it?'

'I've been to see Mrs Whorton. She won't change her statement. Said she saw Ben following Toby on Thursday night, half past seven. Won't budge. Sorry.'

Crabb was pissed off. Not sure whether to blame Bragen's lack of experience, or whether to blame the stubbornness of a horrible old woman.

'Okay,' he said. 'Leave it with me. Thanks. Any luck on the second addresses? Or the vehicles?'

'No one involved owns a van or a hatchback. A few vans and hatchbacks were picked up on CCTV. And they all check out. So far. But we're still looking. Haven't had time to start on the addresses, but that's where I'm heading now. My computer.'

Crabb held his hand up in acknowledgement and farewell. Confused. He'd have put money on Mrs Whorton having been lying. Maybe he was wrong.

But he didn't think so.

Annie hadn't moved. Her eyes still shut. Hadn't heard the door opening, hadn't heard his conversation with Bragen. For the first time, Crabb really wondered what it must be like to be completely cut off from everything auditory. He could hear shouts coming from the custody suite, the raised voices of the custody sergeant as he booked in those just arrested. He heard someone whistling, he heard banging coming from the police cells, a prisoner singing drunkenly. And the ticking of the clock in the room. He heard that too. But Annie heard none of it.

He realised that the idea of total silence frightened him.

Another knock. Sam entered, bowed slightly and took his place next to Crabb.

For the purposes of the tape and the video recording, Crabb took Annie through the formalities, and then said to her, 'I am truly sorry for having to bring you down here, and I can only imagine what you're going through. None of this can be easy, and I can only offer you my sincerest apologies.'

Annie's eyes just looked at him; blank and empty. Embarrassed, he said, 'I have to ask you where you were on Thursday evening – seven o'clock onwards.'

She turned to Sam. 'You don't need to interpret for me. I'll talk for myself, and lip-read Crabb. Thanks though.' Annie looked tired. Too tired and too broken, he thought. Sam sat back quietly, crossing his hands in his lap.

She answered the question, her tone neutral. 'At work. With a million witnesses.'

'At that time? That late?'

'Window dressing often has to be done at night. The shop is empty, no customers. We were setting up a window display. Me and Scarlet. I was there, at the shop, from six o'clock until about midnight. Sarah didn't contact me about Toby until the following morning, Friday: first thing.'

Crabb's abdomen crunched up with shame. His questions outrageously inappropriate in his opinion. He spoke quickly, hoping that speed of communication might conceal the cruelty and unfairness of his questions. He turned slightly from Sam, who smelt like he was overdue a bath.

'And last night. Late, or early this morning, where were you?'

'In a deep sleep on the sofa. Ask Scarlet. She'll confirm where I was. She covered me with a sheet. I conked out, was completely knackered, passed out cold. Exhausted. Totally fucked. Heart-broken. Okay?'

'Absolutely okay. Let's move on to William.' He paused and swallowed, still uncomfortable at having to formally question Annie. But he was covering his official arse. Now he could move on to questions that he really wanted to ask her. He went with his gut and because of his overriding sense of loyalty to her, he carried on her lie.

'Your boyfriend, William Tate – what was his relationship with Toby?'

'William works as a picture framer. His day job. But he also volunteers at the Deaf School – works there on Mondays and Tuesdays. In the evenings. Coaches the football team. Toby didn't really like to play. He did sometimes but preferred to watch. William encouraged him. William liked Toby. Toby liked William. It was as simple as that. Nothing more.'

'Tell me what you thought when you found William. What were your impressions? And I'm sorry to ask. I know it must be very painful. But I have to. I need your input. You were his girl-friend after all.'

She cocked her head slightly and her shoulders lifted. Perhaps in relief that he was carrying on her pretence, or perhaps simply because she was having to struggle to regain her normal mental strength. Crabb thought her strong now, even if she didn't realise it herself. Her face crumpled, like a wadded-up tissue. Unexpected and alarming, he watched her face collapse in grief. But still, her character won out. She managed a coherent, sensible answer.

'What do you mean? What were my impressions? He was dead. That's it. He was killed like Toby. You told me Toby was stabbed in the ear. So was William. Was it the same weapon?'

He saw no point in lying. Nodded. Let the silence lengthen. Let her think about the scene. The staged scene. She waited him out. Maybe too tired to give his question serious thought, or maybe she had nothing to say. He raised his eyebrows. She sighed: a deep and long sigh that seemed to come from her boots. She said, 'I thought it was weird. The whole scene. Fake.'

She swept her hand over her face and stared at him.

'Not my first impression. Not at first. At first I was just shocked. Appalled. Completely fucking freaked out. It was William with a skewer in his ear. How do you think I felt? But afterwards, sitting in the police car with Scarlet, we didn't speak. Sat in silence. And that's when I realised.'

Crabb waited but she didn't elaborate. Needed prompting. 'Realised what?'

She gazed past him, as if picturing something in her head.

'I realised that William sitting there in his chair, in front of his television, ankles crossed, his hands in his lap as if he were relaxed and enjoying a normal evening – *visually*, it was all phony. I knew then that it was staged. It was all about the posing. The setting of the scene. The faked suicide in a cosy domestic sitting room. It's my job. It's what Scarlet and I both do for a living. It was a piece of theatre. Like an installation. It was artificial, something like we'd arrange for a window display at work. We dress and position mannequins, put their make-up on. This was the same.

'William had been positioned like an articulated doll. It was set up to tell a story. But God knows what the story was. As window-dressers, we create a picture, a vision. We make sure it gives out a specific message or tells a story. Dependent on the season, occasion, whatever. It looks realistic but it's false. We want people to believe in it. And they do, because they want to.'

She was desperate for him to understand. And he did. He felt a ripple of excitement but didn't share it. Said, 'You obviously knew William. I didn't. His house looked like he was obsessively neat and tidy. Everything was where it should be. Nothing was out of place. Except the mug of tea next to him. A mug half full of tea. Did you see it?'

Her face crinkled in confusion. 'No. I didn't see that. All I saw was his body.' She stopped to think, to imagine a half-drunk mug of tea. 'He'd never do that. He was a bit on the anal side.' She smiled. 'It used to make me laugh. He was so predictable. Didn't do spontaneous. But he *was* fun. Liked a laugh.'

She stopped. Remembering. Sad.

'But he would never, and I mean *never*, leave a dirty mug out.

Was it on a doily? If it wasn't, it wasn't him who put it there. And it certainly wasn't him who left it there. It's not in his nature.'

There was a sudden silence as she thought about what she'd just said, and what it meant. 'Fuck. Are you saying the *killer* made him a cup of tea? For show? To finish off his tableau of "man relaxing peacefully at home"? If that's what he did, he made a mistake. William would never do that. Even if he was running late, he'd never leave dirty mugs about the place. *Never.* He was too organised. He'd have a heart attack at the thought.'

She made a small attempt at a laugh, trying to enjoy the memory of her friend and his obsessive cleanliness. Not judging him, but re-living him and his habits. Her own words brought back the too recent picture of William's murder. Crabb watched her wrestle with it. He was impressed that she was still able to communicate at all. That she hadn't just curled up and stopped. He wanted to touch her, comfort her, but didn't want to cross boundaries.

She was so beautiful, and he, so ugly by comparison. Physically they were like shit and champagne. He sighed. Told himself that what he felt for her was protective, paternal. Nothing more. To Annie, he must seem like an old and very plain man. He shook his head to dispel the unwelcome thought.

He had almost forgotten the presence of Sam, sitting to his left. As Annie was speaking and lip-reading, the interpreter sat quietly. Not needed. Crabb said, 'I don't think it was a mistake. I think the killer was making a point. Wanted me to see the picture he'd created. Including the mug of tea. But I don't know what it means.'

But I might do. I might have an idea. Because of what you've just said, Annie.

Annie rubbed her eyes as if they were sore. 'I don't know what it means either. Sorry.' She paused and said, 'Why William? He's a grown man. Who's the killer targeting? Deaf

males? What's he *doing*? First, two boys, then an attack on me –
and now I'm not even so sure that I ever was a target, not like the
others. And then he kills William? It doesn't make sense.'

'You're right. It doesn't make sense. And you're not like the
others. You're alive. And I'm sorry, but whether you like it or not,
you *are* involved. Think about who he's killed.'

Crabb took a drink from a bottle of water.

'Toby and William are both people you loved. That's the link.
One of the links. He's targeting deaf people you are close to.'

Annie, defeated: 'But why? What does he want?'

'I don't know.'

'He won't destroy me. Fuck him.' She stood.

Crabb held his hand up. Waved at the chair. 'Sit. One more
question. Both Toby and William showed signs of having been
tied up. But the marks on Toby's wrists were more marked on his
left hand. William's were worst on his right. Can you think why
that might be so?'

She frowned and his heart sank. And then her face broke
into a smile. Tentative, but a smile. Pleased that she had a
possible solution to the seemingly random tying of the hands.

'Left-handed, William was left-handed. Toby right-handed.
Could that be it?'

He smiled broadly, his mind working quickly. Said, 'That
would explain the different bruises on different wrists. The
killer *was* communicating with them, signing with them.' He
stopped, suddenly confused. '*Can* you sign with one hand?'

'Yes.'

Crabb let a silence fall, whilst each of them thought about
Toby and William being tied to a chair. One hand free. Annie
frowned and said, 'That's an awful lot of talking they must have
been doing. Thursday to Saturday. A long time. What were they
talking *about*?'

Crabb shook his head in agreement: it was an unpleasant

image. What *had* they been talking about? Wanting to press on, he brought the interview, if it could be called such, to a close: 'Thank you, Annie. Thank you so much. You've been a huge help. Given me a lot to think about. I think that's it. We'll check with Scarlet, make sure your alibis stand up – I'm sure they will. And my apologies for having to bring you down here at all. You're a brave woman. Can I get someone to give you a lift home?'

'Where are you going now?'

'Going to the school with Sam.' He looked and waited for the interpreter's nod of agreement. 'Going to talk to Ben. And Martin. Ask about Ben's brother. Find out if it was Theo who's turned up. Want to come?'

'Fuck, no. Can't do anything at the moment. I'm going to the pub.' She was already texting furiously and spoke without looking up.

'I need a drink. I'll text Scarlet. Maybe a few friends. Dora, Polly. Whoever.' She shrugged. 'Feel like surrounding myself with people. Is that pathetic?'

He smiled at her. Leant across the table and squeezed her hand. Crossing a line, but he didn't give a rat's arse. 'Of course it's not pathetic. I'm so sorry for everything, Annie. When you feel up to it, get in touch. In the meantime. Look after yourself.'

A weak, sad smile came back at him.

'Don't worry about me. I might turn up sooner than you think. Can't do with sitting around, feeling sorry for myself. I might never move again if I give in now. Need to keep moving. Can't just sit about too heart-broken, too frightened to go out. What would be the point of me living if I allowed that to happen?'

'Good for you.'

'Anyway, I've got to email Sarah. Let her know about

William. Don't want her reading about it in the papers. She'll be upset.'

Annie shook her head and closed her eyes. Crabb watched as she battled to keep from crying. He touched her arm to get her attention.

'Just so that you know, I'm trying to organise a couple of policemen to watch you. Keep an eye on you. So that you're safe.'

She frowned.

Didn't think she needed help. Wasn't used to it.

Get used to it, Crabb thought.

23

Crabb had made sure that Ben was in school earlier that morning. Had rung the headmaster, told him that he needed to speak to the boy this afternoon. Apparently Ben's mother had been called in to explain her son's constant truancy and lack of academic progress. Crabb glanced at his watch as he and Sam hurried on foot to the Deaf School. Hopefully, he'd catch the mother as well.

It was nearing the end of the day and Crabb avoided a mountain of dog shit that stood in the middle of the pavement, directly outside the school gates. Someone had planted a plastic doll, head-first, slap bang into the mass of turd. Drowned in shit. He knew the feeling.

He stopped for a moment to watch the mess of children pour back into the building, their final playtime apparently over. Like measles on the run, they scattered, whooping, making guttural noises, their hands signing, as they flew across the concrete playground. Like an elimination of a plague, the boys stopped playing football, the girls broke up their secretive huddles and they all disappeared, en masse.

It was suddenly completely empty, eerily quiet. Crabb said to Sam, 'You know Ben, don't you? What's he like?'

Sam spoke softly, his hands swinging like a toy soldier as the two men walked: 'I'm afraid I can't give you my views on anyone or anything that is said. Interpreters have a professional code of conduct. To which I adhere. Strictly. I can't be seen to influence either the hearing or the Deaf party. I'm here to facilitate communication between the two. I voice their signs, I sign your voice. My personal views are totally immaterial. That's my job – nothing more. Forget I'm here. It makes the process easier.'

Crabb shrugged. Fair enough. He instead concentrated on the coming interview. He'd already talked to Ben. Today, Crabb would push him. Hard. He almost hoped the boy was telling the truth about not seeing Toby on Thursday. Wanted to prove that bitch Whorton was lying.

And he *did* want to find out about Theo. Why the young man had been pointing at Toby. Hoping that the young man was indeed Theo. If so, it was imperative that he talk to the mother.

As he and Sam walked down seemingly endless corridors, the familiar smell of school dinners hung in the air. Rounding the corner, Crabb saw Ben, standing over a woman.

Sam pointed and said, 'There's Ben. And his mother.'

A tired and dishevelled woman, obviously drunk, bounced off one wall and half fell to her knees. The boy caught her with a smooth and practised ease. Standing behind her, he stuck his fists out underneath the woman's armpits, holding her weight on his forearms. His hands were free and seeing Sam, he started to sign, looking like a mad puppeteer in control of a broken ventriloquist's dummy.

'You remember my mother?' As Sam voiced the boy, Ben swung his mother around, as if presenting her to Crabb: holding her like a rag doll. He dragged her along the corridor in a pantomime dance. The boy's eyes gleamed and he laughed. His hands began signing again. 'We're just one big happy family. Aren't we, Mum? Oh, sorry, forgot. The old cow can't sign. Just nod, Mum.'

The boy took his mother's head and tugged on the hair falling down her back, making her nod.

'Nice to see you again, Crabb,' Ben signed. Sam spoke the words, coating them with heavy sarcasm.

The boy dropped his mother suddenly. Either her weight or his hatred of her suddenly becoming too much. Or more likely, Crabb thought, the joke of his drunken mother had ceased to amuse him. He dropped her as casually as he might have a piece of rubbish.

Crabb inwardly winced as he heard the crunch of Mrs Downing's elbow hitting the floor. He bent to more closely inspect the woman, keeping his face impassive, not wanting to give Ben the satisfaction of letting him see how revolted he was by this whole display. The boy's physical appearance, with his basin haircut and heavy jaw belied the intelligence that shone in his eyes. He was strangely disinterested in his physical appearance. An odd trait in a teenage boy.

Crabb looked around him and noticed a school chair standing abandoned in the corridor. He clumsily picked up Ben's mother and tried to position her on the overly small plastic seat. She slid unceremoniously down, her legs like rubber. Crabb managed to turn the chair sideways and propped her up against the wall. Mrs Downing slid to the side. The interpreter was standing looking at his shoes. Crabb shouted at him, 'Do you think you could give me a hand here, Sam? I don't want her falling off the chair.'

The interpreter was startled and moved quickly to help Crabb, said, 'Of course, sorry. Thought you had it under control.'

Having finally made Mrs Downing as safe as possible, Crabb forced himself not to shout at Ben: the little shit. The boy eyeballed Crabb. He nodded in the direction of his mother who had slumped forward. Her hair hid her face from view.

'She loves an audience. But she won't even remember being here tomorrow. Will you, Mum?'

He kicked her roughly on her shin. Mrs Downing didn't react. She seemed to have fallen asleep, which worked well for Crabb as although he was loath to leave the woman he assumed that she'd be safe enough here and it meant he would have the time and space to talk to Ben on his own. And to watch his reactions.

'Follow me,' said Crabb, and he led the way, back into the playground.

Ben lounged on an old wooden bench, forcing Sam and Crabb to stand opposite.

'Why did you bully Toby?' asked Crabb.

A simple question but one that required a more complicated answer.

'He annoyed me. Fucking little wanker. Such a *good* boy. A mummy's boy. Everyone loved him. He was like a fucking angel. A goody goody-two-shoes. That's why I bullied him. No complicated reason. I just hated him. Simple. He was everything that I'm not.'

Much to Crabb's surprise, Ben had responded with what sounded like the truth. He spoke with a cruel arrogance; as if he couldn't care less how his statements were taken. But Crabb was sure that he spoke the absolute truth. As Ben saw it, he had nothing to gain by lying and didn't understand the inappropriateness of his answers.

'Toby was happy,' said Crabb.

Ben's face took on a youthful expression, thrown by the statement, and then he looked sad. He quickly covered it with anger. It was like watching a mini theatrical show of emotions, all of which danced across his face in rapid succession. A young man wanting desperately to be an adult. But achieving only an emotionally chaotic boy. *He might be a nasty little sod*, Crabb thought, *but he has yet to finesse his spite into anything sophisticated*. Equally, he didn't think Ben was stupid. Far from it. He didn't lower his eyes when signing at Crabb, but held them in a confident stare. He had a certain maturity about him; a charisma of sorts, although a disturbing one. There was certainly more to this boy than met the eye.

'Who do *you* think killed Toby? I'd like your opinion,' said Crabb.

'Yeah, right. Like you'll listen to a sixteen-year-old's point of view. A Deaf one at that.' Ben sat back on the bench, balancing his arms against the backrest. He slowly brought them round to the front of his body to sign, '"I don't know" is my answer. All I know is I saw Toby go past here on Thursday evening. I happened to be walking behind him. I was on my phone. No, I didn't see any loonies picking him up, and I didn't see him get into any cars. I lied to you before. So what?'

'Why did you lie? When I asked you before, you said you hadn't seen Toby. Why the change in story?'

'If I'd told you the truth, I knew I'd get the blame. I get the blame for everything, doesn't matter if I've done it or not. That's why I lied. For a laugh.' The boy bent down and picked up a half moon of a tennis ball which had made its way underneath the seat to die. Ben threw the broken half-ball up and down in his hand, catching it easily, and looked up at Crabb.

'And I saw that old woman from number twenty-two. She pointed at me, at the search party. I assume she told you that she saw me walking behind Toby on Thursday. Just because I kicked her stupid dog. Bet she thinks she's landed me right in the shit.'

He wasn't wrong there. So Mrs Whorton *had* been telling the truth. But Crabb still wasn't satisfied. She was hiding *something*, he was sure. But for the moment, he'd back-burner her.

Ben lobbed the semi-ball into the air, up and over Crabb's shoulder. Crabb heard it land with a splat and said, 'Who was the man you were speaking to outside the school last Wednesday afternoon. Half past four? Was it your brother?'

He didn't expect Ben's reaction. He almost jumped. His mouth dropped open. His body went rigid with shock; sort of jerked to attention. For a moment he looked like the very young boy that he was. Fear had stripped him of all his bravado. 'What man? Don't know who you're talking about.'

He was scared. And he couldn't disguise it. He also couldn't hide the fact that he was lying. Crabb watched as his fear turned to anger. A feeling he was more comfortable with. Ben changed the subject. 'Would I tell you if I'd killed Toby? I could have killed him. I don't think murder's my thing, though. Not absolutely positive on that one, but I don't think so. Or if it was, I would have picked a different method.'

Crabb allowed him this brief interlude from answering questions. It was all about timing. Just let the conversation flow, and it would come back full circle.

'Like what?' Crabb asked.

Ben cocked his head to one side and seemed to give it serious thought. Again, the boy seemed totally truthful and utterly lacking in deceit. Crabb shuddered. Ben was a frightening teenager. Damaged. 'Tell you what. When I come up with a good plan, you'll be the first to know. Can't say fairer than that,' Ben said. He spread his arms out to the sides, in a magnanimous gesture and stood up, throwing back his head with a laugh.

'What do you think of Fiona? Do you like her?' Crabb asked.

'I fancy her. But I don't like her. Can't stand her. She might as well be hearing. Just like Annie. Up their own arses. Fiona with her cochlear implant. Annie with her voice. Are they embarrassed about being Deaf or what?'

'But you let Fiona look after you, didn't you? After you'd met your brother. Theo. That's his name, isn't it?'

Like a cartoon face, Crabb watched the colour drain from Ben's face. It left a sickly pallor. Ben's eyes bulged. Terror.

'It *was* Theo, wasn't it?' Crabb asked.

Ben shuffled his feet, suddenly fascinated with his dirty trainers and the lace that had come undone. Crabb gently touched him on the shoulder – to make him look up. He was wearing enormous baggy jeans and a baggy T-shirt. He suddenly looked too small for them, as if he were physically lost within them.

'Come on,' said Crabb, 'I know it was him. Your older brother. Where is he?'

Ben seemed incapable of communication. He just slowly shook his head. He was like a popped balloon – his life force was, for the moment, dormant, and he sat before Crabb, deflated.

Crabb asked, 'Why are you so frightened of him?'

Ben brought his head up and glared at Crabb. A tear sat unshed in the corner of his eye. He twisted his hands in front of him, his whole posture like that of an infant. He squirmed and kicked his shoes at nothing. 'I'm not scared of him. I'm not scared of anyone. And I don't know where he is. I really don't. He doesn't live with us. I haven't seen him in ages. Years and years.'

From stroppy teenager, to an afraid and pathetic boy. Crabb watched him with interest. Watched him dry his eyes, watched him clench his teeth. Watched him open up and draw back his shoulders. Watched him get his defence mechanism firmly back in place. Ben was back, burying Baby Ben deep inside him.

He wouldn't answer any more questions about Theo. Crabb would have to wait until his mother sobered up and he could talk to them both. Together. It was progress of sorts that Ben had admitted to Theo's existence at all.

Ben winked at Crabb, man to man, and signed, 'And anyway, anyone would let Fiona comfort them, wouldn't they? Have you seen her? I wouldn't mind a bit of that. I've *had* a bit of that.' He fashioned his hands into two cup shapes, jiggling them as if they were two huge melons.

'And what about Martin?' Crabb asked. 'Do you like him? He says you're friends.'

Ben laughed at the question. Derision oozed from him. Utter disdain. 'That old tosser. No. Course not. He's old. Now if you're looking for fools – and sorry to disappoint you, but I'm not one of them – look to Martin. Thick as a plank. Gives deafies a bad name. Although *that's* not hard to do. Look out, here comes the thick deafie.' Ben waved his hands in the air, aping some monstrous being on the loose. 'We don't *think*, Mr Policeman. We leave that up to the hearing and follow like sheep. We just make mongy noises and sound like we're brain damaged.'

Crabb didn't react. The boy laughed and wandered away, not looking behind him. Crabb let him go. Like most things, he'd keep. He wasn't going anywhere. Crabb wanted to give Ben the time to think about his brother, Theo. Theo obviously terrified Ben. So next time Crabb spoke to Ben, hopefully with his mother, preferably in his own house, the boy's fear would have ripened like a fresh peach: just ready for the picking.

'Right, let's go and speak to Martin,' Crabb said, noticing the caretaker's hut. He walked resolutely towards it.

One down, one to go.

24

Martin preened and puffed up when Crabb entered the little shack, obviously eager to show off his own professional space. Like a fat controller in his own little world, he sat on a stool, rewiring a piece of black plastic that Crabb couldn't identify. The Deaf man looked at Crabb, and then with eyes getting rounder by the minute, watched in dismay as his space was further filled by Sam as he also squeezed into the hut.

Martin pulled at his braces and waited, clearly fearing whatever was coming. His foot started tapping as he wiped his palms down his thighs. Crabb spied small droplets of sweat sparkling on Martin's pink scalp, showing through his swept-over thin hair. The perspiration glistened and twinkled with moistness.

Martin was diminished by being on his own. Without Dora and without the Deaf Club. Like a pack animal that had inadvertently drifted away and become separated from the herd, Martin now looked vulnerable to attack. With little or no resources of his own upon which to draw.

'How's life, Martin?' Crabb asked and he watched the man's face for a response as he felt Sam signing behind him, squashed into a corner.

Martin looked unhappy and confused by the simple enquiry. His bovine eyes gazed up at Crabb, rounded in fear and expectation of the unknown. He blinked slowly. Uncomprehending of the situation. Of life in general. Always two steps behind.

'Fine... fine,' he said.

Crabb could feel Sam's breath on his neck as he voiced Martin. Crabb suddenly felt hemmed in. 'Shall we go outside? Too hot,' he said.

He escaped into the playground, wiping his forehead of sweat. He pulled at the armpits of his shirt, flapped them midarm to get a little ventilation circulating. Said, 'I want to know about Ben. Your relationship with him. The truth.'

Martin's eyes looked from him to Sam. Caught their gaze, dropped his own and finally stuck his thumbs behind his braces and pulled them from his body. He attempted a smile. Phony courage. 'He's just a boy that goes to this school. Like a lot of other boys.'

'You said you were friends. Is that true?'

'When I said friends, I just meant that we talk occasionally. Ben sometimes comes and talks to me in my shed. I think he's lonely. He doesn't exactly have a lot of friends. Definitely not with that Toby. He bullied him, you know.'

'I did know. So does everyone else. You're not telling me anything that I don't already know.'

Martin's face remained vacuous, uncertain of the best answer. Crabb said, 'How well do you really know Ben? Do you know his brother?'

Martin blushed and blustered. 'Ben's just like any other boy here. Nothing special. We're just sort-of mates. And no. I don't know his brother.'

Martin glanced up and beyond Crabb's left shoulder. Crabb turned and was surprised to see Annie walking towards them. He could hear the clack of her booted heels as they crossed the space between them. When she was near enough, she spoke and signed, 'I can't get drunk. Typical. Polly walked me over here, in case you were worried.'

Crabb was pleased to see her. He didn't know Martin and her input would be helpful. He said, 'I've just been asking Martin here about his relationship with Ben. Ben visits him in his hut for little chats.'

Relying on Sam to interpret for Crabb, she signed to Martin, 'I couldn't give a toss about whether you're mates with Ben. I want to know what your relationship was with Toby. Simple enough question.'

She signed slowly, and consequently, Sam gave her voice a low but threatening tone. It certainly matched her appearance, Crabb conceded.

Martin answered, shuffling his feet. 'I'm sorry Toby's dead, but what's it got to do with me? *I* didn't kill him. Why would I? I didn't know him very well. Never said I did.'

Crabb caught movement behind Martin and saw Ben approaching the group. It was turning into a bloody free-for-all. The boy raised his hand in greeting, brushing at his thick fringe with his fingers, as he walked across the tarmac. He smiled at Crabb and Annie. Nodded at Sam. 'What's happening? Anyone else been murdered since I've been gone?' Ben looked jaunty and his smile was open and relaxed.

'No,' Annie said. 'How many more dead bodies were you expecting?'

'Who knows? Hoping for at least *one* more. Might perk things up a bit around here.'

Ben picked his nose; didn't bother turning his head – made it a bloody public performance. He smiled innocently, hands by his side: then thrust his finger up his nostril again. Crabb inhaled deeply and focused his eyes just above Ben's hairline.

'We were just discussing Toby. And you. Your friendship with Martin,' Crabb said.

'I told you – we're not friends. I think you'll find old Martin rather preferred Toby, isn't that right?'

Ben placed his hands on his heart and mock-swooned. He laughed and signed, 'I'm too ugly for Martin. Not sweet and naïve enough for him. Not like Toby. I'm the right age though. Fair statement, Martin?'

Martin hurriedly shook his head. Stood totally still as if any movement would betray him. Sam voiced Ben: 'Oh, sorry, Martin. Have I let out your secret? You wouldn't want Dora finding out about your double life, now would you? You, forever seeking Dora's approval. And her friendship. You pathetic wanker. Don't dare pretend that you like *me*.'

He tilted his head at the caretaker. Daring him to give answer. Any answer. Martin looked deflated. Beaten. 'Fuck off, Ben. Shut up.' Then the man shrugged, pretending not to be bothered by Ben's presence. He tried to stare him down and signed, 'I don't know why you're denying our friendship. I don't care who knows. Why would I? You're just a nasty little shit who should be grateful for any friends he can get.'

They stared at each other. Crabb watched as they played out a game. Crabb would put his money on the boy winning. They seemed to be daring each other with secrets. Long-held secrets. Dangerous things, secrets.

Ben signed, 'Yeah, but the question I want answering is, "who do you prefer? Toby? Or me?" And if it's Toby, would you kill him rather than allow your dirty secret from getting out? Is that one of the things you think I should be grateful for. That I *know*?'

'You don't know anything. There's nothing *to* know.'

'Oh, silly me,' he signed. 'It's different now, isn't it, Martin? Now that Toby's dead, that's changed *everything*. He can't tell.

You can play the innocent. But you want to be careful. Keep me on side. Keep you safe.'

Ben stood inches from Martin and cocked his eyebrows. Knowing he'd already won the battle. The boy mock rubbed at his chin as if waiting for an answer. 'Why would you kill Toby?' he said again. 'Come on, Martin. Explain your relationship with little golden boy. All the gory details. He is, or was, just your type, wasn't he? Not like ugly old me.'

Martin flapped his hands at Ben, trying to physically silence him; to stop his signing. He blushed and his eyes skittered around, his movements becoming ever more frantic: a spider trapped under a glass. Desperately trying to think of a lie.

Crabb said, 'What do you mean, Ben? You're not his type? What are you saying?'

'I just said, didn't I? He likes Toby. Liked Toby. I'm just not boy-ish enough. Not as pretty.'

Martin just stood there, looking pale and upset. Drops of sweat ran down his cheeks. A drop dangled from his chin. Crabb waited for it to fall.

Martin swiped at his chin and said, 'What's it matter what I thought of Toby? Or Ben? I only knew Toby from the Deaf Club. Hardly saw him here at school. Ben's just a bloody thug. Shit-stirring.'

Martin was struggling to regain some ground. Sam gave slightly different tones to his voice-overs – to better differentiate between them: Ben's voice he made bullish, aggressive, bragging. Martin's – frightened, weak, flustered.

Ben had all the power in their relationship. Clearly had something on Martin. Something worth killing for? The knowledge of sexual abuse?

But why give it up now?

Martin was visibly shocked at Ben's betrayal. He hadn't seen it coming. Almost stamped his foot, verging on a tantrum, but decided against it, stuck two fingers up to anyone who was watching, and disappeared back into his hut. His behaviour was juvenile and would have been laughable had the circumstances not been what they were.

'What an idiot,' signed Ben. 'Martin's truly pathetic. In fact, all that lot, down at the Deaf Club – they're all pathetic. I hate them.'

He turned and started walking away, and Annie, Sam and Crabb followed him. Sam ran around to the front of the queue so that he could voice, as Annie touched Ben's shoulder and signed, 'What's brought this on? I assumed you liked your Deaf friends. You certainly agree with them in terms of me. You don't like me, because I have a voice, and Fiona because she has a cochlear. Are you actually admitting to having your own opinions after all?'

'None of them is my friend. Not a proper friend. And I don't really mind you, you know. Not really. Just going with the flow. Makes it easier to give in and pretend. Simpler to fit in.'

Crabb said, 'What are you trying to say about Martin and Toby? Spell it out for me.' He watched the boy with curiosity. He didn't need it spelling out. It was perfectly clear what Ben was not-so subtly hinting at. It all felt like a downward spiral.

Ben tilted his head back and stared at the sky. Ignored the question. 'I wish I was hearing.'

As statements went, that was one of the saddest Crabb had heard this morning.

Ben paused and then signed, 'Do you know what I remember most about being a child? I could never work out why every time my mum went to the front door and opened it, there'd be someone there. Every time *I* opened it, there was just empty space, where someone *should* have been. But nobody was ever there. I thought my mum had magic powers.'

He laughed and pointed at Annie. 'You explain it to him. The punchline. He looks lost.'

Crabb raised his eyebrows at Annie. She almost seemed embarrassed. 'He couldn't hear the doorbell,' she said. 'Couldn't make the connection.'

Christ, thought Crabb. *How depressing*. He didn't know what to say, so said nothing. This had to be one of his more chaotic interviews. But out of chaos, the truth would often filter through. Just give it a little patience; let it play out naturally. Don't force it.

Ben reached the steps to the school building, and signed: 'Imagine, if someone like Martin, just as an example, wanted to spy on boys in the shower rooms. It's funny and sad in the same way. He could peep through a hole in the wall – if he'd thought to make one of course – and not worry about any noise he might make. The Deaf make perfect victims.'

He laughed.

'Is that what Martin does?' said Crabb. He battled to keep the disgust from his voice. The thought of Martin, the repellent and pink-scalped Martin, peering, *ogling* little boys, made Crabb feel physically sick.

'I never said there *were* holes, did I? I just said, *if* he'd thought to make one. *If* he were a perv. *If* he hadn't covered his tracks. Remember, he's the school caretaker. He does all the maintenance.'

Annie asked him, 'Why tell us this now? Why give Martin up now?'

'Don't know. Why not? Nothing to lose?'

Crabb wondered if his sudden revelation about Martin was because of the reappearance of Theo. Had *Theo* sexually abused Ben as a child? Is that why Ben had decided to speak out now? Was this Ben's cry for help? Christ. Crabb was being taken down avenues he hadn't seen coming.

Ben signed, 'Martin did also mention, before I forget, that he was a little worried that William might have caught him with his trousers down last week. Well, let's be honest. Having a wank. William does the after-school football on Mondays and Tuesdays. Martin was worried. They'd bumped into each other outside the gym showers. Martin wasn't sure if he'd been seen or not.' He paused. 'Martin's a loser. A pathetic clown of a man. He never gets what he wants. Except possibly in the shower rooms.'

'Did Martin watch Toby?' asked Crabb.

'Don't know what you're talking about, Mr Policeman. Honest, I don't. I'm just a young Deaf boy. I'm only sixteen, your honour. Don't know what you're talking about.' Ben grinned, and signed, 'Why don't you ask Martin yourself? You've probably noticed that he's not a very good liar.'

'Why are you telling me this?' Crabb asked. 'If you knew he was spying on boys in the showers, why didn't you say so before?'

'Wouldn't want you thinking I was involved in any way. Because I'm not. But now I'm looking after number one. I think it's probably time, don't you?'

'If you knew Martin was watching little boys shower, why didn't you tell someone?' said Annie.

'It's nothing to do with me. I'd only get blamed myself. Anyway, it would have been one of those "he said, she said" things; his word against mine. What's that called again? I don't know the word. And I shall deny saying anything to you now. Unless you're recording this, and I bet you're not, you're fucked. Can't prove I knew anything.' Ben bowed theatrically. 'I win,' he said.

Crabb thought the little shit had a point. Difficult to prove his involvement in court. It was hearsay. Crabb knew it. And so, apparently, did Ben. He was a sly little sod. Crafty. Uncomfortably mature for his age when he wasn't being terrified by his brother.

'It's the children that really do it for him. Dirty bastard. Thinks he's covering his tracks – pretending a normal friendship with me. Ask him to show you his hole.' Ben guffawed. And then farted for good measure. He smiled engagingly at Crabb, saluted Sam and bowed to Annie, taking off an imaginary hat and tipping it in her direction. 'Think you might have missed your man,' signed Ben.

Crabb turned and realised that they had wandered to the far corner of the playground during their conversation. The caretaker's shed stood alone in the wide-open space. Looking a long way away. 'Where's Martin?'

'Just saw him disappearing on his bike. He's gone, Mr Policeman. Gone.'

'Bloody hell,' said Crabb, and took out his mobile.

Martin wouldn't get far.

25

Back at Annie's flat, she rubbed at the scar on her cheek. Said, 'Did you know that deaf boys are two to three times more likely to be the victims of sexual abuse than hearing boys?'

She didn't bother to look at Crabb's expression. Knew what his face would say. Shock and revulsion would be written all over it. Said: 'Think about it. What better child to abuse than a child who *can't* tell; *because* they have no voice.'

'I didn't know that. Wish I didn't know it now.'

'Yeah, well. I've just seen William with a skewer in his ear. Tell me about not wanting to know stuff.'

Crabb said, 'All these sexual references. I don't want to get bogged down with them. The murderer is not a sadistic sexual killer. There is no hint of any sexual motivation whatsoever. That is a fact, if nothing else. We mustn't get waylaid with what may turn out to be simple red herrings.'

'There's nothing simple about sexual abuse.'

'I didn't mean that. I was talking merely in terms of how it relates to the murders. I don't think sexual abuse necessarily has any bearing on this case. But the repercussions of it may impact on the investigation.'

Annie tried not to think of William, but her mind felt like it had a million paper cuts slashing out the image of his mutilated body.

Crabb accepted a glass of water. Gulped at it. Said, 'We need to talk.'

Annie shrugged, feeling an almost physical pain from the emotional onslaught she had witnessed.

'I know how you've suffered, Annie. But I don't have the time to personally hold your hand. Although I'm doing my best. Trying to get regular drive-bys of your flat, if nothing else, but we must get to the bottom of whatever is happening here. You can help. Will you try now?'

A reluctant nod, an obligatory murmured, 'of course'. To her surprise, once she'd spoken out loud her willingness to try and help, she felt his words bring her to attention. Maybe she *could* help. After all, she had no choice. It would be her salvation. Her one escape route.

Crabb rolled his sleeves up. Annie crossed her legs on the sofa. Watched as Eric appeared in the short hallway and strolled towards the French windows. He stopped mid-way to wash his bottom – his back leg stuck up like a broken umbrella prong. Briefly, it made her smile. Eric was something normal in a suddenly abnormal world. She said, 'What aren't you telling me, Crabb? What did you mean when you asked whether Toby liked drawing? What's that got to do with anything? There's something you're keeping to yourself and I can't help you unless you spit it out. Tell me the truth.'

He cupped his chin with his fingers but remained silent.

'Come on, Crabb. If you want my help, you'll have to give me something to go on.'

She watched him as he battled with his answer. He sat on the other sofa, and spreading his legs, rested his elbows on them. Took a deep breath: 'I haven't mentioned this before because I thought it unnecessary to upset you further. You've had to deal with enough shit as it is. And yes, I'm aware, the word "shit" hardly covers it. But okay, this is what you don't know. Each victim, including Adam who did *not* have a skewer through his ear, had something placed in their mouths. The same with Toby and William, but different objects were used. Your attacker touched your lips, pretended to insert something into your mouth. It's the killer's signature, but I don't know what it means.'

Clamp and grind of jaws, an attempt to get saliva into her mouth. Suddenly short of lubrication, she finally got out her question: 'What were the objects?'

Crabb held up his hand, taking Annie by surprise. Retrieved his mobile from a pocket, spoke into it, listened and finished the call. 'Unsurprisingly, but thank God, Martin's been picked up. His great escape lasted an impressive twenty minutes. At least the nasty little shit's in custody now.'

Shaking her head in irritation, Annie repeated, 'Disgusting, stupid man.'

Crabb stared into space, before jumping as Annie put some volume into her words: 'Well?'

'Adam Jacobs had a hearing aid put into his mouth. Toby, green pencil shavings and William, the tip of a dog's ear. Do any of those objects, in conjunction with those victims, or even those objects as a group of separate items, do they mean anything to you?'

Annie sat back with shock. Forced herself to concentrate. A hearing aid, green pencil shavings and part of a dog's ear. Sounded like an insane shopping list for a psychopath. Rubbing at her temples, she frowned. And then she *really* thought about it. Tried to tune out the picture of a dog's ear having been placed inside William's mouth. Why a dog's *ear*? Why not it's tongue?

Her gag reflex kicked in suddenly and unexpectedly as the image wrapped its dark tentacles around her mind. Settled like something foetid and rancid. It was only a dog's ear. *Not* a tongue. Only a dog's ear. *Only*. Jesus. Manic laughter fizzed up in her throat. *Keep it in check. I must look mad*, she thought. She gulped from her glass of water. Gulp. Gulp. Sip. Exhale.

Settled her face into a semblance of normality, though wondered why she bothered. Nothing was normal anymore. 'No,' she said. 'They sound completely random and as far as I know, have no connection to any of victims. Apart, that is, from Adam. The hearing aid obviously referred to his deafness. The other things mean absolutely nothing to me. Is it relevant that a dog's *ear* was left? A reference to deafness again, or is the dog the relevant thing?'

Crabb lifted his eyebrows, clearly not having considered the specific choice of the canine anatomical remains left. He waggled his head from side to side, thinking. Always thinking. Didn't answer her.

Annie swallowed more water and said, 'Anyway, the word random is misleading. It's only random to us, because we don't know the connection. But they must mean something to the murderer. They're not random to him. We just have to find out what they mean *to him*.'

'Exactly. Nothing is random in murder. Adam was a boy in the wrong place, wrong time. The killer was reacting to a trigger, something that set him off. Something that set him off and something that after the savagery of Adam, made him then sit down and work out a killing menu; carefully planned down to the last detail. That's my opinion.'

'And the likely triggers are...?'

Crabb blew through his lips, making them vibrate. 'Loss of a job, a divorce/breakdown of a relationship, a death, maybe he lost his house, a tragedy of some kind, an illness. Something that deeply affected him.' He shrugged, frustrated.

'That aside, we have to remember that Adam wasn't skewered. An important point. Put the boy aside for the moment. Concentrate on Toby and William. Killed with skewers in their ears. Symbolism? Is deafness at the root of all this? Is he deaf but wants to be hearing? Does he simply hate the deaf?

'The staging, the posing, the setting up of scenes. What's the killer trying to tell us? Forget the "who", we need the "why".' Crabb was fired up, talking freely, his mind working fast and hard.

Annie held up her hand to slow him. He saw the gesture, ignored it. She repeated the gesture and he took a breath, saying more slowly, 'When I was interviewing you at the station, you pointed out that the staging of William reminded you of your work as a window dresser. It got me thinking. Normally, the aim of posing a body is to shock those that find the body, sometimes to further humiliate the victim, occasionally to show remorse, but this, this is different. You were right. It's telling us a story. A very specific story that I suspect will only resonate with the killer. Both crime scenes have been carefully staged. It will probably be impossible for us, at this point, to understand his motivation, but to the killer, it's what's driving him. He's playing out something that's unique to him. And he won't stop until he's finished. Currently, I'm bloody stumped. That's where I'm at. Completely fucking stumped.'

He stood up and grasped his bald head with both hands. Rubbed gently, giving it a gentle massage.

Annie said, 'We've agreed that Toby and William most likely knew him. But what were they all talking about from Thursday night to Saturday afternoon when Toby was killed? That's what you need to find out. What possible conversation could have lasted that long? Why keep them alive for that amount of time? What was his motive for *that*?'

'Again, exactly. Was he trying to make them admit to something they'd done? Wanting revenge for something they'd done? Wanting acceptance or gratitude for some perceived favour, help, whatever? Were they joining him in some fantasy that was being played out? Was he punishing them? It could be any one of a million things. But it's vital we find out what the killer's *thinking*. Find out what he wants from his victims.'

Annie said, 'Well, he sure as shit isn't getting what he wants, is he? Otherwise why does he need to kill them? Are they failing him in some way?'

Again Crabb up-tilted his eyes, nodded in a 'perhaps' way. Then shook his head vehemently, and said, 'All we know at this point, for a fact, is that the killer is someone who's known to the victims, Toby and William. Adam was merely the catalyst. The starting point. Ground zero if you want to call him that. Poor little sod.

'But the killer knows the victims. He has easy and regular access to the Deaf Community. Or perhaps we can go further and say, he has access to the Deaf Club itself. Someone who is seen frequently, someone who fits in. He belongs.'

Annie softly but quickly snatched up a reluctant passing Eric and held him to her chest; using him as a shield against Crabb's words.

In a community that prided itself in its solidarity the thought that the killer roamed freely amongst them frightened her. She said, 'The killer made a cup of tea for William. Made a mockery of pretending William had killed himself, by superficially slashing at his wrists. Created a mock scene of cosy domesticity. He went to a lot of trouble. What else did he leave with Toby? Apart from the pencil shavings. What else did he add that shouldn't be there?'

'I've been thinking about that. Ponds are always full of general crap that people just dump: a shopping trolley, a forgotten football, a plastic toy boat, empty beer cans, et cetera, et cetera. Impossible to know what, if anything is linked. We need more information on what exactly the killer is doing.'

Annie said, 'Whatever he is doing, whatever bloody game he's playing with his victims, the killings themselves, how he poses them, are important. But so are the crime scenes, don't you think? He feels the need to include very specific things, or actions – like the dog's ear and the phony suicide. He picked a pond and then William's house. The actual places where he left the bodies must mean *something*, surely. As you say, nothing is random.'

Crabb nodded. 'Like he's creating something very special, special to himself. Meaningful. The bodies, where he leaves them, what he does to them, how he leaves them, *must* resonate with him in order to make it work. We might be getting somewhere, Annie. I don't know where, but somewhere is better than nowhere.'

He stood up and took a long last swallow of his water and said, 'Do you know anyone with a dog? A black Labrador?'

'Not that springs to mind, no. I don't think so. No.'

He looked as frustrated as she felt sick. Knowing now that the dog's ear had belonged to a black Labrador. It made it an even more intimate piece of knowledge that she wished she didn't know. Wished she could unknow it. Crabb said, 'And then there's you, Annie. Why is the killer indirectly targeting you? Do you know?'

'Of course I don't know. I'm not a fool, Crabb. I get it. I didn't know Adam Jacobs, but I knew both Toby and William. I loved them both. I am the missing link.'

The doorbell for the Deaf flashed. Annie opened the door to Dora, holding a bunch of flowers. She held her dog like a parcel under her other arm; the Chihuahua all eyes and bollocks and not a lot in between. Polly followed, holding a large bottle of champagne. Charlie Blue stumbled in, bearing no gifts, grinning inanely. Scarlet brought up the rear.

Flowers to remember. Alcohol to forget.

Both worked for Annie, but she went for the latter.

26

The gossip that goes on in the Deaf Community never ceases to amuse. And what potential! Invaluable. The gossip was rife today. It had taken on a life of its own. According to the community as a whole, Annie had been arrested on suspicion of killing both Toby and William. 'Annie is a murderer': the message fluttered from hand to hand, excited, horrified, avid. Whether or not she had actually been charged, would have bothered all of them not a jot. 'Arrest' was a better word than the more accurate phrase, 'helping with enquiries'. But a minor detail conveniently ignored by the gossipers. To them, she was already guilty. Hoorah.

Apparently, the stupid bitch had gone from the police station upon her release, to the pub which she frequents. She drank with her hearing friends and a lot of the little-d deaf and big-D Deaf brigade went along for the ride. One mischievous little-d had told a big-D. And so it had started. The news spread like a raging torrent. A tide of trite and childishly gleeful muck-raking. The Ds and ds had united. What fun. It needed no added fuel from me.

I've been gossip-gathering over the years, knowing that one day I could use these snippets of venom so casually dropped. It was a little like stamp collecting. Only better. More rewarding. But instead of *spreading the gossip like rancid butter, I stored it up. For future use. I piled up gossip like bullets. Ready to fire when I chose to make them live ammunition.*

Gossip is potential gold. To be used wisely. Not revealed as soon as it is known. It loses all potency if not kept under wraps, looked after. Cherished. I dip into my store when and if the time comes. But not before. And long buried secrets are best revealed when least expected.

When they are forgotten.

You see, I know about Annie's secret. I believe I'm the only one who does. I know that she is not the norm sexually. I know that William was also of the same disgusting sexual persuasion. I know that they pretended a relationship. I know all of this, because I had done my homework. Hours, weeks, months, a whole bloody year of traipsing around after Annie and her pretend boyfriend. Watching them on their deviant nocturnal trips.

And because I know, I'd bided my time and then, when the time was right, implemented that particular snippet of secret information. I had used that knowledge to my advantage.

That was why William had been chosen.

And because of his age, of course.

Everyone else still thinks they are sexual partners. That is all that matters. Naturally blame falls upon Annie's shoulders like a sack of shit for the murder of William. Spouses, girlfriend/boyfriends often kill each other. Domestic disputes are commonplace. Suspicion is all that is needed. The romantic partner always a person of interest. She did it to herself.

It could not have been a more perfect set-up. And the fact that their relationship was all a lie, only adds to the irony of it all.

She has done it all to herself.

27

Annie had a hangover. Like her doorbell for the Deaf, her head pulsed out a deep, aching rhythm. She felt a little sick. Dora, Harry, and Polly had stayed well into the evening: Scarlet had gone out for more alcohol.

Just for those few hours, Annie had allowed herself a little self-indulgence, swallowing glass after glass of first champagne, and then far too much red wine. An awful mix. An awful mistake.

But a welcome escape.

And of course, because she'd also drunk in the pub with some deaf people before joining Crabb at the Deaf School, she knew how word would have travelled, from hand to excited hand, that she had been 'helping the police with their enquiries'. Knew that would make her guilty to many. No questions asked. Obviously, Scarlet was always there for her. And Dora and Polly were on side. Charlie Blue had been so drunk he'd been incapable of making any supportive noise. He'd been incapable of communication, spoken or signed. She hoped he felt as crap as she did this morning.

Tuesday morning and she had agreed to go to Ben's house

with Crabb and Sam to speak to the boy again. And to his mother. Get a better feel for brother Theo's appearance. Connected to the killings or not? Coincidental? Crabb didn't believe in coincidences, and Annie tended to agree with him, although Theo's reappearance had stirred Ben up. Made him speak out against Martin. Theo was clearly Ben's trigger.

Dressed, Annie brushed her teeth again, had to stop herself from gagging. Sweat popped out on her face as she swallowed down alcohol that wanted to see the light of day again. *Never again*, she swore.

The doorbell flashed. Quickly adjusting her pale blue 1960s pencil skirt and jacket, she fed Eric, almost sliding on the kitchen floor in her haste.

Annie jumped into the back of Peters' car and closed her eyes, trying not to vomit. She only opened them as she felt the car come to a stop. Looked out of the window. Saw Sam and Crabb; both looking sticky in the heat. Waiting for her.

Ben's mother's house looked sad and deflated. Like all the life had been sucked from it. Annie joined the three others and took in the two-up, two-down maisonette. Net curtains filled all the windows, grey and old and tired looking. The bottom left window was open and Annie watched the nets flutter out of the gap, as if in a last ditch attempt at freedom.

Crabb opened a small gate and in a line, they proceeded towards the front door, Peters bringing up the rear. Annie startled when the front door opened before they'd had a chance to ring the bell.

Mrs Downing stood there. She wasn't obviously drunk; just wiped out. Annie had never met Ben's mother before. Mrs Downing was the colour of her net curtains and just as flimsy. She leaned on the door frame, arms crossed. 'I was just going out. What do you want?'

She coughed. It looked wet and phlegm-filled the way her shoulders heaved; her hand placed on her chest.

Crabb had told Annie that he hadn't informed Mrs Downing of his visit this morning. He wanted to catch her before she'd had time to think up a plausible story. Her son, Theo, had left home when he'd been only sixteen, according to Dora. Crabb suspected that there'd been a very specific reason for his departure at such a young age. Annie didn't think the reason would be a good one for Ben. Her feelings for the younger brother had changed. She almost liked Ben now, as hard as he made it for anyone to do so.

Because Crabb was a kind man, Annie realised he didn't want to embarrass Mrs Downing by saying that they had in fact already met. Knowing that she'd been so drunk the day before that she probably wouldn't remember. Instead he simply said, 'I'm Detective Inspector Crabb, and this is DS Peters. Sam is here to interpret for Ben. I'm sure you've met? And Annie is here, as she knows Ben. I'm investigating the murders of Toby and William.'

'Call me Maggie,' the woman said in a defeated way, her shoulders slumped, her head bowed. 'I know you,' she said, pointing at Annie. 'You're deaf, aren't you? And you, you're the interpreter. Why are *you* here? *I* don't need an interpreter. I'm not deaf. Just my Ben is. Only him, and he's out.'

Annie had no answer for her presence and thankfully Maggie turned her back on all of them, resigning herself to them following her into the house.

'What's this about?' Maggie said, turning wearily as they crocodiled behind her. 'Who are you accusing of what?'

'No one,' said Crabb. 'Really.'

They all followed Mrs Downing down a cramped hallway. The walls were nicotine yellow and the carpet threadbare. They passed a small kitchen. Annie stuck her nose in to have a quick look. Houses said a lot about their owners.

There was a large hole in the bottom of the door, as if a boot had long ago kicked it in. The kitchen sink was empty and the hob slick with grease. An empty glass stood on the worktop, as if abandoned in a hurry, smudged fingerprints still wrapped around it. There was nothing else, other than old cupboards and an even older fridge. A small window looked out on to railway tracks. Annie was depressed just being here for two minutes. She hurried to catch the others up.

Maggie flung her arm wildly about the sitting room, indicating that they could sit wherever they wanted. Crabb perched on the edge of a once-green sofa and Annie chose an armchair with worn arms. Sam sat on an old stool and Peters hovered in the background.

Maggie's face and body was defensive, her arms folded, her chin jutted out; trying for pride but not quite making it. Her hair was dirty blonde, lank; hanging down the side of her pale face in greasy strips like curtains. She swept the wisps away from her mouth, and said, 'Yeah, I know it's not much, my home, but it's *my* home,' she said.

Crabb said, 'Please sit down, Maggie. I just want a little chat.'

She sat down next to Crabb, looking embarrassed and suddenly shy. From her chair, Annie caught the perfumed smell of gin on Maggie's breath. Like lavender infused with alcohol.

Maggie jumped up and said, 'Where are my manners? Can I get you anything? Tea, coffee?' Her expression was over bright, her movements jerky like a wound-up soldier.

Before either Crabb or Annie could respond, she was at the door. Turning, she clapped her hand to her forehead, clearly having just remembered something. The gesture reminded Annie of Ben.

'Forgot. No bloody milk. Sorry, I'll see what else I've got.'

She disappeared.

'That'll be a gin she's gone to get, poor bitch,' said Annie.

'As long as she's not pissed, I don't mind. Whatever gets her through,' said Crabb.

Maggie reappeared, mug in hand. 'Sorry, nothing doing, I'm afraid. I'm just finishing off my coffee from earlier.' She held the mug to her chest, cradling its contents from view. But she couldn't cradle that smell.

'Poor little Toby,' Maggie said. 'He went to the same school as my Ben. And that man, William. Ben sometimes went to football practice with him. After school. My Ben lets me know what's going on in the Deaf World.'

She said this last as if proud that she was up to date with the world that her son lived in. Somehow Annie doubted she was up to date with anything.

'We've actually come about your son, Theo,' said Crabb, keeping it straightforward; clearly deciding against any unnecessary subterfuge. Annie thought it a good tactic. She suspected Maggie wouldn't respond to trickery and would only feel trapped if Crabb were anything but blunt.

Annie watched as the mug almost slipped from her grasp, but she caught it just as it threatened to fall from her grasp. She took a healthy swig and looked wild-eyed at Crabb. 'What do you mean? *Theo*. He's gone. Left years ago. Why are you asking me about him?'

Although the sun was now a definite and hot presence, Maggie wore a brown cardigan. She wrapped it around her shoulders now, tugging it tight across her flat chest, as if she were cold. She held the mug in one hand, and with her free hand, worried at the hole at her elbow; pulled at a loose thread and picked nervously at it – unable to stop.

'Didn't you know that Theo's back?' said Annie.

'Don't you go lying to me. Of course he's not back. Why

would he come back? I haven't seen him in years. I'd know if he was back.' As if realising that her voice had risen, the cords in her neck pulsed, she tried to calm herself down with deep breaths. She perched again on the sofa, and pretended to smile.

'As you can probably tell, me and Theo, we didn't exactly get on. We never did. Not even when he was a little boy. Everyone thinks Ben's the bad one. But that's not true.'

Through her smile, Annie detected the young woman she had once been. Probably not bad looking if you went back a decade or so. Now, she just looked raddled.

'Why are you so angry with Theo?' said Crabb.

Maggie swirled the contents of her mug. 'Theo was never a nice boy. That's all. Better off with his dad. That's why he left. To go and live with my ex. Barry his name was. Better off all round.'

Annie thought she lacked the ability to lie as well as Ben. She waited while Maggie took another swallow of her drink.

'When did Theo start sexually abusing Ben?' Crabb said.

Here was his leap of faith, but Annie knew that he was right. It wasn't really a leap – just a little hop; the seed of information already planted by Ben.

This time Maggie did drop the mug. She could only stare at Crabb. She bent to pick up her mug which lay on its side on the old multi-coloured zigzag carpet. It was faded and about as vibrant now as Maggie herself.

The woman gave herself some thinking time. Dabbed half-heartedly at the wet carpet with the cuff of her cardigan pulled down over her hand. Annie knew she would protest Theo's innocence.

'I don't know what the bleeding hell you're on about. He never did what you're saying. That's sick.'

She bent more furiously to her task, wiping at the wet stain, succeeding only in transferring the fluff from her cardigan onto the carpet. She kept her head down and moved her arm in a circular motion, as if she couldn't stop. The scrubbing became almost frenzied, until Annie crossed the small space between them and laid a hand on Maggie's arm, stopping her.

'I think he did abuse Ben, Maggie,' Crabb said. 'And that's why you threw him out. Sent him to live with his father. To protect Ben. I *know* that's what happened.'

'How can you know? Me and Ben never told anyone.'

Realising she'd just admitted the sexual abuse of her son, she left the room and reappeared with the gin bottle; too upset now to keep up the pretence.

'Suppose you think you're really clever, don't you,' Maggie said. 'Tricking me like that. So what if it is true? I did what I thought was right. I saved Ben. Got rid of that little shit of a boy. Sent him packing.'

She tilted the bottle to her mouth and gulped at it. 'Well, I'm glad you know. I've kept it bottled up inside me forever. Fuck knows what it's done to my Ben. Hasn't done him any favours, that's for sure. But I did my best. What else could I do?'

She looked pleadingly at Crabb. Wanting forgiveness. Deflated, knowing she was losing, too tired to lie anymore, she said, 'Theo's back because he wants money. Nothing else. I told him to bugger off. Knocked on my door... I'm not sure what day it was. Last week some time: Tuesday? Maybe Monday?'

Annie crossed the room and stood next to Maggie. She put her hand on her, let it rest on the woman's shoulder. A reassuring touch. Said, 'Have you seen him since?'

She shook her head. 'He wouldn't dare show his face again. I made it quite clear. Told him to stay away from Ben.'

She shut her eyes, unable to stop a drunken tear from escaping. Annie wanted to comfort the woman, and said, 'I understand you did the best you could at the time, Maggie. I can't imagine how you must have felt. But did you think that packing Theo off to his father's would end it all? What about other children he may have abused? What about when he came home? Like now.'

'Look, I'm not responsible for him. Ask his father what he's doing back here. I've only seen him once since he came back. He's still a little bastard.' She coughed again and dropped her head. Seeming to remember that Annie was deaf, she lifted her head: Everyone ignored Sam who hadn't moved position on his stool. His role so far, redundant.

'How could I know that he'd come back? Thought he'd gone for good. Well, hoped he'd gone for good. Ben was frightened as a child. But I couldn't protect both of my sons, so I chose Ben. Everyone thinks that it's Ben that's a nasty little shit. But it never was him. Theo was *always* a cruel boy. But Ben. He was a different kettle of fish. He's always been my special boy.'

Her eyes had taken on a slight glaze, like lychees dipped in syrup. The gin acted as a natural lubricant for her tongue. She just opened her mouth and the words fell out. 'Ben was always so sweet-natured.' She laughed. 'Difficult to believe, looking at him now. But he was, you know. Questioned everything he did, always wanted to know how things worked, what things meant – ever since he was a little tot. Bright as a button he was. It was only later when he changed. He can't have been more than eight. He started having tantrums for no reason at all. He'd scream and scream. Nothing I could do would quiet him. He'd cling to my legs wherever I went, like a bloody toddler. It was embarrassing. And he was always so angry. For such a little boy. So angry.'

It was almost like she'd forgotten that they were there. She took another slug of her drink straight from the bottle, seemingly having forgotten that she was speaking out loud. No one spoke until the silence became oppressive.

Crabb said, 'But Theo *is* back, Maggie. And he was seen talking to Ben last Wednesday. Outside the school. Ben was frightened. And Ben was seen walking behind Toby on Thursday night, the evening that Toby went missing. Didn't you know? Didn't he tell you?'

Her face drained of all colour. Like uncooked dough, her features became slack and unformed. Her face was tinged with an unhealthy non-colour. As if the blood had literally left her body.

'Ben's seen him? My boy, Ben's been talking to Theo?'

Annie could tell that Maggie's voice had become shrill, her eyebrows raising, her face angled back on her neck. But Maggie couldn't care less.

'How do you know Ben's frightened? Has he said so? Sweet Jesus.'

The fact that Theo had met Ben, made it impossible for her to hear and take in the fact that Ben had been seen walking behind Toby on Thursday night. The implied suggestion of Ben being involved with Toby's death not registering with her.

'Why on earth didn't you tell someone, Maggie?' Crabb asked. 'Someone could've helped you. You and Ben.'

'Yeah, and Theo would be banged up for kiddy-fiddling. Me and Ben agreed to keep it a secret. Neither of us wanted the public shame of it. Didn't want it coming out. So, we sorted it ourselves. I palmed Theo off on his dad, when he was sixteen. Best thing I could think to do. Only way I could keep my Ben safe.'

'But Ben was just a child. Didn't you get him help?' Annie said. She was now sitting back in her chair.

Maggie didn't speak for some time. Just concentrated on tipping the bottle and sipping from the mug which she'd finally retrieved when it had bounced across the carpet. At last she looked up and spoke to Annie.

'I've never told anyone about that time. It's confidential, right. But it doesn't really matter now. Maybe it's right that I tell you. You'll understand Ben better this way. It's not much of a story, but it was too much for me.'

'What happened?' Annie said.

Maggie shuddered in a deep breath and opened her mouth. But nothing came out. A tear rolled down her cheek. As Maggie spoke, Annie guessed that her tone was a dull monotone, her face flat and neutral. 'As I said, Ben was always so happy as a child. A young child, I mean. But he went from being a happy child to being a royal pain in the arse. But I didn't know why then, of course. It went on for years. It broke my heart when I found out. It really did.'

She got up and sat on the floor, and pulled out a packet of tobacco. Her hands shook as she rolled an impossibly thin roll-up.

'And finally, Ben told me. He was twelve and Theo was sixteen. He told me that Theo, had, you know...'

Again Crabb and Annie remained silent.

'Theo had been making Ben do sexual stuff. Ever since Ben was a little boy. And I never knew. I never knew.'

Annie saw Crabb lean forward as if to catch her words. Maybe she was whispering. She sucked on her roll-up which had gone out and absently relit it.

'I didn't know what to do. I was furious. And I mean fucking furious. Theo had always been a cruel boy. Called Ben "The Mistake", "The Accident", "Deaf Boy". If truth be told, I wasn't even all that surprised. I mean I was surprised at the, you know, sexual stuff, but not that Theo was a bastard. Took after his father. *He* did a bunk not long after Ben was born. Because Ben was Deaf. Barry thought it was a reflection of my crappy eggs. Blamed me. Everything was always my fault. And that's what Barry said. He said "You can look after the faulty boy – he's got nothing to do with me. He's all *your* fault."

'And he left. Good riddance was what I said. But him and

Theo always got on. So when I found out what Theo had done, I packed him off to his dad's. Barry was more than happy to have his favourite boy back again.

'But I never told anyone what Theo had done. And neither did Ben. It's our secret. No one needs to know. I don't like airing our dirty laundry in public. It's nobody's business. *I* helped Ben. Well, I tried my best. Maybe I didn't do such a great job after all. I know people think Ben's a bully, but you need to look deeper. Dig a bit.'

She laughed, but it only looked frightening to Annie. More like a rictus grin.

'You'd need a bloody great shovel to dig down to Ben's good bits, his heart, but it's there, believe me. He's a good boy. After the business with Theo, I suppose I mollycoddled Ben. What else could I do?'

Defeated she stuck her chin out aggressively, trying to retrieve some semblance of power. Surprised Annie by saying, 'Anyway, so what if Ben was seen walking behind Toby? What's that got to do with the price of eggs? Ben bullied Toby, I'll admit that. He told me himself. Hated Toby. Don't really know why, he just did. But he's not violent. That I can promise you. I know my Ben.'

Annie got up, went over to Maggie and awkwardly patted her on her arm. 'Thank you for telling us,' she said.

Maggie didn't respond but kept her eyes down, staring at nothing. And then she snapped her head up.

'You don't think Theo had anything to do with that boy's death, do you? Toby, I mean?'

'We don't think anything at the moment,' said Crabb.

He looked surprised when Maggie said, 'Nothing would surprise me about Theo. He was an evil boy. What's to stop him becoming an evil man? A leopard doesn't change its spots.'

'May I ask,' said Crabb, 'if you can't sign, how do you communicate with Ben?'

She smiled weakly. 'Not well. I know a few signs, made some up myself. Ben understands me better than I understand him, but he writes stuff down if I don't get him. Pathetic that I can't sign properly, but there you go. Sums up my bloody life. Pathetic all round.'

Crabb, Maggie, Sam and Peters suddenly all straightened. Their heads turned as one. Maggie, sitting on the floor, reacted the most keenly. Annie knew she'd missed something that everyone else could hear.

She only knew what they'd responded to when she saw Ben enter the sitting room.

28

———

'What the fuck's going on here?' Sam came to life quickly and Annie saw him voice Ben for Crabb and Peters. Annie had almost forgotten Sam was there.

Ben looked wildly around the room, taking in the participants: his mother on the floor, the mug and bottle of gin within easy reach of her; Crabb and Annie both now standing as if they'd been caught out in something they shouldn't have been doing. Peters didn't move from his position against the wall.

'Nothing. Nothing at all,' Maggie said, getting unsteadily up and moving quickly to him. Sam signed for her.

Maggie threw a glance over her shoulder as she went to hug her son. Daring Crabb or Annie to say anything.

Ben looked at his approaching mother. And then at Crabb and Annie. Nodded at Sam. And then back at Maggie. He took in his mother's upset expression, obviously felt the awkwardness of the situation and worked it out for himself. Annie was impressed by Ben's ability to read the situation correctly. Astute, as she'd thought.

'You've told, haven't you? Just because he's back, you've told. You bitch.'

A blush stained Maggie's cheeks as she listened to her child's words. She said, 'I didn't know you'd seen your brother. How could I know? Why didn't you tell me? Anyway, I haven't told them anything. Theo just wanted money from me. I told them I fucked him off. Which I did.'

Sam interpreted all her words with an impassive expression. Annie sighed and watched Ben turn to run from the room, but Maggie wrapped her arms around him. He was a strong boy – clearly Maggie was no match for him – but he allowed himself to be restrained. And then he sank his face into his mother's shoulder. Crabb gestured discreetly to Annie to sit again. They waited while mother and son stood in an embrace.

Maggie wasn't comforting him – the boy comforted his mother. And then he pushed her away.

And faced Annie and Crabb.

Annie hardly recognised the boy. Ben stood, his cheeks flaming – furious. He was wearing the same baggy clothes as the day before, but now his anger made him look physically bigger. Gave him substance. Today he filled his clothes. He stood with his back to Sam, forcing Annie to interpret for him.

'So, Mum's told you. I knew it would come out one day,' Annie voiced.

'Your mother didn't tell us anything, Ben. I already knew,' said Crabb.

Ben's face took on a puzzled expression, his eyebrows furrowed deep over his eyes. 'You can't have known. No one else knows.'

'I guessed, Ben,' said Crabb.

'I don't believe you. You can't have.'

Maggie said, 'Have you told someone, Ben? What's going on? Who have you told, Ben?' She turned to Crabb. 'You can't have guessed. How could you guess a thing like that?'

Ben's cheeks stained an ugly, angry red. An almost identical inherited blush from his mother. His hands were two fists, stuck away under his armpits. Reluctantly, he released them and signed, 'No one. Honest. Who would I tell? *Why* would I tell?'

Annie knew he was lying. Crabb said, '*Have* you told anyone, Ben?'

'No one. Why would I? How stupid do you think I am?'

Annie signed and spoke: 'We don't have to talk about what happened when you were little.' She held up her hand as Ben shook his head. 'We knew anyway, Ben. Your mother hasn't betrayed you.'

Annie caught sight of the silent thanks from Maggie. There was no reason to make her life any harder than it already was.

Crabb took over. 'As Annie says, we don't have to go through it all again. But I am interested in where Theo is now.'

'I don't know. And I wouldn't tell you if I did. He's my *brother*.' Ben was on the verge of tears. Whether they were tears of shame, embarrassment or anger Annie didn't know and it didn't really matter. Ben crossed the room in two quick strides, stopped and squatted. Eye to eye with Crabb.

Annie moved effortlessly and with a practised ease around the room, positioning herself where she needed to be; standing right behind Crabb. Spoke for Ben: 'He's my brother. Don't you get that? Whatever he did to me, he's still my *brother*.'

'Was Wednesday the first and last time you saw him?' Crabb asked, making an effort not to sit back in his seat at the unexpected proximity of the boy.

Ben nodded. He crossed his arms as he straightened.

'And when you were together, outside the school, why was Theo pointing at Toby?'

'He'd seen me bullying Toby. And he asked who he was. Said he looked like a nice boy. But he didn't say it, meaning "nice". He meant, you know, nice in a dirty way.'

He picked at a spot on his face. Avoided meeting Crabb's eye.

Sam slipped around the room and stood next to Annie, taking back his control. Annie manoeuvred herself in turn, so that she could see Sam and Crabb. Sam signed to Annie: 'Who's interpreting? Me or you?'

Annie gestured for him to take over, and she lip-read Sam as he interpreted for Ben: 'Does it even matter? Theo didn't kill Toby. Or William. Why would he? He might be a perv but he's not a *murderer*.' Sam managed to convey the disdain from Ben's signs, using his expression to look contemptuous, a slight sneer to his lips.

Crabb said, 'I haven't accused your brother of killing anyone. Not yet. I'm looking for a killer who is damaged, but intelligent. A man with a brain. Theo needs to be found.'

Annie knew that Crabb was desperate to arrest Theo for child sexual abuse, knew that there was no time limit to charging him. Annie also knew, just from life, that as Theo was obviously guilty of historic sexual abuse, he was almost certainly still doing it. If not to Ben, then to some other poor boy.

And of course Theo could be the killer. He could have abused Toby, been seen by William. A thousand different scenarios whirled around Annie's brain – none of them felt right but she had yet to meet the older brother. She almost hoped that he was the killer. At least she didn't know him. Selfish of her, but it would somehow make her feel better if it turned out that the murderer was a stranger to her.

But if a stranger to her, why was the killer including her, killing people she loved? Attacking her?

Ben unexpectedly slumped his shoulders, and surprised Crabb by saying, 'When Theo pointed at Toby, showed interest in him, I felt hurt. You know, like I'd been dumped or something. I know that's stupid and pathetic. But I felt jealous of Toby. Just for a moment – Toby who'd got everything already. His family all loved him. Why should my brother love him as well? Everybody loved Toby. It's not fair. He deserved what happened to him. Theo loved me.'

He thumped his chest, jabbing his index finger repeatedly against himself. 'Me, me, me.'

Annie inwardly sighed with a deep sadness. Crabb said, 'That isn't love, Ben. Your mother loves you. Theo abused you.'

'But he loved me too. I know he did. And nothing you say can change that. He just showed it in a different way. Not the right way, but I know he loved me. He told me he did.'

Annie watched as Maggie stood, gin bottle dangling from her hand. She absently swigged from the bottle, mug again forgotten. She looked devastated and confused by Ben's support for Theo. She said, 'I sent him away, Ben. So that he'd stop hurting you. He's bad.' She swallowed some more alcohol and said again, 'He's bad.'

Ben signed. 'That's why I instantly recognised Martin... for what he was. Bad like Theo. Like he had a flashing beacon on his head. Bad, bad, bad, it pulsed out. And Martin saw that knowledge in me. Same flashing from me going on, I suppose. He recognised it had happened to me. But I made it clear from the off: don't mess with me. And he didn't. He knew better.'

Annie signed, 'Is that why you told us about Martin now, because Theo is back? Because you were reminded that you were a victim. Like the boys Martin watched in the showers.'

'It's not something I need reminding about. I'm not going to forget, am I? Anyway, I'm not a victim. That's just a pathetic word. I'm me. That's all.'

Maggie automatically cowered as Ben approached her, his hands gesticulating wildly. 'But Theo's my brother. And you sent him away. I loved him. He loved me. And you fucking sent him away. I'll never forgive you for that. Never. I know he was... bad. But he loved me.'

Annie watched as Ben shouted with his hands – spittle flew and the veins in his neck stood out. 'Fuck you. None of you understand. Fuck you all,' Sam voiced for him.

Ben swung his arm out and raised his middle finger at all of them. Turned towards the door, paused, spun around to face Annie. Smiled. 'Anyway, heard you'd been arrested. For murder. Everyone's saying you did it. *I* haven't done anything. Unlike you, apparently. You're the murderer. Not me.'

And then he did leave. A stillness settled on the room in his absence.

Standing, Crabb slipped his business card into Maggie's hand. 'Call, if you need me,' he said.

She dumbly nodded, wiping snot from her nose. She wouldn't meet his gaze.

What a sad mess.

Outside, Sam made his departure, walking away with his hand held high in a backwards farewell. Annie stood with Crabb and his conker-colour haired add-on. She said, 'Ben was lying. He *has* told someone. I don't know how important that is, but he was definitely lying.'

'How do you know?' said Peters.

'Hearing people tend to tighten their lips when they lie, as if they are physically stopping the words from getting out. Ben did that, but he also did the deaf equivalent. He balled his fists, stuffed them under his armpits. Not wanting them to sign out his truth.

'On a more obvious level, he blushed. A triple visual whammy.'

Crabb rubbed his jowls, shook his head. 'I don't know if that's important either. But I do know we have to find big brother Theo, as soon as bloody possible. Get in the car, Annie. We'll give you a lift home.'

As Peters opened the car door and got in, Annie stopped

Crabb with her hand on his arm. 'I've got a mental itch. Something you said. But I just can't remember what it is.'

'The question or the answer?'

'Both. I mean, neither. I can't remember what you said, or asked me, but I remember something, but I can't get it to come to the surface. But I know it's important.'

'Don't push it. It'll come.'

But Annie still worried. She was missing *something* and she knew she needed to know what it was.

29

'What the bloody hell are you talking about?' said Crabb, gripping his mobile.

'We had to let Martin go,' said Peters.

'Didn't they find holes in the shower cubicles?'

'They did. But they were filled-in holes. You know, Polyfil-laed. A recent job. But Martin said that the walls were in a bad state of repair and that he was constantly having to make good. Said the walls were structurally unsound and that it was an on-going maintenance job. We can't disprove it. There was nothing to show that he wasn't lying. Other than what you said Ben told you, we've got nothing on him.'

'Have you sent off Martin's mobile and computer to the labs to check for downloaded porn? Was there nothing that you could have held him on? He's not exactly the brain of Britain. There must have been *something* you could have done to keep him in custody?'

'If there'd been something, we wouldn't have released him. Both mobile and laptop have been sent off. But you know how long that takes. We can't realistically expect any results for at least three to four weeks. And we can't get around the fact, that without Ben's statement, we have nothing but circumstantial evidence against Martin.'

Crabb was speechless. And bloody furious. Martin's sexual predilections, his secret life and actions, *could* be linked to the murders. Martin, Ben and Theo were all inextricably linked through sexual abuse. Crabb felt a strange impotence wash over him.

'Get someone to check he doesn't bugger off before we can arrest him. And we need to find Theo.'

'A big-scale search is on for him. Vice are on it too. They'll find him. The sick bastards always turn up. Find the schools, swimming pools, playgrounds; find the children, find the paedophile.'

Crabb lit a cigarette. Tried to calm down. 'Post-mortem been done on William?'

'Yes. Killed by skewer to brain. Exactly the same as Toby, but better executed.'

Crabb ground his teeth, at a temporary loss. Peters carried on: 'Bragen read me the report. Told me the same snacks were fed to William as was fed to Toby. You know, pork pies, sandwiches, cake, crisps, jelly, et cetera. I was thinking it might be like picnic food. You know... because of the weather. Hot.'

'Well I'm fairly bloody certain the killer didn't take them out to Hampstead Heath and sit down on a tartan rug spread out on the grass. Are you thinking wicker food hamper? A cosy trio? Really, is that what you're thinking?'

Crabb knew he was being unfair. Sucked in air. Snacks. A proper tea. Picnic food. All possible, but which was right? Or was it simply what food the killer had to hand? Relenting, Crabb said, 'Good point, though, Peters. I'll consider it.'

Silence.

Peters said, his voice with a little less conviction now: 'William was killed on Saturday: same as Toby. Probably later.

But because of onset of decomp, Dr Moore says it's impossible to give you the exact hour of death, but certainly within several hours of Toby's death. William also showed identical signs of lividity on buttocks and back. Again, like Toby, presumably left in a chair immediately after death, for some time.'

'What the fuck's the killer doing? Goddamn it.'

'You don't think the murders are sexually motivated, do you?'

'No. I think we've just uncovered Martin's penchant for small boys. As Ben was also abused by his brother, it's not surprising that he recognised something in Martin. And a sick relationship was born between the two. But I'm worried about Annie. We need to keep her safe. I'm not happy that the killer's using her as some form of sick amusement for himself. I need to find out how, why and where she fits into all this.'

'I've asked Docherty again to put a couple of men on Annie, as you requested. Just to keep an eye on her. But he says he hasn't got the manpower. No spare men. So she's on her own.'

Crabb could hear the frustration in his voice as he said, 'No, she's not on her own. She's with me. But if anything happens to Annie, the shit will really hit the fan. Some of it will be coming from the Deaf Community. But most of it will be coming from me. Of that you can be certain. Tell Docherty to brace himself. The fat bastard.'

30

A nnie poured herself and Scarlet one more glass of wine before bed. As Annie sipped from her glass, she picked up Eric. Lifted him up and threw his head and front paws over her shoulder like a favourite fur.

Scarlet was staring at the whiteboard that they used to plan out window displays. It stood in front of the French windows. On it, Annie had written:

Adam – kicked to death: hearing aid in mouth
Toby – skewered in ear: green pencil shavings in mouth
William – skewered in ear: black Labrador's ear in mouth

They both looked at the harsh and stark words. Annie said, 'I don't get it. Can *you* see any connection?'

Scarlet shook her head: 'No, apart from the obvious. You know, the deafness.'

Before Annie could say anything, the doorbell flashed. Glancing at the clock, Scarlet said, 'What now?'

'God knows. Let's open up and see. How much worse can it

get?' But she thought, *a lot worse. Potentially. A lot worse.* It had been a long day. A long week.

She came back into the sitting room accompanied by a dishevelled and sweaty Crabb. He waved at Scarlet in greeting. She waved back, keeping her face turned towards Annie, and said, 'Natty shoes, Crabb. Been golfing?'

He gazed down at his feet; seeming shocked that he was wearing black low-heeled shoes with a red toe-cap. Annie pretended not to notice Crabb blush. A deep, burning red that matched the sunburn on top of his head. He shrugged: 'Nothing. Forgot to change. And no, not golf. Annie, I need to speak to you.'

Annie could see he was excited, hoped he had good news. Wanting to prolong the pleasure of something not completely shite, she said, 'Come on, Crabb. Spill the beans. Scarlet will pour you a drink. What are the shoes for? Dancing?'

His embarrassment threatened to silence him. Finally realising that she wouldn't let him continue until he'd revealed the meaning of his shoes, he sat down heavily on the armchair and said, 'I do Latin and ballroom dancing. Every Tuesday night. Helps me relax. Afterwards, I'm knackered but physically up, you know, like buoyant. Then that buoyancy spills over into mental buoyancy and clarity of thought. Helps me think. Which is why I do it, and why I'm here now. I thought of something when I was dancing tonight. Need you to confirm it.'

'Are you any good? Who do you dance with?'

Annoyed now, Crabb spoke quickly. 'It's not important now. To business. When I was dancing tonight, my partner told me that I stank like an ashtray. Which got me thinking. There were no ashtrays. Not one single ashtray.'

Annie felt her face register complete blankness. 'No ashtrays where?'

'No ashtrays in William's house.'

'That's because he didn't smoke.'

She couldn't understand his excitement at this fact. Looked at him nonplussed. He slapped his thigh in satisfaction.

'I knew it. I didn't put two and two together at first. Knew there was something missing at William's house, but I just couldn't work it out.'

'I'm not really with you. I don't get the relevance.'

'Didn't you notice the tobacco and rolling papers next to the cup of tea?'

'No, I bloody didn't. Just noticed William's body and not much else.'

'Sorry, yes, I get that. But the tobacco was there, and as you say, William didn't smoke. And if you're a smoker you have ashtrays. That's a fact. You've just confirmed that William wasn't a smoker. So, why the tobacco?'

Annie had already brought Scarlet up to date with everything, so now Scarlet said, 'It's another addition from the killer. Like the razor blade in William's wrist, the dog's ear, and the cup of tea. It's another added extra. To portray something specific.'

'Exactly. And *that's* interesting. Tobacco. We have to work out its significance.'

This wasn't exactly the good news Annie had been hoping for, but at this stage, what *did* she expect? The killer caught and neatly tied up with a red bow? Whatever way you looked at it, there was *never* going to be any good news in this whole scenario. Ever. The best that could be hoped for was something that moved the case on. And she supposed this qualified. She was silent for a minute, then watched as Crabb said, 'Taking into consideration all the little extras with each body, it could mean that the victims, both Toby and William, represent other *people*. One who liked drawing, a boy, and a man who smoked, drank tea and possibly committed suicide. So, very specific people.'

Annie kept her facial expression carefully neutral. She

didn't want to engage in a conversation about murdered friends with skewers through their ears and things in their mouths. Tried to get through this as if it were an academic exercise, instead of a very personal tragedy. Tried to be matter-of-fact. Businesslike. Her hair was down, so she got up and went to the table. Found a pencil and secured her hair up and away from her face. *There, a modicum of control.* The authority of the pencil cancelled out the casual shorts and T-shirt that she wore. She sat again.

Crabb jigged his knee with barely contained excitement. Said, 'And the killer's re-enacting some scene. With these people. Or surrogate people. That's what I think. Can't be sure, but it feels right, don't you think?'

'But who do they represent?' said Scarlet.

'I shouldn't really be including you in these theories of mine. Annie's helping me. Me talking to you, including you in my hypothesising, is stretching the boundaries.'

'Bit late now,' Scarlet said. 'But if you want me to leave, just say so. Annie will only tell me once you've gone.'

Crabb glanced through the window, then looked again at Scarlet. 'You're right. Fuck it. Just remember that this is between us. *I'll* pass on anything relevant to my team. And don't blabber to anyone else, okay?'

Scarlet's lips curved in a soft smile, her eyebrows flat. 'Don't worry. I won't tell. Why would I? And I never blabber.'

Nodding, Crabb said, 'If I knew who these surrogate people represented, we'd be halfway to solving this bloody case. All I know is, it's a huge piece of theatre. The killer's playing out some weird fantasy. And he's using his victims like props. Staging their deaths, posing their bodies like mannequins – as you pointed out, Annie. It's *who* they represent to the killer that we have to work out. Both Toby and William obviously represent people who were important to him.'

Scarlet left and reappeared quickly, glass in hand and offered it to Crabb. 'Drink,' she said unnecessarily.

Crabb waved his hand 'no' and said, 'I'm also certain that there will be no telling fingerprints on the tin. The killer isn't stupid. It's to do with the tobacco tin itself. It's a message.'

Annie said, 'It almost feels like he wants you to work out what he's doing. Does he want to be caught?'

'No. I don't think he's finished. Not yet. It's a bit like dancing. I'll use that as an analogy now that you both know my guilty secret.'

Annie saw his long-lashed eyes blink slowly, almost coyly and then concentrated on his mouth again. He said, 'It's like a ballroom dance. The killer is the leader, the man. Guiding us through a sequence of patterns and figures. But only he knows the steps. Consequently, we stumble, not knowing what we're following. He knows the exact rhythm, he knows the notes, knows the rise and fall of the music – we know diddly and we're bloody floundering, tripping over our own feet. We don't even know what dance he's dancing. And at the moment, he's foot perfect. We can't possibly know the final twists and turns that are yet to come – and I'm afraid that there will most definitely be a finish with a flourish.'

Scarlet cocked an eyebrow and said, 'Sounds like we need a dance lesson a bit pronto.'

Annie liked the dancing metaphor. Could visualise it. She closed her eyes quickly, trying to immerse herself in the picture Crabb had created. Opening them, she said, 'You're saying that Toby represents a different child in the killer's head? You're working on the premise that William's role was that of being, amongst other things, an adult smoker who committed suicide, who the killer knew in the past. Adam Jacobs was also fifteen years old. Was Adam a rehearsal? For Toby?'

'I don't think so, no. He was just violence for violence sake.

But I do think the killer's playing with substitutes of real people who he knows. Or knew. Unfortunately, Toby and William were those representations. How or why he's doing it I don't know, don't even know that we're right, but it feels like it fits.'

Annie said, 'Dead people?'

Crabb stopped drinking. Lowered the glass from his lips. 'Yes, dead. They must be. Because of the faked suicide of William.'

'Not necessarily,' said Scarlet. 'Not if he was using Toby and William like puppets or stand-ins of living people. Maybe he wants to change something. The outcome of something? Maybe the man who was William was someone who the killer thinks *should* have committed suicide but didn't?'

'Bugger me,' said Crabb. 'The possibilities are endless. This killer is intellectually violent as well as physically. But however random things appear superficially, they are becoming *less* random. Things are becoming slightly more cohesive. We now think we know that the victims are portrayals of others. It's what I'm going with, anyway. And that's a big leap forward. Gives us a firmer grasp on what's happening. We're just that bit closer to what the killer is potentially thinking. Pity we don't know any of the rules he's playing by.'

'Or the exact dance,' said Annie.

Crabb smiled his agreement, obviously pleased that she'd understood his ballroom explanation. He said, 'And sorry to have to tell you this, but we've had to let Martin go. Nothing to hold him on, although in my mind he's as guilty as sin in terms of peeping at naked boys. And only God knows what else. We'll have to wait until the techies have been through his computer. Takes weeks, but they always find something. Paedophiles can't help themselves, looking at sick abusive videos of children. We'll at least get him on that, plus who knows what else? Just not yet.'

Annie felt too tired and deflated to even make a comment. Crabb turned and studied the whiteboard.

'That list. It's wrong,' he said.

'No, it isn't,' said Annie.

'You haven't included yourself. And you should keep Adam separate. He wasn't tied up. Wasn't kept. Wasn't given any food. Wasn't skewered. Wasn't involved in this re-enactment. You, however, are. Because of your relationships with Toby and William. I'd put you slap bang in the middle.'

He strode up to the board and picked up the marker. 'Here, like this:'

Adam – kicked to death: hearing aid in mouth (Uncontrolled/overkill/opportunistic)
Toby – skewered in ear: green pencil shavings in mouth (Controlled/premeditated) fed snacks
Annie – premeditated attack/knows Toby & William/suggestion of putting something in mouth
William – skewered in ear: black Labrador's ear in mouth (Controlled/premeditated) fed snacks

'Don't make the mistake of missing yourself out. You're very much involved and playing this game, or whatever the hell it is, whether you want to admit it or not. Remember that. For your own sake but for others too.'

Eric prowled across the floor, smelt Crabb's shoes and then jumped onto Annie's lap. She pulled gently at his whiskers, making him yawn. Said, 'I haven't forgotten I'm involved, Crabb. How could I? But what do you mean, for others too?'

'Who else do you love, Annie? They may be at risk.'

Scarlet said, waggling her eyebrows for comic effect, 'Not me. Please not me. You hate me.'

Annie couldn't even dredge up a smile but said, 'It has to follow the killer's pattern so far, so someone deaf.'

Crabb repeated, 'So, who *do* you love, Annie. Think.'

'I don't know. Polly. Dora. Fiona. She shrugged helplessly. 'There are lots of people I love, obviously hearing people as well, but from this Deaf Club, this community, only those three, I suppose. So, start worrying about them. I'll be fine.'

If she said 'I'll be fine', with enough conviction, she could temporarily convince herself that she believed her own words.

Crabb tilted his head to the side, 'Why Polly?'

Annie stood up, suddenly pissed off. 'Why not Polly? She's a good friend. She's different, has her own unique style, is sophisticated, doesn't live and die by the bloody Deaf Club, has a life. She's intelligent, artistic, has her own weird ideas about things, she makes me laugh. I trust her. There, is that good enough for you, Crabb?'

Annie knew that she wasn't really angry with Crabb, but was only directing her anger at him as he was in her firing line. She wasn't sure she was even angry: more frightened. Frightened that at this stage, there were three people whose existence was threatened. Any one of them, or maybe all of them, could die.

Because of Annie.

Because of something that she'd done.

Because she'd pissed off the wrong person.

31

———

ora has spread the good word about Martin. According to the Deaf Hotline, Martin had been stupid enough to go and visit the woman after his release from custody. How I would've loved to be a fly on that wall. Stupid, unsuspecting Martin and the ever-wrathful Dora. He expecting to explain it all away. She, utterly unforgiving.

And now I stand outside Martin's house. The moronic cretin that is Martin, paedophile Martin, has also been arrested. There's a lot of it going about. Apparently, and this is only an assumption, the police lacked evidence to hold him. Astonishing.

I haven't rung his doorbell. There is no need for him to know of my little visit. But I know he is in. I quickly peeped through his net curtains and saw his shadow. Had he seen me, well... it was only me after all. Easy enough to lie about my presence outside his door.

But naturally, I went unnoticed.

He is a sitting duck, with nowhere else to go but home. After all, he would no longer be welcome at the Deaf Club. Frankly I was surprised that he had walked unscathed from Dora's house. Although one can only suppose that there was a definite droop to his shoulders. He's always been a predictably droopy man. Droopy morals.

The Deaf are quick to drop those they consider undesirables. And *he was stupid as well. A stupid undesirable. He'd have to find out for himself just how undesirable he had become. The next time he went to the Deaf Club, he would be snubbed. Vilified. Ignored. Hated.*

I don't want to be caught in the act.

I quickly slip the typed missive through his letterbox. He wouldn't need telling twice. I was more than confident that he would follow the contents of the note. He is nothing more than an unsuspecting puppet. With the slightest of tugs on Martin's strings, he will be off and running. He will react like a dog chasing a stick. And we all know that every dog has its day. I've tossed him a bone.

The whole thing is becoming a comedy of errors.

My Game aim is to make life even more unpleasant for our dearest Annie. The fate of Martin is of no consequence to me. He is doomed. He has doomed himself. Perverted man – disgusting. He'll find no pity from me. Nor, I believe, from anyone.

The deed done, I turn from Martin's door and hurry home.

I have to admit, I'm really beginning to enjoy this unexpected turn of events. It's extraordinary how a few meaningless murders can affect a community. It's truly fascinating. The killings have started a domino effect. Tainting everything, as their impact ripples through Deaf lives.

It is as if the Deaf have been blighted with some contagion. They spread it, without thought, without precaution. They are destroying themselves.

With the airing of their own sad little existences, uncertainty blossoms. Fear abounds and falsehoods multiply. People are their very own cinéma-vérité, starring in their own very grubby vignettes.

It is simply marvellous to watch.

And here I sit. In the Royal Box. I do believe I have the best seat in the house. As befits my role.

32

It was half past six on Wednesday evening. Annie had been cocooned inside her flat for the entire day. Wandered in and out of the sunshine in the garden, feeling bereft. And very alone. She'd insisted Scarlet go into work tonight to finish dressing a window – instead of babysitting her as she'd wanted; assuring her that with the few police drive-bys, and the promise that she wouldn't go out, there was little risk of anything happening to her. She'd made the same promise to Crabb. Felt like a child not allowed out of its playpen. Safe but trapped.

And still with a niggle that wouldn't go away, *something* Crabb had said, but it would not come out and reveal itself. The more she pulled the loose thread, the more it eluded her. Frustrating and annoying.

Scarlet had texted Annie on the hour, every hour. To stop the messages, she got in touch with Fiona, and invited her over for a drink. For good measure, she texted Crabb. Told him that she was with Fiona and both were locked in tight for the night.

In truth Annie craved only silence and solitude. She still felt strangely detached from her own life. It wasn't a life she recognised as her own.

Wallowing, she'd discovered, as she sat down opposite Fiona, was a solo thing. Not to be shared.

Annie now took a calming breath and then a long swallow of wine. Fiona tucked herself into a ball on the deep armchair, her bare legs coiled beneath her. She wore pink shorts with a connecting bib. She was long-limbed, long-lashed, all doe-eyed: all innocence. That was her game, how she operated, playing on her looks for all her worth. *Save me, save me, I'm a damsel in distress. Love me, love me.* Fiona might as well have been saying, 'Love me, help me. Fuck me.'

Trying to relax, Annie conceded that deep down they both needed the company. Fiona always needed company. And alcohol wasn't a bad idea either, except with every mouthful of wine, it became harder to ignore the images of the dead in her head. She wished she could press delete.

Before Fiona had arrived, Annie had hidden the whiteboard in her bedroom. Her knowledge of the three murders wasn't something to merrily hand out, like some tasty canape at a private viewing. Flexing her mental muscles, Annie thought: *I am deaf and I am strong. I am not a victim.*

Her mantra failed to inspire her this time.

She shivered and was saved any more thought by seeing Fiona waving her hand up and down in the air to get her attention. Annie forced a smile and tried to look interested, grateful that she could communicate using SSE.

Fiona sat with her glass of wine in her hand, leant over and placed it on the small side table. The glass teetered on the edge of the table, before Fiona caught it. Wiped the back of her hand across her forehead, '*phew,*' and laughed. Signed, 'That was close. Sorry. And sorry about, you know, Toby. Poor little Toby. I still can't believe it. And William. Fuck, Annie. What's going on?' Her handshapes were slightly sloppy; the deaf version of slurred speech. Her eyes kept on filling up with tears, smudging her mascara.

'I don't know what's going on,' signed Annie.

'What do you think will happen next?'

'What sort of question is that? How would I know?'

Fiona's shoulders dropped. Her eyes dropped. Annie's heart dropped with humiliation. She bent forward and touched Fiona's knee: signed, 'Sorry. That was cruel. Didn't mean to be so abrupt. I have no idea what's going to happen next. It's all a nightmare.'

'How's Toby's mother coping? Is she still staying with her sister?'

Annie nodded. 'Her emails are strange. Difficult, you know. Difficult to respond to. Sarah sounds remote. Like her personality has gone, or she's keeping it under wraps. For the moment, she's unreachable. She's a different person. Maybe forever. She's hiding from everyone and everything. It feels like I can't connect with her. I got no real response when I told her about William. Just a formal email of condolence, as if we weren't good friends at all. As if she didn't even know William.'

Annie drank her wine. Sighed and signed, 'I can hardly blame her. I feel like I can't cope with much more. How must Sarah feel?'

'I know. Awful. Really awful. And by the way...' Fiona flapped her fingers in the air in front of her, balled them into a fist, holding Annie in space, not allowing her to interrupt before Fiona could sign what she wanted. Finally, after draining her glass: 'I shouldn't have to say this, but I don't think you had anything to do with the murders. Of course you didn't. It's just stupid to even think that. No one really believes it, you know.'

'Don't they? Not so sure, but frankly, I'm not bothered what they think. It doesn't matter.'

Fiona looked surprised, so used to being completely

consumed by what others thought of her, it was obviously alien to her that Annie didn't care about idle gossip and petty bitchiness.

And Fiona didn't even know of Annie's own attack. Annie had decided in the long run that her near-suffocation wasn't worth mentioning. To anyone. No value would be gained from its reveal.

Annie and Fiona sat in a sad silence, until Fiona sat up straighter and signed brightly, 'Where's Eric, then?'

Casting her head around half-heartedly, Annie signed, 'Don't know. Out on the prowl. He's always out more when it's hot.'

Fiona smiled, brought her shoulders up to her ears and wrinkled her nose like a rabbit. 'Pity. I could do with a cuddle.'

Couldn't we all, thought Annie, and watched as Fiona flicked her hair behind her ears, her earrings swinging wildly as she tossed her head. Then she bent and inspected her painted nails, blowing on them as if the varnish were still wet. Fiona – her very own plastic friend.

'Can I change the subject, Annie. And how about a refill?' She waved her empty glass in the air. Annie did the honours, didn't bother filling her own. Suddenly, she'd had enough. Fiona signed, 'Why do people treat me so meanly? It's not fair. I'm still deaf even if I do have a cochlear. It's not fair.'

Annie wanted to tell her to stop whining, stop drinking, stop me-me-me-ing, stop having sex with shitty men. Instead signed, 'Take no notice of anyone, Fiona. Just be your own person. And ignore Dora. I know she's against cochlear implants on principle but talk to her. She won't bite. She's kind really. You just need to be brave. Build bridges, or whatever stupid expression fits. Get a pair of bollocks, or the female equivalent. Stand up for yourself. Okay?'

'Wow,' Fiona laughed. 'That told me. Okay, will do. Well, I'll try, anyway.'

Fiona must have been quietly pissed when she'd arrived. Was rapidly getting drunker and drunker. Annie let her get on with it. She poured more wine into Fiona. Realised she was doing what most men did with Fiona – plying her with drink until she was incompetent. She stopped pouring.

Fiona signed, 'Anyway, enough about me, how are *you* coping? I'm so sorry. I don't even know how to make you feel any better. What sort of a friend is that?' signed Fiona.

Annie battled with herself. Even in the safety of her own home; she felt fragile. Her lower lip started to tremble. She threw her hands up in the air. Not in desperation, but in exasperation at her own frailty. Decided to go with the easy and frequently repeated lie: 'I'm okay.'

'Poor you. I wish I could help. I don't even know what to do or say.'

'There's nothing to do or say. Don't worry, I'm fine. Really.'

'Okay, well, have you heard about Dora's party. It's her sixtieth? On Saturday? She hasn't been going on about it because she wasn't sure it was still going ahead. Because of Toby and William, but she's decided it is.'

Fiona's face cleared at the mention of an upcoming party. It was like being with a teenager, Annie thought. Fiona's brain jumping from one topic to another, unsure where to settle, but more than happy at the mention of a party. Any party would do.

'She told me about it ages ago,' Annie signed. 'So, she's going ahead with it then?'

'Yeah. Thinks it would be harder to cancel it than have it. Say's it's going to be in honour of Toby and William. I think that's sweet.'

Sweet. That was one word for it. Annie couldn't help but wonder if it was tasteless under the circumstances. But Dora knew best. Rather, Dora thought she knew best, which amounted to the same thing.

Annie got up to break the conversation and pretended to top up Fiona's glass, and this time, did top up her own. They sat in silence; both trapped in their own sad little worlds.

Annie's heart flipped painfully as the doorbell flashed, like a visual coloured metronome. Fiona raised her plucked eyebrows and tilted her head, silently asking 'are you expecting anyone?' Annie shook her head, looked at the clock on the wall. Half past seven. She frowned and stood up. She didn't like people turning up at her home without letting her know first. Unless she'd actually invited someone, no one was welcome. This was her place of safety.

Especially now.

33

Martin stood in the doorway. He held a bunch of flowers. His usually messy, skimpy hair was slicked down, greasy with gel. The pink of his scalp showed sunburnt through it. He wore a suit and tie with black braces showing behind the lapels of his jacket. His shoes were a highly polished black. They actually gleamed.

Annie felt a nervous laugh trying to escape. She swallowed it. What was he thinking? Did he really think he could win her over with flowers, a cheap suit and even cheaper aftershave?

Did he think that Annie had simply forgotten that he'd been accused by Ben of watching boys in the shower? Of watching Toby? That he was potentially a child abuser? That he'd run away? That he'd been arrested? How thick was he?

She signed, 'What the hell are you doing here?'

His face fell. He looked confused, surprised and embarrassed. He let the flowers drop to his side. 'You invited me.'

'Don't be ridiculous. Of course I didn't. Why would I?' She braced her hands on the door frame, barring him access. Not that she thought he'd try and barge past her. He was too weak, and she too strong. Too mentally strong.

His face took on an immediately more familiar expression. Anger. The theatre of romance forgotten. His face flushed. He actually stamped his foot in temper. 'But you did invite me. See?'

He waved a piece of paper in front of her face. Signed, 'How would I know your address if you hadn't given it to me? You invited me here for a drink this evening.' He signed the last sentence aggressively, as if she were an imbecile, missing what was staring her in the face.

'I don't know your address, so how could I post you anything? Here, give it to me, let me see.'

He held the folded paper back, suddenly reluctant. Signed, 'It wasn't posted. It was hand delivered.'

'I'd still have to know your address, wouldn't I? Give it to me now.'

He passed it over and she ran her eyes over the typed words.

```
Please come for drinks tonight at half past
seven. You know I want you. You're a real man.
I look forward to seeing you. Annie x
```

Her address was neatly typed at the bottom of the note. She felt her face go slack with surprise. Horror even. Who had written this and why? She looked back up into Martin's face. He was smiling.

'See,' he signed again. 'You did ask me for a drink. Told you so. Give it back. I want to show it to the police. It's proof.'

'Proof of what?'

'Proof that I... proof that I like women. Proof that you like me. Proof that I'm not guilty of anything that shitty Ben said. I'm normal. I've always fancied you, you know that. Can I come in?'

Annie felt like shouting at him. Hitting him. *Always fancied her*. What a load of shite. 'I didn't write the fucking note,' she signed. 'And *I'm* keeping it. To show the police. Now, go. Go away, you nasty little arse wipe.'

Fiona took that moment to make a wobbly appearance. She juggled a glass of wine in one hand and used her other as a rudder to guide her down the hallway. She signed with one hand once she'd come to an unsteady standstill. She signed, 'What are you doing here, you dirty bloody perv? I've heard all about you. About what you like to do to little boys. We all know. Fuck off. Leave Annie alone.'

Fiona made shooing motions with her hand and shook her head blearily in disgust at Martin. She tottered slightly but managed to stay upright. She lunged forward and threw the remnants of her wine at him. The alcohol splashed him in the face and dripped down onto his frayed shirt collar. He wiped it away, struggling not to burst into tears. Annie knew that by now the whole of the Deaf Community would know about Martin's arrest. News in the Deaf World always travelled in the same way: fast and inextinguishable. It was like lighting a fuse, watching the flame travel along, fizzing as it went. Blowing on it to try and stop it wouldn't work. It would carry on. And more often than not, embroidered, embellished and exaggerated.

Martin signed, 'But I didn't do it. Didn't do anything. The police made a mistake. That's why they had to let me go. I haven't done anything.'

He dropped the flowers on the floor, and looked beseechingly at Annie, hoping for a reprieve. She didn't react. She noticed that he cast his eyes down and away from his body. It was a perfect picture of a shame that he couldn't hide, whatever he claimed in his defence.

Martin ran his hands through his shiny wet-looking hair. Still wiping the wine from his face and jacket, he turned to Fiona and signed, 'Anyway, what are you doing here? Me and Annie have a date. Don't we, Annie? We do, don't we?'

He eyed Annie, unsure now of her response, but still sticking to his ludicrous self-made script. Or rather, a script written by someone else, to which he was stupidly and pathetically sticking. However improbable it was now proving. Why couldn't he see that? Annie could see the bewilderment in his eyes: thankfully he had gathered that *something* was amiss. That maybe he'd been set-up. Annie could feel her patience begin to drain away. She looked again at the note. Impossible to say who it was from. A plain white sheet of paper, with typed words. Nothing to indicate the identity of the author.

She shook her head. *Unbelievable. Who would bother playing such a stupid prank?* It was cruel. And nasty. And much more than a prank, she realised. She was being drawn into something. Again.

'Go home, Martin. I'm tired.'

He turned to go. She stopped him, looked again at the paper in her hand. She certainly believed that the note had been delivered to Martin. He was too stupid to have made it up. He seemed only mystified by the fact that she hadn't sent it. Hadn't fully grasped that the note hadn't come from her. The penny hadn't dropped.

'I gather you didn't see who posted this?'

He shook his head.

Fiona dropped her glass. It bounced and rolled, empty and unbroken on the hall carpet. She signed, 'Why don't you just bugger off.'

Martin glared at her. Sneered. 'Your friend, Annie here, is no better. The police questioned *her* about both murders. Give me a break. You bugger off.'

He looks like a big and stupid child, Annie thought unkindly.

He couldn't meet her eyes. He signed without looking up. 'The police made a big mistake with me. This note proves it.

They made a mistake with you too. We're on the same side, you and me.'

Fiona laughed drunkenly at the absurdity of his signs, shoved him away, allowing Annie to close the door.

Annie's heart thumped. She felt an odd mixture of panic and anger. Fiona took her in her arms in a drunken hug. Annie allowed herself to be comforted but didn't enjoy the physical contact. Felt soiled by Martin's presence. She gently pushed Fiona away.

They both stood in the hallway. Annie trying to regain her temper. Someone was playing games with her. And she didn't want to play. Suddenly, she felt an overpowering desire to be alone again. She waited, giving Martin enough time to leave, then opened the letterbox and peered through. Just an empty space.

Bending to pick up Fiona's glass, Annie straightened and signed, 'Thanks for all your help but I really need to be alone. Do you mind? I'm really sorry. I'll ring a cab for you. Go home. Go to bed. That's where I'm going. I need to be on my own.'

She leant forward and kissed Fiona on the cheek. Fifteen minutes later a cab had driven away a resisting Fiona, the driver promising Annie that he'd deliver Fiona to the address that Annie had written down.

Sitting back down on her sofa, Annie made her shoulders relax and laid her head back against the cushions.

Thirty minutes later her mobile vibrated in her pocket. The message read:

Here, Kitty, Kitty, Kitty. There's a good boy. Come on. There, there. Who's a good boy then? Eric's a good boy, that's who. Now, come on, Eric. I just want to stroke you. Stop it, Eric. It won't hurt. I promise. See, I told you. *There's* a good boy.

Annie froze.

34

Annie stood up. Carefully. Called Eric's name. Slowly, trying not to panic, she moved quietly from room to room, lifting cushions, duvets, pulling aside curtains. 'Come on, Eric.' He sometimes answered to a whistle. She tried that, but her mouth was too dry. Going into the garden, she called again. Louder. Feeling her voice rise in fear. Ran to the back of the garden, looked under overgrown bushes and foliage.

Sprinted back into the flat, down the hall and out of the front door. Stumbled out onto the pea shingle where her feet skittered and slid on the loose stones. '*Eric.*' Shouting now, stumbling as she did a three-point turn, she continued to call his name. Her breath came in short, painful gasps. Her hand groped in her pocket for her mobile. Wanting to text Scarlet.

And then she saw the bag on the ground outside her front door.

A plastic bag.

A plastic bag with something in it.

She stopped moving and just looked at it as her chest heaved and her heart exploded in terrified bursts.

I don't want to look in the bag. I have to look in the bag. Eric's in the bag.

She wanted to weep, wanted to scream. Wanted to walk away and not see. Not have to look.

But she knew she had to.

Slowly she advanced. The bag was a Sainsbury's shopping bag, tied in a knot; its two loose ends sticking up like rabbit's ears. A piece of paper with typed words was stapled to one end.

For Annie Black.

She carefully picked up the bag. And moaned. Instinctively she knew that the weight was right. Without undoing the knot, her fingers lightly traced the plastic-wrapped lump; knowing already that there was a cat-shaped mound inside. She knelt down, put the horribly heavy bag on the ground and put her head between her knees. Counted slowly in her head. Got to ten and carried on; eleven, twelve, thirteen, fourteen. If she didn't stop counting, none of this would be happening. Twenty-three, twenty-four, twenty-five.

Fuck it.

She bent and loosened the knot but held the bag together – still unready to face what she knew lay inside. Squatting and holding what she knew to be her pet, time seemed to lose all meaning. Unaware of whether seconds or minutes passed, Annie was paralysed with the horror of what lay inside the plastic.

Finally, taking a deep breath and holding it, she looked inside.

And recoiled. The bag fell from her hands and she stifled a sob. Looking away, she blew out her cheeks and then forced her eyes back to the grisly savagery in her lap. This time she squinted her eyes, peeking through her lashes, making the gore still visible, but taking away any clarity and definition. But she could see enough: could see too much.

What was left of Eric lay in a ball of dried blood. His fur was matted and instantly evident were knife marks that had slashed his body like a razor. She fell back, then stood and screwed her eyes shut. Threw her head back and screamed. Neither knowing nor caring about the noise that escaped her mouth, she remained in that position, unable to further investigate the contents of the bag. Eventually, her vocal cords hoarse and painful, she started to shiver. For Eric's sake, she felt responsible for seeing what had actually been done to him. She had to really look.

Her knees buckled and uncaring of the shingle, she sat cross-legged on the warm ground and put the bag in her lap. Again she scrunched her eyes semi-closed, limiting her from a full viewing. Slowly she put her hand inside and gently stroked Eric's face. His tabby colouring was mostly hidden by the blood which had dried in huge gobbets and trails. His eyes were fixed and unmoving. His red collar and name tag were nestled near the top of the bag.

She stroked the top of his head, ignoring the fact that only one ear remained.

The violent death was overshadowed by her grief. She brought the bag to her mouth and kissed his nose. He'd clearly been dead for hours – his body stiff and frighteningly wrong-looking.

Like a perverse waxwork, her cat was a beaten and ruined beast – empty and more dead than she could have imagined. Blood had pooled in the bottom of the bag and congealed in a brownish lump. He'd been carefully placed within the bag, like rubbish, but positioned in such a way that the full horror would not be missed.

Finally she stood, holding the bag to her chest – cradling it like a baby.

Slowly she entered her flat, putting Eric on the kitchen floor.

Not knowing what else to do with him. She ran the cold tap, let it run and run until it was cold. Getting a glass, she filled it to the brim and drank deeply. Life moved in slow motion. Her body seemed sluggish and felt as if it were no longer hers. She made her way onto the sofa, leant back and looked at the ceiling.

A tingling numbness enveloped her. Her limbs felt heavy and not her own. All that she was aware of was her breathing – an automatic physical process. The sensation filled her head. No tears came. Her heart had closed and her eyes were completely dry. She wasn't sure she'd ever cry again. Frightened that were she to allow the tears to come, she may never stop, she refused to give in to her loss. Refused to admit any emotions, barring them free rein. If she allowed one tear to escape, she knew a torrent would follow.

Minutes turned into an hour. Annie didn't move, couldn't move – her mind unable to comprehend the lengths the killer had gone to. He was clearly trying to destroy her and everything she loved. And he was most definitely winning. She swallowed, but other than that, didn't move, her feet placed on the floor, her gaze upward, her ceiling scenery not changing.

Eventually, she texted Crabb.

And then she texted Scarlet.

35

———

Annie stood on the corner outside her flat. She'd been waiting, frightened; alone and desperate to see Crabb. She exhaled with relief as she saw him fall out of the car and come running towards her.

Just his being here already made her feel better. Safer. She ran to him to greet him, needing to get a bit of extra distance between herself and her flat. And Eric. At least Crabb's presence gave her that excuse now. After she'd texted him and Scarlet, waiting for one or both of them, she'd been dithering back and forth between the road and the house. On her own, she'd felt exposed standing on the pavement. So she'd again approached the flat. But not too close. Not too close to *it*. She'd felt like she was caught in no-man's land.

'What's wrong?' said Crabb. His face was tight with anticipation, dreading whatever Annie was going to say. He wouldn't be disappointed. 'Are you alright? What's happened?'

'Come and see for yourself. I warn you, it's not nice.' She beckoned him with her hand. Loitering just a bit. Then she slowed to a dawdle. And pointed to her open front door.

'There. Inside. In the kitchen. It's in there.'

'What is?' asked Crabb. His mouth was tight-lipped and his eyebrows furrowed. His breathing was shallow and he was sweating. Knowing that whatever she wanted to show him was something unpleasant.

'You can't miss it,' she said.

He took her by the arm: 'I'm not leaving you out here alone. Come on.' He stopped. 'There's not someone in there, is there?'

'No, no. It's Eric. He killed Eric.'

She watched him hesitate, his face and eyebrows scrunching up in incomprehension and then he strode purposefully to the door, holding her by the elbow. Unhappily, she took a step into her flat and led the way.

'I got a text. After Martin had been here. It said, "here, kitty, kitty", or something like that. I kept the text. And I found Eric. In that bag. Outside my front door.'

He pulled apart the plastic with the end of a pencil lying on the table and looked inside. He bent further forward still, before recoiling. His jawline worked, and he turned his face away from her temporarily. Composing himself. Pivoting on his foot he faced her. 'It's sick. What bloody sickness *is* this?' he said.

Annie could tell he was shouting. He was clearly upset; whether because of *what* it was, or because it was Eric, or simply because it was yet another attack on something that she loved. Annie wasn't sure.

They both stood in silence and looked at the plastic bag. Crabb parted the bag and took another look. As if to make sure.

'What are you *doing*?' she said. 'It's Eric. You don't need a second look.'

For the first time since finding her cat, her throat clogged with a lump of emotion. Tears fell from her eyes. She couldn't believe that someone could be this cruel.

Crabb stood back from the bloody mess. 'Tell me who you think it is that's done this. Who do you know that *could* do this?

There must be *some*one,' he said, anger now further marring his plain face: his lips drawn back and his forehead ridged with creases. 'You must have *some* bloody idea.'

She suddenly felt very tired. His words threatened to destroy the barrier she'd worked so hard to keep in place since Toby and William's deaths. She didn't want to lose that last piece of her armour. Not now. Tears blurred her vision and she suddenly felt very vulnerable and young standing on the wrong side of normal. She just wanted Eric back. Bending forward, she found herself wailing, tears and snot running and falling from her face. Couldn't stop. Vaguely aware of Crabb's hand patting her on her shoulder, she saw Scarlet's feet walk into her line of vision. Annie straightened up.

'Eric's dead. He's killed Eric.'

Scarlet's face froze with shock. Automatically, she embraced Annie in a locked hold and they swayed together, silent. Finally they parted and Annie let Crabb fill Scarlet in. Leaving them to it, she poured herself a glass of wine. Held the bottle up. An inch remained. Turning, she shrugged her apologies, turned her back and sucked at the dregs from the neck of the bottle. Avoided looking at Crabb or Scarlet. Unable to communicate for the moment, she glanced out of the kitchen window. It felt like the final straw. Stupid. It was only a cat. Only Eric. Not a person: not a young boy or an old friend. Just a cat.

But she still couldn't get it into perspective. It still felt like another murder to her. It *was* another murder. Felt as important and as horrific as everything that it followed. Eric was dead.

She rubbed her eyes; a profound feeling of 'enough' made her want to curl up and sleep forever. Everything that had happened almost overwhelmed her; constant and never-ending shit. She took a deep breath and spoke in a neutral tone, too numb to put any feeling into it. She was all out of feelings. Or too full of them.

'Martin was here this evening. Thought I'd sent him an invitation for a drink. Of course I hadn't. He'd got a note. He was furious. No, that's not right. He was more puzzled by the fact that I *hadn't* sent it. It seemed completely beyond his comprehension. He just banged on about "my invitation" proving his innocence.'

'What did the letter say?'

Annie picked it up from the table. Handed it to Crabb.

'He thought the fact that I'd supposedly asked him for a drink, proved he was a normal man. Not a paedophile. Even pretended that he'd always fancied me. But he'd gone long before I found Eric. He wouldn't have dared come back and leave the bag there after me and Fiona had thrown him out. He hasn't the imagination to kill a cat. Or the malice. He's a nasty little shit, nastier now that I know he's into little boys, but he's stupid. Almost simple. He doesn't even know how much I love Eric. Not sure he even knows I *have* a cat.'

'Who does?'

'Everyone always asks after Eric. Dora especially. And if Dora knows, then I suppose everyone in the community knows. So yes, Martin *could* know about Eric.'

Annie swallowed. *Eric's dead. Shit.* She turned and opened the cupboard, got out Eric's two plastic bowls for food – one blue, the other red. Put them in the sink. Didn't know what to do with them. Didn't want to throw them away. Not yet.

Crabb picked up her phone. Scrolled through her messages.

'Do you recognise the number the text came from?'

'No.'

'Probably a cheap pay-as-you-go mobile. Could have been bought anywhere. Wonder how he got your number.'

'You've already said it's someone in the Deaf Community doing this. Easy enough to ask someone for my number, pretending he'd had it, but lost it. He wouldn't have aroused any suspicion by asking for it. Could even have picked up anyone's mobile who he knew had my number. Found it for himself. Easy enough.'

'I'll have to give it to our tech team. See what, if anything, they can find.'

'I need a mobile, Crabb. It's how I keep in touch. I can't just pick up a landline and speak. I need access to people. It makes me feel safe. Saf*er*.'

'Don't worry. I'll get you another one that you can use in the meantime.'

Annie huffed out her thanks. 'Back to Martin,' she said, 'and Eric. I really don't think this is Martin's style. Eric, I mean. I don't really know him that well, but I don't think it's his style. And I believed him. About the note. He was genuinely confused. Couldn't understand that I hadn't sent it. He wasn't lying. He'd been set-up. Someone's set us both up.'

Crabb picked up the note again, taking it by the corner, using only his fingertips, and held it up to the light, read it, and then read it again, and finally placed it on the table.

'Don't touch it again. I'll get forensics to come round and collect it. I'm sure it will only have Martin's and your fingerprints on it, but we have to check. The police will be coming anyway to deal with Eric. Forensics will want the plastic bag.'

Annie looked at Crabb. He went and sat down on the blue sofa. Put his head back on a cushion and closed his eyes. He steepled his fingers. Pursed his lips. Then he opened his eyes. 'Eric's death. It's especially for you. To upset you.'

Annie snorted. 'Well, of course it's meant for me. The fucking thing was outside my door with my name on it. I don't think it was for anyone else, do you?'

'Someone's playing with you. Martin's an easy and unwitting accomplice. With the right misdirection, you could make Martin do anything. But I agree with you. Martin didn't kill Eric. I can't see him butchering an animal just to make a point. I doubt he's violent. He's spineless and weak. The cat was from the killer. He's trying to frighten you.'

Annie laughed harshly. 'No shit, Sherlock. Great sleuthing. When you catch him, you can tell him he succeeded.'

Scarlet was in the garden smoking. Crabb and Annie sat in silence. She could feel herself getting more and more angry. She couldn't pinpoint exactly why, but conceded she had a lot of events from which to choose that would stir up the fury she felt. It settled in her stomach. It was easier than grief.

'Whatever way you look at it,' she said, 'there's a madman going around skewering the Deaf and now killing cats. My cat. What should I do?'

Crabb massaged his temples. Said, 'Does anyone have some sort of an issue with your deafness? Has anyone expressed annoyance or even a hatred of your inability to hear? Deafness appears to be the one commonality amongst the victims.'

'Annoyance that I'm deaf would hardly be reason enough to include me in all this, surely? It wouldn't be a good enough motive to make me central to whatever the killer's doing.'

'You may not even know the reason why this person hates you.'

'Well, I can't be expected to have an answer for you then, can I? The whole thing sounds like bollocks to me, and anyway, what happened to your re-enactment theory?'

'Oh, it's most definitely still there. I know I'm right. Bloody convinced of it. Last time I saw you, I asked you who you loved. It remains a good question. But I should have asked you, who do you hate? Or more to the point, who hates you? Remember when we first met, after your attack, I asked you who you might have angered? You said you didn't know. I should have pushed you on it, because your name wasn't just pulled out of a bloody hat. You know this man. He is *not* a stranger. This is personal. So I want you to think about it hard.'

Scarlet had come in and heard Crabb's speech. She said, 'You're asking an impossible question, Crabb. If Annie's pissed someone off, or mistakenly feels that something she said or did was an insult, something so trivial and petty that she wouldn't even notice, then how on earth can you expect her to know who it is? I'm sure I piss people off daily. I haven't got a nutter after me. Whoever it is, is clearly mad. Seriously insane.'

Her eyebrows angrily stuck in a sharply defined V, Scarlet made Annie sit down. She put her arm around Annie's shoulders, attempting to soften her expression. Annie put her head between her knees and blocked off the two concerned faces looking at her. She tried to block out her life. What her life had become. But she couldn't do it. The picture of dead Eric sat like a black weight in her chest.

She raised her head, sweeping her hand through her hair. 'I don't make a point of going around making enemies. Certainly not one who would go to these lengths. Male or female.'

'I'm sorry to bang on about this, Annie. But it's someone who you know. They know you. I repeat, it is not a stranger. It can't be. It's someone who you've crossed in some way. You are their target. They know a lot about you. Done their homework. *Think.*'

Annie's face fell even as she tried to cover her fear. She nodded. 'Honestly, I can't think of anyone I've pissed off that seriously. Or even slightly.'

She saw him sigh. He said, 'I'm really sorry about Eric. I'll call Peters. Tell him to bring in Martin for questioning about the note and the cat.' He sat back and took out his mobile.

'What's the point? We all know it wasn't Martin,' she said. 'And anyway, don't worry about me. I can look after myself.'

Scarlet raised her eyebrows in two perfect arches. Said,

'Don't be stupid, Annie. Of course you can't. You're not Super-woman, although you like to think so. You're in very real danger. Okay?'

Crabb nodded his agreement, and said, 'As soon as you accept that for whatever reason, you're the eye of the storm, the better it'll be. Perhaps this all started with you, and it therefore touches people you are connected with, and tonight, the killer's just reminding you, by killing Eric, that, whether you like it or not, you're still involved.'

Ignoring Crabb, Annie said, 'Have we got any more wine, Scarlet?'

'Always.'

'Let's get pissed then.'

Crabb refused a drink in order to deal with the police and the SOCOs who came and took the note and the cat away. Then he sat with her. In silence. Let her drink. Eventually he escorted her to her bed where he remained standing.

He asked her one final question. 'Was Eric microchipped?'

'Of course he was. Why?'

'Just a thought.'

36

The evening had started with Martin's derisory attempt at convincing the divine Annie that she'd invited him over for a drink. As far as he was concerned, that certainly hadn't gone the way he'd envisaged. Poor old Martin. I knew because I was there. Just passing, you understand, but most assuredly there. The residents' cars provided great cover for someone intent on hiding. I found myself face down under a Land Rover with a marvellous view of the entire encounter. Employing stealth tactics, I was able to see everything. A risk, but one worth taking in order to be a witness to my own orchestrations.

And then we'd moved onto the Death Of A Cat. Just a cat. Much like my Snowy all those years ago.

Both of these acts had been a mere diversion for myself. A distraction. Indulgent, but amusing.

But I mustn't allow myself the luxury of having fun. This whole affair is a serious one. Couldn't be more so. So, jolly antics aside, I forced myself to concentrate on the matter in hand.

If I were a religious man I might think there was a little divine intervention going on. Someone up there guiding me. Showing me the way. But I fear it is nothing as other-worldly as that. The Lord does *not lend a helping hand to non-believers. And I am most firmly in the camp of utter disbelief. No, it is not God speaking to me. But maybe one of God's minions is on my side. I seem to have had the most marvellous run thus far. Is it him? On reflection I have to say, no. It is all my own work. Does that make me God? No. That is a patently deranged notion. I am not mad. And I certainly don't need help from him. Or anyone else. I am a true agnostic. Not for me the vagaries of something so intangible and ethereal as a God.*

I deal with facts only.

You can't change the facts. It's not allowed. That is why I have done them in order. Chronological order. One has to follow what was.

I work with what I have been given naturally. My audacity. My skill. And let's face it – my charm. People trust me. Of course it will be the last time they trust anyone, but they don't know that. But at least they cared enough in the first place to trust me. Albeit temporarily. But as I've discovered, when push comes to shove, they don't care or trust *enough.*

I turned my mind to more immediately pressing concerns. I heard something today. It was the steady and unmistakeable sound of the jungle drums. If you closed your eyes you could imagine that it was real sound. The Deaf gossip factory is positively drowning in its frantic signing of a great and imminent event. To me it sings louder than any celestial fiddling could.

The word going round is that there is to be a party. How the Deafies love a party! And I include myself in that. I do love a good jamboree. And I am invited. I can't wait. What an ironic piece of good fortune. I seem plagued by my own good luck.

I have given myself a self-imposed timeline for My Game. Just to keep things neat and tiddly. One week. Seven days. A lot can be achieved within seven days. Take God, for example. I'm sure everyone would agree that what He achieved in that time frame was a feat indeed. Not to be sniffed at. And on the seventh day He created Man.

An interesting coincidence. But not one to dwell on. That way madness lies.

So now there's a party to look forward to. It offers up all sorts of opportunities. Such fun. I'm particularly looking forward to 'my next one'. And I know for a fact that they shall most definitely be attending the Grand Party. Just thinking about my soon-to-be participant, makes me angry. Livid. I shall have to watch that. Anger is a play-ground for mistakes. But I shall endeavour to curb my fury. Fury is bad. It is there, but it is under lock and key. Safe. Until the trigger is pulled. And you know me and triggers.

Believe me − this one deserves a little something extra. Not as much as the ultimate one naturally, but a little extra je ne sais quoi *is required. To give this person the proper send-off they deserve. For I know now that they will fail. In a way, I almost hope they do. And they* will *be 'sent off'. Just like Toby and William. Adam is excluded from this list of the dead. He was just collateral damage.*

This time, the execution will frighten people. Oh yes indeed it will. It might even frighten me.

Just a little bit.

37

———

Annie found herself sitting behind Peters as he drove, Crabb in the passenger seat. It was just after nine in the morning and in truth, she was glad to be out of her Eric-less flat. It felt oppressively empty. Not home anymore.

Absently, Annie played with the temporary mobile phone that Crabb had given her. He'd told her that he'd got someone to add in all her contacts, so she was good to go. She wasn't sure where she was good to go to, but had thanked him all the same. According to Crabb, they were going to visit Maggie Downing again. The mother of two mismatched sons. Annie had agreed to come with him without getting any further details. She asked now, 'Is this professional, bringing me along on an interview?'

Crabb turned in his seat and faced her. Said, 'Maggie phoned me earlier. Wouldn't say what she wanted to talk about, but says she wants you there. With me. Apparently she likes you. You'll be doing me a favour by coming and it's one way to ensure you're safe. I know where you are. I won't tell if you won't. Can always play the Deaf card, and say I couldn't get in touch with Sam. Even though I could and have. In case Ben's there and not in school.'

It was a short drive. Again, Annie felt the house had a disappointed-with-life look.

Ben's mother appeared at the door, obviously waiting for them. She made beckoning gestures, turning her head from left to right, scanning the street. 'Come on,' she said. 'Hurry up.'

Sam appeared at the corner and Crabb mimicked Maggie's hand motions. The interpreter put on a little jog, smiling a non-verbal greeting at them all. Peters joined them and they all piled into Maggie's sitting room, Annie feeling part of an intrusive, although invited, army, invading and taking over territory that shouldn't be theirs to take.

Maggie waved at the furniture, indicating they could all sit. She remained standing – agitated, pent up. Rattled. She said, 'Sorry for getting you to come out here, Crabb, but you did give me your card.'

Sam raised his eyebrows at Annie and she gave him the thumbs-up, nodded – *yes, please sign for me. Too tired to lip-read.* Maggie's words were apologetic, Annie thought as she watched Sam's signs.

Crabb said, 'No need to be sorry, Maggie. What's wrong?'

The woman was wearing the same brown cardigan as before. The only difference was her hair – pulled back, flat and close to her head, with a red elastic band, so it fell into a lank ponytail at her neck. She had the same gaunt features, puckered now in worry. And fear. Maggie entangled her fingers, gripping them, twisting them, lacing them together, tighter and tighter until her knuckles went white. She turned to Annie and said, 'Ben liked you.' She laughed. Annie didn't think any sound came out. 'I know you might not have got that from his behaviour last time, but he does, you know. You should be flattered.'

Annie automatically read her lips and picked up Sam dropping his hands in her periphery. She answered using her voice: 'And *I* liked *him*. Because he let me. *Finally.*'

She smiled to keep it light. Maggie smiled back, but her lip movements never reached her eyes, which skittered around the room, loath to settle on anything; unsure. Still frightened.

Crabb leant forward and said, 'What is it, Maggie? I can't help you if you don't tell me what's wrong.'

Again with the finger-pulling but finally she focused on Crabb. 'First off, I just want to check that you don't think my Ben's in trouble. With you lot, I mean. The police. With the murders. You don't suspect him, do you?'

'No, I personally don't consider Ben a suspect. No, definitely not. Why?'

Annie wondered if Crabb was trying to convince himself with all those negatives, but Maggie seemed desperate to hear only the positives. She pointed at the landline, and said, 'Do me a favour, will you, Crabb? Ring up the school. Check if Ben's turned up this morning. When he doesn't, they usually ring me. But sometimes they don't. The number's written down there, on that paper next to the phone.'

Crabb dipped his eyebrows to show a mild confusion. 'Why can't you ring them yourself?'

'I'd rather you did. The school doesn't like me very much. They think I'm an old drunk, so maybe they feel sorry for me. I don't know and I don't care. Please.' Maggie's face pleaded with Crabb with a despair that seemed familiar to her. Like slipping into an old and loved pair of jeans, her face adopted the expression with ease. 'Go on, *please*.'

'Don't you know where Ben is?' Crabb's mild confusion was in danger of turning into full-on concern.

Maggie lifted her shoulders up and down; a jerky movement. Attempted a reassuring smile – failed. Her lower lip quivered. Said, 'You know Ben. You've met him. You know what he's like. I can't control him anymore. He does what he wants, goes where he wants, when he wants, if he wants. Doesn't tell me nothing.'

'Why are you so worried, then?'

'I just am. Are you going to fucking ring, or what?'

Crabb nodded at Peters who stood and picked up the hand-set, waited, talked briefly into the handset with his back to Annie, and then faced Maggie. He said, 'The school says no, Ben hasn't turned up this morning. Or yesterday. I told them to let us know if and when he does.'

The news seemed to still Maggie's movements. Her eyes glazed over and she sat down heavily on the floor. Annie read her lips, unsure as to whether she was speaking out loud, or merely mouthing the words, 'fuck, fuck, fuck.'

Crabb got down to eye level with her, his back to Annie. Took Maggie by the shoulders. Annie couldn't see his face, so she looked up at Sam and raised her eyebrows, nodded her head at the two on the floor: please sign for me. His face impassive, he nodded and picked up his hands again, interpreted the conver-sation – Maggie saying: 'I don't know where he is. He's not come home before, after a night out, but I'm worried. This time it's different. Normally, if he stays out, he at least rolls in early morning when whoever he's been with turfs him out. And anyway, it's more to do with how he was on Wednesday night. How he was behaving.'

'How was he that night, Maggie?'

'He came rushing in at around five o'clock-ish. Maybe a bit earlier. Could have been more like four. It doesn't matter. He was all pumped up, excited, cocky, pleased. Strangely *powerful*.'

'What did he say?'

'He just made the sign for drinking. I asked him what he was so happy about, but he just laughed and repeated the sign. Waggled his eyebrows up and down as if he was being naughty. You know what I mean, don't you, Annie?'

Annie gave her the thumbs-up, nodding in understanding. Crabb said, 'What worried you so much last night?'

'Like I said. Just his manner.' She paused, and then said, 'You know, like he'd seen Theo.' Maggie lay back flat on the carpet, preferring the ceiling to enquiring faces. Carried on speaking. 'I guessed... No, that's not right, I bloody *knew* he was meeting Theo. Just his mood. Excited in that silly way that he used to get if Theo was nice to him when Ben was little, when he wasn't bullying Ben, you know. Last night, that's what I thought. That was my impression. That Theo had asked him out for a drink. And my stupid, gullible Ben, thought it was a bloody privilege to be asked. Stupid, stupid boy. He's always so confused with Theo. Still, after all this time. Doesn't know what's what.'

Annie watched Sam's interpretation but also concentrated on Crabb's back. He'd frozen momentarily, a fleeting body movement, almost involuntary. Impossible to fake; one of the automatic responses to shock. He stood and said, his face now visible to Annie, 'I saw Ben last night. Staggering drunk, walking along the middle of the road.'

Annie felt her own eyebrows move upwards. Maggie bolted upright, and Annie watched as Maggie's eyebrows reacted, in perfect time with Annie's, hers rising higher up her forehead, like they'd both practised a bloody eyebrow synchronisation routine.

'Was he alone?' Maggie said.

Good question.

'Yes. But I didn't see Theo. I would've stopped if I'd seen him.' The policeman looked embarrassed now, dimples a long, long way away.

'Are you saying a drunk deaf sixteen-year-old on his own, isn't good enough to stop for? What did you do?' Maggie asked. 'Just left him to it?'

Crabb's face coloured and his eyes lowered fractionally. Just for a second. He ground his teeth, working his jaw muscles. Trying to save face. Annie was curious as to his answer. 'There was an emergency, Maggie. I placed Ben on a bench, made sure he was okay, and yes, I left him there.'

Internally, Annie winced. It sounded like Crabb had left Ben like a forgotten umbrella. Worse, she knew that she'd been the reason for the policeman's desertion of the boy. Her text to Crabb for help.

Maggie was understandably angry that Crabb had effectively dumped her son: 'What do you mean, you just left him there? *Made sure he was okay*? How did you do that, then? You can't even sign. How do you know he was okay? Christ all-fucking-mighty. What were you thinking? He's only sixteen. Sixteen and pissed and *Deaf*.'

Crabb retreated into police-speak, distancing himself from what sounded uncomfortably like abandonment of a minor. A drunk, deaf minor. 'I had no choice, Maggie. As I said, there was an emergency, I had to prioritise. I'm sorry. You're right, I should have made sure he got home safely. But he was alone. I didn't see Theo. And I did call it in, got someone to pick him up. By the time they got there, he'd gone.'

'What were you *thinking*? What about all these murders? The killer could have got Ben. How do you know he hasn't? He's got Ben, hasn't he? Hasn't he?'

Annie stood and caught the now standing Maggie in her arms, unaware of whether she carried on repeating the awful words. Held her tight, squeezed her tight, calmed her. Let go, looked into her eyes, said: 'Does Ben have a place where he goes when he wants to be alone? A special place, maybe. Or he might just be nursing a hangover. Sleeping on the heath, or some-where. It's not cold.'

Maggie shook her off. 'He's always alone. Don't you get it? Of course he doesn't have a special place. He has no friends. The occasional shithead will go drinking with Ben, but no one he knows. Not knows properly. He's alone and he's out there. He's not in school and he's not here. So where the fuck is he?'

Maggie started hitting Crabb in the middle of his chest, her small fists bouncing uselessly off him. She wouldn't stop shouting, over and over again, 'You've got my son killed. Ben's dead. It's your fault. It's all your fault. Where is he? Where is he? You want to pray he's only missing, you bastard.'

Annie turned her back on the room, looked out of the window so she couldn't see any more.

Sometimes, she thanked God she was deaf and could tune out the audible pain of others.

38

Crabb and Peters drove Annie home. The last time Annie had leant forward from the back seat, she'd seen Crabb shouting into his mobile, the veins in his neck throbbing, pulsing with anger: 'Find Ben. We have to find Ben. Organise search parties – work outwards from the area he was last seen. I want every man available on this. Find him, for Christ's sake.'

Like a coward, Annie looked away and out of the rear passenger window, trying to ignore the urgency that thrummed off Crabb. 'Find Ben, find Ben, find Ben.'

The words – a manic rhythmic heartbeat; frantic, desperate, furious. Frightened.

Upset for Maggie, worried for Ben, unsettled by Crabb's desperation, distraught by all the deaths, she bent down and texted both Dora and Polly. Fiona would be working. No point in asking her to come around during the day. But Annie needed to be with people with whom she felt, well... deaf. She'd been fielding texts from her hearing friends for a week, and she'd fobbed them all off. Apart from Scarlet.

Annie needed to immerse herself in the Deaf World. With

the killer on a rampage, she wanted to be around the community. She just wanted to be there.

Because it was her fault – all of it. In the eyes of the killer, she was somehow responsible. She was to blame for his madness. For that she had to pay the price by at least seeing friends whose lives she was inadvertently impacting.

She wanted Dora and Polly together, in her flat: both of them at risk because of her. Needed to see them alive and breathing.

Scarlet would be at home, refusing again to go to work, wanting to shield Annie from yet more death. If Annie wasn't with Crabb, then Scarlet was her cover. Her protector.

It was half past eleven when Annie finally and with relief, opened the door to Dora and Polly who arrived together. With no obvious police presence in tow.

The heavy quietness of the flat had been suffocating since her return from Maggie's. After Eric's death, Scarlet had retreated into a fearsome silence.

Now, Annie gave the women glasses of ginger beer which she poured from a jug full of ice cubes.

Scarlet sat in silence, only slightly raising her eyebrows in recognition of the two guests.

Dora gathered her fat around her hips, as if she were hitching up stockings, before collapsing her large frame into the sofa. Polly gathered her folds of pashmina, the colours dazzling and frenzied, around her neck and shoulders. Rearranged her bangles which snaked up her thin wrists. Both sipped from their glasses. Waited for Annie to sign. Obligingly, she did, also giving voice to her words. Because she knew Scarlet was listening.

'Ben's missing.'

Dora's face shifted, the blood initially draining from it, and then infusing it with an uncomfortable, shocked red. *'Mean what? Missing? Impossible.'*

Annie interpreted for Scarlet. 'What do you mean, missing? He can't be.'

'He went out drinking last night, and hasn't been home since. Isn't at school today. Never came home.'

Annie watched as Polly tilted her head, her hand flat on her chest as if her breathing had been temporarily halted. She signed, 'What's going on? Is Ben's disappearance linked to the deaths of Toby and William?'

Annie lifted one shoulder, unsure how much information she should be giving out, how much was considered by Crabb to be within the realms of their secret consultation. Decided it didn't much matter. Everyone would know soon enough about Ben. Why hide the facts? It wasn't as if she really knew anything anyway. She signed and voiced, 'The killer seems to be targeting people who I love, or those with whom I have a special relationship.'

Dora placed her Chihuahua on the ground where it stood and trembled. Dora didn't know that Eric wasn't here anymore. But it annoyed Annie now – that arrogance that she had. Every time that Dora came here, which wasn't often, that presumption that her bloody dog took precedence over Eric, always irritated. Eric had always made a hasty exit when Dora's dog came. Not now. No crouching Eric, hiding cat; no arched back, no flattened ears, no puffed-up fur like a dandelion clock. No Eric at all.

Annie ran her tongue around her teeth, giving herself time, stretched out her calf muscles, rubbed her scar and restrained herself from kicking the Chihuahua. Overwhelmingly and disproportionately angry with the woman, she concentrated instead on Dora's puffy but elegant hands as she signed, 'But you don't love Ben. That's rubbish. He can't be missing. It's too much.'

Dora's eyes filled with tears that didn't fall, but sat instead in the bottom of her eyelids, like a mini wave, teetering. Annie shook her head sadly, 'You're right, I don't love him. But we sort of came to an understanding. Made friends if you want to put it like that. And yes, he *is* missing.'

Polly signed, 'Poor boy. What a life. But how do you know he hasn't just gone on a teenage bender? He's certainly got reason to do a bunk what with everything that's going on.' She rearranged her bangles before signing again: 'And why is the killer targeting people you love?'

The million-dollar question.

And then Polly's eyes gleamed with understanding. She wagged her index finger at Annie – not in reprimand, but instead showing her sudden realisation; her mouth open in an 'aah' lip-pattern. 'So *that's* the reason that Dora and I have ourselves our own police groupies? Now and again – when they bother. Because we're your friends? Because we're potential targets?'

Annie nodded again, feeling the guilt ooze and slither through her, but relieved that it was out there now. She physically winced when Dora signed, 'So, all this is your fault, then? The killings, everything. Why? What have you done?'

When Annie voiced Dora's signs for Scarlet, when she spoke the unkind words, Scarlet looked up and glared at the older woman, her brows a black slash above her eyes, and said, 'Don't you dare speak to Annie like that. Who do you think you are? Of *course* it's not her fault. How could you even say such a thing?'

Dora sat back on the sofa, shocked in turn as Annie interpreted Scarlet's words. Her face coloured again, and she looked suddenly upset. As if she might cry. Really cry. Finally she signed, '*Me, blunt. Deaf way.*' She carried on, 'Sorry, I say it as it is. You know me, Annie. Me and my big mouth. Stupid. I didn't mean it. You know I think of you like a daughter. I love you.' She blushed at having to communicate her truth and avoided looking at Scarlet.

Polly leant forward, her eyes bright, and signed, 'Ben's missing. That's what's important. More to the point, I rather presume that to be in Annie's group of very special people, well...' She spread her hands out in front of her, palms upwards. 'I suspect the criteria for being included in that particular gang is that you're Deaf. Am I right?'

Annie nodded. She felt she had been doing far too much nodding, like a mechanical toy. She signed and said, 'We have to find Ben. Where would he go? Have you any ideas, Dora? You probably know him best.'

Dora seemed mollified by this fact and flashed a smile at Scarlet. Signed, 'Sorry, Scarlet. Forgive me. Too much Deaf Pride. I didn't mean to be so harsh. I know you're Annie's best friend, so that means that you and me are fine.' She signed, *'You, me – linked.'* She put her two thumbs up at Scarlet, who stared back at her. In neutral. Unforgiving. Her collarbones and shoulders stuck out sharply, accentuating her thinness. Accentuating her frostiness. Dora carried on: 'But back to Ben. I'm still not convinced by him going missing. I mean, if the link between the murders is you, Annie, you can't include Ben. You might have made your peace with the boy, but you're not *mates*, are you? He's closer to *me*, and that's not really saying much. He's a sad boy. Lonely.'

She picked up her dog, as if for comfort, stroked it and signed, 'Has that Theo done something to him? Nasty little bastard. Nothing would surprise me in terms of Theo. He's...' She waggled her fingers, seeking the right sign. '...odd. Frightening. Not quite right.'

Annie held her hands aloft, ready to sign something, but stopped as she caught sight of Scarlet's face. Her flatmate had been looking up at Annie, now fully involved in the conversation. But then Annie watched as Scarlet's gaze dropped from

Annie's face, shifted downwards – transferring her eyes to something behind Annie.

Scarlet's expression froze.

Instant fear kicked in Annie's stomach, churning like a changeling baby wanting a speedy exit.

'*What*? Why are you looking like that?'

Annie turned and looked wildly around her, behind her. And then she saw it. Couldn't believe what she was seeing.

Eric walked through the conservatory doors, into the sitting room. He was doing a weird sort of dance, his whiskered nose grappling with the thing tied around his neck, fastened by a piece of ribbon. He pawed at it, tried escaping from it, and side-stepped into the room, worrying at the alien thing, moving like a dancing crab.

Ignoring the white square around his neck for the moment, Annie screamed in delight. She bent down and knelt at Eric level, picked him up and squished him into her chest. He started to struggle but she wouldn't let him go. She breathed him in, Eric's smell filling her nostrils, his whiskers tickling her face. Eventually she held him up in the air at arm's length, laughing with relief, incomprehension, and pure joy. 'Where have you *been*, little man?'

He struggled, his back legs bucking helplessly. She saw the wodge of tightly folded envelope secured to the ribbon around his neck by a staple gun. Eric's head moved from side to side, trying to rid himself of the white rectangle. He wasn't in pain, but Annie wanted to relieve him of it, wanted to calm him.

Annie reversed, Eric in her hands, and shoved Dora up the sofa using her hips. She put her cat between her legs, clamped her thighs together, making it impossible for Eric to move his torso and head. Reaching over him, she tried undoing the knot, her fingers shaking. Unable to untie it, she pulled the neatly folded envelope free – uncaring as she tore it. Before she released Eric, she kissed him, hard, on the space between his ears, ran her fingers around his neck to check for injuries and satisfied that he was unharmed, happily let him run off into the kitchen. Scarlet was already there, waiting to feed and water him. Sat on the floor, stroking him – a soppy expression on her face. Annie said, 'Scissors,' pointing at Eric's neck ribbon. She made chopping motions with her index and second finger. *Cut.*

Annie wiped tears away from her face and settled back, making herself ready for the message. At this precise moment in time, she didn't care what the fucking killer had to say – Eric was alive. Anything else she could cope with. It felt like a reprieve of sorts. A temporary happy ending. Ignoring the puzzled looks from Polly and Dora she read the note, neatly typed on an A4 piece of paper:

You must allow me the theatrics of this demonstration, Annie. I left you a vivid and colourful example of what I could have done. Proof of how easy killing your cat would have been, had I chosen to do so. Tabbies are all visually much of a muchness. Especially when they wear your cat's stolen collar. And have been brutalised to such an extent.

Just so you know, Eric didn't miss you. He was quite happy with me. I'd go so far as to say, happier with me. That cat would do anything for a treat. Even come to a waiting stranger's hands.

But I return him to you. Purely because I want to show you that I am not a monster.

I'm sure Eric's unfortunate stand-in

fooled you. As, alas, I appear to be doing. Fooling you with consummate ease. Give me the grace by taking your current situation seriously. But not too seriously. Because what is the point?

It's nearly time.

It's nearly over.

It's too late for you to be that serious about anything.

You've left it too late.

39

———————

B en. *I had to give him some respect. Credit where credit was due.
That was only fair. He'd come up to me on the street. He must
have been following me. Waited for me outside my flat. And then, as
bold as brass, he'd approached me. I looked enquiringly down at him,
trying for avuncular. Watched his eyes roam around, not wanting,
perhaps not daring, to look me in the eye. He signed, 'You told.'*

*'Told what to whom?' I assumed an expression of complete incom-
prehension and waggled my index finger from side to side: 'What?' I
looked thoroughly perplexed, because I was.*

*The boy was embarrassed, suddenly reluctant to say his piece.
'You know.'*

*I had gone for 'I've been struck by a thunderbolt facial expression'.
It wasn't difficult. I shook my head in real puzzlement.*

*More eye avoidance, and then the signs came flying from his
fingers like unwanted dirt. 'You told the police.'*

I found myself growing impatient with him. 'Told them what?'

'You know. About the sex. You know...'

*I didn't help him out. I was interested to see where he was going
with this. He shuffled his feet and rubbed his nose. Looked over my*

shoulder. *Signed without making eye contact. 'You told the police about the sexual abuse. No one else knows. Only you know. You told.'*

He exhaled and hung his head in shame. And blushed.

So there it was. The accusation. Finally. Like getting blood from the proverbial. And here's the joke. It wasn't I at all. The accusation was false. I am not one to betray secrets just because I can. Where would be the fun in that? But he thinks the accusation is true. Ergo, we have a problem. We have a loose end. And loose ends have to be cut. How do I know who else he may reveal this falsehood to? I do not want any unwarranted attention drawn to me.

I like to think that I can think whilst caught on the hop. And the back foot was undoubtedly where I now found myself. Of course I rallied. Rose to the occasion.

I shook my head in negation. 'Not me, Ben. I didn't tell anyone anything. Why would I? Maybe the police just worked it out for themselves.'

'How could they? How could they guess that?'

'Sexual abuse has come up with Martin. Perhaps the police just joined the dots, made a leap of faith. Unfortunately for you, they guessed right. But believe me, Ben, I would never betray you. Never. I can keep a secret. You know that.'

I put my two first fingers to my lips – schtum. Then, making a quick decision, signed, 'Why don't you come to my house. My other house. My real house. We could chat there.'

I waggled my eyebrows to indicate delights to come. 'I have beer there. Lots of it. We can have ourselves a little party. Just you and me.'

'But it's only the morning. I haven't even been home yet. Mum will be worried.'

I wafted my hand in front of my nose, and said, 'You smell like you've been out all night. Got a hangover?'

Ben grinned, feeling like a man. 'Yeah, got a crap hangover. Slept on the heath all night. Feel like shit.'

'Well, we can certainly fix that. Hair of the dog and all that. Follow me.' I smiled encouragingly.

And of course he followed. Why wouldn't he?

The boy had never been to the house before. No one had. Well, except for Toby and William. And they'd never left. Neither would Ben. Couldn't have a loose end out there, unravelling all over the place.

And so it was, that a second boy entered my world, my life, my reason for being.

His mind was fixated on the coming beer. Nothing would put him off that.

And of course, he looked forward to drinking with me. His mate. His chum. We were brothers-in-arms, staring adversity in the face and laughing. I offered him a feeling of solidarity. To enhance that, I slipped my arm around his shoulders and gave him a virile, manly squeeze.

Ben is big. And heavy. I recognise a liability when I am presented with one. And he most certainly fit that category. I needed to minimise the risk of all-out combat with him. Not minimise it. Eradicate it completely. He and I in a physical altercation — it would be no contest. I knew my limits. I wanted to avoid any actual fisticuffs. Because I would lose.

I was also slightly peeved at having to deal with him at all. It was like having to do some tiresome domestic chore.

We stood in the kitchen. Seeing the kitchen through Ben's eyes, I realise that things were indeed more than a little messy. And he only contributed to it. But he didn't seem fazed in the slightest by the less-than-perfect state of the worktops. The unwashed plates and mugs. Didn't notice the bolted down chairs.

Didn't even notice my dog.

He was blind to everything other than his own immediate needs. He turned to me and signed, 'Where's the beer, then?'

'Sorry. Where are my manners? There's a couple in the fridge. Help yourself.'

The boy ambled over – confident. Sure of himself. If only the poor fool knew. Beer would be the last thing on his mind. His dying thought. How very pedestrian.

I looked around. Several things came to mind. But I settled on an old cast-iron skillet which hung from a rack above the stove. I didn't have to tread quietly. Or creep about the place like some mouse. I was bold with my movements and intent. It wasn't as if Ben would notice my approach.

As he squatted in front of the open fridge, the interior light illuminated his face. He looked almost angelic with his cherub-like basin haircut. He reached in, eager – greedy. Focusing entirely on his alcoholic prize. I quickly slipped on a pair of latex gloves.

He didn't hear me coming. Too concentrated on his goal. The pan hit him squarely on his temple. It felled him with one swift blow. Just to make sure, I hit him again as he lay on the floor.

And then I put my face to his. I certainly couldn't feel his breath upon my cheek. I placed my hand on his chest. As if locked in some lover's clinch, our faces touching, I looked down the length of his body. Nothing. His chest didn't rise and fall. It had stopped. Dead as the proverbial dodo.

I smiled. Content. Satisfied. Triumphant.

Now what to do? I sat back on my heels, pan still in hand. I wasn't going to skewer this one. He wasn't part of the Game. He didn't warrant nor deserve the symbolic gesture.

But I could most certainly do the 'what-have-we-here?' in his mouth part of the Game. It would be a waste not to. Waste not, want not as I always say. And I'd thought of a little something. A little something that would sit well on the tongue. It amused me. But the timing was critical. I needed to make the very most of this opportunistic slaying.

My amusement at my plan was tempered by the fact that I seriously doubted whether anyone else would get the joke. But a moot point. It's not all about the laughs. And really, I am past caring what others think. This one's just for me.

And of course, it's especially for Annie.

I'm going to make it mind-bogglingly gratuitous. There will be no hidden meaning, no symbolism. Just me having fun.

I'm going to completely gross Annie out.

Simply because I can.

40

Saturday morning, the day of Dora's sixtieth birthday party. A party. It seemed surreal to even contemplate a birthday party. Balloons, streamers, cake and crisps. All wrong. Murder and parties. They didn't go. Like vomit and roses. Big clash.

Scarlet was working, leaving Annie feeling guilty at dumping the responsibility of the shop on to her flatmate's shoulders. But what else could she do? She certainly didn't have it in her to work.

So now Annie sat with Eric fast asleep on her lap. He had made himself secure and as small as was possible, one paw over his eye as if bothered by the light. The reappearance of Eric was the one ray of light in her mind, but her thoughts were still singed and blackened by too much death.

She'd played with a dry piece of toast, finding it impossible to swallow.

Glancing up at the whiteboard, she looked at the last line that she'd added. *Jesus Christ. It's all completely unthinkable.*

Adam – kicked to death: hearing aid in mouth
(Uncontrolled/overkill/opportunistic)

Toby – skewered in ear: green pencil shavings in mouth (Controlled/premeditated)/fed snacks
Annie – premediated attack/suggestion of putting something in mouth/knows both victims
William – skewered in ear: black Labrador's ear in mouth (Controlled/premeditated) fed snacks
Ben missing???

Staring at the whiteboard, she knew that there was something that she still couldn't quite remember. Something she'd just read. *Note to self – tell Crabb.* The doorbell flashed into the room, relieving her of the pressure of looking at the stark words. She almost ran in the hope that it was Crabb and peered through the peephole. Prayers answered. The DI shuffled into the flat. Held his thumb up in greeting.

She smiled in return. Lying. Got right down to it: 'Do you think they'll find Ben? Alive, I mean.'

'God knows. I can only hope so.'

Pointing her mug of coffee at the whiteboard, Annie said, 'There *must* be something that we're not seeing. Something so obvious we're missing it.'

The more Annie stared, the more the words looked strange and indecipherable. Completely unrelated. A random scrabble of letters meaning nothing. She continued to read the words; over and over again. Crabb stood next to her. Angled his head. Looked up at the ceiling. Said, 'You know what's been bothering me? The food. The snacks. Both Toby and William were fed "snacks". What does "snacks" mean?'

Annie frowned. 'Don't be stupid. You know what a snack is.'

'But in *this* specific context. Cakes, jelly, sandwiches, pork pie, jelly. Snacks. Like a picnic.' He sat down. 'But not a picnic. That doesn't feel right. We're missing a trick.'

Annie shook her head, lost in the conversation. Her mind

felt sluggish, unable to keep up. Crabb said, 'What sort of cake do you think it was?'

'How would I know?'

'Just wait. Wait. Let me think.'

Obligingly, Annie kept quiet and waited. Watched as Crabb stood up and made a phone call. His back to her. Ending the call, he spun round. 'I knew it. Just spoken to the pathologist. Asked what sort of cake it was. The food in Toby's stomach was barely digested as he was killed almost immediately after eating. Sorry.' He held up his hand, acknowledging the detail he'd gone into was difficult to listen to. Said, 'It was cake with icing. Standard sponge, jam and cream. With *icing*.'

'So? Why the excitement over icing? Lots of cakes have icing.'

'Birthday cakes have icing. I knew it. I fucking knew it. It's not just *snacks*. It's birthday party food. With a *birthday* cake. Dora's party tonight made me think of it. I'm right aren't I? It's bloody birthday party food.'

Annie felt her eyebrows stay suspended. Not convinced. Slowly she lowered them as she considered the theory. 'Not bad,' she said. 'Not bad at all. You may have got it. I'll add it to the list. It's definitely possible.'

'I think it's definitely more than possible. I think it's probable. You don't normally give a grown man that sort of food – it's what a child would be given. As a treat. A celebration. A birthday party. That's what the killer's doing. Re-enacting someone's birthday party.'

'Yeah, but whose?' She paused. 'If you're right. It's one giant leapfrog of a theory. You can't *know* you're right.'

'Yes, but supposing I am? It changes everything.'

'Does it? Where does it get us? Big deal, the killer knows someone who's had a birthday – useless information. Or he was the birthday boy himself. Again – big deal. That rules out no one and rules in everyone. Everyone has a birthday.'

She didn't know why she was being so negative. Crabb might be right. She left him looking pleased with himself, explaining that she was taking out the rubbish. He nodded vaguely at her, caught up in his theories.

Annie adjusted the shoulder strap of her striped vest and put on her flip-flops to take out the black bags: her once-weekly routine.

As she neared the rubbish area, she noticed that her bin was not where it should be. It wasn't quite flush with the wall but was instead standing slightly further out than it should.

She wrinkled her nose as she approached the black bin. The lid wasn't properly closed. *Strange.* It should be relatively empty. This was the first rubbish she'd put in there since they'd been emptied on Friday morning. But something was stopping the lid from shutting. She hesitated as she got nearer.

The smell of decay floated around the bin area.

Her bin.

Full of something that shouldn't be there. She closed her eyes. Turned her face to the sky. Felt the heat on her face. She thought that it might be the last thing she enjoyed for some time.

She forced herself to move closer. Within touching distance. She hesitated. *Fuck it*, she thought, and still at a distance, stuck her neck out to better understand what she was seeing.

A pair of trainers was her first thought, sticking out from a roll of carpet. It took several seconds to realise that the shoes still had feet in them. In fact, an entire body was attached. The figure was scrunched and crammed into the bin: its limbs lying awkwardly. They looked broken although the part of her brain that was still working with some clarity thought this was more an optical illusion. It was merely the stuffing of a big body into such a small space that looked upsetting. And so very wrong.

Careful not to touch anything, she took a step closer: almost on top of the bin now. To get a better look.

Now she could see only too clearly.

She gasped. Clutched at her throat. Stumbled back. Regained her balance. And then just stood there. Rooted to the spot. She knew she'd have to check again. To make sure. She greedily sucked warm, fresh air in through her open mouth. Tried to stop the dizzy feeling.

She walked towards the bin again. She bent and looked inside.

It was Ben.

He was dead.

The side of his head was smashed in and covered with dry blood.

And his eyes were missing.

She bent a little closer. And then she saw it. The real, full, unthinkable damage done. To a boy. A child.

His mouth was full. Full of his own eyes. The eyeballs had filmed over, but they were definitely eyes. They stared up at her: forever blind. She couldn't help but notice that they had ghost-like threads running from them. As if they had been ripped from his sockets, taking all tendons, nerves, and muscles with them. In one fell swoop.

And now they sat in his mouth, distending his lips: too much to fit comfortably. His mouth stuffed with two eyeballs. His eyeballs.

She concentrated on not being sick.

Carefully she backed away. Frightened that if she made an unexpected noise or movement, it would somehow re-energise the boy. Make him leap from his plastic coffin, like some ghoul released from the depths of hell.

She walked away, back into the house and back to Crabb. Said, 'I've found Ben. Dead. He's in the bin.'

Crabb paled. Rushed from the room. Leaving her alone.

It was only as she sat back on the kitchen chair that the scream finally came. She screamed until her throat hurt and her head throbbed. She screamed and screamed and screamed. And then her voice deserted her. Unexpectedly and suddenly. Leaving her numb, physically and mentally.

She stood up shakily and ran her face under the tap, then allowed the water to drip from her face. She found Scarlet's stash of cigarettes in the third drawer down in the kitchen. Her hands scrabbled frantically for them; they fell from her grip again and again as her fingers trembled. Finally, she managed to light one.

Drops of water fell onto the table whilst she sat drawing deeply on the cigarette, as if it could save her.

41

Scarlet hovered about the place, unable to settle. Disappeared into the kitchen.

Annie was with Crabb in her sitting room. Déjà vu. Sunlight came through the French windows, the whiteboard casting a rectangular shadow onto the carpet. He sat next to her on the sofa, holding her hand stiffly. She felt rigid. Paced up and down. Annie turned to him: 'Ben in a bin?' she said, her voice and expression full of disbelief.

She giggled and then stopped abruptly. Knew that hysteria was just hovering under the surface, ready to erupt at the slightest provocation. It sounded almost like a joke. 'What do you call a boy in a bin? Ben. Ben has been binned.' Alliteration gone mad.

She needed to keep calm. Her hands started to shake in Crabb's. He reassuringly squeezed them. Looked into her eyes. 'Drink some of that,' he said, nodding at the mug of sweet tea beside her.

'I don't want any. Again with the bloody sweet tea. It doesn't cure anything. Believe me, I know.' Annie pushed it away and put her head between her knees, feeling faint. Looked up only when she felt a hand on her shoulder.

Scarlet stood over her and was pushing a healthy slug of brandy at her. 'Drink this.'

Annie coughed and spluttered at the harsh taste but took another gulp. She held the empty glass out to Scarlet. 'More.' She sipped at it this time.

Gradually her breathing calmed and she finally met Crabb's eyes. 'I'm okay. Really. I'm fine.' She knew she was lying but allowed herself to pretend a bravado. It made her feel better. Grounded her.

Knowing that Crabb wanted to go outside, wanted the facts from the pathologist, from the team of police officers and SOCOs, she said, 'It's okay. You can go. I'm fine here with Scarlet.'

Glancing at her friend, Annie realised that Scarlet looked as frightened as Annie felt.

'But before you go, Crabb, why wasn't Ben skewered? Like Toby and William?'

Crabb's face attempted a sympathetic look. 'I don't think Ben's part of the pattern,' he said.

Annie turned on him quickly. 'Not part of the pattern? Based on *what*? Did you see what he had in his mouth.'

'I saw, Annie, I saw. Firstly, there's no skewer. That's an important omission. It means something. I'm guessing he *had* to be killed. But he's not included in the killer's grand plan: Ben's like Adam. Collateral damage.'

Annie felt like she might be sick.

He said, 'From the injury to Ben, the taking out of his eyes, I'd guess that he was killed because he saw something.'

Annie threw herself back on the sofa and slumped down. Locked eyes with Crabb, who had gone back to perch on the armchair opposite.

'That's not necessarily true,' she said. 'That he'd seen something. Remember, you're talking about Deaf victims. It might mean that he'd seen something like a conversation. He could have, for want of a better way of putting it, "heard" something.'

'Yes, of course,' Crabb said and nodded. 'Or it could be just a sick joke from the killer. Putting Ben's eyes in his mouth. "I'm looking at you" type of thing. Just to completely freak you out. This man's very, very sick.'

Annie up-tilted her chin, acknowledging his words. Crabb said, 'Do you think they'll cancel the party tonight out of respect?'

'No. They won't cancel it,' Annie said. 'I think the community is frightened. Too much is happening too quickly. They'll feel safer all together. It doesn't mean they don't care. It'll turn into an opportunity to respect the dead. A celebration in itself. Grim, but kind.'

She shook her head: weary. Bone weary. Dead weary. Her voice felt one dimensional. *She* felt one dimensional. But carried on: 'And don't be surprised by the number of people there. I can guarantee every Deaf man and his dog, plus children, will be there. Even hearing children and the occasional hearing husband, wife, partner, whoever, will be there. Some of the older ones from the Deaf School will come. The Deaf love parties. It's one of the only opportunities they have to get together and just be who they are. Signing without hearing people staring at them, as if they're something from a circus show.'

She stood. Said, 'I need to be alone.' Annie moved quickly to her room, suddenly aching to be on her own. The adrenaline after finding Ben, still swamped her, like a burst water pipe: it coursed around her body like raw sewage. Frantic, she reinforced her feeling of relative safety by moving into the corner of her bedroom, her back to the wall. Hiding. Making herself small. Her knees bent. She huddled. Sitting there, she felt violated, emotionally raped. Wanted a shower. Couldn't. Couldn't be naked – too vulnerable, too exposed.

It seemed like forever, that she squatted there, waiting for rescue.

And then she realised the only person who could rescue her was herself. So she stood up. Pretended anger. How dare someone try and frighten her? She wouldn't put up with it. As she'd told everyone, she'd be fine. She always was. She was a survivor. Alone now, with all her personal things around her, everything familiar and hers, she felt better. Stronger. She had a fight on her hands. But she was ready. Bring it on.

'Come and get me, you bastard. You want me, here I am,' she said out loud. 'Here I am.'

She looked at herself in the mirror, crouched as if ready for combat. She knew she wasn't, but still faked it. She smiled at her reflection. *Fuck it*, she thought.

She strode back into the sitting room to be with Scarlet. Crabb was still there. He rubbed his eyes and said, 'The killer murdered Ben in the most brutal way possible. The eyes in the mouth are of course important. Maybe the killer saw him as a threat? So best to get rid of the boy. No messing. Quick. It prob-ably just amused the killer, putting Ben in your bin.'

'Yeah. Cracking sense of humour,' said Annie. She kept her face deadpan: dead. 'People are dying, Crabb. It's enough I've agreed to come to the party tonight. Don't ask any more of me. And Ben. Poor Ben. Bloody hell. Will you tell Maggie?'

She spoke slowly. Ignored the fact that Crabb wanted more from her. She didn't have more. He nodded. 'Of course.'

Crabb seemed to have momentarily switched off. She saw him watch Eric stroll past. Saw him smile to himself. He dug into his pocket and handed Annie a small red box. Inside was a tissue-wrapped package. She raised her eyes in question. He said, 'For Eric. Sorry it's not red but thought you might want a different coloured collar. It's blue,' he said. Unnecessarily. He blushed. Said, 'I couldn't get the exact same name tag either but hope this one will do. It says "Eric".'

Annie's eyes swam with tears as she unwrapped the new collar and name tag. Her whole face lightened. She put her arm out to him, to thank him. 'You knew, didn't you, Crabb? How did you know? You're not even surprised that Eric's back. Alive.'

'I'm bloody relieved, though. After the cat's body was checked late last night for any forensics that the killer might have left – which he didn't, by the way – I asked them to see if the cat was microchipped as you'd told me he was. He wasn't and it hadn't been removed. So I knew it couldn't be Eric. I was hoping he'd turn up. Wasn't sure what to do if he didn't, but he did. Thank God.'

'But why? Why didn't he kill Eric? Why kill a random cat? How did you know?'

'Because this man is a game-player. He's killed Toby. And then William. Now Ben. He wouldn't bother with killing your cat. Too easy. It would be like underkill for him. Not enough impact. He's killed four people, so killing a cat wouldn't be worth it. Better to upset you. Tease you. Exert and display his control over you. He's just taunting you. I went with my gut, and thank God, I was right. Think of Eric, now. I'm not saying forget all the dead, but at least enjoy the return of your cat.'

'He's not a person, I know that. He's just a cat. But I do love him. Thank you so much, Crabb. Really. You're a sweet man. And a clever one. Thanks.'

Crabb did a huffing movement with his mouth. Embarrassed. He stood up and said, 'Anyway, I appreciate you coming to Dora's party tonight, Annie. I really do. I need you there with me. You know these people better than I ever will. I want you to tell me what you see.'

She returned a resigned shrug, turning Eric's new collar in her hand, and said, 'Okay. Give me a lift. That way I can get drunk if the need arises.'

Crabb nodded his thanks and said, 'I just need a quick chat with the pathologist. Why don't you have a rest?'

Annie remained silent. Had nothing to say. About anything.

42

Crabb hated to leave Annie, but he couldn't mother her now. Or whatever it was that he was doing to her. His brain was still going through the birthday food theory. He should have got it earlier. He knew it made sense. With Toby's singed hair, a birthday cake with candles seemed a more than probable theory. Had he been forced to blow out birthday candles at some macabre party? Had his loose lock of hair, as described by his mother, caught a quick lick of the tiny flame? Had William joined in with the blowing out of the candles?

Was this indeed all about a recreation of a birthday party? If so, a recent one or a long-ago one?

And why?

Why would anyone want to recreate a birthday party?

Still thinking, he joined the disaster outside.

Dr Moore grunted at Crabb's approach and spoke before Crabb had even asked the question.

'I'll give you a rough estimate of time of death. Nothing else until after I do the post. He's been dead no more than twenty-four hours. And probable cause of death – please note the use of the word "probable" – is blunt force trauma to the head. Unless I open him up and he's got galloping cancer, in which case I'll review my findings.'

Crabb thanked him sourly.

The pathologist's voice dragged Crabb's attention back. 'His eyes appear to have been forcibly and manually gouged from their sockets.'

'Is that possible?' said Crabb, not looking at the body. 'I mean, without cutting. Just pulling them out? No tool or specialist equipment needed?'

The pathologist looked up at Crabb. 'That's what I said, yes. Manually ripped from his face. What specialist equipment did you have in mind? Over-the-counter-manual-eye-poppers?'

Crabb looked back at Dr Moore and kept his facial expression neutral. He didn't know what he'd meant; conceded that it wasn't the most intelligent question he'd ever asked. He went to turn from the pathologist but Dr Moore spoke, making Crabb stop.

'So, your Deaf *friend*,' the pathologist stressed the last word, making it sound vaguely salacious, 'has found yet another body. What's she doing, going for a gold medal for the most corpses found by one person in one week? She's doing a bang up job.'

'What are you insinuating, Moore? I think that even you can concede that Annie has been through more than enough for one person in the last few days. Have you no sensitivity *at all*? She's a *victim*.'

Taking Crabb by surprise, the doctor suddenly sprang to his feet and spoke, his voice rising in anger: 'Do you think I enjoy this?' He waved a hand towards Ben. 'This is the second child that I'm going to have to do a post-mortem on. Do you think I like cutting up little boys? Children? Why don't you do your job and catch this fucker?'

The man had a heart after all it seemed, but Crabb replied,

'Fuck off, Moore. I'm doing my best with very little to go on. You do your job, I'll do mine.'

The pathologist turned his back, saying, 'Seems to me your little woman friend is behaving like a fucking cadaver dog.' He laughed, which then turned into more of a snicker, and Crabb turned away from him, disgusted.

A noise from one of the windows above Annie's flat made Crabb look up. DS Moss, whom Crabb recognised from the station, had opened the casement window and was shouting his name.

'Thought you might be interested, sir. Got a neighbour here, a Miss Henrietta Garber, who saw a man arrive with a roll of carpet in the middle of the night. Do you want to talk to her?'

'I'll be right up.'

Once he'd reached the first floor flat, Crabb found himself having to bend his head down in order to speak to a tiny woman – beady eyes and white hair, her hands clasped on top of a cane, her feet planted shoulder-width apart. She must have been in her seventies. Her hand shot out from its perching point and grabbed his.

'I'm Miss Garber. I've just been speaking to your sergeant, here. I'm told I might have seen something interesting last night. Pity I didn't realise it at the time.'

She smiled helplessly and Crabb's heart sank a little. 'What did you see?'

'I wouldn't even have mentioned it if DS Moss here hadn't asked me outright, "Did you see anyone on foot or in a car or van last night?" But I did. I saw a man. A man getting out of a white van.'

'Can you describe him? Did you see his face?' Crabb attempted to rein in his excitement, kept his face impassive but receptive.

'Sorry, no. He wore one of those hard hats that workmen

have. A white one. And I only saw him from above. I thought he must be a little hot with that hat on, bearing in mind this heat, and because that was precisely why I was at the window myself at three o'clock in the morning. Too hot. Trying to get some air. So I never saw his face. He kept his head down. No reason for him to look up, I suppose. I just assumed it was someone putting rubbish in our bins. Admittedly, a strange time to be dropping anything off, but people do work such strange hours now, don't they? I'm so sorry if I've been a stupid old fool, but it seemed all quite normal to me.'

Crabb wondered how anyone could think it normal to be depositing a roll of carpet in the middle of the night, but she spoke again as if she'd heard his disbelief: 'It was what he was wearing that made it seem... well, not suspicious in any way. After I first spotted him, with the carpet on his shoulders, he disappeared from my view, I now know, into the bin area, and then he reappeared and just walked away. Without said carpet. My point is, I didn't really think anything of it as he was wearing a yellow high-vis jacket. *And* the hard hat and white van. Naturally I assumed it must therefore be somehow official.'

'Can you describe the van?'

'No, sorry. I'm not very good at cars. Or vans. It was just a white van, you know, a normal white van. No markings or anything. I'm so sorry.'

'Don't worry, Miss Garber. Thanks anyway. I don't suppose you saw him limp? Or notice any other obvious physical disability?'

Miss Garber shook her head. Crabb realised they were still holding hands. He squeezed hers a little tighter, and said, 'If you wouldn't mind, the sergeant here will take down all your details and someone will come around and take a statement.'

'Thank you, and again, I'm so sorry.' Her eyes filled with

tears. 'Such an awful thing to do. To kill a boy. Is it true? Was there a boy in that carpet?'

Crabb smiled at her gently, not wanting to cause her further distress. Squeezed her shoulder and left. DS Moss caught up with him in the hall. 'If I may, sir? I've been working on this case. More in the background. Chasing things up, you know, statements, interviews–'

'I haven't got time for your résumé, Moss. What do you want?'

'That's what I'm trying to tell you, sir. I've been taking statements from the deaf, as I know how to sign. With an interpreter, to keep it legal,' he added quickly, 'but I'm a CODA.'

Irritated, feeling the pressure of time, Crabb said, 'What's a CODA?'

'You know, I'm a Child of Deaf Adults. It's just an expression really, an acronym. But it means that I'm a fluent signer as both my parents were deaf. Thought I could be better used tonight at the party. Lots of officers are coming down, about ten others I think, including Peters, but I thought I could look after someone specific if you needed me to? Because I can sign.'

Crabb had already gone over the basic surveillance teams for tonight but if Moss could sign properly, could pass as a deaf person, he had just the job for him. A little juggling would be on the cards, but now Peters could look after Annie, Fiona and Polly. Crabb didn't think they'd be unhappy going around as a trio. Not after the discovery of Ben's body. He nodded at Moss: 'As you can sign, you can look after Dora Potts. Take her with a pinch of salt, be nice – she can be a little on the sharp side, don't let her out of your sight, hold her hand if need be, but whatever you do, don't lose her. Not for a minute, got it? Do not let her out of your sight. At all.'

'Yes, sir. Thank you.'

'Re-double efforts on white vans. Check surrounding CCTV

and yes,' he held his hand up, 'I'm well aware that this road has no cameras but check the area – can't have been that much traffic on the road at three o'clock in the morning. Something *must* have been captured somewhere on film en route to one of the dump sites.'

Moss nodded quietly, writing in his notebook. Crabb said, 'The other officers coming down to the party tonight – any of them sign?'

'Not like me, no. Two have a bit of sign language, but it's very basic. It'll be better than nothing though.'

'Will it? I don't want them looking like bloody incompetent fools, with flashing bloody Belisha beacons on their heads, *looking* like policemen. They need to blend in; a bit of subtlety wouldn't go amiss.'

'Noted. And before you go, why did you ask Miss Garber if the man had any disabilities?'

'Because the killer has a sense of humour. He's pretended a limp already. Can't you see me laughing?'

43

As they entered the Deaf Club at half past eight that evening, Crabb, Annie, Fiona, Polly and Peters came to an abrupt standstill. The sheer volume of people stopped their progress. The hall was packed with revellers already in brittle and jangled high spirits who were rooted to the spot, drinking and signing. All the lights blazed. There was a general smell of alcohol and sweat.

Crabb didn't think the vanity of the killer would be able to resist the temptation of showing off tonight at the party. He was a grand-stander. And now there was an audience to perform to.

He hoped he'd done everything possible to keep people safe. Specifically the four women: Annie, Fiona, Polly and Dora. Annie and the three people who meant something to her in this strong but insular community.

He worried and cared about all the potential suspects, but Annie was his number one priority, because Annie was the number one priority for the killer.

Game on.

He turned to Annie, who was jammed up behind him. Squashed behind her, both Fiona and Polly. Immediately behind them, Peters tried politely to avoid too much physical contact with Polly. Like a bloody courteous queue for the toilet.

At Crabb's request, Annie was wearing a straw hat – easy to keep track of. He said, 'You weren't joking. Wasn't expecting this many people.'

Music thumped out of huge speakers, and Crabb had to remind himself that he didn't need to shout at Annie.

Placing her hand on the top of her hat, she gestured with her head, indicating that they should push on through the throng. Try and find some space. Crabb nodded and held his hand up in greeting to people as they squeezed their way across the room. The Deaf turned to watch their progress: a lot of the faces showed relief at Crabb's presence. As if they somehow felt safer now that there was someone official here. As if Crabb could protect them.

Although superficially it all looked very jolly, you didn't have to look too hard to see the unhappy leaks that had sprung in the Deaf Community. The fear behind the gaiety was visible. Strangely Ben's death had made more of an impact than any other death so far.

Everyone was playing a role, it seemed to Crabb. A 'let's pretend we're not frightened' game. But their forced smiles failed to reach their eyes, their laughter failed to conceal their nervousness, their signing looked frenetic. Party hats were perched on heads, but managed only to look disturbing, mawkish and surreal. It all felt false and out of place.

He turned to Annie. 'Why's the music so loud if everyone's deaf?' Crabb covered his ears and still found himself shouting. It was impossible not to.

'We can feel the bass. And that's why everyone's waiting for the fireworks tonight. Something to watch *and* feel.'

She seemed less taken aback by the crowd; she had after all warned him of the expected numbers. He'd listened to her but hadn't envisaged *this* many people. Hoped his lack of understanding about the Deaf and their love of parties – and the sheer volume of people he had to police – wouldn't come up and bite him in the arse.

Annie melted into the heaving mass. Crabb tried to grab her but she was gone. He panicked and gestured at Peters to follow the three women as they moved as one, further away from him. The young policeman nodded and disappeared into the crowd.

Great swathes of bunting and streamers festooned the room. People's hands flashed through the air as they communicated fiercely, holding on to their glasses or cans of beer and signing with one hand. To Crabb, their signing looked like a mess of many hands, painting pictures that he couldn't see. A private viewing – accessible only to those in the know.

Most were dressed in shorts and T-shirts. Once alabaster skin now turned an unbecoming lobster red was the general sore impression on display.

Blue and red balloons danced in tethered couplets in the air. The blue ones emblazoned with the word 'Happy'; the red ones, 'Birthday'. Some had become detached from each other had floated in solo flight upwards, coloured umbilical cords dangling in their wake. A small collection of 'Happys' were stuck to the ceiling. A few burst 'Birthdays' lay shrivelled on the floor like used and discarded condoms.

Ahead of him, he saw Annie and her two friends. Peters hovered behind them. Glancing around, Annie saw him and made a 'follow me' motion with her hand.

He pushed politely, and then not so politely to keep up; aware that amongst this crowd was the killer. But how to recognise him? How to stop him taking another victim? Crabb felt an unease settle and flutter in his stomach. Felt the weight of responsibility on his shoulders.

As he passed through the crush, people looked uncomfortable, as though they were too frightened to leave. Too frightened to stay. There was too much manic laughter. Too much drunkenness so early on. It all felt on the verge of breaking. Hysteria lurked too near the surface. A mob mentality threatened: people presenting a united front against an unknown enemy.

The community felt ready to shatter around him.

He watched as Annie waited for him, his progress slow. Trying to think how to control a crowd this big. He didn't have the resources. Ten undercover coppers. It wasn't enough. No way.

Fucking fat Docherty and his budget.

Finally he stood by her side, hot, sweating. Worrying. The three women each held a glass in their respective hands – Fiona looking blank, Polly old, and Annie, young and vulnerable: eyes blank, her expression unfathomable.

Crabb said, 'I don't want you taking that hat off this evening. Makes you easier to spot, harder to lose.' He smiled, wanting her to relax. 'I'm making you sound like a parcel whose delivery status is being tracked.'

'It's a fair analogy. I'll try not to end up in the lost and found,' she said.

He'd had to lean in extra close to her in order to hear. He pulled away quickly, embarrassed by their proximity.

Crabb lifted his nose. Identified immediately the smoky smell of a barbeque. Motioning for his entourage to fall in behind him, he followed the smell, weaving in and out of the crushing crowd. Found himself in a courtyard. He turned to Annie who trailed behind him, like a toddler, her head down. She looked unhappy and frightened. He squeezed her hand, acutely aware of the precarious safety of this female crocodile line under his protection. Hoped... no, more than that, *prayed* that he and his team were enough to stop further bloodshed.

The courtyard was bigger than he had imagined, although

little effort had been made to make it anything other than a place for bins, and smoking. He looked around in surprise at the space.

A large and messy space crammed full of people.

A perfect venue for a party.

A perfect venue in which to hide.

A useless place to be if you wanted to watch people. The crowd was just too big. He stumbled and realised that he had almost trod on a child. Irritated, he asked Annie, 'Where's Dora?'

'Should be out here, I'd expect. For the fireworks. And the barbeque afterwards.'

They both glanced around but couldn't see her. Crabb texted Moss. Got an immediate response:

Don't worry. Dora's with me.

Crabb could see the pockmarked Edward. He stood behind a huge gas grill set up along one of the walls. With fork in hand, and paper hat on head, he alone looked ready for action, immune to the dark mood that gripped most of the guests. He smiled happily, alone and totally oblivious to the strained atmosphere.

Edward looked keen to start and prodded and poked at his assorted meats, checking and re-checking the flames. He was clearly enjoying himself. Either he did not care about the down-beat feel that surrounded him, or was not aware of it. Crabb guessed that the former was nearer the truth. He wondered why.

Out of nowhere, Dora appeared, carrying a bowl of lettuce leaves under one flabby arm and under the other, her dog was squashed and held in position like a rugby ball. She nodded at them: her smile tired. Worried. Frightened. Stopping to kiss Annie she managed a thumbs-up without dropping food or animal, nodded in a sort-of apology, before carrying on to her destination. She looked older, her body stretched with a tightness that looked ready to pop beneath her pink flowered dress. Conversely, her fat face sagged more than usual, like a rubber band that had lost some of its elasticity overnight.

Depositing the lettuce on a trestle table, she immediately found a seat, collapsed onto it and held the dog securely on her lap. She was out of breath and looked lonely sitting there on her own until DS Moss went over to her. Started signing. He'd appeared smoothly and confidently out of nowhere. At ease. At least someone was. But he shouldn't be. The situation was not one to be at ease in. Crabb said to Annie, 'What's he saying to Dora?'

Annie peered across people's heads, until she had Dora and the young man in her sights. 'I can't believe you're only sixty. You look amazing. Sure I couldn't get you a drink?' She spoke the words and rolled her eyes. On hearing Annie's interpretation, Crabb thought the sergeant was overdoing the charm just a tad – smarmy little git but was happy that he was showing some initiative. He just hoped he wasn't showing off and wallowing in his own brilliance – that he fully understood his task. Keep his eye on Dora. At all times. It wasn't rocket science.

Crabb glanced at Annie. She was safe. Ditto Fiona and Polly. Dora was being looked after by Moss. All he needed now was an interpreter. Quite a few had been asked, but he looked out for Sam. Wanting to stick with what he knew. It was now up to him to do what he did best.

Understand the people who surrounded him. Get a feel for them.

Find the killer.

44

The air was sticky and Annie's hatband was sweaty. She wore her hair down and bits of wayward straw felt more and more prickly as the minutes ticked by: she stopped herself from scratching her scalp. Thinking of Scarlet, she wished that she'd asked her to come tonight, but had instead asked her to babysit Eric. Stupid really, but it was one thing less to worry about.

Those that could had crowded into the courtyard and it was now absolutely packed. Annie was swept along by the sudden surge of people and got separated from Crabb. She turned in panic and with relief found Peters beaming down at her. He held his thumbs up to her. She nodded sadly but was grateful for his presence. She looked around for Fiona, who had also got detached from their little group. Fiona had been immediately surrounded by four, then five men: excited, predatory, anticipatory. Like kids round jelly. It seemed Fiona wasn't Deaf enough to be accepted in the Deaf Community, but she was deaf enough to fuck.

Looking at Peters, she realised they were now a group of two; but she could see Fiona move away from the men and take hold of Polly's hand. At least they were both within touching distance. Nearly. Annie felt alone.

One person lost in an ocean of people.

She watched Dora stand from her seat, dog in hand, and take centre stage, gazing out at her birthday audience. Her normal expression of superiority had deserted her, her face somehow haunted and distressed. Dora waved her hand, in a queenly manner, to summon Sam. He stepped forward and stood opposite her, his back to the crowd. Whatever Dora wanted to say, she wanted the hearing partners and children to hear it. And the policemen who stood awkwardly, ill at ease and uncomfortable.

It was to be a toast to the dead, Annie guessed, and Dora wanted it heard. The older woman held a glass in the air and Annie could see Sam speak out the words for all the un-deaf.

'This is a toast for a boy called Adam Jacobs. I didn't know him. But he is dead. As is Toby, William and Ben. We miss them. We will always miss them.'

People lowered their heads in respect.

A short and sweet eulogy. But what else could you say? Absolutely diddley-squat; Annie knew that much from personal experience. After she had found Ben this morning, Fiona and Polly had come round. For support. Whatever that meant. But Annie had almost wept when she had seen Fiona. Her old school friend had held her, hugged her and kissed her on the cheek. Polly had done much the same. But this was the first time that Annie had seen Dora since Ben had been found. She looked sad and defeated; clearly not enjoying her birthday.

Or life in general.

Four women bound by one maniac.

Four dead young men bound by that same one maniac.

Christ only knew how many other lives had been affected, but the grief in the courtyard felt heavy. A solid thing.

The crush of people didn't move for a good two minutes as they stood, their heads on their chests, their hands clasped together, their drinks placed at their feet. It felt like forever. Some openly cried, others were dry-eyed, and still more just looked frightened and bewildered.

Dora raised her head and without smiling, scanned the faces before her. Her flock. The expressions that Annie could see were loving, and in return, Dora's face reflected their emotion. She signed, 'Enjoy the fireworks and thank you for coming.'

Annie found herself squinting in the sudden darkness and reached out to make sure Peters was still there. She didn't bother turning around as she recognised his hand as it perched on her left shoulder. Possessive.

She watched Edward, now armed with a box of extra-long matches, as he made his way to the desolate patch of dried baked earth at the back. He laughed merrily. Annie thought he was at the wrong party.

The air quality and mood subtly changed: it bristled with a desperate anticipation of something nice, something normal to come.

The Deaf unashamedly and gratefully threw off their collective sadness like an unwanted shroud and instantly switched their faces from grieving and frightened men and women, into overexcited children. Most were already holding their burning sparklers in their hands, swirling them in huge loops, making patterns in the night air.

Someone thrust a sparkler into her hand and lit it. She looked down at a small deaf man who she knew quite well, who smiled up at her and nodded, as if they had entered into a secret pact, before disappearing into the crowd. Annie smiled back, grateful. Not sure what she was grateful for, but she silently thanked him for his acknowledgement of her. Perhaps of her pain.

More likely forgiveness that it was she whose bin Ben had ended up in. That fact was known by everyone. It made her feel like the Grim bloody Reaper. The bringer of death into the community. Shrugging the thought off, she scanned the faces around her, wanting to be with someone she knew. Anyone would do. It was too late to find a friend or get nearer to Fiona and Polly. The fireworks loomed nearer, as Edward held a long flaming match in the air, his hands clasped together, as if it were an Olympic torch. Despising his inappropriate happiness, she briefly closed her eyes.

Self-consciously she stood there, holding her own sparkler. Isolated. Peters dithered behind her not wanting to intrude. She couldn't carry on ignoring him. He was standing on her heels. Pivoting, she faced him and with relief saw a very sober Fiona hand in hand with Polly. The two women approached, under the watchful eye of Peters. Annie smiled at them and said, 'Thanks, Peters. You're making me feel safe.'

He wasn't. It was a lie. But she wanted to be kind. He nodded once at her. Looked ridiculously young. Stupidly flattered. She said, 'You *are* allowed to talk to me. Otherwise it'll become awkward, you hovering at my shoulder and me cowering like a big girly.'

'I'd never call you a big girly.'

She smiled at him, more warmly: 'No, you're right. I'm not a big girly. Never that.'

She watched as Peters' face flushed in the light of her sparkler. Giving it to him she watched as it died immediately in his fingers and he smiled self-consciously. Fiona slipped her hand into Annie's, Polly placed her hand around Annie's waist and they all gazed up.

The fireworks had started. Jumping Jacks were lit and banged and popped with vigour and colour. Soon fireworks shot high into the sky, falling like tears of light, weeping reds, blues, and greens into the night. The smell of sulphur came to her; it hung in the air with no breeze to move it. White plumes of burning rockets were visible against the black of the evening.

She quickly glanced around her. Every single face was angled skyward. They looked utterly enthralled by the spectacle. As the rockets started, she could feel the excitement swell. The deep bass of the booms as the rockets exploded made the Deaf laugh with delight. They oohed and aahed at every explosion. They were spellbound. Very few were signing. They all seemed captivated by the visual and auditory spectacle before them. A lot of them held their hands to their chests as a particularly loud firework banged its way out of sight, high into the sky, leaving sparkling entrails in its wake. Then it fizzled and died.

Annie needed to escape the crush of people. Felt suddenly hemmed in and claustrophobic. Nodding at Fiona and Polly, tipping her head in the direction of the side door, Annie pulled her attached DS along behind her. They all slipped out of the door into the alley and escaped the party. Peters trying to pull her back, but then following as she gave him no choice.

She wanted to watch the finale in the alleyway on her own but had to admit that she did feel a bit safer with the young policeman at her side. Fiona and Polly stood a few feet away, more relaxed now that they too were free of the physical constraints of too many people. They all turned their faces upward. Waiting.

Annie held her breath as the bangs grew in size, each one getting bigger and bigger. The last rocket actually made her jump – the air and ground unexpectedly shuddering with the vibration. It was like a clap of thunder. She placed her hand to her chest as she felt the deep resonance of the noise reverberate within her body. She watched as the last fountain of colour fell, glittering and sparkling and finally spluttering out into oblivion.

And then there was nothing. Only the smell lingered and a faint pall of smoke.

She turned and the four of them continued to walk down the alley at the back and around to the front of the Deaf Club.

As she rounded the corner, she bumped straight into Martin, and couldn't help the little squeak of surprise that escaped her mouth. He was drunkenly crying and tried to grab her. She was too quick for him and retreated a pace or two. His signs were sloppy, his brain too drunk to make clear gestures. But Annie understood him: 'I want to see Dora. Tell her I'm sorry. It's not my fault. She doesn't understand. Please get her for me. It's her birthday. She's my friend.'

Peters stepped between them, pushing Martin away from her. 'Get back, Martin. Go on, back.' Peters made shooing motions with his fingers, and then placed both his hands on Martin's shoulders steering him backwards and away – out of Annie's space.

Martin looked a mess; his shirt was untucked and his hair was greasy. His eyes were wild and skittered about the place. He was clearly frightened at being out in public. Even he must understand that he was no longer a welcome part of the community. He'd been deleted.

She turned her back on him and glanced up to find a flock of Deaf faces, angry faces, jutting forwards in their direction from the shoulders of a large group of men who stood outside the entrance. The skin on her arms puckered with fear as the fine hairs on them stood to attention – flight or fight.

The anger wasn't directed at her, but she knew it was coming. Physically coming. They were going to beat the shit out of Martin. Martin the paedo. Martin the murderer. Martin the big bad bogeyman.

Why had he come? What had he been thinking? What did he expect? For*give*ness?

He was a fool.

She held her breath as the front doors opened and more men, looking for a fight, approached en masse. They spilled out like ants but advanced like beasts: lips drawn back, furrowed brows, balled fists. She saved herself at the last minute. Swerved the tide of flying fists as they descended upon Martin, who was still too near her. Side-stepping around Peters, by-passing the mob, giving them a wide berth and aiming herself like an arrow, intent on its target – she ran to the relative sanctuary of the motionless Fiona and Polly.

'Move, move,' she signed to them. 'Get in inside. We'll go round the back again. *Move.*'

The two women ran in front of her, but Annie came to a stop. Maggie Downing, Ben's mother, stood there; as still as a statue, ashen, stony-faced. Annie gently but firmly pushed her back, out of the way of the violence. But Maggie stood her ground.

'What are you doing here, Maggie? Come on. We've got to go. There's a fight. You'll get hurt. Come inside.'

'Do you think I care? I came here to see my Ben's world. His Deaf World that I was never a part of. Is this it? I was hoping it would be a happy world. A happi*er* world. That's what I always hoped it was for him. But this...' She pointed over Annie's shoulder at the accelerating brawl. 'They're just animals. It's not what I imagined for my child. This... this fighting. This hatred. This disrespect. My son is dead, and people are fighting. They're off their faces, out of control like it's any old party. They've already forgotten. They've forgotten Ben's dead. I know it's Dora's birthday party, but it was also a party for my son. His last party. I came here in his honour. I wish I hadn't.'

'They haven't forgotten, Maggie. They haven't. I'm so sorry.' Her words felt cheap but still she hadn't discovered any words that were strong enough to convey sympathy to a mother for the unimaginable death of her child.

'Don't feel sorry for me. I'm going now. I shouldn't have come. It was just a way to feel closer to Ben. But it was a mistake. I didn't think I could feel any worse. Any more sad. But I was wrong.'

She pushed past Annie and calmly skirted the tangled mass of people throwing punches at Martin. Then she turned again. Said, 'Why your bin. Why put Ben in *your* bin?'

Again, Annie felt guilt cut through her and decided to lie. Wanting to distance herself from the responsibility of Ben's death. 'I don't know, Maggie. Really I don't. I'm so sorry. If there's anything I can do.'

Again with the platitudes and clichés. Maggie just stared at her, her sober eyes unwavering. Then she said, 'It doesn't really matter, does it? Anyway, bye.' Turning, she passed the fight: unafraid and untouchable. And she walked away into the night, her head bent down, watching her own feet as they stepped slowly away from the Deaf World.

Annie felt like screaming with frustration. She put a hand to her head, holding her stupidly jaunty straw hat in place. She felt like a badly dressed mannequin – wearing clothes that did not meet the overall specifications of the brief. It bothered her. Feeling out of place in this particular landscape she quickly took off the hat.

Peters ran up to her, out of breath, pink-faced, panicking. He looked wildly around him, trying to herd her away from the violence – wanting help. He said, 'Where are Fiona and Polly?'

'Don't worry. They're inside. Safe. Well... I say "safe", but are they? Where is safe, Peters? Do you know?'

45

Crabb checked on Dora. Surprisingly, he spied her at the edge of the main group, looking hemmed in by all those who'd strained as near as they could to the fireworks. Now that the display had ended, the previously solid wall of people relaxed subtly as a gentle movement amongst them began.

Dora stood awkwardly as if physically tired, having lost her seat, shifting her weight from foot to foot, her little dog quivering in her arms. She moved it up to her shoulder, patting it on the back, as if she were about to burp it. Moss continued to sign at her. She looked bored and irritated by him. Didn't sign back.

Crabb was surprised that no one had thought to make her comfortable. She clearly needed to sit down. Then as if sensing his thoughts Moss tapped her on the elbow and pushed a chair towards her. She sat down gratefully. She clung on to an empty glass, and fake-smiled at people from her seated vantage point, as they wished her well, continually patting the head of her trembling dog.

Next to her, Crabb immediately spotted two plods who were pretending that they didn't know each other. They were making efforts to mingle but as neither could sign well, it was a sorry performance. They kept on inadvertently bumping into each other and then feigning unfamiliarity. His eyes moved over them, embarrassed by their inability to be undercover party guests. He doubted that anyone here tonight could mistake them for anything other than what they were. Only Moss had the nerve to carry off signing and look natural about it. He was sticking to Dora like peanut butter to the roof of the mouth.

And then Crabb heard it. In the far corner a commotion rippled through the crowd. There were shouts, the sound of breaking glass. The music continued to blare but a physical torrent of people was spilling out of the building, propelled by an unknown force, pushing them further into the courtyard.

He saw Fiona and Polly struggling towards him, flying in from the alley door, throwing hurried glances over their shoulders. His heart missed a beat. Where was Annie? He pushed aside a man, vaguely realising that it was Charlie Blue – the interpreter who fitted in like wallpaper. A good description from Annie. Always there, often on the periphery, but a nothing sort of a man. Crabb manhandled his way past Edward, who at first pushed back, thinking it a game.

'Move,' Crabb shouted at him.

And then there she was, Annie; calm, unflustered. Alive, thank God. Peters held her elbow, Annie struggled to get out of his grasp.

'What the bloody hell's going on?' said Crabb.

'Martin's here,' said Annie. 'Getting the shit kicked out of him. Big fight. Out at the front.'

'Stupid man. Bloody *hell*. What's he doing here? Was he expecting to be welcomed back to the fold as if nothing had happened? What an idiot,' said Crabb.

'Maggie was here as well.'

Crabb was confused. 'Maggie? But why? Is she in trouble? Was she involved in the fight? Is she hurt?'

Annie shook her head. Simply stated, 'She's gone now.'

'Did you see Theo? Is he here as well?'

'I didn't see him, no.' And then she went to stand next to Fiona and Polly. Annie picked up someone's glass of unfinished wine and drank it. Stared at him defiantly.

'Keep hold of Annie, and the other two, Peters,' Crabb said. 'Do we need backup?'

The DS nodded.

'Sort it now then.' Crabb grabbed two policemen and told them to follow him. A third policeman appeared, speaking frantically into his radio, all of them going against the crowd towards the front. Finally they reached the main doors.

Martin lay, in a foetal position, his arms covering his head. A group of men kicked him. Like a football. Booting Martin in the back, on his legs, aiming for his face. They weren't holding back. It was savage and brutal. The three coppers waded in. Crabb grabbed a man by his shirt collar. There was a lot of scuffling, irate hands signed at him. He ignored them, pulling the men off one by one.

At last, there was just Martin left – lying on the pavement. Unmoving. Bleeding. Whimpering. At least he was still breathing. Crabb told one of the policemen to telephone for an ambulance. Even as he said it, three police vans drove up. They squealed to a halt and out spewed policemen in riot gear. Quickly assessing the situation, they took over and Crabb stood back, breathing heavily.

Now he had the number of officers required. He hoped it wasn't too late.

He left them to it and re-entered the hall.

Complete bloody chaos. Some were rooted to the spot, others advanced, wanting to watch the fight. Still more were clearly frightened and were moving as far back into the Club, into the courtyard, as possible. Crabb swore.

He looked for Annie again. Worried. He felt flat-footed, as if he had forgotten his dance-steps, unsure what was meant to follow. Pulling himself together, he started moving. Slow, slow, quick quick, slow – easing himself through the crush. Finally, there she was.

Annie stood apart from everyone else, ignoring Fiona who was crying and shaking, and a stern-looking Polly who comforted her. He grimly made his way towards them.

Moss grabbed him roughly by the shoulder. Something in the man's eyes made Crabb pull up sharply. Crabb looked at him, daring him to say the unthinkable. How badly wrong could this night go?

Moss wiped the sweat from his face; his features were drawn, suddenly gaunt. He had difficulty meeting Crabb's eyes. 'I've... I've lost Dora. She's gone, sir. I'm sorry. I don't know what happened.'

Crabb closed his eyes. Forced himself not to panic. Tried to remember when he had last seen Dora. The fireworks had just finished. She'd been sitting on a chair. About ten minutes ago. 'Are you sure she's gone. What the bloody hell were you doing? How could you possibly lose sight of her? Jesus fucking *hell.*'

Moss kept his eyes down, staring at his shoes.

'That wasn't a bloody rhetorical question, sergeant. How did you lose Dora?'

'She said she was thirsty. Asked me to get her a drink. So I did. I was only gone for a minute or two. It must have been a few minutes later when I heard the fight break out. I went back to her straight away, but she wasn't there.'

Crabb clasped his head with his hands. He spoke slowly. 'Why didn't you get someone else to get a drink for her? You were meant to stay with her. You weren't supposed to be her bloody butler. *Christ.*'

'I realise that now. Obviously I shouldn't have left her. Totally my fault. I'm sorry, sir. God, I'm sorry.'

Crabb didn't have the time to make him feel better about it. He was working it out. The time between the fireworks finishing and the fight starting was about ten minutes. Maximum. Add on another five minutes. Fifteen minutes. It was enough time. Enough time to take her.

He spoke to Peters who had appeared at his side. Told him to let the police outside know that Dora *might* be missing. He didn't care if he was being overcautious. He *hoped* he was being over-cautious but as he cast his eyes around the still-packed court-yard, he saw no sign of Dora Potts.

'Where's Dora's dog?' Crabb asked Peters, having to raise his voice. 'And turn off that bloody music.'

The young man shook his head in answer. 'I'll start looking for the dog, sir. And Dora, of course.'

Crabb nodded. 'You,' he grabbed a passing policeman in riot gear by the arm, 'look for a dog. A Chihuahua. Now.'

The heavily vested policeman tried not to show surprise at the request, nodded and before going off on his own, spread the word to his colleagues. Crabb watched as, as a group, all their eyes fell to ground level: dog hunting. Striding up to Annie, he said, 'Did you see Dora when you were outside?'

'No. Only Maggie, Martin and the fight. What's happening, Crabb? Someone said Dora's missing. Please tell me they were wrong. Maybe she needed to be on her own, was too hot, too overcome. Too something. Help me here, Crabb.'

'It doesn't sound like Dora, does it? Leaving her own party. She's gone and we've got to find her.'

He went over what had happened. There was no reason for Dora to have left her own party of her own accord. She wouldn't have left without saying goodbye. However sad she'd been, she would never have left her guests like that. It wasn't in her nature.

And she wouldn't have gone anywhere without her dog.

Someone turned the music off and in the sudden silence, Crabb watched frenzied signing spread like a rampant disease, touching everyone at the party. Looks of panic took hold and faces sobered. The Deaf stood immobile before deciding to start searching. They moved suddenly and swiftly, backtracking into the Club, spreading out as much as possible. Disorganised. A mess of people making everything worse, more confused. He needed order. Crabb pointed at Peters, 'You, stay with Annie. Moss, with me.'

Pre-empting the muddled searchers, Crabb made his way to the front door, physically pulling people out of his way, and managed to stop any more of them exiting the front by standing steadfast at the door with his arms held out, barring their way. He grabbed Moss as the nearest available signer with a voice, told him to interpret, and said, 'Stop. Everyone stop.'

He held his hands out, palms facing down, floated them up and down in the air, trying to calm the group, whose hysteria was palpably rising. They pushed and shoved and sweated.

'The police are here. They will search for Dora. Who *may*, or *may not*, be missing. I want you all to stop panicking. Just stay where you are. Do not leave. Please.'

They had all watched Moss' signing but Crabb could only watch with dismay and mounting anger as Dora's birthday guests, not to be deterred, gathered in hastily formed groups. Secretive, huddled signing and then, as one, they turned and made for the back exit in droves. *For Christ's sake.* Reinforcements in the form of six policemen arrived. Crabb angrily sent them out of the front and round to the rear of the building, saying, 'I want both exits blocked. No one is to leave. It is imperative that everyone is accounted for and questioned. But some of you...'

He pointed to the coppers overdressed in their riot gear.

'...get outside, see if you can see Dora. She hasn't been gone long. Ten minutes, probably fifteen, twenty now. Fat woman, white hair, wearing a pink flowery dress, with her dog – a Chihuahua.'

Twenty minutes. A lot could happen in that time.

Annie came and stood next to him. 'You know what they say, don't you, Crabb? It's not over until The Fat Lady Signs.' She laughed bleakly and then burst into tears.

46

I had been cooped up in the fucking Deaf Club for hours. Interminable hours. Playing along. Smiling. Nodding. Outwardly upset and distressed. Inwardly laughing.

The world had not stopped turning as she followed me out. The air had not shifted. Not even imperceptibly. As if her very existence had been in question.

It had been easy enough to trick her with promises of a birthday present for her dog. I just needed a hand, I told her. She trotted happily behind me – as much as her girth allowed, intent only on getting something for her ridiculous pet. Fear forgotten. Not even considered.

I had deposited the fat bitch here. In The Cupboard. Under the stairs. At home. At last. Under lock and key. I had made her little guest room sturdier. Impossible for her to escape from. Reinforced it for extra safety and my peace of mind.

I needed her to feel it. The fear. The total absence of light. The blindness. The panic. Hopefully she would also feel the wet of her own urine, the stench of her own shame.

And then I had gone back to the party. Just in time for jelly. I was *back almost before she had gone missing. I even kindly offered to search for her. I enjoyed the irony of the situation.*

Now, back at home, I had finished my baking. Another perfect cake. It sat and cooled on its rack.

Finally I went to bed at about six o'clock this morning. I was ready to sleep the sleep of the just. I changed into my pyjamas and padded barefoot around the recently rediscovered bedroom. My brother's bedroom. Touching things that were now remembered vividly again. The nostalgia was like a layer of dust: it coated everything. I lightly trailed my hands over framed photographs, ran them through clothes hanging in the wardrobe, stroked sporting trophies. I took from a shelf a shiny cup declaring some remarkable display of swimming prowess. My brother, Ewan, hadn't been that good in the water. Obviously. He'd proved that himself. With a little help from me. Proved it beyond a doubt.

I exhaled, holding my mouth close to the faux silver until a mist of my breath created a cloud. I drew a smiley face in the vapour and then erased it with a sweep of my fingers. And then for the first time, I actually touched the bike. It was leaning against the bedroom wall. I caressed the crossbar and the handles. I sniffed the saddle. Breathed the smell deep into my lungs. Savoured it. And then I kicked the bike. Viciously. It crashed to the floor. I watched its wheels spinning for some time before I got into bed. I fell asleep as soon as my head hit the pillow.

It was good to be really home.

Finally.

47

I'd gone down to inspect her just after I'd had my lunch. Another hot day, but it was time now. Didn't want the old girl suffocating. It was as hot as hell.

She'd been long enough in the Cupboard. Unfortunately, she had not wet herself and she didn't look as broken as the other two had. But she looked angry. Outraged even.

I looked down at her.

God does indeed work in mysterious ways. His creative powers had gone a little awry with His creation of this woman. In her nakedness, she resembled one of those strange albino whales. Unformed and unfinished blubber. Bleached white. It was as if He had got bored and forgotten to create any visible definition on this mighty mammal. I had an amorphous blob under the stairs. Her whiteness looked like spilt milk. And we all know, there is no point in crying over that. I untied her.

She sat in my kitchen. Tethered. Naturally. I might be kind but I am not a fool. The woman was proving fascinating. In stark contrast to her two male counterparts who had come before her, she it was that showed only fury when released from beneath the stairs. A handsome fury at that. I found myself, against my better judgement, in awe of *her strength of character. And a little chilled. It was an unexpected turn of events. I mentally doffed my cap to her. She was already in character with little prompting from me. She waved her free hand, forcing me to look at the kitchen in all its glory. It indeed looked resplendent.*

'This place is filthy. Disgusting. Rubbish everywhere. What are you thinking, you dirty little man?'

Momentarily thrown, I made no reply.

Her face had utter contempt written all over it. I could have killed her. Literally. There and then. But I refrained from doing so. I ignored her. Instead, watched her facial expression change. Wily.

'Why not let me clean it up for you? Won't take long, and then we can enjoy that cake. Did you bake it yourself? Looks better than my baking efforts.'

I had obviously given her too much credit too early on. As we sat in silence after my non-response to her ridiculous chattering, I realised that I had allowed my own emotions to override common sense. I suddenly saw her for what she was. She wasn't in character, as I'd first thought. Had first hoped. This was her character. She wasn't playing at all. She was just being herself. A subtle but important point. I must not fall prey again to her physical presence. Not react like a child.

But she's physically perfect. I have a doppelgänger for tea. That was all it was. They were like two peas in a pod. Two fat juicy peas. It should have made the Game easier for her. But it wouldn't, I knew.

It was her facial expressions that upset me so. Complete disdain. Disapproval. Disgust. And yes, there it was again, a flash of pure hatred. It frightened me. After all this time, I reacted in exactly the same way as I had when a boy. It was as if she still knew which buttons to press. And I responded accordingly.

But there was nothing to fear from her. I had to remind myself of that stark but obvious truth. I it was who was in command. I was no longer that cowering little boy. Nobody will call me 'Cupboard' anymore. Never again.

Deep down I knew that she was totally incapable of making this The Perfect Day. Making it like it should have been.

Instead she just sat there. Gave me that look that I knew so well. It made me furious. So can you blame me? Really? Can you?

Perhaps that was why her particular fate was already sealed in the most visually stunning and stupendously grisly way. With her, I was going out of my way to make a particular point. Whatever she did, even if she pretended to play the Game, even if she were to actually pull it off successfully and play the Game perfectly, she will suffer. Disproportionately so.

Each death now felt like a vindication. A victory. And this time, with this woman, I wanted revenge more than anything. To wipe that smile off her face. Forever.

This time I decided to change the order of play. Why? The answer was simple. I wanted her to feel all of it. I wanted it to hurt.

We'd been at it for most of the afternoon. And well into the evening. She'd certainly provided more fun than the others. Had displayed a certain sophistication that had been unexpected. But good for her. At least she had shown an understanding of sorts.

But I knew that I was making it an unfair contest. Barely listening to her answers. Her questions were slightly more amusing compared to those of the chaps and certainly worth a moment to listen to.

But no more than that.

I wanted to get on with it.

Inevitably, she started to complain that the ties were too tight. Her left hand was going slightly blue I had to agree. It looked painful. I'd be the first to admit that maybe I had manacled her to the chair rather too well. Maybe I was fearful of her physical size and her presumed strength. Silly, really.

I patiently explained that she should not worry about her hand.

There were bigger things than that to worry her. But she did keep on so. She waved her right hand around wildly. Got angry. And her signs became wheedling. Crafty. She tried to trick me. But to give her credit, she never begged. Not like the others. Again, I tipped my hat to her stoicism.

She seemed to understand that the pleading, the whimpering, the wails for mercy would be ignored. The others had lacked the grace to beg for absolution for their sins. They had begged in their craven way for mercy only. Merely fearful of their own imminent deaths. This woman had more style. She was a game old bird.

And she certainly wasn't stupid. She tried talking to me as if she were my mother. Not a bad assumption, but most definitely a wrong one. She made calming faces. Soothing signs. Stupid platitudes fell from her hand as she realised, too late, that she'd got something wrong.

Her signs suddenly fell over and over each other; pouring from her one free hand, like a waterfall of sudden comprehension. She knew she was lost. She had played and failed at the biggest reality show in town.

But she wouldn't shut up. Still tried to placate me. I think my temper was evident.

I signed at her. Very slowly.

'Stop talking to me as if you were my mother. You were never that. You might play at that role in the Deaf Club, but we're not there now. We're here. My world. My Game. Don't you know who you are? Don't you get it?'

Her fat face looked tired with utter incomprehension. Sadly she shook her head. Wearily she signed, 'Who am I? Tell me.'

'Think older than my mother.'

She blinked. Stupidly. I sighed.

'You are the mother of all mothers. Understand now? Remember what you did to me? All those years ago. You made me like this. All of this is your fault. It was all your idea. You started it.'

She dipped her head.

I lifted her chin up and signed again, 'You started it, and I'm finishing it. You won't even apologise to me. Don't even know what you're meant to be apologising for. So, we reach the end. With fuck-all help from you. It was all your idea. You thought of the Game. You suggested it would be fun. Isolating me. Destroying me. Remember? Get it now?'

I think she did. Finally, Granny got it.

It was her arrogance that really sealed the deal. She just had to have the last sign. On and on she banged.

'I apologise. I really do. Please accept my apologies. I'm sure I was wrong. I'm often wrong. Forgive me. Let's have another cup of tea. And how about another slice of your delicious cake? Perhaps another one of your jam sandwiches? Or maybe a pork pie. Please. Sit down and we'll chat some more. Make me understand. I'll listen properly this time. I can be whoever you want me to be.'

I knew she didn't mean it. She didn't know what she was apologising for. I hated the desperateness of her signs. I went out of her line of vision and reappeared.

It was the sight of the cleaver that finally shut her up.

But then I stopped. Was I being too hasty? I put the cleaver down and just looked at this vast pile of a woman sitting at my kitchen table.

Maybe she was a keeper after all. Maybe. Maybe not.

48

They all stood on the pavement of a quiet residential street in the early Monday morning light, struck dumb by what lay before them. Even Dr Moore had the grace to keep his smart comments to himself. Crabb turned to check on Annie, the cuffs of her pyjamas visible under her jogging bottoms and baggy top. Her hair was scraped back in a ponytail and she sat with her head between her knees. Scarlet's arm was wrapped around Annie's shoulder; her own expression utterly devoid of emotion. A blank, white slate of a face.

Annie had been sick and Crabb could see her shaking from where he was standing. Slowly bringing her head up she met his gaze. He held up his thumb to her and smiled. She just shook her head sadly.

We're all waiting for someone to say something, realised Crabb. It was difficult to find the right words or the right questions to ask the doctor. It was pretty bloody obvious what they were all gawping at, but the cause of death wasn't immediately clear. He *hoped* it was the skewer. But the sheer brutality of the killing made it almost irrelevant and Dr Moore would tell them as soon as he knew. Crabb only hoped that Dora hadn't suffered too much. Although that was unlikely judging by the carnage that lay before him.

Another body meant another victory for the killer. Crabb inhaled slowly: a deep and heavy sigh left his body. As a rule, he rarely knew murder victims prior to their deaths. It was a new experience for him and he decided he wasn't a fan. It was all-too intimate. Too close for comfort.

It was overkill gone mad. Both the spectacle and the shock value had been ratcheted up, along with the gratuitous savagery.

Crabb wondered if the actual road had any meaning, was perhaps another message from the killer.

Docherty was there. He had seen the body and turned away, pretending that he wanted to stretch his legs and think. This time, Crabb couldn't blame him. Peters sat on a wall, away from anyone else. He tried to look composed but his hands were shaking as he wrote on a pad. The SOCOs drifted around in silence. Uniformed police had cordoned off the road. Crabb was left with the doctor.

And Dora.

Dora's corpse was so grotesque that it took Crabb's eyes some time to register what he was seeing. He took a deep breath and tried to refocus. Concentrate. It was too much. It shouldn't be. But it was.

She lay on her back. Her legs were spread-eagled and her dress lifted up to reveal large white knickers. Dora with her dress pulled up. She would have been mortified. Crabb tried to ignore the callousness of this act. It was a good excuse not to look up at the atrocity visited upon the woman's face. She had undoubtedly been posed but it was the first time that such sheer cruelty had been quite so obvious. The killer had shown no personal attachment to any of the victims. Devoid of empathy, sympathy or compassion. A true-blue dyed-in-the-wool psychopath.

Crabb asked the photographer to get a move on. He wanted Dora covered. In life, she had had an overabundance of pride, which too often leaked out; frequently misconstrued as something harsh and abrasive. Sometimes hard. But deep down, Dora had been kind and soft. Caring. Most definitely modest. She deserved if not a little dignity than at least a modicum of respectability in death.

He made himself look up. At her face. At her mouth.

Her lips were spread open obscenely to accommodate the thing that had been stuffed inside. The *things* that had been stuffed inside. Two things. Her jaw had been broken and looked untethered; unhinged from the rest of her face. Her mouth was stretched to its capacity and was ripped like paper at the corners. Someone had yanked it open with such force that her upper lip covered her nostrils. The nose had been lost in the ruin of her face. Her eyes remained open and glassy. They pointed upwards, seeing nothing.

From out of the hole in her face stuck eight digits. The thumbs were presumably tucked inside, behind the teeth. Eight fat fingers dropped like obscene over-sized maggots – pressed together; the right palm resting on the back of her left hand: her knuckles on both hands facing outwards. A large gold band on her ring finger was buried into her flesh, the metal cutting into the swollen skin.

Her nails were blue. Her right index finger had a streak of dirt underneath it. The nail on her left ring finger was chipped. The hands fell out of her mouth, as if cupping her chin.

What remained of Dora's arms were crossed as if in prayer on her chest. Two bloody stumps, severed at the wrists, stuck out from her white cardigan sleeves. They were pulled up so that all could see the violence done to her.

There was a skewer in her ear.

Crabb winced. He hoped that Dora had been dead prior to

the amputations. He almost didn't dare ask the doctor but knew he must.

'No. She was alive. She would have died from massive blood loss. The skewer itself did not cause her death,' said Dr Moore. 'Obviously I'll confirm after post-mortem.'

Crabb had never seen the pathologist looking so sombre. The man looked pasty, tired and for the first time, upset by his job. He moved slowly and meticulously, resting on his haunches as he bent over the brutalised woman. He handled Dora's body with reverence. He worked in complete silence, his dark hair a mess of curls. Crabb watched the top of his head as he again started his visual scan of the body; starting at her head and working methodically downwards, to her feet.

The doctor looked up at Crabb. 'What was this maniac thinking, Crabb? I've never seen such… such *ferocity*.'

Crabb could only shake his head. The photographer had finished and Crabb gently pulled down Dora's dress. He arranged it neatly just under her knees. He knew it was silly but he could give her back *some* pride. Although it hardly seemed worth it. A wasted gesture.

'I don't suppose there's any sign of her dog. A Chihuahua? Furry little rat thing. She never went anywhere without it,' Crabb said.

The pathologist looked at Dora's body. 'Unless he's sewn the dog up inside her, I can see nothing dog-related. One should be thankful for small mercies considering the mess I'm looking at.'

As Crabb stood upright from straightening her clothes, he caught a pungent whiff.

'What's that smell?'

'Alcohol. She reeks of the stuff. Smells like a brewery. Her clothes have been doused with it. Someone's poured a bottle all over her.' Dr Moore bent closer to the body and sniffed. 'Rum, I think.'

Crabb realised his hands were damp from the alcohol on her dress and he wiped them on his trousers. Covering her in rum was another piece of dramatic art intended to baffle the police.

'I'll let you know re stomach contents,' said Dr Moore.

Crabb nodded sadly. He thought that the killer, in his slaughter of Dora, must have been awash with blood. Caked in the stuff. Unless of course he'd washed and changed his clothing before dumping her body. But he guessed that the killer had instead chanced it. Was now taking stupid risks. Was losing his grip on reality. Crabb was relying on his experience. He didn't know he was right, but it *felt* right.

'I've got to catch him. *And* find the bloody primary crime scene. What a bloody mess.' He hadn't realised that he had spoken aloud until he felt the gloved hands of Dr Moore patting him on his calf. 'You will.'

Crabb looked down in surprise and nodded at the doctor before turning towards Annie. She and Scarlet had joined Peters and they now all sat on the wall looking empty and sick. Scarlet's bony hand swallowed up Annie's small hand. Both of their knuckles showed white with the strength of grip. They reminded Crabb of two frightened children taking comfort in holding hands. They both sat straighter as Crabb approached. He squatted down in front of them, turning towards Annie. Annie remained silent. Her skin was a sickly grey pallor.

'I've never seen anything like it,' said Peters.

Crabb said, 'Would you like to go home, Annie? You don't have to stay. I'll arrange for someone to take you. And stay with you.'

She vehemently shook her head but didn't bother to answer him directly. 'I could do with a fag. Feels like a good time for a vice. And sex is obviously out of the question,' she said flatly.

Crabb nodded; didn't bother smiling and he lit up a cigarette for himself. He offered the pack to both the women. Both accepted and inhaled deeply and gratefully.

'Was Dora a big drinker, Annie?'

She didn't reply immediately, concentrating on watching the white smoke stream from her nose and mouth in a plume of puffy white smoke. She coughed and looked at the cigarette; seemingly surprised at the effect. But she inhaled again.

'Did Dora drink?' Crabb repeated.

She frowned and swallowed, and then shook her head. He didn't press her. There was no need. He thought he had the answer. Was getting a better handle on the Game. Someone the killer knew had drank themselves to death and Dora's body replicated that death.

Eventually, Annie shook her head again and said, 'No, not really. Dora liked a social drink, but she didn't *drink*, drink. Why?'

Crabb kept it simple: 'Someone's poured a bottle of alcohol all over her. Rum.'

'She didn't like rum.'

They left it at that. Crabb wished he hadn't asked her to come to the crime scene – he'd had to cajole her but had made sure that she hadn't seen Dora up close. But she'd seen enough. Seen too much. Poor bitch. Fuck it. His fault. A mistake, but he was desperate – hoping that perhaps Annie would notice something specific about Dora's murder, its location. She hadn't. Crabb had to keep focused and stop worrying about her. He at least now had an answer: the alcohol was definitely just for show. An addition. Like the tobacco, the mug of tea, the pencil shavings, the dog's ear. All to make a point.

They all watched Docherty roll towards them, his upper thighs clearly rubbing together. He looked unusually drained and at a loss. Even his beard had lost its shine. Broken Santa. His lack of understanding of the case transparent, the inability of the police to catch the killer out there for all to see. But to give him credit, he asked, 'Any ideas, Crabb? I don't know what to do.'

'If it's any compensation, I suspect the killer has become sloppy. He'll have left forensics, I'm sure of it. I think he's losing control. The fury *looks* the same as that perpetrated on Adam Jacobs. But far *too* much fury is on display here.' He shrugged. 'I suspect some of it's for show.

'Appearance-wise, this murder *feels* more disorganised. The manner of this death is too much. Verging on idiocy. He'll have left something of himself behind.'

Crabb turned and looked again at the mess that had been Dora. Said, 'It almost feels like he's given up. Perhaps because he's nearing the end of his game. He's unravelling. The final act will be following shortly. Unless I stop him.'

Crabb realised he was speaking aloud and Docherty was looking at him blankly. 'What are you talking about?'

'I've told you the killer is playing a game,' said Crabb impatiently, 'and you chose to ignore me. Thought I was being fanciful. You wasted time by "not wasting" your precious "resources". If you'd really wanted to know what was happening you should have listened to me before. I just need to work out the connection between the victims and stop the last person from becoming one.'

'And how do we find out what that connection is?' asked Docherty, sounding plaintive. He'd patently given up trying to pretend that he was in control.

Crabb didn't bother answering Docherty's question; it was both stupid and rhetorical – the DCI had lost the ability to keep up appearances. His voice was barely audible. Crabb turned away from him. It wasn't his job to babysit his superior officer. Let him cry on his own.

Crabb, Annie, Scarlet and Peters all remained in silence,

averting their eyes to avoid looking at Dora's body as it was being moved. She was in transit to her final stop.

Crabb fleetingly felt alone. He felt the responsibility of the case, the entire burden of solving it, leave the DCI's shoulder – where it had only ever temporarily perched – and land squarely on his. He braced himself, swept Annie into the crook of his arm and walked away with her and Scarlet, without looking back.

He had a nasty feeling that the killer was saving the last dance for Annie.

And he was buggered if he'd let him have her.

49

———————

Scarlet sat next to Annie on the sofa, her arms crossed. She stared at Crabb, making him feel uncomfortable that he was visiting them yet again. Her presence was intimidating. But he needed Annie's help. She was his way into the Deaf Community. She was his key. And now he had to turn it.

It was evident that Annie hadn't slept in the hours since he had dropped her and Scarlet off. Her hair was still unbrushed and in a ponytail, and her pyjamas were still visible under her clothes. She said, 'I need a bath. I swear to God I can't bear to see another body. Every time I close my eyes, I see Dora.' She rubbed at her scar. 'I see all of them.'

Her colour was a sickly grey and her eyes filled with a line of tears. But she didn't allow them to drop.

Crabb sighed with sadness. He knew he couldn't do anything for her, other than treat her gently.

'I need something to concentrate on,' she said. 'Something to distract myself with. So, after my bath, when I'm clean – though I feel that's impossible at the moment – we'll get down to some work. Okay?'

She left the room and Crabb smiled to himself. She was one

tough cookie. He sat in silence with the frightening Scarlet. Neither talked: she probably didn't want to, and he because he didn't quite dare.

An hour later Annie was once again sitting in front of the whiteboard. Crabb stood with marker in hand, intent on all the information that had been written down. No one spoke for a while. Scarlet sat on the sofa – silent. Eyebrows in repose. All were lost in their own thoughts. Staring blankly at the written words.

And then Crabb saw it. 'Bloody hell,' he said, as he spun round to face Annie. 'I don't believe it. I've got it.'

'Got what?' said Annie.

'What he did to Dora. I know what it means. She's been made to eat her words.'

'What?'

Annie threw Eric off her lap and stood up.

'Fuck me,' said Scarlet.

Annie said, 'That's it. Christ, how disgusting is that? Why would he *do* that? How fucking mad *is* he?'

'Mad, and getting madder,' Crabb said.

He turned his back and carried on drawing arrows between the names of the victims on the whiteboard, his mind working furiously as his hands methodically drew and redrew.

'Explain,' said Annie. 'What are you doing?'

Scarlet threw her empty cigarette packet to get Crabb's attention. It bounced off his shoulder and Eric pounced on it. 'Come on, Crabb. What gives?'

He turned. 'Dora,' he said. 'The killer stuffing her hands in her mouth. She's been made to eat her words. Literally. It's how she communicates. What better way to visually shut her up?'

He nodded slowly to himself. It was a plausible and interesting theory. The woman had been known for her unwillingness to suffer fools gladly. Could be impatient, sometimes to the point of callousness. It might very well be a symbolic gesture by the killer to silence her. To make real his fantasy – shut her up forever. Or whoever she represented. Crabb knew that the issue of deafness was key to the killer. And Dora used her hands to sign.

He nodded again. 'That's it exactly,' he said. 'And I think the things put into the mouths *are* specific to each victim.'

Annie said, 'What do you mean? William didn't have a dog, and Toby didn't particularly like drawing. So how's that specific?'

'It's specific to the killer. It's what they mean to him that's important. How they are linked to each person in *his* mind. Remember, he's mimicking or recreating the deaths of *different* people. Toby, William and Dora are only *substitutes* for who the killer is really murdering in his own head.'

'How do we find out what the killer's thinking? Who *are* these fantasy people?' said Annie.

'Therein lies the answer.'

Scarlet said, 'And he's obviously gone a bit berserk with this one. Too much, don't you think? Violence was completely off the scale.'

'*Something's* set him off. Made him change his behaviour,' said Crabb. 'But I'll guarantee that Dora will have been fed on birthday cake and jam sandwiches. She'll have been given her own little birthday party. Or rather, his version of one.'

Crabb watched as Annie sat down again and closed her eyes. Refusing to lip-read. Let her head rest against the back of the sofa. She swept tendrils of her dark hair from her face with irritation: having just been washed it was soft and kept falling across her eyes. Crabb thought she still looked beautiful through her grief. She opened her eyes and said, 'You've definitely checked everyone's birthdays?'

Crabb nodded at her. 'No one has a birthday that falls within the time frame of the murders. But *some*body's bloody birthday is being played out. Again and again. I know I'm right. And yes, I agree about the violence shown against Dora. Maybe Dora set him off in some way. Her personally, I mean.'

He turned back to the whiteboard and neatly wiped away all the lines of text. Wrote three names boldly in the centre: Toby/William/Dora – skewered

Then he changed the linear form of the names and put the names in a vertical line. He looped an arrow from Toby to William to Dora. Added Annie's name with a question mark.

'Subtle,' said Scarlet.

'What do you see? Don't think too hard about it, just let it come,' he said.

The two women gazed intently at the board, as if something would miraculously pop up, giving them the answer.

'There's something there – there must be. It's probably simpler than we're making it,' said Scarlet.

'Toby was left in water, with pencil shavings. William's wrists were "slashed". Dora reeked of alcohol,' Crabb said. He stopped and looked at the board again.

'I suspect the killer forced Dora to drink, but we'll have to wait for the post-mortem. He spilt the contents of the bottle over her body. Deliberately. Dora wasn't a drinker. But whoever she represents in the killer's mind, was. And that's a fact.'

Eric lay across the threshold of the French windows like a draught excluder.

'Isn't there anything we can *do*?' said Annie. 'Feels like we're just kicking our heels.'

'But we are doing something. Don't underestimate the power of thought. We've worked out the game, we know it revolves around a birthday. We're nearly there, Annie. I promise you.'

Scarlet rolled her eyes, not shy in showing her disbelief.

Annie just looked sickened by all the ugliness.

50

Annie was tired. And it was only mid-morning. She, Crabb and Scarlet sat in the garden, she only dimly aware as Crabb talked incessantly into his mobile, shouting out orders, organising this, doing that, marshalling all his generals. Peters came and went, following instructions from Crabb which she didn't bother to watch.

She didn't think she'd ever been this tired in her entire life. She turned as she saw Crabb reach for his mobile again. His face clouded as he read it. 'Bloody hell,' he said.

'Who is it?'

'Ben's mother. Maggie. Here, read it for yourself.'

She took the mobile, already feeling a dread at what it might say.

Come to my house Crabb. Now. Theo here. I'm frightened of him. Please come now.

'You better go. She sounds desperate,' said Annie, handing back the mobile. She knew she probably seemed disinterested and unfeeling. But her heart was thumping with fear.

Crabb shook his head at her, already standing, knowing he had no choice but to go. He'd already let Maggie down by leaving Ben drunk on a bench. He kept that guilt to himself, saying, 'I have to go. She trusts me. And you're coming too. You're not staying here on your own.'

'Yes, Crabb. I am. Scarlet's here. Please don't make me come.' She realised she was almost begging and felt angry with herself. She was used to being strong. But four bodies in one week had nearly destroyed her.

Scarlet stood up and said, 'Leave her with me, Crabb. Don't make her go with you. I'll look after her. I promise.'

Annie was overcome by the sensation of dizziness – falling into a deep hole: her mind filled with the pictures of Toby, then William, Ben, and finally, Dora. Then they merged into some mad and frightening vision, all blurred together as if they were overexposed photographs, all running into one awful snapshot.

Crabb said to Scarlet, 'She'll be safer with me.' He took Annie's hand. She grudgingly allowed herself to be led from the garden and into the car. At the last minute, she dug her heels in.

'Really, Crabb. Come on. The bogeyman isn't going to get me. I'll lock myself in the flat and not open the door to anyone. Just me and Scarlet. We'll be alright. I don't need a babysitter the whole time. I just want to be left alone.'

'Get in the car. You're not going out of my sight. Go on, get in.' Crabb held open the driver's door to his car. She didn't move.

'We haven't got time for this, Annie. Just get in. I need to see Theo. Arrest the little bastard for sexual abuse. *Interview* him for Christ's sake. Check where he's been, what he's been doing. Get him in fucking custody. He is a suspect in four murders. This is important. Do it for Sarah. Now, move your arse.'

Annie got in, thinking the Sarah reference was a cheap shot. She realised she was sulking but didn't care. She was angry that Crabb had felt the need to remind her of Sarah. As if she needed fucking reminding. It was the one thing that kept her going. Finding the killer of her best friend's son.

Crabb quickly did a three-point turn, sending an arc of pea shingle spraying up from his tyres. They drove to Maggie's house in complete silence.

She allowed her thoughts to turn more fully to Sarah. As bad as Annie felt, it couldn't possibly compare to how Sarah would be feeling. How she would no doubt always feel with the loss of her son. She decided that she'd go and visit her, be with her, as soon as this was all over.

And there was the continuing nearly remembered niggle that still eluded her. After thinking it to death, *over*thinking it, she couldn't identify what that lost memory was. She didn't stop to worry about it now. It would come.

They pulled up outside Maggie's house and parked, remaining in the car as a frightened Maggie appeared at her front door. The woman was terrified and even from here, Annie could see tears pouring down her face. She'd lost her son as well, Annie remembered, and shuddered.

'I can't go in, Crabb. I'm sorry. I really can't. I can't bear to see more grief. I just can't.'

She saw Crabb hesitate. Saw him look from Maggie and then back to her.

'I'm sorry,' she said again and angrily wiped at her eyes; surprised to find herself crying. 'I refuse point blank to move. You can't make me. It's too much. Enough.'

'Okay. Calm down, it's alright. I'll go in on my own and be as quick as I can. But I'm locking you in and taking the keys. So you can't get out of the car. You *will* stay here. Okay? I'll be as quick as I can.'

Annie nodded gratefully. 'Thanks,' she said. 'I'll be here waiting for you.'

Crabb gave her an awkward pat on her shoulder, got out of the car and locked the doors. She offered up no resistance to being locked in and settled back, feeling safe, watching him hurry towards the house.

Finally he was gone and sitting on her own, she breathed deeply with relief.

Watching Crabb disappear into the house, she rolled down the window. It was hot. At least she'd had the sense to put on shorts and a T-shirt.

She became obsessed with the minute hand on the clock on the dashboard. It moved incredibly slowly, as if time itself was heavy and resistant to moving forward. Seven minutes went by. Rolling the window further down, she was desperate for the mild breeze that barely rustled the leaves of the trees. She felt like she was being baked on a low simmer. She also wanted a cigarette but didn't want to smoke inside the car. Hemmed in, the temperature rose. A slow suffocation. Sweat trickled down between her breasts.

That did it. *Fuck it*. She wound down the side window as far as it went. Turned in her seat and faced the gap. Putting her feet out through the window, she then followed through with her legs. Rolling over so that she was facing downwards, her arse half in, half out of the car, she grunted and pushed on the seat with her hands. She slithered out.

Having successfully escaped, she leant against the car, smoking and feeling better. Enjoying the warmth from the sun and the very soft breeze that only whispered around her body. But it was enough. She closed her eyes and relaxed – glad to be on her own but safe, with Crabb close at hand.

Her eyes flew open as she felt a hand touch her elbow.

She jumped and put her hand to her chest, surprise and shock making her heart leap. 'What are you doing here?' she signed.

He made a sort of 'come off it' mouth gesture, compressing his lips and tilting his face back from her, as if his presence should be expected. Signed, 'Don't look so surprised. I've come to collect you. We have an overdue appointment. A date, if you prefer to call it that. But not a romantic one. Come on, come on. No time to waste. There'll be food, wine and time to make merry. Well, perhaps no wine but that's of no consequence. It's party time. Celebrate now for tomorrow we die.'

He laughed and his face lit up.

Her mind stuttered to a shocked halt. Stupidly she had time to think, *now* I remember what I wanted to tell Crabb. The niggle that wouldn't go away. 'Do you know anyone with a dog – a black Labrador?' That's what Crabb had asked her, the thing she couldn't remember. *Now* she remembered. The man in front of her had had a dog. A long time ago, but he'd definitely owned one. A black Labrador.

She saw him draw back his arm and realised that there was a fist coming at her face. Hard and fast. She stood there dumbly – waiting for the contact.

I sat and reminisced. Took the time. It was important. Respectful. Crucial that I got in touch with my inner child. I made myself remember. Remember everything.

It was the morning of my birthday. A teenager at last. I had no great illusions that it would change anything. And I had spots. Really bad ones. I tried not to squeeze them, but I couldn't help it. I was so embarrassed by them. Of course, after I had squeezed them, my face just looked worse: red and inflamed.

But, anyway, that morning I woke up feeling unusually excited. After all, Ewan had got a six-gear racing bike two days ago, for his fifteenth birthday. Surely my first year as a teenager would warrant something as grand and exciting. I usually got books. And I'd have to tell Mum the titles so that she could go out and buy the right ones. But that morning, I thought I might be in for a real treat. A special present, that I had hinted at to Dad, more than once.

I was, as usual, the first one up. I couldn't concentrate on a book that morning. I paced up and down the hallway, wandered into the sitting room, and then the kitchen, waiting for the family to get up.

I stood at the bottom of the stairs. Looking up. Willing them all to hurry. Finally, I saw slippered feet, shambling along to the bathroom.

That would be Dad. Then Mum got up. I saw her open Ewan's door a crack. I didn't know what she said, but Ewan was up and out of bed quicker than usual. The house actually shook as my grandmother planted her feet squarely on the floor, as she got out of bed. I tittered. My mother, father and Ewan descended the stairs, in a line, followed by my fat grandmother. Surly and taciturn as usual.

I hurried away from my vantage point at the foot of the stairs, suddenly self-conscious. They smiled at me, as I dithered in the hall. They all wished me a happy birthday. Except my grandmother. She just looked at me with 'her look' – her face without expression, and yet somehow loaded with it. As she walked past me, I jabbed up two fingers at her fat back as it wobbled down the hall. Of course, no one saw me. I giggled again. I rushed into the kitchen first, pushing past them, with my fingers crossed in front of me, so that they couldn't see. I'd told my parents, well, Dad at least, exactly what I wanted for my birthday. I'd even told Ewan. My heart thumped with excitement.

We went through the card giving, and I exclaimed over the witty inscriptions. I stood there, awkwardly, waiting for the big moment. I felt flushed with anticipation, and couldn't help myself hopping from foot to foot.

After what seemed like forever, Mum handed me The Present. I knew immediately that it wasn't what I had asked for. It was totally the wrong shape. The parcel was hard and rectangular. I ripped open the paper, discarding it on the floor. How stupid was my dad? I had shown him only last week – pointed right at it, and told him that was what I wanted. He'd nodded and smiled, tapping his nose in a secret squirrel sort of way. In a 'we-shall-have-to-wait-and-see' way.

What I was now looking at was a school pencil case. Full of coloured pencils. I'm thirteen. Ewan got a bike, and I got coloured pencils.

I felt my face drop. I couldn't hide my disappointment, and even worse, I could feel a tear start to form in my eye. My father didn't even look at me – just carried on rolling his stupid stinky roll-ups. Mum was already picking up the wrapping paper from the floor. Only my grandmother continued to watch me. I think she was waiting for the tear to fall. I briskly wiped it away and signed 'thank you'. I left the room, feeling betrayed. Cheated. Angry.

Much later, about teatime, Mum asked me and Ewan to go to the shops. For my birthday cake. She'd forgotten to buy one. She counted out her pennies and put them in my hand. I couldn't help but feel that she did even this grudgingly.

Celebrations for Ewan's birthday had started early. A whole week of special treats for him before his big day. And a party. With his friends. Lots of them. Mum had made a huge birthday cake for him, with candles. There were plates and plates of his favourite sand- wiches. There were crisps and jelly and miniature pork pies and everything. My parents and grandmother even went to the trouble of buying fifteen balloons and tying them all around the house. They had blown on those party streamers, covering my glowing brother with party string. It had all been very merry.

For him it had been merry. For me? Not so much.

Now I felt left out of my own birthday. But nothing new there. And obviously no friends had been invited to my non-party. I didn't have any anyway.

Now my mother was asking me to go out to get my own cake. I was so furious I couldn't speak. I just quietly put on my coat, and left with Ewan. He pedalled his shiny new bike, and bounced his football as he went. Slowly, so that I didn't have to run. Showing off his hand— eye co-ordination. His sporting prowess. What a dickhead. We decided to cut across the heath.

Ewan had to get off his bike and push it, as the path was too bumpy to ride, too uneven to bounce his ball with any degree of accu- racy. We both walked in silence. Ewan knew that I was upset about the pencils, and so wisely kept quiet. The rain had been drizzling when we left the house, and was now falling heavily, drenching both of us. But Ewan just carried on bouncing his ball and steering his bike with the other hand. Bounce, bounce, bounce. It was beginning to annoy me.

Bounce, bounce. And then the ball hit a stone and unexpectedly veered off course, and came hurtling towards me. Instinct, and pure luck made me catch it. I laughed with surprise, and Ewan smiled. And then, feeling emboldened, I hoofed it as far as I could. Albeit in a rather girly way. We both watched its splendid arc, and then its perfect descent, plummeting down and landing in a nearby pond. It landed with a splash and disappeared. Ewan scowled, and dropped his bike where it fell, and ran after the ball. I followed on, laughing. I couldn't get over my skill: first catching it, and then kicking it properly — straight into the pond, as if that had been my intention. I sniggered again. It wasn't every day I got one over on Ewan.

Ewan waded into the pond with no hesitation, his hair already plastered to his head from the rain. I sat on the bank, watching his efforts, interested in the outcome. The water rose up to his midriff, and he waved his arms about to keep his balance. Every time he approached the ball, it bobbed just out of his grasp. Each time his hands came into contact with it, it tantalisingly bobbed on the surface of the water, slipping beneath his fingers, before floating even further out of his reach. Finally though, after several attempts, of course he caught it. He turned and waded slowly back towards the bank. It was still pouring, and I squatted on my heels. Ewan was now furious. Before reaching the side, about six feet from where I was squatting, he chucked the ball to safe ground. He then bent forward and put his hands on the bank. They immediately lost their hold in the slippery mud. Down he went, his face disappearing under the water. Taken by surprise at the unexpected loss of his grip, his feet slipped from under him. He resurfaced. Really angry now.

He tried to get out again. And again he slipped. This went on for three, maybe four more attempts. Ewan was tiring. I held out my hand to him. A look of relief filled his face. He reached up for my hand. Just as our fingers touched, I pulled my hand away. Disbelief crossed his face. And panic. And seeing him like that, I realised that Ewan really needed me. For the first time. Me, his younger sibling. Ewan needed my physical prowess to save him. I sat back for a bit. I held out my hand again. Ewan reached for it. I snatched it away at the last minute. I just wanted to see what he would do. See how long it would take before he started begging. I pretended to reach out to him for a third time, but Ewan had stumbled further back. The mud seemed to be sucking him down. His face kept on bobbing up and down, disappearing into the water. I watched. As his head disappeared under the water again, he made a last futile gesture, a last kick for freedom, and reappeared just once more, before vanishing for good. I laughed.

Stupid cunt. He'd had it coming though. I sat there, for about thirty minutes, wet and cold. So cold. Waiting to feel something. But I didn't really feel anything at all. I walked over to his bike. I kicked it. It wasn't my fault. My face was wet from the rain.

It certainly wasn't wet from crying. My eyes had never been drier.

52

Crabb stood inside Maggie's sitting room. The woman couldn't stop crying and Theo told her to shut up. The young man said, 'You must be Crabb. How are you? I've heard a lot about you.'

'And I, you.'

Theo ran his hands through his hair and waited, leaning on one hip. Maggie stood as if impaled to the wall. Wanting her son gone.

Crabb held his mobile in his hand, ready to ring Peters. He needed to let him know that Theo was here. Acting calmly, not wanting Theo to realise he was going to be arrested, Crabb held out his mobile and started to punch in the numbers. The beautiful young man was clearly under the impression that, with Ben dead, there would be no one to accuse him. He thought himself safe.

Crabb looked up and through the open window. He could see his car.

And it was empty.

He'd never believed it when people said they felt like their heart stopped with fright. Now he believed. Shouting to Maggie to wait there, he'd be back, he bolted from the house.

He ran to the car. Looked inside. It was still empty. He'd somehow, stupidly, hoped Annie was lying down in the footwell.

Where the *fuck* was she? He should have known she was incapable of sitting still and staying in the car. Noticing the open passenger window, he recognised her escape route. *Christ. Christ al-fucking-mighty.*

He opened the driver's door. Her bag sat on the passenger footwell. He quickly up-ended it – no mobile. He tried to remember if she had had time to bring it with her when he'd led her out of the flat. He couldn't remember. He fumbled with his phone and texted her.

Waited.

Nothing.

Panic seized him. He squatted down on his haunches, endeavouring to get his breathing under control.

There was absolutely no way that she would have gone for a walk without telling him. He was also sure her own self-preservation would have kept her there, wanting to stay close to him. Sauntering off wouldn't have entered her head.

Had she gone willingly? No, for the same reasons he'd just outlined to himself. He rang Peters. His hands shook. So did his voice. 'Peters? Annie's missing. Get a search organised now. And I mean *now*. Then meet me at her flat. I need you. And fucking hurry up.'

'Where did you last see her?'

'She was waiting for me in the car outside Maggie's house. I locked her in. She got out. There's no evidence of a struggle inside. The car's still here.'

Crabb felt guilt and fear nudging at him. 'I'll search on foot the immediate area, but she wouldn't just walk off. Which means the killer must have her. He'd have put her in a car. That's the only way he'd have got her away. I was only gone ten minutes. I'll check anyway, but it's a waste of time.'

'Calm down, Crabb. Go back to the flat. I'll see you there,' said the DS. 'And try not to worry.'

Crabb cut the connection without replying and started running quickly but methodically up and down the road, scanning streets that branched off. Stopped quickly. He was on a fool's errand. He sprinted back to his car, turned on the engine and pointed it in the direction of Annie's flat.

Just in case she'd returned there. As highly un-fucking likely as that seemed.

Scarlet opened the door and seeing his expression, she said, 'What's happened? Where's Annie? Why are you so freaked out?'

'She refused to come into Maggie's with me, so I locked her in the car. Didn't occur to me that she'd escape. Is she here?'

For an answer, Scarlet slapped him in the face. Hard. 'What have you done? Of course she's not here. Why did you take her? Fucking hell, Crabb, what have you done?'

He pushed past her, down the hall and into the sitting room. Wanting to prove to himself that she wasn't here. Knowing that of course she wasn't here. He spoke out loud to himself: 'God-al-bloody-mighty. Where *is* she?'

Crabb watched as Scarlet hugged herself, her eyes round with shock. What had he done? Why had Annie decided to get out? What was she thinking? He went into the garden and tried texting her again. Nothing.

He rushed back into the sitting room and stood in front of the whiteboard. He lit up a cigarette and tuned out his panic, his fear, his anxiety, his dry mouth and focused entirely upon the four names on the board.

Desperation swamped him. Scarlet was silent but accusing. He could hardly blame her. His heart continued to thump erratically.

He silently accused himself. For everything.

53

*A*nnie gave me the ability to make all my dreams come true.

She was right on so many levels. She fit the part. She was the part. Always had been, without me even really realising it.

Simply by being herself, she had precipitated her own downfall. Made herself integral to me. To me and my family.

As she breezed through life, her ability to blend in, *happy in either world, be it Deaf or hearing. She was everything that I was not.*

She made me feel like a victim again.

Like a little boy.

Like my mother had made me feel.

Completely unwanted and redundant.

It must have happened about a year ago, now. Well, that's how I remember it. When I noticed her not noticing me. She had snubbed me, waved me away with a dismissive gesture of the hand. She didn't even bother making eye contact. Just waved in my general direction. And with that one casual hand movement, I was catapulted back into my childhood. Her consummate arrogance, her carefree attitude; she had not even considered how her actions might impact upon me. So horribly like Mummy.

Now, I am pleased to state, she *is feeling the impact. Feeling the hurt. The emotional distress.*

I have systematically destroyed her. As I have been destroyed. Slowly, slowly, I went about my campaign; learning her habits, her routines. I have been unrelenting. Even I have noticed the small cracks appear in her armour. I have made little dents in her, and now I shall break her completely. She will play the Game.

She will not stay too long under the stairs. I want to play the game with her. Now.

I shall of course play it out properly. It would be a shame to veer from the agenda now. I shall play it to the end. But the point has been lost. Somewhere, somehow, I've lost the will to win. I suspect it is because I already have.

This one will just be the final nail in the final coffin. Hammering home my point. Which shall of course be wasted on all. Again.

Mind you, she could be different. I have to have faith. For what else is there?

But I want her to fail. She deserves to fail.

As she has failed me.

54

Crabb ignored Peters, who sat solidly on Annie's sofa with his laptop, typing with one hand. The other held his mobile into which he spoke hurriedly. Officers ran in and out of the flat – Annie's house had become a temporary headquarters.

Scarlet paced back and forth, squeezing the cat to her. Silent. White. Bloody terrified. Refusing to leave in case Annie returned. But Crabb ignored her. Had to. Ignored her as she walked past him, still holding Eric, mumbling that she'd be in her bedroom if Annie turned up.

He deleted the question mark next to Annie's name. She was no longer a question mark. The killer had her. Crabb stood back and looked at the list. Again he added 'Adam' and 'Ben'. He now had a chronological list of murder victims. And he had Annie's name. Not *yet* a murder victim.

Adam
Toby
William
Ben
Dora

Annie

He rubbed the names out and rewrote them.

He deleted Adam and Ben. Moved Dora's name next to William's. To make a circle. A full circle, he thought vaguely.

Toby

William, Dora

Annie

There was something complete to it now. As if before it had been a mathematical equation with too much data. Too much wrong information: there only to misdirect and confuse. Now he had the whole formula. It was there to solve. Or was he merely seeing things as he wanted to see them? He could theoretically keep on adding names, filling out the circle, ad infinitum. But it *looked* and felt complete. Crabb cocked his head. He added another question mark in the middle.

Peters' whispered voice interrupted his thoughts. 'There's a full-scale search on for Annie. The whole works. The police are interviewing everyone again. Double checking, in case we missed something. Somewhere. Anywhere. And they've picked up Theo. He's in custody.'

Crabb heard but was too intent on his work to reply. He registered that all it might take was the realisation of a little detail missed, the spotting of an anomaly. A contradiction. A lie. Anything.

He knew he could solve it. Right here, right now. He finished his cigarette, stubbing it into an already full saucer. Added his stub to the countless cigarettes that Scarlet was smoking.

Fuck. He *had* to find Annie.

He thought back to how the case had started, how it had

unfolded. He continued to leave out Adam and Ben. So, what was he left with?

The murder of a little boy – Fifteen years old.

And then the murder of a young man – Thirty-seven.

Followed by the murder of an older woman – Sixty.

And now the disappearance of a young woman – Thirty-seven.

Four names. Four characters. The answer was there. He felt intuitively that it was within his grasp.

'I'll put then in gender order,' he said. He grunted to himself and rewrote the names.

Dora
Annie
William
Toby

He looked at the column. 'Bloody hell,' he said.

'What?'

'Look, Peters, come here.' Crabb pointed excitedly at the board. 'What do you see? Forget the gender thing. That's not it.'

The DS scrutinised the names. Tilted his head, as if to get a different angle. Shook it in bewilderment.

'I don't get it,' he said.

Peters carried on shaking his head with incomprehension.

Crabb wiped the names off the board and rearranged them: the oldest at the top.

Dora

Annie, William

Toby

'Got it. That's it. Same order, but not gender,' said Crabb.

'Annie and William are the same age. It's not *who* they are as individuals. But what they represent *as a whole*.'

He stood away from the board, to better see it. Looked at Peters, who continued to look confused. Crabb said, 'It's a *family*. I can't believe it. Fuck. It's a family. It's that simple. You add the name of Annie, and it's a family.'

Peters slowly nodded but still looked unsure. Crabb wasn't convinced that he was seeing the whole picture.

'Annie *is* the missing link. Always bloody has been. He could have taken Fiona, for example, but he wanted Annie. Specifically, Annie. She was involved emotionally with all the victims. The killer has been leading up to this. Leading up to Annie. The final one.'

He sat down on an armchair and looked at the whiteboard.

'These four names are real people. They are not related. But their ages show that they *could* be,' Crabb said.

His voice was getting louder and louder as the pieces fell into place. As he began to understand it.

'The killer is recreating a family. A deaf family.'

He stood back and let his own words sink in.

'Dora as the grandmother, William and Annie as the parents, and Toby as the son.'

He watched as his sergeant's face cleared, his brains catching up with the new information. Finally saying, 'So, whose family is it?'

'Well, that's the bloody question, isn't it?' Crabb said.

He started pacing the room, muttering to himself.

'And he's re-enacting something that happened to this family at a specific time. So they'd be the age they were then. Like recreating a birthday party. His own?' Crabb said.

He nodded to himself.

'That's it. That's it exactly. They'd be the ages they were when this *something* happened. But it has to be more than a birthday party. It was *something* that affected the whole family. The killer would have been a child then. And now he is punishing his family. But for what?'

He carried on walking in circles and talking to himself. He said, 'The *something* that happened: it has to be linked to a birthday party, bearing in mind the stomach contents. A forgotten birthday? A child's party with no guests? An abused and lonely child who is now trying to recreate the whole thing as an adult? No, no, no. That's not it. It's not *enough*. If it was only a crap birthday party, why the skewer, why the things in the mouth, why the faked deaths?'

He smacked the side of his head and pulled at his earlobe. And then he got it.

'I know. Fucking *hell*. It's something that happened *at* the birthday party. Now *that* sounds right. Something that involved the whole family. Something that has to be put right.'

Peters said, 'Who's the killer then? A brother?'

Crabb stopped. He nodded quickly. 'Could be. Could be any male family member, but I think you're right. Has to be the brother: a close blood relationship.'

He could hear himself talking faster and faster as the idea gelled into something solid.

'That's why each killing had a feeling of something being staged. Toby was found in water, as if drowned. William with his fake slashed wrists, as if a suicide. Dora who was found dead, eating her own hands and covered in alcohol. Drank herself to death? The pencil shavings, the dog's ear, the hands. The specific meanings of those I don't know. But we have a murder or accident in water, a suicide, and death by alcohol. What do you think?'

He found himself completely unable to stop moving. His heart still beat erratically and his mind veered again and again to a picture of a tied-up Annie, one hand free.

'Come on. Time's running out. What's the most obvious thing that affects a family? That devastates a family? As a unit. Think,' said Crabb.

Peters brought his eyebrows together as if in a parody of deep thought, but his eyes skittered about the room. He wasn't concentrating. He was panicking. Crabb tried to get him back on track; said, 'Death of one of them? A child? A child's death could destroy a family. All parents die. It's expected. It's only natural. It would affect a family less dramatically if this is all because of a parent's death. We'll go with death of a child then.'

He tried to settle the adrenaline coursing around his body. Tried to stop sweating. Said, 'And that child was Toby. Well, Toby *represents* that child's death. By drowning,' he repeated.

He sat on the sofa again and put his head in his hands. If he didn't work it out soon he'd have no chance of finding Annie in time. He let his brain clear and then silently went through various scenarios in his head.

Why would a person, a man, recreate a family? He worked on the premise that his theory was bang on. So, a death of a boy. A deaf boy. But who was the original boy who had died? What had set the killer off on this fantastical game? A dead boy dumped in a Hampstead pond. That was the starting point.

Crabb swept at his bald head. Again and again he ran his fingers across the dome of his head. He felt it calming him. Focusing him.

A killer replicating what had happened to his own family. It was that simple. How many deaf boys had been murdered on Hampstead Heath over the years? Or maybe, bearing in mind it had been a drowning, it could have been recorded as accidental. Surely there can't have been that many?

'Look up all deaths of fifteen-year-old deaf boys on Hampstead Heath,' Crabb told Peters.

'Going how far back?'

'As far back as bloody necessary. And bear in mind, it's going to be the drowning of a boy, so it's more than possible that it would have been ruled accidental. Go back years. Just do it and hurry up.'

In his excitement, Crabb found it difficult not to hover at the DS's shoulder as his fingers flew over the keyboard. The man didn't type as fast as Crabb wanted. Then again, no one could type as fast as Crabb wanted.

'Come on, come on. Hurry up,' Crabb said and lit another cigarette. 'I bet he's killing them in the order they died. I can save Annie if I'm right. He's still got to play his game with her.' He paused. 'In the killer's head, Annie is his mother. I'd guess he's the surviving sibling. It all fits.'

Crabb noticed that Peters' hands trembled over the keyboards. He swore.

'Bloody crap,' said Crabb. 'You're trying to type too fast. Just calm down.'

Peters' fingers frantically backspaced and retyped a word. 'My fingers have turned into toes,' he said.

'For Christ's sake. I've told you, calm down. Pull yourself together. I'm relying on you here,' said Crabb.

The young DS gathered himself. He breathed deeply and then resumed typing. 'Sorry,' he said.

Crabb told him*self* to breathe: Peters wasn't the only one on the verge of panicking. Annie had been missing for just over two hours. He had time. He unclenched his teeth. His mouth was dry. His head ached.

He didn't allow himself to think what would happen if he was wrong.

55

Bound and gagged, locked in a cupboard, Annie found time had become static. She might as well have been floating, suspended in a vacuum. She thought it was like that old question about whether a tree makes a sound in the forest when it falls if there is no one there to hear it. Time, she discovered, was like that. With no starting point, who was to say if it was any later? Did it only exist if you had something against which to measure it? Like light.

Or another person.

There was nothing to fear from darkness. Darkness was only the absence of light – it wasn't a physical threat. It couldn't harm her. Closing her eyes made her better equipped to deal with the situation. *I'm making it dark; I have darkness, darkness doesn't have me.*

Her arms and legs started to cramp and her mouth was dry. So dry. It was difficult swallowing with the rag in her mouth. She could smell her own sweat. It was hot. Stiflingly hot.

Her eye hurt where he had punched her. Annie thought about the man who had kidnapped her from outside Maggie's. The man she had seen around the area for years.

She thought furiously. Went through her options. She knew he had kept Toby and William for a couple of days. The man had obviously coerced them into *doing* something: that much she knew – Crabb was right, a game or a test of some sort that the killer had created.

And happy fucking birthday to someone.

Let them eat cake, she thought and almost laughed. Hysteria wasn't something she wanted to contend with so she went back to breathing calmly.

Toby would have been too frightened to go along with anything. She could only imagine his fear. Too young to understand some sick game. Probably locked in this same cupboard. Blanking out that vision, she concentrated on William. He would have refused to follow instruction. Either based on his lack of imagination or simply out of sheer bloody-mindedness. And Dora? Well, she would have refused to participate in anything that was not within her control. She would have died fighting; clinging on to her pride and her principles.

The more Annie gave it thought, the more evident it became that she would play along with whatever he wanted. However warped. At least she knew that no one had been sexually abused. That being the case, and rape not an obvious threat, she would do whatever she had to. Lying on her side in a comma shape, she wondered what she'd ever done to the man to warrant this attention. That warranted all these murders.

She jumped. Felt the vibrations of footsteps overhead. Descending. Knowing that she was trapped directly underneath the stairs, she cowered at the very back of the space. Where the ceiling sloped down and the area was at its smallest. But she couldn't burrow her way into invisibility. She'd run out of hiding space. Wanting to close her eyes like a child, she played the juvenile game: if she couldn't see him he'd be unable to see her.

Curling into a ball, foetal, she waited for him to open the door. Eyes now wide open.

A sudden burst of sunshine hit her in the face, making her squint. He stood over her in silhouette. Blinking furiously, she tried to adjust her vision, adapt from darkness to light. Saw his outline in front of her, his face close to hers. Smiling down at her, he signed, 'Come on, then, Mummy. It's playtime.'

He gently removed the tape from her mouth. She lacked the spit to forcibly eject the rag from her own mouth so let him pluck it from her. With a flourish. As if producing a rabbit from a hat. He looked gleeful as he untied her. Rubbing at her sore wrists and ankles, she crawled out on all fours.

'There, Mummy. Better?' he signed.

She forced her face into some semblance of normality. Mummy? Had he really just called her *mummy*? She refused to allow him to see her terror. Held his gaze boldly. He seemed slightly perplexed at her reaction. Or non-reaction. *Good*, she thought with some satisfaction.

He shrugged, as if unconcerned and again signed down at her, 'It must be a relief to be out of that sweaty little Cupboard. No one has liked it. I know *I* hated it, but you already know that. You enjoyed Granny's little game. Remember?'

His eyes danced with merriment and he laughed. His laughing was more frightening than his usual calm and set features that she had become used to over the years. Now he seemed overexcited. Like a boy. As if he couldn't wait for something. She didn't allow herself to think what that something might be. Was in no doubt that she would find out soon enough.

Ignoring what he was wearing, she allowed him to take her hand. She bit down on her lip, angry that she had no choice. He was stronger than her.

As they left the cupboard under the stairs, she looked to her right – down three little steps. They led to a sitting room. She only got a passing glance at the room; a worn and shabby sofa with old, lacy covers that sat crookedly on the arms. They were so old they might as well not have been there. They looked like fingers of grey material clinging desperately on to the last stages of life. Glancing up at the window – so grimy that she couldn't see outside, she felt him tug her hand. Swallowing in a mouth that was so dry it hurt, she had no option but to meekly follow him.

They stopped at the doorway to the kitchen. The smell of dog hit her. Her eyes swivelled around the room – and found the source. A large, overweight black Labrador lay curled on a red tartan rug on the floor. There was something wrong with its breathing. It was struggling, wheezing. The animal was in pain. She looked closer. The dog had been bleeding; its ear sat awkwardly at the side of its head. The tip was missing. Refusing to let her mind remember where that tip had ended up, she quickly turned her gaze away.

She thought, *I have survived great loss at the hands of this man. And I will get through this. No matter what.* But she wasn't as convinced as she wanted. Sadly, it was all she had.

Next to the Labrador, curled into a ball, was Dora's dog. The Chihuahua looked dishevelled and trembled, although it was only sleeping. She saw its flanks rise and fall softly.

She carried on her scan of the kitchen. *Remember, keep your face neutral*, she told herself. *And stop trembling.*

It was filthy. It smelt of old people. It was an indefinable but recognisable odour. The smell of tired human flesh, washed a little less, cared for a little less. Loved a little less. And there, if she inhaled a little deeper, she could just catch a little whiff of hope that someone would not have to carry on living for too much longer. It was the smell of a slow surrender. The not bothering to disguise one's own dying smell with flowery powders and perfumes. Just eking out the last few days, hours, minutes of one's life.

There were unwashed plates and coloured plastic cups thrown in the sink. Paper plates with the remnants of food still stuck to them had been casually tossed and left on the kitchen worktops. Swathes of streamers were Sellotaped from all four opposing walls and met, drooping in the middle of the room; sad and deflated. He'd obviously intended that they hang from the central light fitting, but gravity had won. The decorations were discoloured and old. As were the balloons that lay only semi-inflated and on the floor.

Looking more closely around her, she saw that all the decorations were old. Really old. Like years and years old. A large banner was strung from the centre of the room, nailed into the ceiling with tacks. It declared a rather pathetic 'Happy Birthday' – its colours faded and the 't' in birthday ripped; the 'H' was missing entirely. The number 'Thirteen' was still legible. But only just. The innards of festive poppers had been trampled into the stickiness of the old lino floor and lay like damp autumn leaves underfoot. They looked trodden in for eternity.

The kitchen floor itself was only superficially dirty in some places. There were areas that although dusty, were vaguely clean underneath. She guessed it had been a relatively recent descent into complete chaos. A plummeting and frightening descent. Annie forced her eyes to travel on.

There was a large pool of dried blood. A *very* large pool. Big red bootprints had been smudged across the floor. She let her eyes pass over the blood as if it was not an uncommon sight. But inside her head, she screamed and screamed. She struggled to maintain her non-expression. Tried to ignore the hammering of her heart which thumped at the base of her throat.

He nudged her in the side and she turned and looked at a birthday cake which sat in pride of place in the middle of the table. It looked fresh, and beneath the bad smells, she thought she could still detect the smell of baking. The cake was obviously home-made. It had that slightly off-kilter look that came from its layers not being quite symmetrical. The icing was slap-dash; its execution hurried.

He poked her in the ribs again and signed 'Mummy' at her. Raised his eyebrows as if unsure of her response.

Again with the 'mummy'. She'd chosen to ignore it the first two times he'd signed it. But now she really *heard* it. With all its potential meaning and associated madness. As she saw it signed, her stomach lurched a little.

On a practical level she wasn't old enough to be his mother. Not by a long shot. *He* was older than her. Not by a lot, but definitely older. Okay. Now she knew that *this* was part of the game. An important part.

She had no choice. She'd play. Lifting her hands, she signed back, 'Yes, darling. What do you want?'

Waiting, she held her breath. Was that the right response? His face told her it was. He was ludicrously pleased. He clapped his hands together and started a macabre dance in front of her. Annie watched, keeping her face blank – hiding her distaste and fear. Allowed just a little pretend-love to shine from it. It made her want to vomit. It was hard to keep it up, but she persevered.

He stood there, a grown man squeezed into a child's school uniform. Insanity oozed from him. His very male and hairy thighs bulged obscenely from his shorts. The sleeves of his blazer come to his elbows and the material was ripped down the back. Hair sprouted from the top of his shirt. A ridiculously small school cap perched on his head. *It makes him look, well, mad*, she thought stupidly. A grotesque and crazy dancing dummy. Annie shivered and felt sick. Counted to ten. Slowly. She started to tremble again.

Trying for a kindly, mummy-type expression, she signed, 'What's your name?' *Name you what?'*

'Don't be stupid. You know me. What are you *talking* about?'

He roughly threw her onto one of the chairs around the table. Tied her left wrist to the arm. She looked down and noticed that the legs of the chair had been bolted to the floor. On this hot day the plastic slats of the chair make her flesh sticky immediately. She crossed her legs, attempting to pull at her shorts to cover the bare flesh of her legs. Her heart thudded in her chest and her mouth was still dry; arid with apprehension. *Appear normal*, she told herself. *Pretend you're enjoying yourself. I'm just having birthday tea with a nutty uncle. Or more accurately, a nutty son.*

She said it over and over to herself, chanting it like a mantra. If she thought it enough times, maybe she could convince herself.

Realising her mistake, she too late understood that she should have called him by his name. He's changed his age, but not *who* he was. She'd have to learn the rules of this game. Quickly. She already knew the basic and obvious premise of the festivities he was playing out. Crabb had been right. All she had to do, was not rock the boat. Agree with everything. Suggest pass the bloody parcel – whatever it took. She signed, 'Happy birthday.'

His grin was wide: too wide to look anything other than fucking mental. He clapped his hands together excitedly and signed, 'Go on. Sing the song. The Happy Birthday to Me song. Sing it now.'

Pausing, she was at a loss. Finally, 'Do you want me to use my voice, or sign it?'

The grin evaporated, like a burst bubble. 'Take your fucking pick, Annie. I'll leave it up to you.'

Frightened by the sudden use of her real name, confused,

she decided to sign the song only. Remembered that Crabb had said deafness was key to the man and his game. Oddly, she felt embarrassed at having to perform this to him. Almost shy. What a strange combination. Fear and coyness at the same time. She wouldn't have thought it possible. Mind you, she'd never have thought it possible that she'd be tied to a chair, surrounded by filth, a dried blood pool and a man in boy's clothing. A man-boy. She felt herself starting to shiver uncontrollably, her hands fumbling and shaking. He didn't appear to notice.

He lowered his head when she had finished signing. She could have sworn she saw him blush. He wiggled his foot from side to side, pivoting the toes of his right foot from side to side, his heel suspended in the air. Looking at him, she couldn't work out whether he really believed himself to be a child, or if he could adopt this posture, shrug it on like an old jumper, and carry it off so well merely through practise. Annie knew it was important to get the answer to that question. And the quicker the better.

She involuntarily reared back in her seat as he approached and tore her hand free from its armrest, fumbling with the ties in his haste to get her up and out of the chair.

'Come on, Mummy. As a thank you for that, however fucking belated, you deserve a tour of the house. I'll show you everything.'

He pulled her from the chair and Annie fell into step behind him, walking across the kitchen. She stepped over the blood, not looking at it. Trying to forget that it must be Dora's. Tugging gently at his hand, she stopped him. Commented on the lovely decorations.

'It all looks wonderful. Everything is perfect.'

Wanting him on side, she wasn't sure if she'd gone too far. But he seemed pleased enough, although distracted – almost feverish. He nodded and leading her out of the kitchen, they entered a small room, directly opposite.

It was the first relatively clean space she had seen. It was superficially 'normal' looking and other than a whisper of dust that speckled the surfaces, it also seemed non-threatening. A room not long abandoned by its resident, but rarely visited by others. Next to the single bed with its ring binder was a side table with boxes and boxes of pills. In neat and ordered piles. A pamphlet from Macmillan Nurses lay next to an empty jug. Tissues and a glass of water stood within easy reach. The water was scummy – untouched for months and months. A film of dirt had settled; flecks hung stagnant in the liquid, almost grey with age.

Above the bed, a large wooden cross was nailed to the wall, next to a picture of Jesus Christ.

The walls were covered with photographs of a good-looking boy; from baby pictures up into his early to mid-teens. Various poses, but all of them showed him smiling or laughing; sometimes boldly and unashamedly looking directly into the camera – grinning, laughing, posing. A happy boy. A larger photograph of him sat in a gilt frame next to the bed. She bent forward to read the inscription above. 'My Son.'

Annie nodded and smiled as if she knew what it all meant.

The man turned her towards the en suite bathroom. Clearly adapted for a disabled person.

'You were a very sick, Mummy. Shame, really, that we lost touch. I didn't have the pleasure of actually seeing you when you were ill. But that was your choice. Not mine.'

He smiled at her. 'Although I rather think I would have made the same choice as you.' He held his hands out with his palms facing upwards. 'To tell you the truth, we haven't seen each other since I was a young man. Do you remember? No? Well, let's not sully things now with sour memories.'

She was caught by surprise when he took her hand in his again, pulled her out of the sick room and into the hallway. He almost ran her up the stairs, his excitement making him trip: dragging her. Eager, eager to show her the rest of the house. So fast, she could barely keep up. The further they got from the little bedroom, the filthier the house became. Her free hand trailed up the wall as she was hauled up the stairs, steadying herself. She pulled it away as she felt the greasiness. A huge curl of ancient wallpaper peeled away from the wall, and she had to duck under it.

Annie looked up. Cobwebs hung in every corner. A thin strand of silk brushed against her cheek as they rounded the top of the stairs. Flapping wildly at a spider's web, she gasped with disgust as her hair stuck to it. A fat black spider which she had disturbed ran down and across her chest. She flailed at it, cried aloud, finally managed to flick it from her. Trying to balance herself on the newel post, she nearly missed its reassuring solidness as he whipped her around the corner. He dragged her at such speed that she stumbled. At one point she fell to her knees, grazing her shin on an up-turned carpet tack. He hardly noticed. She had become a forgotten attachment so intent was he on his destination.

Pausing outside a door, panting slightly, he stood for a moment, as if wanting to protract the wait. Annie found herself expecting some revelation. And not a good one.

A piece of yellowed paper was pinned to one side of the panelled door – Keep Out!!! Next to it a Chelsea banner, its tassels dusty and old.

The man drew his breath in expectantly, held it for a few seconds and then threw open the door. It banged back against its hinges on the wall behind it. And having no choice, she stood there and looked. It was a teenager's room; the owner long gone. She saw strangled memories, locked in a long-ago time. There was a framed photograph with a boy holding aloft a trophy. He was grinning. It was the same boy in the photograph that she had seen downstairs in the sick room. This is the son's room. A dead boy's room, she guessed.

It appeared shrine-like. Untouched. A mother trying to keep the memory of her child alive? But there was no love here anymore. Only despair and sadness. Ivy crept in through a crack in the wall next to the window frame and coiled through the gap; sliding, reaching and crawling up and across the ceiling.

She guessed that nothing had been changed or moved in here for many years. It was an inactive room: as frozen and paralysed as its ex-inhabitant. The once plain blue curtains were now moth-eaten and tattered. An old bike had fallen on its side. A pair of scruffy trainers, one with a sock still in it, lay as they had been thrown, however many years ago. One lay on its sole, the other on its side. Both were still tied in a hasty knot. An old Chelsea top was slung over the back of a chair. Posters of football players were pinned to the walls.

The shelves were full of sporting trophies, although the cups were dull. It was all shabby and forgotten. Although cluttered, the room felt only empty. It was as if the boy had been simply plucked from his room and only the memory of him lingered.

The one thing that indicated any life at all was the bed. It had clearly been made recently – the blankets tucked with neat hospital corners, the covers stretched taut over the mattress. Trampoline tight. Folded pyjamas peeked out from under the corner of the pillowcase.

The man touched her arm.

'This is Ewan's room. Now it's mine.'

Her brain stumbled and she knew she looked vague. He flung his arms in the air, suddenly furious: signed, 'Ewan. My fucking brother. Your son. Keep up, Mum. Fuck me.'

He looked at her with utter contempt. She tried to excuse

her blunder but the damage was done. How to rescue the situation? Frightened, she attempted to make soothing noises and gestures. Signed, 'I knew that. Of course I knew that. Silly me.'

'Yes, very silly you. A word to the wise. Do *not* fuck with me, Mummy. You fucked with me before. Don't you dare to presume to do it now. Not ever again. Okay?'

Her mind moved, in turn sluggishly, and then in erratic frenzy. She could think of nothing to say to calm him. His body was bent forward in anger. Dressed in his boy's clothes. Staring at her with his man's fury. Complete panic overwhelmed her. Shut her down. She whispered up a silent prayer. To her dismay, she couldn't stop the one tear as it fell from her eye, showing him her weakness. She felt its wet path trickle down her cheek. *Think, woman. Think*, she berated herself. But her mind had temporarily taken a holiday. It had deserted her. Given up.

Annie closed her eyes, needing everything to stop.

Crabb felt himself tense. The sound of Peters' fingers hitting the keys had suddenly stopped.

'Look,' the DS spoke and Crabb heard the happy surprise in Peters' voice; felt his own spirits rise, the excitement kick in. His headache immediately left him and he felt fresh with hope. Crabb said, 'What? What have you got?'

'You were right. It's all here. Everything. It's one of those "memory lane" features – rehashing an old news story.'

'Well fucking have the grace to tell me. I need to know now.'

Peters read aloud from the information on his screen.

'Nineteen ninety-five. On July 28th, a body of a deaf fifteen-year-old, Ewan Fletcher was found in a small pond on Hampstead Heath. The death was ruled accidental. He'd been playing on the heath with his younger brother. The boys' deaf parents and grandmother were unavailable for comment.'

'Bloody *hell*,' said Crabb. 'It *is* the younger brother. Christ!'

Crabb strode around the room. Fletcher. Crabb had him. Now, please God, let it not be too late.

He angrily swore to himself, to Peters. '*Fuck*. He was always there: there – but in the background. So easy to forget he even existed. He's been floating around this bloody case like a ghost. Invisible.'

He was furious. Had never even *considered* this man as a potential suspect. Not even entertained the notion. Everyone, including himself, had purely and simply forgotten him. Crabb had heard him, but not seen him. Not really looked at him and *seen*. Simple as that. *Everyone* had missed him. But Crabb knew he was only trying to make himself feel better. He *should* have thought of it. So much time wasted. So many lives wasted.

'Did DC Bragen even include him in the checking of addresses and cars?'

Peters shook his head. 'Didn't think to. Thought he was one of us. You know – in a position of authority.'

Jesus, what a cock-up. The DS kept his head down, embarrassed by their omission. Crabb said, 'What's his address?'

Peters told him.

'That can't be bloody right. I know those flats. There's no way the killer could come and go with all four victims, keep them there and then take them out of the flat without being seen. It's just not doable.'

He forced himself to sit down, his head throbbing again. Said, 'Go back to the article about the drowning. Check if it gives any more details about the family, when they all died, who died last and more importantly where they lived.'

Peters read out loud: '"Mrs Edna Fletcher, née Brown, died 1st April last year. She never moved out of the family home." It's a local address. Just round the corner, in fact.'

Crabb stood up and peered over the DS's shoulder. Looked at the computer screen. And there was the address. Crabb stopped breathing.

'Fuck me. That's the road where Dora's body was dumped.'

'That's either brave or seriously stupid,' said Peters. 'Or overly arrogant.'

'Or he's losing the plot. Doesn't care. Annie is his main prize. His "mother". Shit.'

Just for a second, he felt paralysed. Couldn't move. But then he got his act together. He said, 'Right, I've got to go. Now. Now this minute.'

Crabb rushed to the door, hearing Peters' voice behind him: 'Crabb, wait! We can get the hostage unit on it. I could arrange backup cars to be dispatched now – they could be there in five minutes.'

Crabb was already dismissing what Peters was saying. He was doing it his way.

'Crabb, stop. Just fucking stop.'

Crabb was so surprised to hear him swear that he stopped in mid-stride.

'You need to know this. There's a follow-up piece. Several stories following the family and what happened to them. The father committed suicide shortly after the death of Ewan, only six weeks later in fact, by slashing his wrists. He'd moved out of the family home already. And the grandmother... hang on.'

Crabb angrily pulled at papers on the table and found his discarded car keys underneath. He grabbed them and stood impatiently waiting for Peters to finish. He knew he had to be briefed fully. Have all the ammunition possible. But it was diffi-cult not to just run from the flat to find Annie.

Peters continued talking, calmer now and more in control: 'The deaf grandmother continued living with the mother, her daughter, Edna, until her own death. The grandmother died from alcoholism at the age of sixty. Wait, wait. Here – the mother died from cancer last April at the same address.'

'The same age as Dora. Hence the rum. A full house. I'm going now. I've got enough. And there's the trigger. The mother's death last year. Same month as Adam Jacobs was kicked to death.'

He was trying to work out his plan of action as he moved across the sitting room.

'What about backup? You can't go on your own. Don't be a fool.'

'I am not having the entire force descending on the house mob-handed. With armed backup. It's overkill and not necessary. I can talk to him. I understand it now.'

He took a breath. He could envisage it all playing out with disastrous consequences if he informed the DCI. Trigger-happy policemen. Overexcited and adrenaline-fuelled officers on the rampage. Annie might get killed with a bullet clean through her head. Guns were never a good idea. Not when words would do.

'How do you know it's not necessary? It's a risk. What are you planning to do – *reason* with him? He's mad.'

'But I know him. I know the Game. I know the rules now. And I'll win. Without any guns. Organise what you need to, Peters. But do not, I repeat, *do not* allow *any* officers, armed or not, to storm the house. It's imperative that I have time with him. I can talk to him. We need to make sure Annie is still alive. And stays alive. I can convince him to give her up. I know I can.'

And he *did* know he could. He needed to take the initiative away from the killer, on his own. He was more than confident that he could do it. Although he was nervous. Frightened for Annie.

'Right, I've got it. Come *on*. Is there anything else?'

Crabb jiggled his keys in his hand, impatient and getting more bad-tempered the longer the DS talked. But he knew he had to listen. To make sure he was fully equipped: he needed to get the psychology right before he went steaming in there, confronting a killer.

'Ewan drowned on his brother's birthday.'

The birthday connection at last.

'July 28th, so why didn't he plan all the killings around that date? And what about the pencil shavings, and the dog's ear? What do they mean?'

'The actual date of his birthday doesn't matter. He was recreating it, in his own time. Wanting all his victims to be there. And they all failed him. But it's definitely all about *his* birthday. And whatever happened on that day. I'm not sure of the finer details. But I'll find out.'

He moved quickly towards the door, swerving past an officer who was standing there talking into his radio. The sound of running footsteps behind him, made Crabb turn. Scarlet caught hold of his sleeve.

'Do not make me slap you again, Crabb.' This time she smiled to take the edge off. 'But if you screw this up, I'll never forgive you.'

How much had she heard? Enough obviously.

'I won't screw it up. Promise.' He pulled her away from the officer in the hall. 'Keep Peters from giving up where I've gone. He's young and naïve. You're not. Give me two hours. At least. Look after my DS. I'm trusting you with that.' He smiled briefly. 'And no, you won't slap me again. Ever.'

He slammed the door behind him and ran to the car, started it, and took a deep breath. Trying to hurry but equally trying to remain calm. Get it all right in his head.

The skewering *was* a symbolic thing all along. The killer obviously had serious issues about being the only hearing person in a family of deaf. He'd been making a very special point.

Crabb forced the car into gear and tyre-screamed his way from the block. He went through everything in his head, speaking aloud in the privacy of his car: He wondered what Annie was doing. What she was being made to do. Put his foot on the accelerator.

Finally he turned into a quiet cul-de-sac and parked several doors down from his destination. Quickly he rang Mrs Whorton, the old bag of a neighbour who'd said she'd seen Ben walking behind Toby.

'Mrs Whorton? DI Crabb here. When you gave your statement, did you omit anything?'

'No.'

'Perhaps you saw someone else in the area at the time? Near the school? Maybe a vehicle? Did you see Toby get into a van?'

There was a pause. Heavy on the quiet venom. Finally, 'Well, you appear to know that I did indeed see Toby get into a van. But that was hardly worth mentioning. After all, the boy was with one of us. A figure of authority. A good man.'

'And who was it?'

She told him what he already knew.

Crabb disconnected the call, cutting her off. Nasty bitch.

He now realised how close this house was to the Deaf Club. A mere couple of minutes. Time enough to steal Dora and return without being missed.

Pulling up at the address, he opened the car door and got out. Jogging up the street he wiped his sweaty palms down his trouser legs. He could feel his heart thudding uncomfortably underneath his shirt.

57

———————

As we stood in Ewan's room, I watched as a lone and rather pathetic tear escaped her eye. I watched its progress down her face, as it tumbled over her scar. The teardrop left a wet mark, not dissimilar to a snail's trail, in the trough of her blemished skin. It disappeared into the heat of her neck. I waited for more. Tears seldom travelled alone. They were pack animals. Find one, and you'd find a million in its wake. Waiting quietly. Just around the corner. I waited politely for the deluge to come. But no. Nothing.

Fascinating. The teardrop turned out to be a real live, honest to goodness solo act. A one hit wonder. Maybe she was exerting some control over her tear ducts. Control indeed. I carried on looking at her. More interested now than angry. She closed her eyes. I prided myself that patience was one of my many virtues. I waited until she thought it right and fitting to open her eyelids. To look upon me again.

I didn't have to wait long. She did, however, surprise me.

She looked me straight in the eye and signed, 'What are we waiting for, Birthday Boy? Maybe we could have a cup of tea? And some of that cake you made. Personally, I'd prefer a drink. A glass of wine would hit the spot. As it's your birthday.'

Feeling slightly disconcerted by her manner, we went downstairs fairly amicably. I let her lead me by the hand. Always good to lull a person into a false sense of security.

We took our seats at the table. I didn't bother tying her down. It wasn't necessary. I knew she wouldn't make a run for it. We both knew that she wouldn't get very far. I was quicker. Bigger. Stronger. She semi-stood and gestured at the cake. Signed, 'Shall I be Mummy?'

Was that her idea of a joke? Or was she being serious? Difficult to know. I really had to hand it to her. She was giving me a run for my money. I decided to ignore her facetiousness, if that is indeed what it was. I signed back, 'You remember what you always told us, Mummy. Sandwiches first, cake after.'

'How about that glass of wine then?'

Shocked at her request, I looked up and past her: remembering. Mummy and Daddy did *have a glass of champagne at Ewan's birthday. To celebrate with pride the birthday of their adored son. But this wasn't Ewan's birthday. It was mine. There* should *have been champagne, but of course there'd been nothing.*

Nothing fanciful about my birthday. So why was Mummy asking for a tipple now? What was she playing at? My parents had had nothing as magnificent or joyous as a glass of anything to toast my birthday. Perhaps the woman in front of me was prepared to make a real go of it. Finally, give me the birthday that had been so catastrophically ruined. I signed, 'I'm afraid I haven't any wine. A beer? I have several of those in the fridge.'

'But it should be something special. It's your birthday after all. Let's just stick with the tea, then.'

I nodded. Felt the Game boundaries blur. I had never had anyone who had grasped the concept so quickly. Bringing it back into my control, I signed, 'What sort of son am I?'

I sat back and folded my arms. Waited for a nonsensical response.

She paused, then signed, 'You are my son. My special son.'

She was coming up with all the right answers. Although she hadn't got it fully. Not quite. But she would. I didn't bother informing her that she had answered well. Instead I threw her a curveball.

'If I'm so special, bring me my birthday sandwiches.'

She looked panic stricken. Funny really. Not knowing where to look for the sandwiches. Finally she worked it out in her fucking tiny pea brain. Yes, that's right, Mum. In the fridge. Amazing deductive reasoning going on there. She took hold of the plate and brought it to the table. And it was positively laden with a mountain of sandwiches. With all the right fillings. Egg mayonnaise. Cheese and chutney.

And of course, jam. My favourite. Nothing quite beats the jamminess of a jam sandwich.

'And what about my cake, Mummy? How did that go?'

She sat down again. Reverted to her blank face routine and took the cling film off the plate of triangular delights. Delaying. I helped her. Gave her a clue.

'Did you perhaps forget my cake? Did you?'

Suddenly enraged, I banged my fists on the table, making her jump.

'Did. You. Forget. My. Cake?'

She shook her head, signing frantically. Of course she hadn't forgotten the cake. There it was, she pointed at it. She'd made it last night. As a birthday treat. Home-made. Especially for me. She'd made it herself she repeated, her hands gabbling in their terror.

I had to hand it to her. She was putting on a great show. A fine performance. She deserved a rosette. Best In Show. I could staple it to her forehead as a going-home-present.

Although she was participating, my annoyance with her was growing. I could feel the early stirrings of fury rumble uncomfortably in my stomach. It didn't sit well. I couldn't understand it. I should be happy. Finally, I had the opportunity to explain. To someone who clearly had some passing semblance of a brain. But all I felt was anger.

It didn't bode well.

I sat down again. Belatedly realising that I had been standing. Shouting and signing down at her. I just wanted the right fucking answer. Was that really too much to ask?

I watched her. She faced me square on. Not dipping her eyes in fear. I actually saw the light in her eye as she got it. It was a fleeting brilliance that shone from her. A sudden gleam that appeared momentarily in her face. I smiled. Shrugging, she held her hands up in an admission of guilt.

'You're right. I did forget your cake. It was unforgivable. But I see that you've made one yourself. Good boy. It looks much better than anything I could have baked. Really, well done, you.'

Bravo. A million times bravo.

I smiled again. She smiled. Good God, it was turning into a love-fest. I'd have to nip that in the bud. But not yet. Much to my amazement I discovered I was actually beginning to have fun. I'm not sure how I felt about admitting that. But I was loath for it to end. We were having quite a merry old time of it. No one was more shocked than I. High jinx all round. Anyone would think it was my birthday.

I laughed in delight.

We were positively chummy. I realised I had a chummy mummy. I giggled. We were going great guns although I wouldn't use that expression to her face. Didn't want to alarm. Although guns are far too violent and crude a weapon for me. Not my thing. No, not at all.

But I had to keep everything in context. Not get carried away with my own hilarity. She was still my final contestant and would have to carry on playing.

'Why, precisely, did you forget my cake? Careful how you answer this one. I must accept your first answer. Your time starts now.'

I turned to look at a pretend watch on my wrist, counting down the seconds as they ticked by.

She was a cool customer. And she was proving her mettle. For that I had to respect her. I watched with growing fascination as she calmly took a sandwich. And then another one. She even offered me one. Audacious. She's a cool one, as I said. But clearly playing for time. Understandable. Under the circumstances.

I already know she had an inherent confidence. Self-belief. Whatever. Three hurrahs for her. She raised her eyes to mine. And there, again, that light shone from her eyes.

Realisation.

58

Annie's fear had ebbed and flowed throughout the afternoon. She had found herself in the troughs of despair that had made her feel physically sick. Then she would peak with a strange kind of elation when she'd got an answer 'right'. It was hard keeping up with the constant barrage of questions. But now she had an answer to give. And she knew that a lot rested on it. A life-changing answer was required. She couldn't afford to get it wrong. Why *had* the bloody mother forgotten to make the stupid cake for this man?

She took a sandwich. Egg mayonnaise. Bought herself time. Tried not to think of the filth in which this sandwich had been made. The bread felt as if it were increasing in size, becoming more impossible to swallow with every bite. *It's mind over matter*, she told herself. The bread was fresh, the filling as it should be. Breathe and chew. Not hungry at all, as un-hungry as she'd ever been, she took another sandwich; this time a jam one. She offered him the plate. He laughed and also took a jam sandwich. He was doing a lot of laughing. In all the wrong places. At all the wrong times.

She cast her mind back to the mother's room. Ewan's room. Her brief glimpse into the sitting room. Was there anything she'd missed? There had been *something*. In all the rooms she had seen – *something*. She struggled to remember. It had been an object that she herself was used to seeing. Something commonplace. Annie dipped her eyes, mind tumbling in panic.

And then she saw it in her mind. As clear as a bell.

Literally.

The bread in her mouth suddenly felt like a blockage. She gulped at it and concentrated – tried not to gag at the cloying sweetness of too much jam. Not answering was not an option. Answering the question wrong meant infuriating him. And might bring about her own possible death. Annie was still not clear what the end of this game was. Was it possible that she could win? If her answers were correct? The odds were not stacked in her favour. She could only hope for rescue. Relying on help did not come naturally to her.

Inhaling into the depths of her soul, she eventually decided to go for broke, and signed, 'I forgot to make you a cake because you're hearing. You're an embarrassment of a son.'

His eyebrows shot up his forehead in shock. Lowering them quickly, he waved his hand in a circular movement, indicating that she should expand.

Annie knew that within predominantly deaf families, a hearing child was sometimes viewed as something to be ashamed of. Deaf parents often wanted their children to be Deaf. Like they were. She signed, 'I'm Deaf. So is Daddy. Obviously Ewan is Deaf. But you're different. You're hearing. I'm ashamed of you. That's why I forgot to make your cake. Because I don't care.'

She stopped. Had she gone too far? He sat opposite her. No reaction. Nothing. A great belt of fear whupped her in the stomach. She shook. Felt tears threaten again. And then she just waited.

Should she make a run for it? But where would she run *to*? The front door was too far away. She was at the mercy of this man and how he chose to react to her answer. If he *was* the only hearing boy within a deaf family, would he acknowledge that truth? Or would he lie? Because he was angry.

He did a slow hand clap: his face expressionless. Carried on clapping. And clapping.

She waited.

And then he spoke, his eyes staring straight into hers. He didn't bother to sign now. Making her lip-read. As if he was terribly weary.

'Oh, congrats, Mummy. Hats off to you. I am overwhelmed by your brilliance.'

Nodding and keeping her face non-threatening, she could only wait to see what he did next.

'What gave it away? *Mother*.'

Annie noted the spite. His face screwed up as he said the last word. She signed, deciding to carry on being as deaf as possible. If he wanted deaf, he'd get it.

'I saw the flashing door bells for the Deaf. In your mother's and Ewan's room. Your room now – I understand that. And there was one in the sitting room as well. I just guessed that your father was also deaf. Deaf tend to marry deaf.'

'*Your* mother's room? Now, now. Don't forget to play the Game. *You* are my mother. Here to atone for *your* sins.'

Annie realised she was nodding too vigorously and changed it to an understanding tip of her head, gently; up and down, up and down – soothing, accepting.

'Do *not* patronise me. With your understanding nod. And you forget one person. A very, *very* important person. Not one to be ignored.'

Annie was stunned into silence. Who was he talking about? She made herself think. She'd been cast as 'Mummy'.

And then she got it. It was obvious once you made the connection. William was Daddy. Toby was Ewan. And Dora. Who did Dora represent? She went over the ages in her head, knowing she had to get this right. Dora was the grandmother. Couldn't be anyone else in this sick game.

'Your deaf grandmother,' she says.

'Indeed, *indeed*. You are excelling yourself. You're positively showing off. You have my utmost respect. But that can always change. You'd do well to remember that. But I appreciate your efforts thus far. Well done.'

He clapped again. Briefly this time. And he smiled again. A tired smile and spoke again: 'If I was being fair, I could put it to you that we have reached an impasse. A stand-off, if you will.'

They were stuck. Apparently.

'But who's to say that I *am* fair? In the circs. We still have round two. The important round. It is critical. Do you understand the enormity of what we are now going to attempt? But how could you? It remains the great stumbling block. No one has been able to do it. Haven't even come close. Maybe here you can shine. And shine you most certainly have been doing. So far. You have that in your favour. So for me, just one more little sunbeam is required from you. A last and solitary ray. Just for me.'

Annie asked him to sign what he'd just spoken. He raised his brows as if dealing with an incompetent. He signed it.

'Comprende?'

Annie just looked at him. Waited for some outlandish request. He signed, 'All you need do is apologise. A simple thing. But for those who have gone before you, an impossible task. You need to say "sorry". For my life. For the culmination of said existence – specifically apologise for my thirteenth birthday party.

Which never was. Because none of you loved me enough. You need to give me back that day.'

'I'm trying my best.'

'You are. I've already complimented you on the fact. What do you want – a fucking medal? It's a simple request. You have nearly reached the finishing line, Mummy. With all your limbs intact; unlike some. That's a blessing. And you have been punished. You have experienced the cupboard. You did it to me, because *your* mummy told you to. So I did it to you. It's always nice to be reciprocal, don't you think? But time waits for no man. Shall we proceed? I've got some new balloons. And of course I have to apologise myself. *There's* a thing I didn't think I'd hear myself utter. Not in this Game. Apologise for what, I hear you cry? What could he possibly have to be sorry about?'

Slowly she shook her head, not knowing the answer.

'The paucity of guests, Mummy. I'm sorry there aren't any. Again. Ironic really. Fantasy is mimicking my reality now. I *did* have some guests this time around. As I'm sure you've heard. But I killed them. They send their excuses.'

Holding his gaze, she realised that he was rushing. Hurrying through the last rites. The final round of the Game. Rushing was not a good thing. Whatever she did – be it blow up balloons, cut birthday cake, play 'pass the parcel' – she suddenly knew with a stark certainty, that he would kill her anyway.

He seemed quietly angry. Depressed. Defeated. Fatalistic. But mostly angry. It simmered silently, but not silently enough. He couldn't hide it. She knew it would be unleashed soon. He said, 'All I wanted was a proper party where I'm loved and got all the presents I asked for. A special day, like Ewan's was. A fucking apology for the useless day that it was. Long overdue I think you'd agree. That's all I want. A "sorry." And some cake. And a puppy. That's all I wanted. Not much for a young boy to want, is it?'

He disappeared. Out of her immediate line of vision, panic made her break into an immediate sweat. He had changed. Although he'd pretended delight that she'd grasped the rules of his Game, he was unsettled. Wanted it over.

So now it was the end. He was angry and he was dangerous.

What could she say to save herself? How could she excuse his shitty thirteenth birthday party when she didn't even know what had happened? She'd got the gist but knew there must be more.

She picked up a jam sandwich and started pulling it apart. Slowly.

The doorbell for the Deaf went off. Annie looked up. Prayed that it was Crabb. She literally prayed, heard the words in her head. *Please, God. Please, God. Please, God, let it be Crabb.* Annie sat, heart thumping as he leapt from his seat opposite her and tied both her hands to the armrests. He also bound her ankles to the chair.

'Now, who do you suppose that may be?' he said.

'Guests. Birthday guests. It *is* your thirteenth birthday, after all,' she said, now having no choice but to speak.

His good humour was back. He said, 'Oh, stop teasing, you. Silly Mummy. Have you invited imaginary friends? Friends for me? *What* a surprise. You're certainly coming up trumps.'

He looked around the kitchen and told Annie to sit tight. On his way to the door he glanced back at her, waggled his eyebrows and said, 'The plot thickens.'

He adjusted his tie and smoothed down his hair, his school cap left on the table. She thought his mood-change alarming. So quick. From a quiet fury to manically happy. He'd never been normal, but now he was seriously mad. Frighteningly mad.

'It's turning out to be quite a party,' he said. 'And I suspect I know who's at the door. I have to admit I would have expected him to let me know he was coming, but manners these days appear sadly lacking.'

Whoever it was, their presence had certainly cheered her mad host up. Disproportionately so. Worryingly so. She closed her eyes again.

59

———

Crabb waited impatiently. He'd already noticed the white van in the driveway. Had quickly peeked in. Room enough for a wheelchair. Presumably the mother's.

And the owner's own car – a small green Fiat – was parked beside it. Used to take Annie. Less conspicuous than the van.

Crabb had rung the doorbell. Waited. Nervous. Finally, the door swung open slowly and a man's face popped around the frame. The face smiled and the man said, 'Aha. I was right. I knew it could only be you. What a treat.'

Crabb recoiled at the appearance of the man standing before him. He was dressed like a boy in a school uniform, but there the resemblance of desired-youth stopped. Abruptly and jarringly. The man dwarfed his boy clothes, exploding out of them, so tiny were the shorts and blazer. Even the tie was too small. Crabb watched the man and assembled his face – going for relaxed calm.

'Hello, Sam. May I come in?'

'Be my guest. And I mean that quite literally.' The interpreter held the door open and then turned back towards Crabb. 'What, no balloons?' he said.

Crabb smiled his apologies and hurried to catch up with Sam. He had disappeared quickly into the house, leaving Crabb flat-footed. Trying not to run, trying to maintain a calmness that he didn't feel, Crabb followed quickly.

Sam stood behind Annie, a skewer in his hand. Crabb watched as the interpreter brushed the metal spike across her ear. Keeping his face neutral, Crabb said, 'May I sit?'

'But of course. Pick a chair, any chair. And welcome, welcome.'

Crabb sat, wondering why Sam wasn't bothering to restrain him. Tie his hands. Incapacitate him in some way. Maybe he didn't feel threatened. Arrogance oozed from him.

Crabb gestured towards his cigarettes in his pocket. 'May I?'

'But of course. I'm delighted that at least somebody has an obvious vice. At last.'

Sam pushed an ashtray towards him, appearing relaxed. But appearances could be misleading. The interpreter sat, very close to Annie. Too close. Said: 'Well, apart from your birthday greetings which I take as a given, is there anywhere in particular that you'd like to start? I'm sure you have questions. Fire away.'

Sam slowly sipped from his mug of Earl Grey tea. He took a jam sandwich and offered the plate to Crabb.

Shaking his head, he said, 'You killed the boy on the railings.'

'Indeed I did, Crabb. I did kill the poor unfortunate. It was a practice run. Getting my eye in. Or boot, on that occasion.'

'You lost control. You were angry, weren't you?'

Sam said nothing.

'You were angry because your mother had just died. Your Deaf mother. All your family are Deaf.' Crabb spoke quietly, keeping his voice on an even keel.

Sam smiled, held his arms out from his sides. Added a defeated shrug for good measure. A demure bowing of his head.

As if admitting being caught out in a lie. Sam raised his eyes to focus on Crabb's. Almost coyly.

'Mea culpa. My family were indeed Deaf. I stand before you, guilty as charged on that count. And yet, my mother here, Annie to you, she's one step ahead of you. She worked it out for herself: all on her lonesome with only a little encouragement from me.'

He smiled quickly at Annie as if they were bound by something personal.

'I'm what is commonly known as a CODA.'

Crabb sat back and blew smoke into the air. Said, 'An acronym. Child of Deaf Adults.'

Crabb saw Annie's eyebrows rise up in surprise at his knowledge. Discreetly, he gave a quick thumbs-up to her and she acknowledged him with a nod. She was pale but looked physically unhurt. He said, 'And your grandmother is also Deaf. In fact, that makes you the only hearing person within your family.'

'Right again. I am half deaf, if you will.'

'*Does* it make you half deaf?' He lit up another cigarette. 'Or does it make you half a person only? A nobody? Not all there.' He held his hand up, not wanting any misunderstanding. 'And I don't mean "not all there" as in mentally incapacitated. There is no doubt that you are a clever man. Very clever.'

'Thank you for the flattery. It will get you everywhere. But let me tell you how I came to be nothing. Even the great Dora Potts knew nothing of my existence as a child: I was kept quiet as an embarrassing, dirty secret by my Deaf family. But that aside, going back to your point, I am half something. As you so astutely pointed out. Although I would have put it more eloquently perhaps. But you've hit the nail on the head. I am half a person, if you will. Half hearing, half Deaf. Two halves in this equation, however, do not make a whole. It's most unfortunate. They cancel each other out. They in fact make a nothing. Again, as you so rightly deduced.

'I belong in neither the hearing world, nor the Deaf. I have no station. Deaf or Hearing, it is immaterial – I am invisible to both. Accepted by neither. Therefore, one could question my very existence.'

'Unlike Annie,' Crabb said. 'Who very much exists. In both the hearing and the Deaf worlds. She has friends, lots of them: some who are deaf and others who are not. But you don't have any friends at all, do you? You're all alone. Invisible, as you say. Shall I tell you why I think you picked Annie as your focal point – your substitute mother?'

'No. *I* shall tell *you*. This is my story. All mine. How dare you presume to think that you know anything about me.'

Sam leant forward, pointing the skewer in Crabb's face. 'I fucking hate Annie. She is everything that I despise. I loathe her with every fabric of my invisible being. Do you know what she is? She is everything that I am not. Everyone loves her, whatever their bloody position on the audiological spectrum. But she uses me. Constantly. When she wants or needs an interpreter, she'll deign to acknowledge me. When she either feels like using her voice or lip-reading, she drops me, casts me aside without a please or thank you. Making me completely redundant. As if I suddenly am surplus to requirements. A non-person.

'Just like my mother. Annie victimises me. Again and again. She is a constant reminder of my nothingness. My whole family were the same. As soon as I was no longer useful, I was dispatched back to nothingness again. Annie repeats the trend.'

He leant further forward, the skewer only inches from Crabb's face. 'Did you know that I had to interpret for Mummy when she had ovarian cysts. When I was eleven, twelve years old, Crabb. So young. Think of it. And when my services were no longer required, back to being ignored. Just like Annie ignores me now.'

Crabb sat back. Sam was shouting, his voice suddenly filled with hatred and an all-consuming anger. He stretched across the table and pinched Annie's arm between his index finger and thumb. Hard. Crabb could almost feel it bruise as he watched Sam press his fingers ever tighter. He waved the skewer at her neck. Crabb partially rose from his seat but Sam stopped him with words: 'Annie *is* a somebody. I wanted to make her a nobody. She is everything that I am not. Everything that I should be. She treated me just like my family did. But I've made her pay.'

Sam up-ended his mug into his mouth, then spat the dregs into Annie's face.

She didn't react. *Good for her.*

Sam's voice returned to a more normal pitch – the fury gone.

'It's ironic, really. Here I am, attempting to replicate my family, and here is my nemesis, unwittingly mimicking the abhorrent behaviour of my mother just by breathing. She is mimicking all of them.'

'You think she deserves this? Your life isn't her fault. So what now? What are you going to do now?'

Crabb tried for a non-threatening, empathetic pose, sitting back and crossing his legs. Gently nodding as Sam started to speak.

'I don't expect you to understand. You in your ivory tower: languishing happily in a world where you belong. You lack the capacity to see beyond your own pathetic life. See the sadness in others.'

Sam got up and took a step towards Crabb who instinctively flinched.

'I was ignored as a child, ignored and dismissed by my

family, and then, time and again, ignored and dismissed as an interpreter. By Annie.'

The interpreter surprised Crabb with his speed, and he could only watch as Sam slapped Annie's face. Crabb jumped up. Sam held the skewer to Annie's eye.

'Sit, Crabb. Just sit and listen. I haven't finished. You have to understand, as an interpreter, I'm good at being a ghost. Not seen by others. Coached from birth. It is an attribute to be applauded. And I'm simply fucking marvellous at being a nobody. Instant success in my profession.' He held his hands out from his sides. 'Lucky me. I have been well-trained in that particular field.'

'Don't look too pleased with yourself,' Crabb said. 'I think your story is a sad one. I pity you. But I do understand you. I understand the Game.'

Silence. Crabb looked over to Annie again. Her face had a strange look on it. One he couldn't decipher. The three of them continued to sit there, the skewer still in Sam's hands. Crabb broke the silence. 'Tell me about your thirteenth birthday. That's when it all started, wasn't it? This mission of yours.'

'It also depends on what you blithely and oh so glibly refer to as "it". Being locked up underneath the stairs for years? For no reason. Maybe that was it. Having to wear pretend hearing aids in public so as not to embarrass my family? Could that be it? Only being allowed to sign when we all went out in public on riotous family outings? No speaking in public allowed? Do you think that could be the elusive it? Having to interpret the medical crises of my mother's gynaecological problems. An interpreter when it suited my family. Then back to a nothing. How does that rock your boat? Or maybe the death of my brother? Was that it? The fact my less-than-perfect mother forgot my fucking birthday cake? Could that possibly be it? My fucking useless birthday present? Fucking pencils. Pencils.

Instead of a dog. I got pencils. Ewan got a bike. All I wanted was a puppy. Perhaps that's it. What say you, Crabb? Is that the "it" to which you refer?'

Crabb merely nodded, feigning control. Exuding a serenity he didn't feel.

'As you can see,' Sam gestured towards a dog – 'I finally bought a dog for myself. My own puppy. I bought my own birthday present. Years later. And now look at him. Earless for the cause. Ironic, don't you think?'

Sam stood again. His voice had risen. He daintily dabbed at the corners of his mouth. Where spittle had gathered. He had grabbed Annie's hair and held the skewer to her neck. Again. A miniscule pearl of blood showed against her milky white skin where the tip had penetrated.

And then he just sat down again.

Crabb swallowed, his mouth dry and said, 'You've been creating a surrogate family. A better family than the one you had.'

Sam gently bowed his head.

'But why?' Crabb asked. 'To what end? May I guess?'

Sam laughed. Laughed hard. Seemed to enjoy Crabb playing the Game.

'Guess away.'

'You want your birthday as it should have been. You've been trying to replicate that day, to make it perfect, but all your players failed to play their parts with any credibility. They failed. They didn't stand a chance, did they?'

Sam tipped his head graciously. Assuming it a compliment. 'I wanted my birthday to be as special as Ewan's. But enough. Move on. Do you know what revenge means, Crabb?'

'I do.'

The interpreter glanced over at Annie. She didn't respond at first. Sam prodded her – wanting a reaction.

She turned and looked at him. With her pretend-nothing face on. She blinked. And a little scorn squeaked out of her face, her mouth twisting just a little at the corners. Dislike for Sam. Hatred and disgust. *Watch it*, Crabb thought. *Don't push it.*

Sam said, 'Ooh, you look just like Mummy.'

Crabb said, 'Revenge, Sam. Tell me about revenge.'

'I asked them to surrender their identity. And become my pretend family. My better family, who would love me for me. To give me my one day back. My birthday. You'd have thought they'd have leapt at the chance. For their very lives depended upon it. I let them know that fairly early on. So that I couldn't be accused of cheating later.'

He laughed and looked at Crabb. And then at Annie.

'It was a game of "happy families". Everyone knows how to play *that* – surely? Except possibly my real family. Failures all. That's why I re-enacted their deaths. Their giving-up deaths. Nothing to be proud of there. Pathetic to the end. All of them. I wanted revenge on all of them.'

Crabb said, 'You killed Ewan. You drowned him. It was evident from your murder last year, of Adam Jacobs, that you'd killed before. You showed such a complete lack of under-standing or empathy. You simply didn't care. However you killed Ewan, it doesn't really matter. I think you were responsible. But it was ruled an accident. You weren't caught. And then it all went downhill from there. Your family disintegrated. All you've been doing is trying to recapture what you destroyed. Ironic.'

'I? Killed Ewan? That entirely depends upon your interpreta-tion of murder. Murder by omission, possibly. Nothing more. And most categorically not my fault. Who could've predicted that the Great Ewan was such a crap swimmer? Him with all his aquatic cups. It was his fault. Not mine.'

'It never is your fault, is it, Sam?' said Crabb.

'I wanted a replay of my thirteenth birthday party. How it

should have been. With me getting everything I always wanted. I wanted it to be like Ewan's birthday. Perfect. But you can't change what was. So I wanted an apology. That was the crux. An apology. A heart-felt apology for the way I was treated. For the non-birthday I received. That's all. Do you realise that I bought my own banners and streamers?' He gesticulated around himself. 'With my own pocket money. The day after my birthday. And I've got them out every year since. To celebrate. On my own. Alas – every birthday: not a guest in sight. No presents. No fun. So this time, this year, this birthday, I wanted my family here.'

'But your birthday is July 28th. Why kill this month?'

'Because I can, Crabb. Because I felt like it. Because the date doesn't bloody matter; it didn't matter then so it doesn't matter now – it could have been any day of my choosing. Call it my unofficial birthday if it irks you so. The whole Game should have been completed within a week. Ewan's birthday festivities lasted for a week. But I ran over that seven-day period simply because of silly distractions with Martin and Ben. But no matter. It's the principle of the thing that matters. Why bother with real dates? No one bothered with my real birthday so it may as well be when I want it to be. It makes no difference. It is neither here nor there. Maybe I just couldn't wait.'

Crabb didn't respond.

Sam continued, talking as if to himself. 'As that proverb says "old sins cast long shadows". How true that is. Shadows are dark places. People get lost in the dark. I admit that over the years I have indeed been lost. Some would argue that I still am. But who isn't? Really. Who isn't?'

60

———

I stood up. I had never been so tired. I could barely remain vertical. All I wanted was to lie down. Forever. The melancholy of all things done. It comes to the best of us. But I had to finish. And finish with a flourish.

I'd been told all my life that I was worthless. Let's see if they were right. Maybe they were. That would be amusing. The final irony. After this long and arduous journey. Maybe they were right all along. Deaf is best.

I stood behind Annie. She sat like a sack.

I noted with some amusement that Crabb sat straighter in his chair. Believing that he could change the outcome. Outrageously silly.

I controlled the outcome.

I pressed the skewer to Annie's ear. Slid it across her cheek. Caressed the bridge of her nose. Smoothed it across her closed eyelids. Whispered it across her lips. Softly, softly. It was like love. I didn't mean sex. Or even making love. It was a simple love. But I was only guessing. Forgive me if I got it slightly wrong. I was a novice in that area.

I gently moved Annie's thick black hair to one side. The skewer rested on her ear lobe. A flesh coloured bullseye beckoned.

'You can console yourself. You have saved the girl, Crabb. I know she was your priority. Not I. And I would have killed her — more out of boredom than anything else. And to finish the Game. But now, it all seems a million miles away. Everything does. I am a beaten man. Congratulations, Crabb. You win.'

I planted my fist on the table. The one holding the skewer. I could see that Annie felt the thump on the table. She frowned. Looked at my fist. And then at me. There was that gleam of realisation again; she knew what was coming. I was glad she looked at me. I held the skewer upright and rigid. Planted my feet on the floor: my shoulders square on. Looked into Annie's eyes for the last time.

I ignored Crabb as he leapt from his chair. Too late, old man. Too late. I had that victory at least.

I smiled at her. She didn't smile back. And then I began my downward arc. Fast. Aiming for the tip of the skewer. My head flew through the air. My ear hurtled towards the sharpened tip. My brain slowed and I saw everything clearly. And I prayed. Prayed it would go deep.

Make me Deaf. Make me Dead.

61

———

It was raining.

'So, come on, Crabb. Let's talk. Here. Have a drink,' Annie said, handing Crabb a huge goblet, overfilled with red wine. He remarked that it was an obscenely large glass and she told him not to worry. It was over. Finally.

Annie thought that the woman she had been before all this, was slowly making its return. Although often swimming in alcohol. But she wasn't about to give herself a hard time: five dead people, four of whom she had known, three of whom she had really loved – all dead. She wasn't a believer of psychiatry, nor of 'talking' therapy of any description. She would recover and be happy again. And she'd get there in her own way. Pissed or not. Back at work now, things would never be normal again, but she could at least go through the motions.

They both sat in silence for a few minutes; Scarlet adding her own unique presence. A drenched Eric came in, looking as though he had been out partying all night, his fur drenched sticking up in spikes. Crabb bent down and stroked him; clearly having grown fond of the cat over the days he'd known Annie.

'What's the latest on Sam?' asked Annie.

'Alive, breathing, but not responding. If he recovers, he'll no doubt end up in a secure psychiatric unit. If he doesn't, he'll stay where he is. A vegetable. For all intents and purposes.'

'Self-inflicted skewering is obviously harder than you'd think. Or harder than Sam thought anyway.'

'How do you feel after your week up in Oxford with Sarah. Better?'

Sarah had been waiting. Waiting for her son to be released by the police. Waiting for Toby to stop being evidence. Waiting to get his body back home. To become her son again. She had waited and waited. So she could bury him. Now she could do that.

'I suppose I feel a bit better,' Annie said. 'I'm still struggling to come to terms with all those deaths. Toby, William, Ben, Dora. It'll take me time to get back to my usual dazzling self. But I'm getting there.' She tried a smile. 'Sarah helped. We sort of helped each other. She's a strong woman.'

'As are you, Annie.'

They sat quietly for a bit, eating Twiglets and drinking. Scarlet remained quiet – silent but there, in the armchair. Always, thankfully, there. Her eyebrows were at rest– peaceful and untroubled now.

Annie put her hand on Crabb's knee. 'Thank you for saving me.'

'Think nothing of it. It was a pleasure.'

'And it's Toby's funeral next Wednesday. You're coming to that, aren't you?' she said.

He nodded and looked sad – defeated. She wanted him to engage in conversation and not wallow. Annie squeezed her still-resting hand on his knee and said, 'The denouement, Sam's finale, *was* spooky. The whole thing. To say the least. Completely bananas. And I didn't see that coming. The skewer in his own ear,' she said.

'Seriously fucked up. And all because he didn't get a puppy for his birthday. Remind me, if I ever have children, like *that'll* ever happen, but *if* I had the immaculate conception, remind me to give any child of mine anything and everything they ask for. Especially if he asks for a puppy. Safer that way. I wouldn't want to create a monster.'

Annie was aware that she was slightly pissed. So what. It was an escape. Crabb rolled up the cuffs of his shirts and leant forward.

'But Sam was locked in a cupboard. Had to pretend he was Deaf. Wasn't allowed to talk in public, et cetera, et cetera.'

'Are you condoning his behaviour? There are loads of people who are abused as children who don't turn into raving loonies. That's no excuse. It would be like me saying Sam had a good reason for picking me to torment. I *did* make him invisible. I *did* use him. I never really thought of him as a person. Just an interpreter that I didn't need. So sue me.'

'Of course I'm not condoning anything that he did. Just pointing out that his life was hardly peaches and cream. That's all,' said Crabb. 'The whole thing was a disaster. And a fucking sad one. For all those included. *What* a mess. Sam was so damaged. Damaged by his family. A cold man. Living in his own, lonely world. He was losing it slowly and quietly, all through the investigation and I missed it. I made a mistake in never considering him as the killer.'

'Stop being pathetic, Crabb.'

'I should have picked up on his coolness, his remoteness, the almost complete non-way he was treated by the Deaf Community. Like he was an outsider. Which, of course, was precisely what he was. His entire life. None of the Deaf treated him like a friend. Not one of them.'

'Don't try and make me feel sorry for him. You won't. And you're not infallible, Crabb. You at least saved the girl. That'll be me. Remember that. It's important. You couldn't have saved the others. You're not God.'

She locked eyes with him. Eager that he understood. And he did understand. He smiled at her.

'I'm just sorry I let Sam get you in the first place. I'm damn sure you'll think twice about escaping from a car window again.'

Annie smiled blearily. 'Yeah, not the most intelligent thing I've ever done, but there you go. Sam didn't kill me, because you saved me. Now get a grip. And about Ben. I've been thinking. I think Ben told Sam about his sexual abuse. Accused Sam of telling. Didn't realise the police had worked it out for themselves. Sam had to clean house. Poor Ben. Christ, what a person to choose to confide in.'

'Ben didn't have many friends. Maybe Ben saw Sam as a safe bet: separate to him, an authority figure, but someone that he thought he could trust. And Ben's brother, Theo. Bastard. At least we got him,' he said.

Crabb nodded at his own words, drank and said, 'Theo's a nasty fuck. Seriously nasty. They found him holed up in a squat. With his own laptop full to bursting with photos of himself, actually *on screen*, abusing children. It's probably the best result we've had all round, putting that shit away. We'd have had problems proving that he'd abused Ben because Ben was dead. Would have been one of those "he said, she said" things. So at least a happy ending there.'

Annie leant back on the sofa.

'*And* you caught a serial killer, Crabb. Get some perspective. You should be celebrating. You worked it out. Why are you so depressed about it?'

'Because the whole thing's so bloody sad, that's why. And I was too late for some people.'

'Yeah, but not for me, Crabb. You couldn't save everyone.'

'The whole thing has been so... so disgusting. The behaviour and madness of the people involved. I never get used to other people. Humans – they're a strange and not particularly nice species.'

'It's over. Really. And thank you, for everything.'

But it would never be over. Not for her. Not for Sarah. Not for the Deaf Community.

'Don't be ridiculous. Thank you for all *your* help. We were partners.' He took another crisp. 'At least my DCI is happy. Like a pig in shit. Taking all the glory.' He shrugged. 'Let him. I don't care.'

He offered Annie a cigarette. She shook her head. Said: 'I've given up. Anyway, let's all go out and eat, Crabb. I'm starving.'

'And let's have a toast,' he said. 'To all of those Sam killed. To all those that died.' They all held their glasses aloft.

Annie said, 'I'll drink to that. I'll always drink to the people I love. For the rest of my life, I'll drink to them. And I shall never forget them. Never.'

62

I've *been in a coma. For some time. I believe I've even had an operation. A little tinkering of my brain went on. A bit of damage control after the effects of the skewer.*

And now I'm playing dead.

Unfortunately I just cannot control my brain activity. I can't help reacting to auditory and physical stimuli. Most annoying. The old brain just keeps on ticking away. Clever little thing. It really is most extraordinary. Against all the odds. My brain works as well as it ever did. Maybe better.

But for the moment, I'm playing vegetable. They can't make me open my eyes. Nor force me to talk.

And I shall be mute. By choice. For I know I can talk. I've practised. When I'm alone. Connected to a sea of tubes and drains, I lie in bed in the darkness and whisper.

I quite like the idea of being forever silent. It has possibilities. Having the power to speak. But not. Interesting.

Of course, at some point I shall have to open my eyes. But in the meantime, I lie here. Plotting. A new Game is afoot. And have no fear — it will be better than the last one.

I promise.
But shh, don't tell anyone.

THE END

ABOUT THE AUTHOR

Jocelyn Dexter was born in Blackheath, London. She worked as an interpreter for the Deaf for seven years. Whilst doing this, she completed her MA in creative writing at Brunel University and wrote her first book. She enjoys sunbathing, shopping, meeting people and wants world peace.

ACKNOWLEDGEMENTS

First of all I'd like to thank Bloodhound Books, specifically Betsy Reavley for picking up my novel. Particular thanks go to Clare Law who edited my book and made it cleaner, sharper, better. The entire publishing team has been welcoming, friendly and efficient – my thanks to all.

I'd also like to thank Kerry Billington, a profoundly deaf woman, for whom I interpreted for many years. My protagonist in this novel is loosely based on her. Kerry signs, has a clear speaking voice and has lip-reading skills which are simply remarkable.

Special thanks of a different kind, go to verathediva.com – a Latin & Ballroom dance school based in Clapham, London. Going quietly but happily insane from sitting on the sofa writing this book, dancing cured me of a potential inability to move at all. Glued to laptop, stuck to sofa. Strangely, I discovered that in terms of writing a book, immediately post dancing, my brain was always more alert, enabling me to bask in my own imagined dancing brilliance (tongue firmly lodged in cheek) and more importantly, I found that I was able to write better; grey cells reinvigorated. Mentally, more on the ball: physically, more on the balls of my feet. I am very grateful to the whole team, especially, Edurne Golderacena for her patience and tuition, and her son, Gorka.

I feel obliged to explain that my author's bio, is in fact, my Miss World Acceptance speech – for those who don't know me personally.

But most of all, thank you to Francesca. For everything.